Whom Shall I Fear?

Whom SHALL I *Fear?*

ANNE CLARE

PUBLISHED BY Anne Clare

Whom Shall I Fear?

CHAPTER 20 includes an excerpt from Lieutenant-Colonel John McCrae's 1915 poem "In Flanders Fields".

COVER DESIGN AND INTERIOR FORMATTING: Amanda Ruehle

Apennine Mountains
Rome
Adriatic
Sea
Termoli
Cassino
Naples
Taranto
Mediterranean
Sea
Sardinia
Messina
Sicily
ITALY

Dedication

To those who served,
and to those who waited
and prayed for their return

Part One

One

Sergeant James Milburn stumbled on a corner of threadbare carpet. The thud of his loose shoe striking the baseboard echoed against the dark wood walls.

Fool. They'll find you in a minute if you're not more careful. Wishing for his broken-in, tight-laced boots, he crept on.

The hall stretched before him, morning light streaming through thick leaded windows and ribbon-thin cracks around the frame of the front door.

Freedom was in sight.

Something white fluttered—there—through the doorway to his left.

James froze.

Easing his stiff neck around, he turned, eyes searching. The white fabric fluttered again, and he exhaled in relief. *Only a curtain. Must be a draft in the dining room.*

He glanced behind one last time as he reached the door. Neither of his elderly jailors made an appearance, and he allowed himself a small smile as he turned the knob.

The door opened with a deep, protesting groan.

James's relieved sigh turned into a muttered curse.

Footsteps echoed on the floor above.

Abandoning caution, he flung the door open and rushed through, letting it slam behind him.

His right elbow bumped the brickwork surrounding the entrance.

Pain shot through his shoulder and he flinched—the drugs were wearing off. He slowed to adjust his sling, glaring at his prison over his shoulder.

Thrush House crouched over him like a great brick toad, squat and ugly. Of course, it hadn't been chosen for looks, but for size and location—lots of room for convalescents, far from the bombings in London.

Rounding the corner of the house, James hesitated near the edge of the kitchen garden and listened for sounds of pursuit—a cry warning him not to overexert, the creak of that blasted front door, footsteps pursuing him for more treatments.

Nothing. Had they lost interest in him already? After all the fuss from the staff when he'd arrived yesterday, some inattention would be a relief. Most likely they assumed that hunger and the need for medication would draw him back soon enough.

They're right about that. But for now, for a moment, I can imagine I'm free.

He stretched his long legs and walked, drawing the dew-damp morning air deep into his lungs. Nothing to hear but birdsong and the soughing of the wind through the oak trees behind the house. He lingered in their green shade and closed his eyes, savoring it for a few moments—until the quiet began to press on his ears, unsettling and dangerous.

Quiet left too much time to wonder.

How are the boys making out? How many others were lost on the march to Messina? How many did I fail?

James swallowed, hard. He could almost taste the dust, feel the acrid smoke burning his throat. Quickening his pace, he hummed a soft tune to fill his ears and tried to shake the memories.

Circling the house, he reached the gaudy iron curlicues of the front gate. It stood open, and the dusty lane beyond beckoned. He ran his hand through his fair hair, considering.

I could just walk out. Not that there'd be any point. He laughed aloud, a short, bitter sound. There wasn't much in this lonely stretch of northern Cumberland, and he'd been ordered to rest.

If there was one thing he knew, it was how to follow orders.

The persistent ache in his shoulder called him back to the house, back to the sterile, echoing halls that smelled of disinfectant, and the chattering tongues of the Red Cross Nurse and Mrs. Jenkins, the housekeeper.

James pursed his lips, ignored the call, and continued his walk.

Beyond the gate, a tall laurel hedge bordered Thrush House's grounds, separating it from the neighbor's, Stoneglenn. The hedge looked worse for the recent conscription of the ageing gardener's son. Bits of twigs and loose leaves dangled from forlorn branches. A bit further on, one of the plants was nearly dead, with only a few defiant limbs standing upright.

Thwack!

A long silence followed the odd noise. *Thwack!* Another long pause. *Thwack!*

What in the world?

The noise came from the other side of the gap in the hedge.

He only meant to walk past—a quick, casual surveillance. Instead, his feet slowed, and then halted as he stared.

The scene framed by the pathetic branches was like a magazine photo from happier days. A girl stood at one end of an impeccably groomed tennis court, dressed in white, poised for service.

Thwack! Decent serve—not brilliant, but in bounds. Tucking her tennis racquet under her arm, she trotted around the court to retrieve her ball, and prepared to serve from the other side. *Thwack!* Back to the beginning again.

Up at the crack of dawn to practice tennis during war-time? Hasn't she anything better to do?

She was a fairly attractive girl—not the sort to stop you on the street, but easy on the eyes. Rather short, slim waist, pleasantly curvy where she ought to be. With a few dark, loose curls that had come undone, she made a pretty picture.

Not keen to be seen lurking, he was just turning to continue his walk when a miss-hit ball flew directly towards him. He threw his good arm up to deflect it from his face and realized that he'd missed his chance to disappear unnoticed. *Oh blast…*

The girl saw him and jumped, fumbling and nearly dropping the racquet. Her wide eyes blinked, then took in his convalescent blues. "Oh…good morning?"

Heat flushed his ears and the back of his neck. "Good morning. Pardon me, I didn't mean…I was surprised to see someone else up this early."

She gave a shaky laugh. "So was I!"

"Yes. Well. Sorry."

"It's all right. I'm sorry that last one almost got you. Where did it—ah." She came towards James and retrieved the ball from a little hollow under the laurel branches. "I simply can't get my swing right, but as the birds woke me up again, I thought I might just as well practice."

"Birds?"

She laughed again, sunburnt nose and cheeks flushing pinker. "Oh, I've a nest of baby birds on my window ledge—starlings. They have me up with the lark every day, or up with the starling I suppose…" She trailed off, and James realized he'd been staring at her smile.

He wracked his brain for a response. "You don't mind?"

"Oh no! I like the morning, and they're awfully adorable, such tiny little balls of fluff except for their enormous orange mouths! It's been a bit warm, not being able to open my window, but I wish Charles would…" She stumbled to a halt, sobering. She glanced over her shoulder.

"What?"

"Oh, my cousin keeps wanting to have the nest moved, so I won't be bothered. And I keep explaining that I like having them there… I'm sorry. I don't mean to babble on like this, and I haven't even introduced...bother. I'm doing this all wrong, aren't I?" She stuck the tennis racquet under her arm and stretched out her hand. James leaned through the gap, grasping her fingers awkwardly with his left. "Evelyn Worther. Evie."

"James Milburn."

"You're *Sergeant* Milburn then, here to convalesce? We'd heard you were coming..."

Just then there was a "Hallo!" from behind her.

Her back stiffened and her grip tightened, knuckles white before she released his hand. Her smile was a little too quick as she said, "Oh, that must be my cousin."

A man limped into view. He managed to swagger even as he leaned on his black cane, his handsome face arrogant under his lacquer-neat dark hair. He was dressed impeccably, looking as if he'd just come from business in town.

"There you are, Evie." His voice was a languid drawl. "Have you been practicing without me? After last week I'd think you'd know better than...who..." He trailed off as his eyes met James's.

The man's confidence vanished. The color drained from his face as he stared.

Puzzled, James stared back. *Do I know him? I could swear I've never seen him before.*

Evie's brow furrowed, and she stepped towards the man. "Charles? Charles, this is Sergeant James Milburn, here to convalesce at Thrush House. Sergeant, this is my cousin, Charles Heatherington."

Charles blinked and reached across for a hurried handshake. "Sergeant. Welcome to our little corner of the world. A bit quieter than where you've been, I imagine."

"Yes...a bit."

"Quite. Well, if there's anything you need..." Charles left the offer hanging and draped his arm across Evie's shoulders.

She stepped forward, and his arm fell to his side. "Oh, yes. If there's anything that we can do...books or anything..."

"Thanks. It seems like the place is pretty well set up."

Charles stepped up beside her. "Glad to hear it. Well, Evie. Shall we get in a bit of practice before breakfast? If you don't mind, Sergeant?"

She bit her lips, then molded them into a smile. "Of course, Charles. If you'll excuse us, Sergeant Milburn?"

James nodded, but Charles had already taken her arm and steered her back to the court. With one last glance from those blue eyes and an apologetic smile, she was gone.

James turned to walk back to Thrush House.

Couldn't ignore the shoulder much longer anyway. Maybe they'll have breakfast, and then I can get a letter out to Davy...

His steps slowed. He listened for noise from the other side of the hedge, but could only hear quiet voices, and the *thwack* of the tennis racquet.

EVIE WATCHED SERGEANT MILBURN GO. Poor man. He looked so ill and drawn.

I don't imagine I helped much, blathering on like an idiot. It's just as well Charles found me. She shook herself back to the present and gave her cousin her attention.

"I'm sorry, Charles, what did you say?"

"I said that you're out and about dreadfully early again, Evie. You really ought to let me do something about those dratted birds."

"Charles, I told you that I don't..."

"Yes, I remember. I just hoped you'd see sense. Have you been practicing your service?"

"Yes. You were rather abrupt with him, you know. Sergeant Milburn."

He had the good grace to look apologetic. "I didn't mean to be. I'm just a bit tired of meeting people who'll be leaving again directly. I daresay he didn't notice. Now, remember what I told you last weekend about the placement of your feet..."

Charles's leg made it difficult for him to move quickly, so having a real game was out of the question. After an hour, he declared that he thought Evie "had a real possibility of improvement, if she would only let him practice with her more." Evie had nothing much to say to this, so they returned to the house, not daring to be late for breakfast with their Great Aunt Helena.

Over the luxury of half a hardboiled egg and toast with their allotment of butter scraped across it, Charles told them the latest news.

"Operations in Sicily are going swimmingly. With any luck, our men will go over the Straits of Messina and Italy will be out of it. Or maybe we'll go for Sardinia and Corsica." He paused for breath and a drink. "Either way, with such an easy campaign under their belts, they ought to be able to press forward almost at once."

"Easy?" Evie spoke up. "What about the troubles with the landing, and those poor men in the gliders, released too soon and drowned? And with the malaria as well as the Germans..."

Charles brushed all these difficulties away with a wave of his hand. "What of all that? What of a few casualties in war?"

"What I meant was—" Evie began, but Charles was off, and there was no stopping him.

Sitting up even straighter, his eyes took on a far-away look. "Why, at Dunkirk we thought we were all lost, the British Expeditionary Force finished, and our home left undefended. But we didn't give up..."

Evie sighed and returned to her breakfast.

She appreciated the courage of the soldiers at Dunkirk who had kept the enemy at bay so that troops could be evacuated back across the Channel, and of the sailors—many of them civilians—who had kept bringing men off until the very last. However, she had heard Charles speak exhaustively on this subject many, many times.

She picked at her toast and imagined breaking in to his speech, perhaps having an actual conversation. There would be no opportunity. Once Charles got going, he was nearly impossible to derail, and Evie was tired of trying.

She looked over to Great Aunt Helena. *She* at least could always command Charles's attention.

There was no help from that quarter. Only Great Aunt Helena's veined hands—clamped onto the edges of the newspaper—and the top of her steel-gray wave were visible.

Evie sipped her tea, grimacing at the bitter aftertaste, missing her cream and sugar. *Just another weekend.*

After breakfast, the smartly-uniformed Molly pushed Great Aunt Helena's chair into the library. While Charles followed them, Evie slipped into the music room, gathered her books, and escaped out the French doors.

Past Stoneglenn's hedgerow, a mossy stone wall adorned with a few straggling remains of spring's little golden Alison flowers and draped with ivy coming into bloom bordered the road into the village of Thrush. Birds called to each other, singing in the branches and the fields. The hills on the horizon hinted at the beauty of Wordsworth's beloved Lake Country. Summer was here, and the countryside rejoiced.

Evie saw little of it.

She couldn't get Charles's insistent voice out of her head.

Whatever am I going to do *about him?*

She wandered past the cottages huddled on the outskirts of the village. Further along, the same few dress goods slumped in the shop's window display. A poster of "Mrs. Sew-and-Sew," the government's rag doll mascot, declared "Make-do and Mend!"

Evie stared absently.

Charles had always been difficult. One memory surfaced from her childhood summers, when all of the cousins had descended on Stoneglenn. Charles had been in a snit about something to do with the fishing excursion the other boys were planning. Evie, several years younger though she was, felt sorry for him and had sat and played checkers with him all afternoon.

When the others had returned, Charles's eldest brother, Roger, had pulled her aside. "Evie, you're awfully good, the way you put up with Charles. You know, though, you can't always get on with everyone. Sometime you've got to stand up, or he'll push you as far as he can."

Poor Roger. He'd always tried to look out for everyone else. He'd been the general of all their games, and the medic for any of the small ones who were hurt. Evie shivered, though the sunshine was warm. She prayed again that Roger's death had been quick and painless and increased her pace.

If only Charles wouldn't push so. If he could only let things be as they were before.

She turned down the street to the church by way of the post office and nearly collided with Sergeant Milburn, who was coming out of it.

Startled, she stumbled back. He caught her elbow and steadied her. "I'm very sorry, Miss Worther."

"Oh no. It was my fault. I was wool-gathering," Evie said, flustered. *Goodness, he's tall!* His hazel eyes and lean face were inscrutable, and she couldn't tell if he was irritated with her or amused.

The postmistress, Mrs. Davies, leaned out the door. "Hullo, Evie, nothing new yet today—no papers, no reports. Is there anything else you're looking for? I was just on my way out."

Collecting her wits, Evie said, "No, nothing else. Thank you, Mrs. Davies. Will you be at the next meeting?"

"Yes! The salvage drive is a grand idea. I think we'll do well. Julie's pleased to lend a hand." She waved farewell.

Evie waved back, then looked over to Sergeant Milburn, still standing by. "We've been trying to keep an active Women's Voluntary Service going. We're planning a salvage drive for Monday."

He smiled, a nice smile that softened his serious face. "My mum does some WVS work. It's a good organization."

Evie shrugged. "Yes, well, it's something useful to do way up here." Sergeant Milburn blinked, and she flushed. "I don't mean...you're right, Sergeant. It *is* a good organization. We've just had so many people moving away for war jobs, it's hard to keep anything going."

"Everyone's on the move these days."

"Most everyone anyway." Evie shifted her books. "And those of us who can't must carry on."

"Can't?"

Evie, you need to stop babbling! "Oh, it's just my great aunt. She's determined that I won't leave Thrush until the war's finished." She shrugged. "Anyway—I'm walking to the church, if you'd like to see it." Forcing a careless laugh, she added, "There isn't much else to see here."

"Thanks." He fell into step beside her. After a moment, he cleared his throat. "So. Where'd you go if you could?"

"Well..." Evie floundered, unaccustomed to having someone ask her opinion. "I don't know, exactly. I'd like to be able to find someplace where I can do my bit for the war effort. Nothing I've been able to do up here seems to be enough. But I don't mean to complain."

The sergeant shrugged his good shoulder. "I don't see that there's any harm in wanting to do some good. Don't you think you could just..." he shrugged again.

"Just go, if I really want to? I suppose. But..." She searched the dust at her feet for the right words. "I'm...grateful to Great Aunt Helena. She's done so much for me, and she and Charles are all the family I have left, and either way, I'll be twenty in a couple of years and I'm bound to be called up then, if it's not all over. Not that I want it to go on so long, of course, it's just...I do wish that I could help..." She trailed off in a small voice.

"Family's hard to cross. Mum was none too pleased when she heard I'd enlisted." He grinned. "Good job I didn't tell her till it was all done."

Evie laughed. "Oh dear. Has she forgiven you?"

Nodding, the sergeant kicked at a loose stone. "But she's watched my brothers like a hawk ever since."

Neither of them spoke during the rest of the short walk to the church, but as Evie bade him farewell and went in to practice, she glanced back over her shoulder.

He's quiet, but he seems awfully nice. I wonder if we'll see him tomorrow.

CHARLES DRESSED WITH EXTRA CARE for supper Sunday evening. At his suggestion, Great Aunt Helena had invited the residents of Thrush House to dine.

Something about the new man worried him. Maybe it was the way he'd looked at Evie, even sitting near her this morning in church. Maybe it was that first impression, that first glimpse through the hedge when he'd seemed terribly familiar.

It was just a trick of the light. He doesn't look much like Roger at all. Still...it gave me a turn. Imagine, if he *were suddenly resurrected.*

Charles straightened his tie, frowning into the looking glass. *In any case, I don't suppose there's anything to worry about. There've been plenty of convalescents over at Thrush House, and Evie's never been one to lose her head over a uniform.*

Still, he hadn't cared for the way Evie smiled at the man. Scrubbing his hand across his face, he sighed.

Evie. He'd hoped something frivolous like time on the tennis court might bring back some of the old days—the fun they'd had in the summers before he enlisted, before the war, before France.

He wished everything with her hadn't become so complicated. But it had, and he would do what he must. He squared his shoulders.

Things are going too well. Can't let some sad-eyed soldier interfere.

Leaving his room, Charles met Evie at the stairs. He noted that she looked particularly lovely in a reworked rose-colored gown and her mother's pearls. "You really make everything do very well, Evie."

"Thank you. Can't look shabby for Great Aunt Helena's table, can we?"

"Certainly not!"

"Did you get a new jacket? It's very smart."

"Yes, thanks. It took some finding." He took her arm but paused on the top step. "Evie, I've been thinking."

Evie glanced at him out of the corners of her eyes and said nothing.

"I'm not sure that I like seeing you up in front of everybody, playing for services. It's good of you to pitch in and all, but really, don't you think it seems a little *plebeian*?"

She laughed at him. Irritating when she did that. "Oh Charles, don't be silly! Since Mr. Phillips joined up, we haven't had anyone to play the hymns. What harm does it do for me to play a little music?"

"In front of the congregation, it doesn't seem quite dignified for a girl like you."

She started down the stairs. He had to follow or release her. Taking a step too quickly, he flinched.

Evie stopped at once. "Oh Charles, I'm sorry. Is your leg..."

"It's fine," he lied. "But I wish you'd take what I'm saying more seriously. Do you even listen to me?"

She sighed and continued walking at a more moderate pace. "Of course I do Charles, but really. 'A girl like me?' What reason do I have to put on airs? Everyone is pitching in where they can these days—my, just think of Lady—"

"Well, with your family connections—"

"Connections?" She interrupted him, laughing again. He gripped his cane, trying to keep the annoyance off his face. "Of course, there's Great Aunt Helena, and I know with you being Uncle Raymond's heir, but I'm just a charity case..."

"Ah," he said as they reached the bottom, slipping his arm free, and taking her hand. "But if your position were to change," he squeezed her fingers, "mightn't that also change your view of things, and the way you'd want people to see you?"

Evie pulled her hand away. Her voice was low, and she didn't meet his eyes. "I haven't any idea of my situation changing so dramatically."

She turned towards the opening front door, and so didn't see the dark cloud that momentarily marred his features, or how closely he watched her face and the sergeant's as they greeted each other. He frowned at what he saw.

Thrush House's owner, the retired Colonel Bryce, claimed Evie's arm as they all went in to dine. Sergeant Milburn and Father Carter found their seats while Charles brought in Great Aunt Helena, who remarked that in the old days they would never have had such an unbalanced party. "Four men to two ladies, indeed!"

This led to general discussion of the changes war had brought into their midst, with reminiscing from the older set of their Great War, the one that was to have ended all wars, if only Hitler and Mussolini and all the rest had concurred. The colonel's white sideburns bristled as he shared some of his favorite stories, some amusing, and some truly dreadful.

Milburn, being the newcomer, was asked many questions, which he answered in as few words as possible. Yes, he'd served in North Africa during Operation Torch, then in Sicily. No, he'd been invalided back before the end of the campaign. No, he hadn't seen the particular Indian officer the colonel wondered about. Yes, he was now attached to the 8th Army as part of the 78th Division. Yes, he preferred the sights on the newest Lee Enfield rifle, and so on.

Charles listened with half an ear, more interested in Evie's reactions. Always wonderful at parties, she seemed the same as usual. She listened to all the colonel's stories, laughed at the minister's small jokes, and managed their Great Aunt better than anyone else he knew. She didn't talk to the sergeant much or ask him any questions. Charles couldn't decide if this was a good sign or not.

The men retreated to the terrace after dinner. As the colonel lit his cigar, he asked Charles, "So! Any wedding bells yet for you and that pretty little cousin of yours?"

Charles glanced to see Milburn's reaction. Did his shoulders stiffen a bit? He decided to dig. "Sergeant, I suppose I should explain. Evie and I are not really cousins, not in the regular sense. Great Aunt Helena's older sister was Evie's grandmother. Her husband, Uncle Raymond's younger brother, William, was my grandfather, so she is my Great Aunt as well. We just all called each other 'cousin' for years and years. It was easier than figuring out the technical designations."

The sergeant nodded. Charles took a puff from his cigarette. Turning back to the colonel, he continued, "No, nothing of that sort on the horizon, Colonel. Or, I should say, nothing yet."

The colonel slapped his shoulder. "Well, don't wait too long. Girls like that don't keep. Thought a couple of the last batch of convalescents were going to make a go for it, but I suppose it all came to naught."

Charles smiled, his lips tight. "She is only eighteen. Given time, I'm sure we will finalize our plans."

"Pshaw. My Essie was 17 when I married her, God rest her. I say, marry 'em young. What do you say, Milburn?" He turned to the sergeant with a jovial grin. "Got a sweetheart or two waiting at home, I imagine—going to make them wait too long?"

"I haven't really considered all of that yet, sir. I've my duty to my country first. Maybe once that's done I can think more about the future." Stiff, formal and dull. Charles relaxed.

The colonel shook his head and muttered, "Youth is wasted on the young. Well, that's the end of that cigar. Shall we go in?"

Reentering the house, Charles positioned himself at Evie's elbow. Milburn positioned himself on the other side of the room near the eastern window, though with the blackout curtains in place there was nothing to see.

The colonel positioned himself next to Great Aunt Helena, who immediately bent his ear. The others were not left to wonder about the direction of her discontent; she broached her topic loudly enough that they could not avoid inclusion. "I am sure that you agree with me, Colonel, that my great niece has no business gallivanting around the countryside alone while we are at war, hauling garbage no less."

Evie spoke up. "I shan't be hauling garbage, Great Aunt Helena. Salvage. Tomorrow's the day for the salvage drive. And I'm not going alone. Mrs. Davies' oldest girl, Julie, is coming."

"Fine protection, that! How old is she, eight?"

"No, she's twelve."

"Well that makes a great difference."

"She'll be a great help lifting things, and really, I won't be going that far. Just around the houses in the neighborhood."

The colonel cleared his throat. "And how do you intend to get this salvage home? No petrol to be had, I should think."

"The Davies are going to loan us their horse and cart. Colonel Bryce, I hope you'll reassure my great aunt. *You* know how important the war effort is, and there hasn't been a hint of danger anywhere near here."

He stroked his chin. "I've got a deal of dictating to do tomorrow, or I'd be happy to go along. Really, Helena, I don't see that the girl will be at any risk, and it's good for her to be able to do her part. Send her one of Raymond's pistols, and what about you, Milburn? You'd go along and make sure the ladies are safe, wouldn't you?" He turned on the sergeant.

Charles frowned, irritated. "Colonel, I hardly think—"

Evie began speaking at the same time. "It's not necessary," she protested. "And isn't Sergeant Milburn supposed to be convalescing? This wasn't meant to put anyone out…"

Nodding, Charles stepped forward. "Nor should it. I have a meeting I can't miss tomorrow, but perhaps, if it were done later in the day, or if we put it off—"

Evie shook her head. "But Charles, it's all planned. If we try to change things now—"

"Nonsense!" Colonel Bryce's voice boomed over all. "Sitting on a wagon seat for a few hours? It'll do the young man good to be out of doors. What do you say, Milburn? Will the doctors be aghast?"

With all eyes turned towards him, the sergeant opened his mouth, and then closed it, glancing over at Evie and then back to the colonel. "If Miss Worther doesn't object, I'm certain that it would be all right."

Charles sputtered, trying to find the words to offer some other alternative, and Evie started to say something, looking as if she meant to object again, but Great Aunt Helena's imperious voice overruled them all. "That will do very well. What time will you come by for my niece?"

As they settled the details, Charles watched Evie. She said little more, but her shoulders were stiff and her lips tight as she smiled her good nights.

Well, that's something.

The room empty and quiet again, he gripped his cane's handle a little tighter, then leaned over to ask in her ear, "Would you like to take a walk? The moon is shining."

She pulled away. "No thank you, Charles. I'm really very tired."

He pursed his lips and nodded, swallowing his irritation. Great Aunt Helena was watching, chuckling at his discomfiture as Molly came down to take her to bed.

Charles bade them goodnight, and went outside, alone, pacing the grounds in the dark.

Go on and laugh.

I'll be the one laughing, soon enough. After all, you can't live forever...

Two

THE DREAMS FOUND JAMES THAT NIGHT.

Biting teeth of rock shards dig into knees and elbows and belly as he chokes on dust and the volcanic stench.

Ping! Patter, ping! *Stones strike his helmet with jaunty, semi-musical notes—counterpoint to the mortar explosions and the silent percussion of the ones that find his limbs.*

The whistle and shriek from behind—covering fire, at last. The mortars pause. Time to move on. Sliding hands under chest, trying to press-up… this should be easy…stars flash, small galaxies behind shimmering waves of nausea.

"Sergeant, you all right?" A hand on his elbow, coated in dust and dirt until it is the same color as his sleeve.

Up, time to get up. The boys need their leaders, not weaklings, groveling on the ground. Lips move, but his voice sounds strange and detached.

"I'm fine. C'mon."

Forward, forward, each step heavier… heavier… teeth grit, fists clench around the rifle, eyes squint ahead through the fumes and flashes, dust and scrambling forms of khaki-clad men blear together.

A stumble, a stagger back.

Disbelief as the red stain blossoms out of the neat hole in his battledress. Rifle drops from nerveless fingers. No pain, not yet.

One coherent thought—Blast, how am I going to aim?

The boys around him drop to the ground. Why?

The shell's shriek registers in his sluggish brain.

Slowly, he follows them to the ground. Too slow…

James jerked awake. He blinked, disoriented and listening for the scream of artillery, but the small, dark room was silent. He breathed deep, nose wrinkling at the smell of disinfectant, willing his heart to slow.

Only a dream. I'm a long way from Sicily. Only another dream.

The soft mattress was inviting under his shaking hands, but he pushed himself to standing. Pale early morning light shone through a gap around the blackout curtains. His body told him that it was time to get up, even if his mind told him there was no point.

I'm useless. They're all over there, and I'm here doing what? Chaperoning a country salvage drive.

At least after last night I'll know better than to think too much about Evie.

A SMILE HOVERED around the corners of Evie's mouth as she dug out Father's old trousers and a scarf for her hair. Charles had departed for his office and wouldn't return until the next weekend.

Salvage drive day—finally, something useful to do! No tennis practice, no arm slipped around my waist will I or no… unless Sergeant Milburn is cheekier than he seems to be.

The thought sobered her.

Trying to brush it away, Evie set out for the kitchen in high hopes that Cook had managed to produce some of her famous scones this morning. Rather than travel indoors, she slipped out through the French doors in the music room and passed into the flower beds, observing her own hard work with approval. It had taken years, but she had worn Great Aunt Helena down and been allowed to help in their tending. Orange marigolds, deep red begonias, bright sunflowers, and a rainbow of dahlias smiled from behind their neat borders. Flower gardens were out of fashion, particularly in London where every free space—even window boxes and pots by doors—was crammed with vegetables. This was unacceptable in Great Aunt Helena's garden.

Down the path a little farther, the herbs wafted enticing scents of lemon, mint, basil and rosemary. Evie plucked a piece of parsley to chew on.

She walked into the little orchard Uncle Raymond had planted that spread all the way down to the old carriage house at the edge of the grounds. The apple trees had finished their bloom, the new apples were swelling, and she thought hungrily of the fresh fruit to come. Everything had been picked and stored jealously last year, making up for the fruit that could no longer come in due to the blockades. As this year's harvest approached, last year's canned goods were running low.

The enlarged kitchen garden led all the way up to Stoneglenn. The family home reared up, age-stained blocks of local stone dark against the bright sky.

Reaching the house, Evie turned and surveyed it all. She sighed.

It was a beautiful morning here, so tidy and perfect, and an utter lie.

How many men have passed through Thrush House now? How many broken bodies and minds? And poor Sergeant Milburn—he has ghosts behind his eyes...

The world was broken, even if she couldn't see it from here. Even if she couldn't do a thing to mend it. Her nails bit into her palm.

Her reverie was interrupted by Cook calling out the kitchen door, "If you're going past the raspberries, see if there are any ripe, won't you?"

Kneeling on the dusty brick pathway, Evie lifted the fringed green leaves on the raspberry canes, wary of thorns, searching for the crimson flash that would herald ripe fruit. She found a small handful and brought them with her into the steaming kitchen.

Something smelled lovely, and Evie's stomach rumbled. She made a beeline to the counter where scones sat cooling, depositing her meager harvest on the work table.

"Cup of tea, duck?" asked Cook, settling her sizeable bulk on one of the narrow kitchen chairs. Her graying hair was pinned back with a severity which would brook no nonsense, but her smile was warm, and her eyes—set deep behind her large, rosy cheeks—were kind.

"Yes, please, Cook. These scones smell wonderful!" Cook's real name was Mrs. Fisk, but she had worked at Stoneglenn nearly thirty years, and this fact was rarely remembered, even by herself and her husband.

"Ah, well, no cream for 'em, and no egg to wash them with, but they'll do for tea, I suppose."

"I don't think I'll be staying for breakfast. Would you mind if—"

Cook laughed. "Make a plate for two. And I've packed a few biscuits in the hamper just there for you to take along this morning." Cook poured out the fragrant tea. She shifted her bulky frame, took a sip, and launched into the morning's gossip.

Mrs. Jenkins of next door and Cook were great friends, having known each other since girlhood. Evie had wondered: if the two of them were to compete at talking without drawing breath, which would go down first? The two had already had lively conversations about Thrush House's new resident.

"He's a fine looking young man, she says, but she can get hardly two words out a him! Ah, that's the way it 'tis sometimes. My uncle John now, he had a bad war, never really himself after, and slept with his bayonet under his pillow." She shook her head, grave. "What a pity this sergeant wasn't here last month so there would have been others of his kind for him to visit with, it's so frightfully empty over there right now. Not that we want more wounded, but I imagine they're full up enough in London."

Pausing to take a sip of tea, she gave Evie a sharp glance over the rim of her cup. "And what did you think of him? I didn't get much of a look the other night—is he a handsome young man, handsome as your Cousin Charles was in his uniform? Now, his was a long convalescence..."

A little warmth crept across Evie's cheeks. She shrugged. "I suppose so, though you can see that he's been ill. Fair, not dark like Charles, and taller."

"And did you find him close-mouthed, too?"

"Oh, he's quiet but he seems nice enough. Speaking of..." Evie checked the clock, gulped her tea and waved goodbye, taking the hamper.

She reached the front door just as Molly was opening it for Sergeant Milburn.

Seeing the dark shadows under his eyes, Evie frowned. *I wonder if he really should be doing this.* She tried to make her smile encouraging. "Good morning, Sergeant. Shall we go?"

As they started their walk to the Davies', he cleared his throat. "I hope you don't mind me coming along. They all seemed set on it last night."

"Oh no. I'm sorry that you were pushed into it, though." She shrugged with a resigned grin. "Great Aunt Helena has her ideas. If you hadn't agreed to go, she might've tried to insist that I call off the whole thing."

"Would you have?"

Evie blinked. "I couldn't very well, could I? Everyone's planning on it. It would have been a bother to figure out a solution, so I suppose I should thank you for sparing me that."

A drowsy, gray-dappled horse was already hitched to the wooden cart, the Davies' Julie holding its harness in an iron grip. A tall girl with the thin, stretched look of a child who has grown rapidly in a short time, Julie's eyes got big at Evie's introduction of the sergeant. Her mouth snapped closed after a choked, "'Lo." She clambered into the back of the wagon, finding a seat beside the boxes for sorting the salvaged goods.

"Would you like to drive, or shall I?" Evie asked, stroking the mare's nose.

"You know where we're going, and if I'm to be ready to spring into action at any time, I suppose I'd better just ride." He said the last with a dry half smile that surprised her into laughing.

The rutted country roads stretched ahead, empty. Fleecy gray clouds hung low overhead, but no rain was forthcoming. Gusty breezes bent and tossed the wild grass heads and tangled the girls' hair.

"Did you both have breakfast? Cook sent some biscuits." Evie reached down to the picnic hamper at her feet with one hand. She passed a warm biscuit to the sergeant. He handed it back to Julie, and then he took one for himself.

He nodded to the pistol tucked carefully into the top of the hamper. "You know how to use that?"

"Oh yes. The colonel took charge of the Home Guard in the area and made sure that each household had some means of defense. He was very thorough. He set up shooting practice for those of us who hadn't done much before." She added, embarrassment mingling with a touch of pride, "He said my aim was quite good."

"Better than with a tennis racquet, anyway?"

Evie laughed again, surprised by the flash of humor. "Yes! Though I didn't do well with a rifle. The recoil left my shoulder sore for a week." She sobered. "And not that I've ever shot at anything living. I'm not sure..."

"If you could?" he finished for her. His face was impassive, his eyes distant. "Yes, it's different."

An elderly couple met them at their first stop and showed them the salvage ready to be collected. Evie and Julie—and the sergeant doing what he could one-handed—helped load up. Into one box went empty tins and other scrap metal, the second was for kitchen waste, the third for boiled bones, and the last for paper.

There was a small sack for rags. The wife of the house laughed and said, "Sorry, dear, we've got none to spare!" She pointed to neat patches on her apron and her husband's pant knees.

The harness jingled as they resumed their journey. Evie clucked to the horse, who increased speed for a moment and then resumed plodding. "I didn't hear last night, where were you serving, before..."

"North Africa, then Sicily."

"North Africa! Was it all sand and wilderness like in the newsreels?"

The sergeant gave a sharp laugh. "No. I'd seen the newsreels too and was all set for blistering deserts and sandstorms. We landed in Algiers in November, so we didn't have the heat, but the rain and mud were enough trouble. Everything got bogged down, including supplies. Worst Christmas dinner I've ever had, counting the first year my sister made the pudding."

He grinned at her, hazel eyes bright, and then froze. Clearing his throat, he dropped his gaze to his shoes.

She fixed her eyes back on the road. "Were you ever sent to France at all? Two of my cousins were there."

"No. We were tossed out before I could be sent over. Where did your cousins go afterwards? Maybe I met them over here..."

"Well, one was Charles. He was wounded in the retreat, you know. Invalided back. Great Aunt Helena had him come up here to finish his convalescence—we were worried about that leg for a while." She hesitated. "The other was Roger, his brother. He didn't get out of Arras."

The wagon's wheel thumped into a rut in the road, and Evie focused hard on the reins, grateful for the distraction.

After a moment, the sergeant said, "I'm sorry for your loss."

"Everyone's lost someone." She sounded brusque and she regretted it, but she didn't want to explain. Quickly, she moved on. "But you—you were wounded on Sicily? How did you end up here? Are you going to be sent back?"

"After I'd spent some time in field hospital, well, between the malaria and the shoulder, they weren't sure when I'd be fit for duty. Since we've got the Mediterranean again, I was invalided back and then sent up here when I was well enough—making room for others. The last doctor said I should be good as new within a month. Hopefully I'm healed quickly enough to go over with the next reinforcements."

"So, you want to go back, then?"

"My mates are still over there." His jaw was tight, his eyes focused straight ahead. Evie asked no more questions.

They finished in the early afternoon, pleased with their accomplishments, and Mrs. Davies had them all upstairs for tea. The sergeant moved slowly on the stairs, careful to keep his sling from bumping the wall. Evie didn't say anything, but she made certain he had everything he needed to hand.

Seated next to the thin, silent Julie, Mrs. Davies bubbled over with enthusiasm. "Well done, Evie! And I hope Julie was a help to you. What shall we plan next? What do you think about setting up a clothing swap? Or they're always looking for metal for the factories, so maybe an aluminum drive? And I wish we could send something to the cities where the bombings have been."

"I think any one would be wonderful. The clothing swap might be nice for the families with growing children, you and the Smarts, and the Bradleys. Anything extra could be sent to the bombed-out areas."

Mrs. Davies nodded. "Here, Sergeant, would you like some bread and jam? I'm afraid it's Wheatmeal loaf, frightfully nasty, coarse stuff, but what can we do? They've got to use all of the grain, but I surely do miss good white bread." She took a slice for Julie's plate, skipping her own. "The jam helps—carrot jam, if you can believe it. It came out rather well, I think. The boys were all for planting more and more carrots after seeing those flyers about the RAF pilots and how they improved their night vision with 'em." She looked past Evie, out the window. "Those morning broadcasts from the Ministry of Food with the recipes and all are a great help. Is your cousin, Mr. Heatherington, involved with those at all, Evie?"

"He hasn't ever mentioned it."

"It's a grand thing that he's gotten that position." She paused, then commented in an offhand fashion, "He'll likely be ready to settle down soon, don't you think?"

Oh, for heaven's sake. Why not just come out and ask? She kept her voice even and pasted on a smile. "His work seems to keep him very occupied."

Mrs. Davies smiled knowingly. The sergeant downed his tea.

CHARLES SIPPED THE MUG of tea he had brought to his desk and idly twirled a pencil between his fingers. He tried to focus his attention on the half-completed paperwork before him. The pencil stayed poised over the form.

I wonder what she's doing now. Wish they hadn't sent Milburn along with her. We don't even know the fellow, but I know soldiers. I certainly wouldn't be sending a girl like Evie out alone with one...and the way he looked at her...

"You'd best look busier than that." He glanced up as Gladys rushed past in a swirl of red skirt, pasteboard box of ration booklets in hand.

"Oh?"

"I just heard we've got a visitor coming in. Lord Woolton himself! Checking out how things are running and all that. Time to smarten up!"

Charles felt a surge of excitement. Lord Woolton! As Minister of Food, the man had done a brilliant job of boosting the image of the Ministry and getting the public behind the necessary rationing policies. More importantly, he was a man of influence. Charles straightened his collar, smoothed his hair, and made certain that his cane and stiff, injured leg were visible.

Silver-haired and as friendly-looking as his voice on the wireless suggested, the older man in a slightly oversized dark suit came walking by only moments later, visiting with another employee. He approached

Charles, who rose, and they were introduced.

At Charles's last name a broad grin spread across Lord Woolton's face. "Heatherington. So, Raymond Heatherington was..."

"My uncle."

"Yes! I knew your Uncle. Good man. The last time we met, I recall he introduced me to another nephew—in the Army. Roger Heatherington."

Charles kept his smile fixed in place. "Yes sir, Roger was my brother."

The other man caught the past tense and gave a sympathetic nod. "Ah. Fine young man, very impressive. Didn't make it back from France, I take it?"

Shifting his leg with a grimace, Charles replied, "No, sadly not."

"Well, well. Pleasure to meet you..."

"Charles."

"Charles." He was already looking past him, ready to move on. "Keep up the good work."

Charles eased himself back down, leg throbbing. He stared at the papers on the desk for a moment, unseeing.

It always comes back to Roger.

Roger. Roger in that dark alley, shouting at him to get moving amid the rumbles and roars of the approaching enemy. Roger in his last moments, his eyes wide and shining in the firelight as he realized that he was going to die, and then, empty.

Charles closed his eyes on the image, then took up his pencil. He twirled it between his fingers, then caught it in a tight grip, snapping it in two.

JAMES DREAMED OF AFRICA.

Boots thud, scrub crunches underfoot. The odd metallic clank or grumbled murmur carries over the faint sound of running water, as the men shift their materiel, rifles at the ready.

Cross the river, hold the bridge—simple orders.

Streaks of pale color creep into the gray sky. The light grows until the rim of the sun breaks over the horizon dead ahead, dazzling eyes and casting long shadows.

Not far now.

The fellow ahead stops short and curses. The way to the river is clear, the banks a mere two hundred yards away.

Two hundred yards without a tree, a bush, a hope of cover. Two hundred yards of easy shooting for the Germans, waiting for them on the other side.

Got to do it. Ready, run. The drumbeat of footsteps follows.

The bullets whine by. A man cries out and falls to his right, another to his left. Head down—got to run, even in mud-heavy boots and bogged down with equipment, bent nearly double—almost there!

The river bank opens and down they plunge into the shocking cold.

Hold the rifle high, push against the current. Glance about—not as many men as before, but enough if they can cross—

The far bank. It's too steep, too high.

Men cry out down the line—they cannot get up.

The men can't get up to the top, and Jerry fires down at them, fish in a barrel.

Dive for the far shore—across! His fingers scrabble at the earth of the bank, trying to get a grip. Bits of dirt fall, coating his hands and stinging his eyes,

And then the slip, falling to the scarlet-tinted water.

The frigid river water rushes into his mouth, nose, ears. His sodden clothes pull him down.

Can't stop!

Up! Burst through the current, panting, wiping water-filled eyes.

Where's the rifle?

Groping through the water, his hand bumps something heavy and dark, floating on the surface.

Reggie Cartwright.

Enlisted man. Hardly a man. Small in life, smaller in death, wide eyes staring out of his round baby-face at a sky he can't see.

Swallow it down—it can't matter now. Stand up!

Reg isn't alone. Tom, Peters, Ryan, Davy, Harry, Jonesy, and scores more. All the men lie there, all dead, bodies torn, broken and lifeless, scattered on the muddy banks, or floating, limp arms and legs bobbing gently on the eddies of current.

It's over. It's all over.

I've failed them all.

Nowhere to shelter, nowhere to dig in, no way to retreat. The shell whistles as it falls…

James threw back his covers and sat up, soaked in sweat and gasping. Unable to lie down again, he paced the room until his heart slowed to its normal rhythm.

"It's not true," he told himself, his voice thin and unconvinced. It had seemed so vivid, like a premonition. "But we're not in Africa anymore. And I just heard from Davy. It's not true." He muttered the reassurances. Then, listening to himself, he wondered if he were half mad.

Striding to the window, he jerked the curtain aside and peered out. He hated the blackout curtains. They made him feel shut in, trapped and blind. If something were coming, he wanted to see it, to face it.

Staring into the inky night, he hissed, "Dear God, I've got to get back!"

Morning came too soon, softened by a fine gray drizzle. There was no chance the staff would allow James outside, but for once, he was pleased to have a reason to be trapped indoors. Dark circles under his eyes had greeted him in the mirror as he shaved. Tired and low, he decided that it would be best to avoid Evie.

What's the use of hanging around a girl that I find so… anyway, a girl who's already spoken for? Even if she weren't, I shall be here for less than a month. It would be pointless to try to have any kind of relationship. Pointless, and selfish, and distracting.

In good weather this would be no mean feat, being neighbors in a ridiculously small village, but the rain would give an excuse for him.

The colonel was dictating his memoirs, the nurse had gone into Thrush, and Mrs. Jenkins was overseeing a thorough kitchen cleaning. Wearily resigned to solitude, James had just settled into an overstuffed library chair with a book when he heard a knock at the door.

He wasn't left to wonder who would be out on such a dreary day. Mrs. Jenkins showed Evie in. She looked like a child caught wearing her parent's clothing in an oversized, mannish McIntosh and toting a worn canvas satchel. The damp had made the curls around her face escape her broad brimmed hat and wreathe her forehead.

James rose politely, as Mrs. Jenkins pressed, "Let me take your wet things, Miss Worther."

"Thank you. I don't intend to trouble you for long." She pulled the coat off and James caught himself admiring the way her dark green dress—*None of that, now.*

"Nonsense," said Mrs. Jenkins. "I'm needed in the pantry with Betsy, but shall I make a cup of tea for you and Sergeant Milburn?"

Evie hesitated, and James avoided her eyes. She said, "None for me, thank you. I'll just be stopping in for a few moments."

"Very well." Coat and hat in hand, Mrs. Jenkins departed.

Evie stepped further into the room, holding the satchel before her in both hands. "I'm so sorry to bother you, Sergeant."

"No bother." He met her gaze but didn't move.

"Great Aunt Helena was very insistent that I return the colonel's gloves that he left Sunday evening, as well as a few books that we had borrowed, only it seems that he is dictating his memoirs again this morning."

"Yes, and not to be disturbed."

She took another small step forward, hands twisting on the top of the bag. She tilted her head. "May I leave them with you?"

"Of course."

When he made no move to take the bag, she placed it on a convenient small table. She looked up and studied his face, brow furrowed. "Have you any plans today?"

He held up the book. "Reading. And I want to get some letters written."

"Are you right-handed?"

"Yes."

She gave him a rueful half smile that he wished he could return. "It must be a challenge to learn to use the left."

"It's slow going." James kept his reply clipped, hating for her to think him rude, but reasoning that it was for the best. He dropped his gaze to her shoes.

She shifted her feet, seeming uncertain if she ought to stay or go. "Still, it's good that you're making the effort. I'm sure they're anxious about you back home. It's a pity you couldn't go to a convalescent home nearer your own people. Are you writing your family?"

"No. I mean, I do, but today I'm writing a mate in Sicily." *Assuming*

Davy's still alive to get it.

His voice betrayed his worry. Evie stepped forward. "It must be terribly hard, being so far away and not knowing what's going on… over there."

The empathy in her voice raised James's eyes to hers. "Yes, it is."

He turned away from her and walked to stare out the window. The frustrations and fears boiled over into words he hadn't intended to say. "I've trained with and served alongside some of those fellows for years. And leaving my platoon… it's like I've just walked out on them."

He heard Evie move closer. "But you haven't. You were wounded, and ill, and not being in top form—you couldn't even fire your rifle with your shoulder like that, could you? You would've been a danger to them more than a help."

"Yes, that's so." His shoulders slumped, then straightened. "And soon I'll be back."

"Waiting is dreadful."

He turned to her. Her eyes were sad and distant. He offered what he hoped was an encouraging smile.

She brightened and returned it. "I had wanted to tell you, there's a new show playing tomorrow night over in Farthington—the next village over. It's less tiny than Thrush and has a cinema. I was going to bicycle over, or a family just west of here sometimes drives a cart and picks people up by the church. Would you like to go, too? It's, well, it's something to do, and even if the newsreel is a bit outdated, maybe there'll be something different than you get from the papers and the wireless."

James hesitated, wavering. Evie smiled at him.

Evie was out of breath when she met him at her door Wednesday evening, her face rosy from washing and traces of dirt under her nails. "Sorry, I was working in the garden and lost track of time. Taking advantage of the rain stopping, you know. We've planted lots more vegetables and they're taking off wonderfully."

After a day spent in gray, idle isolation, her bright cheerfulness was like a tonic. James couldn't help smiling back. "That's grand. We always had an enormous garden. Didn't always appreciate it growing up, mind you, especially since Mum always sent us out to weed when she said we were being too rowdy."

Evie laughed merrily, and they departed for the church and their ride. The taciturn driver sat hunched under a great coat despite the warmth of the evening sun peering through the tattered fragments of clouds. James handed Evie up, breathing the fresh, sweet smell of her scent: lilac.

They crammed in next to a couple of girls and a boy who looked a few years younger than Evie. They greeted her, looked James over, and then leaned their heads toward each other, talking and laughing in low voices.

Evie turned to James, pressed in close. "Is your arm all right?" He reassured her, and she added, "You were saying you all got sent out to the garden. Do you have many brothers and sisters?"

He shrugged his good shoulder. "One sister, two younger brothers. She married, but her husband was in the Navy—he went down with the *Hood*."

Evie made a sympathetic noise. James added, trying to lighten his family sorrows, "She still runs the village pub. Between that and their two boys, she keeps occupied."

"And your brothers—didn't you say your mother's keeping them at home?"

"Well, sort of. They're both too young to be called up. Hal's in the Home Guard. He tried to lie about his age and enlist early, but the village's too small and a fellow went and told Mum. She brought him home by the ear. Probably for the best. He's young for his age. Doesn't understand what he'd be getting himself into." He shifted, lips pressed together, picturing Hal's eager face and idealistic speeches. "Hopefully, it'll all be over before he's old enough."

"How long..." Evie hesitated, then said, "Is there no chance to see any of them while you're here?"

James shrugged again. "It's hard to get Dad off the farm. I hope... well, maybe Mum and some of the others may be able to come and see me off."

They pulled up to the cinema, a dingy building tucked between a chemist shop and an ironmonger's. Its once jaunty yellow paint peeled and cracked around the wide doors.

Inside, Evie was accosted by a couple of girls, one of whom whispered loudly, "Ooooh! Who's your date?"

Evie widened her eyes and shook her head. James feigned deafness.

Turning to him, she introduced Mary and Sophia—sisters, and friends from her childhood summers at Stoneglenn. Red-lipped Mary, cigarette in hand, lounged along, cool and disinterested. Mousy-haired Sophia—though she'd tried to make up for her pale complexion with extra make-up—tended to fade into the background.

Once introductions had been made and seats found, the sisters fell to giving detailed accounts of the sorrows of rationing, the gain and loss of boyfriends, and the fates of various mutual acquaintances.

Intermittently they recalled James's presence and tried to include him, but he soon made excuse to go and see if there were any concessions to be had.

He returned as the lights dimmed but hesitated just behind the girls' row when he heard Sophia ask, "Where's Charles? We never see him anymore."

He didn't particularly want to think about Charles, nor did he want to eavesdrop, but curiosity kept his feet still and voice quiet.

"Working. He comes up weekends to visit Great Aunt Helena."

Mary snorted and then coughed on the smoke. "Yes, I suppose he's got to suck up, but I'm sure it's not only dear Great Auntie on his mind. Has he proposed yet?"

"Oh, yes, has he?" asked Sophia, her voice dripping apprehension.

James's heart stopped.

Evie bowed her head, examining her fingernails. "I don't know why everyone keeps asking that."

Rather than a snort, Mary tried an expressive shrug with more success. Sophia exhaled.

Evie sighed. "Look, he hasn't. Not in so many words. But, well, he has hinted. And I've done my best to discourage him."

Mary took a long drag. "Well!"

Sophia cried, "Oh, but why, Evie? He's so handsome and self-assured and charming!"

"When he wants to be," Mary said.

Ignoring her, Sophia continued. "Don't you think, maybe…?"

Evie shook her head. "No, Sophie. I know my own mind and whatever he is, he isn't for me."

James knew he shouldn't feel so relieved. *Just because she doesn't care for him doesn't mean that you have a chance—and besides you've got no business…*

Mary threw her arm around her sister. "Old Sophie always liked him though, didn't you? Maybe when Evie says no, you can console him!"

Sophie shrank into her seat.

Mary leaned across her, close to Evie, and lowered her voice, though James could still just make out the words. "What about that sergeant of yours? He's awfully nice looking, so tall and tanned, and such sad eyes. He looks like he could use a nice girl to distract him from his cares…"

A flush of heat rising up his neck, James cleared his throat and walked forward to join them. Evie jumped as if she'd been stung. Mary laughed, gave him a saucy grin, and leaned back into her seat.

During an intermission, Sophia leaned over and whispered in Evie's ear. James heard Evie whisper back, "What about Mary?" Sophia's reply was inaudible, but something about it must have displeased Evie. She frowned as she turned to him, but then relaxed her face into a smile. "Excuse me—can we get past? Sophie and I will be right back."

He stood to let them pass, noticing Evie turn back to give Mary a curious look—not quite frowning but with a little worry line between her brows. Returning to his seat, he bumped elbows with Mary who had scooted over next to him. "Oh—excuse me."

"That's alright." Shaking her golden hair back and smiling, she observed, "It must be pretty tiresome, stuck for your convalescence out in the middle of nowhere."

He stared at the cigarette in her hand. "It's quiet."

"You know, we aren't very far away. It's tricky to find a ride, but if you'd like, I can give you a number where I can be reached just about any time. I work in the telephone exchange, but the other girls will cover for me." She batted her eyes and leaned closer. "I'd be happy to show you around. I'm sure we'd have some laughs."

James shifted away. "Thanks, but I'm only here for a few more weeks."

"Well then, why waste time? Come down this week!"

The far arm of the seat dug into his side. "I don't think..."

Mary raised carefully penciled eyebrows. "Wait, a few weeks, and then you're back to the front? How frightfully—what? Thrilling? Dreadful? I *would* like to know what it's all really like over there." She leaned closer still.

"I'm not sure you would."

In spite of his cool tone, Mary tried one last tack. "Well, if not that, then I'm sure we can find something to talk about to keep your mind off it all."

James gave no more ground. His courage had always risen under attack. He met her eyes. "Mary, you're a lovely girl. I'm sure you'll find a fellow who'll be able to stick around, but that's not me. So."

She blinked, then leaned back and took a last drag from her cigarette, face betraying nothing, eyes appraising. "So." She nodded. "You're that sort." With a grin, she shrugged. "I suppose I can't object that she fancies you, then. Too bad." She shifted her weight so that she was no longer confronting him. She took out another cigarette and offered it to him as he blinked in surprise.

"She?"

Mary rolled her eyes. "Innocent as kittens you two are, and you with a couple of years abroad, too." She held out the cigarette again, and he shook his head. With a shrug, she continued. "I imagine you do well enough as a soldier, but you don't know much about girls, do you? Of course Evie likes you."

"But…"

"Charles," Mary nodded, "wants Evie. But she'll make up her own mind, never fear." She fixed him with a stern glare. "You must promise to be very good to her. She deserves it."

This speech left James open-mouthed. He managed a weak, "I…" but there came Evie and Sophia, intermission was over, and he was left sitting, relieved that the lowered lights concealed what he was certain was a foolish grin spread across his face.

CHARLES SMILED showing too many teeth—a shark, scenting blood in the water. "Well, Chester. Your records are certainly…interesting. Would you like to try to explain any of these items?"

The little man in his ostentatious green suit worked his hat between his hands. He fixed his eyes on a point over Charles's shoulder. "No, sir, Mr. H. You know I run an honest business. Never any trouble with the Ministry before…"

"Well, then, if this is all above board, you won't object to my taking these records in. I'm sure everything will be satisfactory."

A bead of sweat trickled down Chester's florid face. Charles ignored him and began gathering the papers.

Chester seized the edge of the box. "Wait! I may have, I mean, one of my under clerks may have—you know how hard it is to find good help, right, Mr. H? Incompetents, most of them, who's to say they mightn't've gotten some ration coupons confused for others, or miscounted..."

"Hmmmm. Interesting." Charles continued his work. "Of course, even if mistakes were made I'm certain that the Ministry would like to know. After all, as long as you have the goods in hand, how can I be sure you aren't going to be trying to make a little extra profit on the side? I hear that spivs make good money, no matter how unfair your black market is to the law-abiding citizenry."

Chester leaned in close, hissing rapidly, breath foul with fear through his broken teeth. "No way I'll be able to unload all this quick enough. I'm a little fish, Mr. H, just trying to get by, just like everyone else. Even the coppers look the other way these days most times...c'mon, can't a bloke catch a break, just once, please... I've some lovely things on hand if you're needing anything..."

Charles kept his eyes fixed on his box a moment longer, pretending to study the contents, fighting the smile that was threatening to return.

I love it when they squirm.

When he had regained his composure, Charles looked up. "Just what are you suggesting?"

"I just need time, Mr. H, just time to clean up this mess."

"So, you think you can bribe me for more time?"

Chester hesitated, eyes measuring. "Certainly not, Mr. H! As I said, I'm an honest businessman! But some of this lot, well, I don't know what to do with it now it's here, and I figure a favor for a friend...I just want us to be reasonable..."

Charles allowed himself to look less disapproving. "Hmmm. It *is* late and there isn't anyone to check through these records tonight anyway, I suppose. It might even take a day or two to get through all of it." He set the box down. "What did you have in mind?"

Four

A GRAY SKY and a fluttering white sheet of notepaper greeted James as he paced Thrush House's grounds on Wednesday morning.

He paused at the gap in the hedge, staring at the paper which had been folded over once and impaled on one of the skeletal twigs. Large, looping letters addressed the note to him.

Pulling it free, he read the signature and grinned.

Good morning! I wondered if you'd like a walk into the village today.
I am visiting a friend and could use the help of your good arm.
If you are willing, please meet me at a quarter of 10 at my gate.
-Evie

Mystified, but not displeased, James checked in with the staff at Thrush House. Far from the jailors he'd fancied them a few days ago, they seemed pleased to see him getting out, provided he followed the doctor's orders. Assuring them that he would, he left for Stoneglenn's gate.

He was greeted by a large wicker hamper sitting alone in the weeds by the dusty verge of the road. Moments later Evie appeared, lugging an identical one.

"Good morning!" she called, breathless but smiling. "I'm not sure what your doctor's orders are. Will that be any trouble for you?"

James hefted the hamper in his left hand and assured her that it would not.

"Oh good! Molly usually goes with me, but Great Aunt Helena

won't spare her, and I can't quite manage both of them."

She set the hamper down, her smile becoming uncertain and her cheeks flushing. "Thank you for meeting me. I—I hope you didn't mind the note. It seemed to cheer you up, having something to do last night, so I thought..."

"No, I didn't mind. You're right. It's nice to have something to do. And it's nice to be useful. Where are we going?"

Evie picked up her load and started walking. "On Wednesdays Great Aunt Helena sends some extras to a war widow in the village." She shifted her grip. "It's been pretty rough on her, so we all try to help out."

"She's fortunate to have you."

Evie shrugged. "How could we not help? Anyway, she's a lovely person. I always enjoy the visit."

James felt a pang when Mrs. Smart opened the door to Evie's knock with a smile on her broad, unlined face—she was an even younger widow than his sister Janet had been.

Handing over her hamper, Evie relieved her of the baby she held, who blinked and then burst into noisy tears. Unabashed, Evie plumped him on her hip and handed him a little blue flannel bear from her pocket. He calmed while James helped Mrs. Smart unload.

She exclaimed over the soap and various foodstuffs. "Oh, Evie! Wherever did you get this?" She held up some dark blue cloth.

"Charles. He always manages to find whatever's needed. I guess that comes with working for the Government. And look in there!" Evie pointed to a basket nestled carefully in the top of the other hamper. "Eggs! Mr. Claridge had some to spare, and we hadn't used our allotment. They beat the powdered ones anyway."

"Oh, and sugar!"

"Yes!" Evie lowered her voice to a whisper. "Enough for a birthday cake, maybe?"

"Perfect!" Mrs. Smart embraced her. Then she quickly covered the hamper as running footsteps announced the arrival of two more children—auburn-haired girls, ages about five and seven.

"Miss Worther! Miss Worther!"

"When can we come to tea again, Miss Worther?"

"I like your dress, Miss Worther!"

"Did you bring more jam, Miss Worther?"

The smaller girl noticed James and stood staring, one finger in her mouth. Her bolder sister stepped forward. "You're a soldier, aren't you? Did you know our papa?"

Their mother murmured, "Now Lucy…"

James knelt down to her level. "I don't know. What was your papa's name?"

"Peter Smart. He was a very brave soldier. He died in France, and he's in heaven now."

Poor little mite. "No, I wasn't in France with your papa, but I'm sure you're right, and he was very brave. Are you very brave, too, and a helper for your mum?"

She stood taller. "Yes, I am! I can watch my sister and brother now because I'm big, and I even dust!"

"Well, that's very good," James said, smiling.

Giving him a grateful look, their mother shooed the children back outside and James and Evie over to the little table. "You'll both stay for a cup of tea?"

The baby had cuddled against Evie's shoulder and dozed off. James pulled his eyes away from her fingers idly stroking his soft curls as Mrs. Smart asked him about where he'd served. The girls burst in occasionally—individually to report grievances and in pairs to see what the grown-ups were about. When the baby started fussing, Evie and James took their leave amid many thanks for visiting.

A short distance down the road, Evie thanked James, too. "It must have been a little awkward, not knowing them at all. It was kind of you to stay so long."

James shrugged it off. "I'm pleased I could be of some use."

"Yes—that's how I feel, too. I hate to think of those little ones never knowing their papa…" She bit her lips, and for a moment James was certain that she was thinking about something besides the Smarts' sorrows. She shook herself back to the present, pulling out a handkerchief and dabbing at the wet patch the baby's mouth had left on her blouse's shoulder. "At least we can try to make sure they're provided for."

"Pity, really. Maybe it's better…"

"What?"

"I was just thinking about my sister. At least the boys were a bit older, but it won't be easy for all of the 'Mrs. Smarts' to be independent again. Maybe it would have been better if they hadn't married in wartime." *And maybe it would be better if I were less of an idiot and stopped hanging around you.*

Evie frowned and shook her head. "I see what you mean, of course, but she didn't marry in wartime. The girls were born before Peter went over. And even in peace there aren't any guarantees."

She looked out over the fields, up towards the hills. Heavy clouds shrouded their green heads. Her voice sank. "We lost Father when I was ten. I suppose it was a result of war—he served in the Great War and his lungs were never quite right afterwards. Still, while I'd agree that some people get a little, well, *hasty*, in the end, don't you think you've just got to make the best plans you can and trust God to make it right?"

The question that had gnawed at James since Tunisia sprang to his lips. "Do you think He will? Make this business right somehow?"

Stones crunched underfoot. Evie glanced over. "Don't you?"

"I try to. But, you haven't seen…" He groped for the right words. The blood. The blasted, broken bodies. The empty, hollow eyes of men who'd seen more than any man could take. The rows upon rows of hospital beds. The evil that one man could do to another.

He sighed and stared at the roadside. "There's an awful lot of ugliness in the world that you haven't been exposed to. I'm not denying God, but it's been difficult to see… how He would allow it to happen." Kicking a loose stone, he looked over at her.

She was fishing in her pocket. Drawing out the crumpled handkerchief, she dabbed again at her still-damp shoulder and then shook her head. Rather than return the handkerchief to her pocket, she held it, working it between her fingers. "I…I wondered that when Mother died. It seemed like losing Father ought to be enough…" Her voice broke, but she took a moment, then lifted her chin and continued. "But then Father Carter suggested reading Job—what ugliness he lived! And yet God hadn't left him. Even though Job couldn't understand it all, there was a greater plan."

James shrugged his good shoulder. "He didn't get to see the plan for a good long time, though, did he? Davy, one of my mates, he always brings up one verse, a psalm I think—"Wait on the LORD: be of good courage, and he shall strengthen your heart; Wait, I say, on the Lord.'"

"Yes! Psalm 27, it's my favorite." Evie recited quietly, "'The LORD is my light and my salvation; whom shall I fear? The LORD is the strength of my life; of whom shall I be afraid?" She trailed off and shrugged. "And then it ends like you said. Wait."

James gave a wry half grin. "So, I guess we wait. And see."

Evie laughed, a sad sound. "I get so tired of waiting." She turned her face away from James, and they finished the walk in silence.

EVIE HURRIED UP to her room, pleased that no one stopped her on the way. Closing her door, she sank down on the yellowed, embroidered coverlet, resting her cheek against the faded roses on the wallpaper. Unable to hold back the flood of memories, she shut her eyes and let them wash over her.

After Father's death, Mother had moved them to London. She'd held Evie on the train ride, whispering in her ear that there was nothing to fear. Mother had dressmaking experience and would find work. Evie would continue school, and life would, though slowly, return to normal.

Normal. Since Father's illness nothing had seemed normal. He had been a quiet man, gentle, and well-read. Evie had never fathomed how he had managed to woo her fiery mother, but the two of them adored each other. When his illness set in in earnest, they had fought it with doctors and treatments, slowly draining finances in the process. Nothing they tried mattered. He slipped slowly away.

At least I got to say good-bye. Evie impatiently brushed an errant tear off her cheek. With Mother there had been no chance.

Once the war had begun, Mother had taken a job sewing uniforms instead of dresses. She had gone to work as usual. Late in the afternoon, the sirens had started.

The neighbors had taken Evie to their Anderson shelter in the back garden. It was a dark little hole, with a cement foundation buried in the dirt and a roof of corrugated metal arching over, covered in turf. The light of an oil lamp on the center table wanly illuminated their pale faces. It was a wet day, and she'd tucked up her feet, not wanting to get her stockings dirty in the puddle on the floor—Mother had said they were nearly through their ration of soap.

At last, the all-clear sounded. She and the others had emerged, crumpled and blinking and looking around for any damage.

At first, Evie hadn't been surprised that Mother was late coming home. Her shift had been due to end near the time of the raid.

As the time stretched on, she had begun to wonder, pacing their little hall, rushing to the door at any noise.

When the truth came, she'd just sat on her neighbor's couch, dry-eyed, holding a rapidly cooling cup of tea and staring at her skirt. Mother had been looking at the hem yesterday to see if it could be let down any more.

The train ride up to the country had been brown and gray, full of khaki-clad men and somberly dressed people under leaden clouds. The man and woman in the seat behind her were telling the couple across the aisle how they had been diverted from their last train due to an unexploded bomb on the track. Evie had huddled into the corner of her seat, chilled and alone.

Alone. Evie sighed as she returned to the present. She wiped her eyes and smoothed an imaginary wrinkle in her pillowcase.

Great Aunt Helena had tried to make the big house a home, in her way. She'd provided this room, food, clothes and occupations to keep Evie busy. And Evie had made the best of it, tried her best to love her Great Aunt and cousin, to do her duty wherever she could.

Still, the chill of that full but empty train car had never left Evie's bones. She had never escaped the feeling that she was a guest here—not a resident—disconnected, drifting.

But now—now I'm not the only one. Now there was the sergeant—quiet, serious James with his strong hands and his thoughtful eyes, as unmoored as she was in these peaceful fields. James, whose expressions she was just learning to read with some confidence—from the melancholy looks reflecting his pain and loneliness to that grin that surprised her with its humor and warmth, lighting up his features every time it appeared.

Of course, he would be leaving soon, too.

She sighed and flopped backwards onto her bed. "Evie," she told herself sternly, "you're an awfully silly girl."

AT THRUSH HOUSE, James was surprised when Colonel Bryce took a break from memoir writing and made an appearance at tea. The colonel spent less time eating and drinking than grumbling, cursing, and beating his leg with his riding crop because the wireless was broken, and he would miss the evening programs.

His mood improved quickly on the receipt of an invitation from Mrs. Heatherington stating that, having been informed of the colonel's misfortune (in the mysterious fashion that news travels in small communities), the men were invited to join the ladies at Stoneglenn for that evening.

The invitation was duly accepted, and the small party assembled. The room was all wood and brocade, decorated in the fashions of a generation ago, and Mrs. Heatherington presided in her chair like a queen on her throne.

Evie was over at a side table, preparing some refreshment. James sidled across the room toward her, but when she straightened and turned, he froze, hands in pockets, avoiding direct eye contact.

After the way we left things this morning, what do I say? "Hullo Evie! Sorry I made you talk about your father's death. Better now?"

Mercifully, the colonel marched over with a hearty, "Well now, Miss Worther, and you sergeant, what do you think of all this then?" He left no time for awkwardness, quizzing them on their thoughts on the Allies' next moves, so that he could debunk them with his own well-polished theories.

Just as he was getting a good head of steam up, Mrs. Heatherington called him over. "What is your opinion, Colonel? What station shall we listen to? Home Service or the Forces Programme?"

The colonel hesitated. "Well, Home Service has the more serious topics, I think, but I'll bet you, Miss Worther, would rather listen to the Forces Programme—see if there's any new music, or if *It's that Man Again* is on?"

"I think that would be lovely." Turning to James, Evie asked, "What do you think?"

"I'd like the Forces, if everyone else agrees." As all was arranged, he added, "The comedies are my favorite."

"Oh, yes, though some of the dramas are rather good—did you hear the one..." As all was made ready and the stately wireless in its shining wood veneer crooned the first strains of the evening's entertainment, Evie sat on the sofa, a hard, brocaded affair, and took out her mending basket. She smiled up at James, who was perfectly happy to forgo the more comfortable seats surrounding to join her.

THE NEW PART for the colonel's wireless would not come until Saturday, when Charles would bring it from town. Mrs. Heatherington graciously invited the gentlemen to join them each evening until then.

Thursday night, as the colonel and Mrs. Heatherington discussed the musical program for the evening and Evie knit something yellow, James found himself telling her about his home. He swallowed a wave of homesickness as he described the sprawling farmhouse in Lancashire where his family had resided for generations, mainly raising sheep.

While counting her stitches she said, "It sounds beautiful. When this is all over, do you intend to go back?"

"Yes, God willing. I'm the eldest, and it's expected, but I love the old place, and I love the work. It's hard work, but it's good. My brothers, now, I don't know that they'll stick to country life. They've always said it was too slow for them. Me, I can't imagine anything slower than being trapped behind a desk or indoors in a factory all day."

"Yes, I can't imagine you having to sit all day—you can't even stay indoors much to recuperate. I see you pacing around over there at all hours. Not that I'm *watching* you over there, I just..." She closed her mouth, opened it again, and looked away from James's broad grin to examine her knitting needles. "I mean I see you. When I'm outside. Sometimes." Silence descended as the number on the wireless ended, and she focused furiously on counting her stitches until the music resumed. Appearing eager for a change in subject, she looked up with another question.

"How did you end up leaving? Were you conscripted?"

He shifted in his seat, then shrugged his good shoulder. "I had just turned eighteen when they declared war and expanded conscription. My best mate was called up, so I went, as well."

"But wouldn't you have been exempted? Essential workers…"

"Well…" He shrugged again. "I've no love of fighting, but if Tom was going, I was bound to go over, too. I'd not leave all of my mates to serve while I sat at home shearing sheep..." He met Evie's shining eyes, and he finished in a rush, "It just seemed like what I ought to be doing. The right thing, and all that."

Her busy hands slowed. "Did you and your friend end up serving together?"

"All the way into Tunisia." Clearing his suddenly thick throat, he said, "He didn't make it through."

Evie's needles stilled. Reaching over, she put her hand over his for a moment. He started, then nodded thanks.

The song playing in the background ended, and she jerked her hand away, glancing over her shoulder. The colonel and Mrs. Heatherington were still deep in conversation. Turning back, she picked up her knitting again, but held it limp in her hands. She bit her lip, then ventured, "Were you…were you able to be with him when…"

"No." James paused and then continued speaking, almost to himself. "We were assaulting Medjez. Had to cross the river and take the far side of the bridge. There was no cover near the river, and the bank on the far side was high. Those who made it across found some shelter in the cactus groves—nasty business—tanks headed our way, and we couldn't keep the ground we'd gained. We gave it all back, retreated to the other side."

He swallowed, remembering the frustration, the fear. "I found, after it was all over, that a bullet had nicked my leg. Nothing serious but it needed dressing. Any kind of wound festered so quickly there. The medical officer who did it up told me. He knew Tom and I'd been mates. He'd helped carry him off." He shrugged, as if he could unload the weight on his shoulders with the careless gesture. "Sounded like it was quick. Tom'd knocked down one of the boys when he saw a grenade headed their way. Couldn't clear himself out fast enough..." His words ran off into silence as he stared into his empty hands.

Through it all, Evie said nothing. He cleared his throat. "Sorry about babbling on like this."

Looking up, he met her suspiciously moist eyes. Alarmed, he clumsily offered, "There now, I'm sorry. Don't..."

"No, please, don't be sorry." She gathered herself, dashing the back of her hand across her eyes, and taking a deep breath. "I'm all right. It's just all so awful. I wish..." Hands spread wide, she paused, groping for the right words. "I wish I could *do* something. I wish I could..." She heaved a sigh. "I'm so sorry, James."

"Well, that's war. I didn't mean to go into all of that." He gave her half a smile.

"What's that?" The colonel came over, beaming. Evie surreptitiously wiped her eyes again. "Telling our young Miss about the glories of battle?"

"Something like that, sir."

"Quiet down! The next show's starting!" ordered Mrs. Heatherington.

James and Evie exchanged a look and settled in. *I could imagine that aunt of hers leading a charge. No one'd dare to step out of line.* He grinned to himself, until the announcer mentioned the date.

His grin faded as he realized that two weeks out of his month at Thrush House were gone.

Five

SATURDAY CAME, and with it, Charles. He produced gifts for all the ladies of the house: chocolates for Great Aunt Helena, a tin of biscuits for Molly and Cook, and Evie's favorite scent in a cut glass bottle. He looked very pleased with himself in a new dark suit. Evie wondered how he'd have any clothing coupons left for the winter.

In high spirits, he offered, "Great Aunt Helena, do let me push you around the grounds a bit. It's very fine out. I've asked Cook, and she says that she can manage a cold luncheon on the grass. It'll be like old times."

To Evie's surprise, Great Aunt Helena agreed.

During their stroll, the matriarch critiqued Evie's work on the flower beds with relish, gave advice on the care of the kitchen garden, and once again exclaimed against Evie's suggestion of a chicken coop. "Think of the smell, child. And the noise."

"I was thinking of fresh eggs. And meat."

Charles said, "Never fear, Cousin Evelyn, I will see that we do not lack, without you needing to tend livestock!" He gave her a bow, and she laughed in spite of her irritation.

Oh, why can't we always get along this well?

After the meal, Evie excused herself to go and practice for Sunday. Charles frowned. "Evie, after last week I thought we'd agreed that you didn't need to be doing that anymore."

"You agreed, Charles. And Father Carter is expecting me to play."

Charles's frown deepened. "Well. I hope you will consider my advice before he is expecting you again next week. And after all, I suppose we can practice your tennis later this afternoon."

"Yes, of course." She stifled a sigh.

"I'll walk you to the church anyway, shall I? If Great Aunt Helena will release me."

The old woman, watching the exchange with interest, said, "Oh yes, please go. After all the fresh air this morning, I am quite ready for a rest. Just send Molly down."

Evie hesitated. "That would be very nice. James—Sergeant Milburn, that is—will likely be joining us, at least as far as the Post Office. Oh, here he is already!"

Great Aunt Helena chuckled at Charles's expression as Evie, avoiding looking at either of them, hurried over to greet James.

By the time he joined them, Charles had slipped on a welcoming smile. He shook hands and exchanged pleasantries with the other young man.

As they walked, he positioned himself in the center of the party and conversed with James—or more accurately, at James—all the way to the Post Office. To the barrage of questions and observations the other man launched at him, James responded with a 'yes,' an 'I don't suppose so,' and several non-committal shrugs.

Leaving him there and continuing on, Charles observed with amazement, "What a dull fellow! One can hardly get two words out of him! Still, I imagine it makes him a good soldier—they say 'go', and he goes without inconvenient questions."

Evie took a deep breath and kept her annoyance in check. "He's reserved, but don't you think you're judging him harshly for knowing him so little?"

"And do you know him so much better?"

"We've been thrown together a bit this week. You know how it is whenever the colonel's house is being used."

"Oh, I do. This war has a way of throwing all sorts together, doesn't it? Do you even know what he did before a uniform smartened him up?"

"His family has a farm in—"

"Oh for…a farmer?" Charles rubbed his forehead. "Tell me it's at least their own land—he's not a tenant, is he? No wonder he hasn't much to say—"

"Charles—"

"I hear you took him over to the cinema, too. Hope he behaved himself there in the dark."

Evie stared at him, open-mouthed. Heat flooded her face, and, choked with anger, she could only say, "Charles, don't be disgusting."

She walked into the church without another word.

"HALLO, SERGEANT! Mind if I walk back with you?"

James paused, waiting for Charles to fall into step with him, and adjusted his long-legged pace to the other's limping gait.

"Evie's in no mood for an audience just now," Charles said, voice low and confidential. He gave a rueful chuckle. "Women. Honestly, half of the time I don't know what they want, and I'm not sure they do either."

James managed a faint smile and said nothing.

"So." Charles nodded towards James's bad arm. "What happened?"

"Took a bullet to the shoulder. Tore things up pretty well."

"They sent you back for that?" Charles's tone was careful, polite, but it still set James's teeth on edge.

"Some tricky shrapnel. Had a rough go of malaria at the time, too." He shrugged his good shoulder. "It wasn't my call."

"Mmm." They walked in silence for a few moments. Charles cleared his throat. "Full recovery predicted?"

"Hopefully. We'll see what it does to my aim."

"Infantry, then?"

"Yes."

"Back at it soon, I imagine."

"Two more weeks, if all goes well."

Charles shook his head. "Well, if it doesn't maybe they can find something in the rear echelon."

"No." James didn't realize how harsh the word sounded, until he noticed Charles's curious glance. "What about yours?" he asked, changing the subject and nodding towards the cane.

"Explosion during the retreat to Dunkirk. Bad enough for a permanent discharge, but I can't complain. My brother died in it."

"I'm sorry."

Charles just nodded, face grim and unreadable.

James knew that look, and asked no more, but, spurred by the other man's loss, he volunteered, "I've got two brothers. God willing this'll be done before they can go."

"Yes." Charles shook himself back to the present. "Family. Aren't they, in the end, who we're fighting for? That's one reason," he said with a sidelong glance at James, "that I feel so strongly about Evie. We are the only ones of our generation left. With the loss of her parents, she's been adrift in the world. I'm, well, rather protective of her. Sometimes it makes me come on a little strong, I'm afraid." He gave an apologetic laugh.

James said nothing, but squared his shoulders and lifted his chin, looking straight ahead. *Here it comes. I suppose I deserve it.*

"Evie is so tender-hearted. I've worried about her heart being broken in this war." Charles paused, but James didn't respond. He continued, "I could easily see her being hurt by someone making promises to her that he wouldn't be able to keep. I, on the other hand, am determined to be here, to look after her, no matter what." He stopped, caught James's eye and held it. "I'm sure you understand."

"Yes. Of course."

AS A THANK-YOU for the evenings at Stoneglenn, the colonel had invited his neighbors over for the evening. There was some debate whether Great Aunt Helena could make the short journey at night, but between Charles, Molly, and Evie, they managed it.

Charles could hardly conceal his delight. Milburn was almost silent. Charles watched from across the room as Evie tried to talk to him a few times and was answered in monosyllables.

That's right. Back off and leave her to me.

He felt a little sorry for Evie, who looked bewildered and hurt. She soon ceased her efforts, sitting near the colonel and giving his stories attention in a wooden imitation of her usual self.

It'll be better for everyone in the long run. Everything will work out just perfectly—just as I've planned—and she'll come out of if all right.

He tried to make up for the silence of the other two and flattered himself that he kept the party pleasant. However, when the programs ended, no one seemed inclined to linger.

As he helped Great Aunt Helena into her wrap, he glanced over his shoulder. There stood Evie in the corner by the door, leaning towards Milburn, hands clasped, eyes anxious.

"James, is everything all right?" she asked in a low voice.

"Of course," he replied, voice polite and distant. "Good night, Evie."

Charles could hardly suppress a smile.

He felt less exultant in the morning. Dark circles shadowed Evie's eyes, and he tried to be extra attentive at breakfast. At the service, he sat back near the wheezing pipe organ. He watched the way her eyes kept darting towards the front, where Milburn sat by the colonel.

Maybe I can find her some chocolates this week.

The men from Thrush House disappeared almost as soon as the service was done. Great Aunt Helena, fatigued from the previous day's activities, had issued no invitation for supper.

Everything was moving in the right direction. Charles couldn't resist one more nudge. Before he left to catch his train, he said, "Now Evie, will you please promise me to speak to Father Carter this week about finding someone else to take on this music business?"

She sighed wearily. "I'll see what Father Carter says."

Six

STEADY RAIN FELL from oppressive gray clouds Monday morning. The weather matched Evie's mood. Trapped indoors, she tried practicing on Great Aunt Helena's gracious black piano. It only reminded her of Charles's nagging.

Irritated and unable to focus, she rose and walked to the window. The deluge was so thick that she could barely make out the laurel hedge.

"What's the matter with James?" she asked her reflection aloud.

Charles, the back of her mind whispered.

"No. Why would he..." But she knew exactly why he would.

She tried to cheer herself and set out into the house to see if she could be of use, but playing chess with Great Aunt Helena only reminded her of more pleasant games played with Father, and helping in the kitchen only reminded her of cooking with Mother. She kept telling herself that she really didn't miss seeing James today *very* much. She finally sat down in the sitting room, watching the rain and resigned to being miserable.

The telephone rang, and Evie was summoned. Upon lifting the receiver, Evie smiled for the first time that day.

JAMES HEARD THE QUICK knock at the door and guessed who it was. He sighed, put his book down, and stood.

Evie paused at the library door. He couldn't help but notice that her cheeks were flushed pink above her white blouse, but her eyes looked tired, as if she hadn't slept well, either. Waiting, unsure of what to do, he stood silent while she studied his face in return. Giving a little nod she came forward. "Hullo, James!"

He forced a smile. "Hullo, Evie."

Evie frowned and put her hands on her hips. She opened her mouth, closed it, and then strode to the chair opposite him and sat. The set of her chin and the sharp look she gave him were reminiscent of her great aunt. "James. Whatever is the matter?"

Clearing his throat, he asked, "What do you mean?"

She folded her arms and stared at him.

He sighed and sat as well. "Look. Evie…" He couldn't meet her eyes. Dropping his gaze, he examined her right foot, which was tapping the worn rug. Unfortunately, it was also attached to her pretty ankle, which was not something he wanted to notice. He shifted in his seat and examined his folded hands instead. "Evie, I'm here for less than two weeks, and then only God knows where I'll be or what will happen."

The foot tapping stopped, and her chair creaked as she leaned forward. "I know that, James, which is why I hoped to see you while you were here. I thought we were…friends."

James swallowed the lump in his throat and forced himself to look at her. Those blue eyes looked so hurt and uncertain that he could hardly bear it. He swallowed again and tried to keep his smile steady. "Evie, I'd love to be your friend. You…you deserve all the friendship and kindness you can get. But I don't want to make things harder on you when I go. You've lost enough people."

She dropped her gaze, pursing her lips. "Did Charles say something?"

Scrubbing his hand through his hair, James pushed himself to his feet. He walked to the window, putting some space between them, and looked out at the rain. "What *about* Charles?"

Her reflection in the glass shook its head. "No."

He knew it wasn't his business, but he turned, leaning against the window frame, and asked anyway, "Why not?"

Evie sighed and looked at her hands. "Lots of reasons. I don't love him—not like that. Isn't that enough?"

"Maybe, but feelings can change—"

"No."

He blinked at her vehemence.

She continued, her voice hard. "I will not marry Charles. Not ever. We wouldn't—we wouldn't get on well together."

"He seems nice enough..." The words soured on his tongue, so he hurried on. "In his way. And fond of you."

"Yes, he seems that way."

"But?"

Hands working in her lap, she bit her lip. When she answered, she sounded as if she were reciting out of a textbook. "I know enough about his character to know that I would be unhappy with him."

James raised an eyebrow. "That's cryptic."

"He's family." She frowned down at her hands. "I haven't much of that left." Her voice broke.

Fishing in his pocket for a handkerchief, he came over and sat down across from her. He offered it to her. "I know, but...well, you can keep mum, but I'll probably imagine it's something much worse than what it actually is. Human nature."

She took the handkerchief and knotted it in her hands. After a long pause, she nodded, slowly. "All right. We've known each other our whole lives, Charles and I. He could be pleasant, as long as he was able to run things. He'd get terribly frustrated when the others wouldn't go along and, well, odd little things would happen..." Shrinking into her chair, she shrugged, trying to laugh, though it came out flat. "One summer our cousin Penny's favorite comb was found broken in the garden. It was right after she was teasing Charles about...oh, I can't remember. But another time, there was a terrible row when their father found cigarettes in Roger's pocket, but Roger never smoked. And then Susannah's kitten got out of the house. It took us forever to find the little thing, but it had locked itself into the carriage house." She shrugged again. "Funny things, which Charles may not have done, but...well, there were things he said..." She trailed off.

James's knuckles cracked, and he took a breath and relaxed his fists. *Sounds an unpleasant, spiteful, little blighter.* "Surely he's matured?"

"I hope so. He certainly still likes his own way. What's it to him if I play organ, or serve well at tennis, or—oh, lots of little things."

Playing devil's advocate, James asked, "Doesn't everyone rather like their own way, though?"

"Yes, but...there was a fly in the milk. The delivery boy didn't apologize fast enough, and he pushed until he got him sacked. Or the way he talks to clerks, especially if they make a mistake, or how he talks about people after being so polite to their faces. He can be awfully unkind underneath the polish."

She sighed. "Still, he's family. I try to be patient with him. He's lost nearly everyone, too. His own brothers—you know he was there when poor Roger died? And he couldn't save him. I can't imagine... We all loved Roger."

She uncrumpled the handkerchief, wiped her eyes and shook herself. "But marry him? Everyone assumes it's coming. Him, most of all. They push and push. He's Great Uncle Raymond's heir, after all, so if there's money involved—and there's lots of it, between Uncle Raymond's house and grounds here and the other holdings, and then there's all the money on Great Aunt Helena's side—what does it matter what I say or what I feel? But I just couldn't bear it, James!" She threw up her hands, eyes pleading for understanding.

His fingers twitched, wanting to reach for hers. *But all of this doesn't change the fact that I'm leaving.* He kept his hands still but gave her what he hoped was an encouraging smile. "All right. No to Charles then."

Evie studied his face for a moment, and then managed a shaky smile. "It is a relief to finally explain all of that to someone." She busied herself, smoothing the handkerchief back into neat folds. "I hate having to talk about him like that. He isn't always awful. We had plenty of good times, too. I wish he'd just let things be as they were."

They sat in silence, until Evie broke it with an "Oh!" Brightening, she fished something out of her pocketbook. "Here," she held out a handwritten note, "is something jolly that I came to tell you about—if you're going to talk to me again, that is."

"It doesn't seem that you'll give me much choice." He grinned.

"Mary rang me up. There's going to be a dance in Farthington this Friday night! I've written down the details. There's a door charge and it's all to help war widows and orphans. I haven't gone dancing in... oh, it's been a long time. I love dancing, but I always feel so awkward at those things, going on my own. If only," she looked away from him to examine the unremarkable brass lamp on the table beside her. "If only someone would ask me to go."

Only two weeks left. James shifted in his chair. "I don't know, Evie. I'm no great shakes at dancing."

"Who says I meant you?" She arched her eyebrows. "I was thinking of the colonel."

James guffawed.

"Honestly, I'm a dreadful dancer, but, oh, James, wouldn't it be fun?" Her eyes shone bright as stars.

Two weeks. "What time do we leave?" He added, with some satisfaction, "And, I should be rid of this awful sling by then."

THE WEEK PASSED. Evie practiced her music, visited the Smarts, did her WVS work, read the news from the Front, worked in the garden, amused her Great Aunt, and saw James often. Every morning they walked to check the post together. In the evenings she stitched; she had found a dress of her mother's that would fit just right with only a little taking in.

She finally informed Great Aunt Helena on Thursday that she would be gone Friday evening. When the old woman heard why, she raised her eyebrows. "Does Charles know you're going dancing with the sergeant?"

"No. We haven't spoken since last weekend."

Great Aunt Helena's eyebrows nearly disappeared into her gray fringe. "Are you going to tell him?"

"Of course, when I see him. I'm not doing anything wrong, Aunt Helena. Charles and I are not—well, anything besides relatives, anyway."

Great Aunt Helena looked like a cat with a bowl of cream. "Tell him while I'm in the room, won't you?"

FRIDAY CAME AT LAST. Evie appeared at the door, and though that nagging voice—*only one week now*—attempted to give James pause, she commanded his full attention. Soft red lips, smooth dark hair, dark flower print dress that hugged her curves just so and brought out her eyes, the gleam of her gold cross on her white throat, silk clad legs—and crowning all, that brilliant smile. He was lost.

The neighbor's cart was again the commissioned chariot to the dance hall. When they arrived, they saw that the event had attracted a crowd. As they made their way through the crush to the door, Evie took his good arm and the crowd pressed her close against him; his heart flipped. A photographer was mingling, flash bulb illuminating pairs of laughing, happy faces.

They smiled for the photographer, and then saw Mary and Sophia plowing towards them, each with a young man in tow—American troops. Their smooth, shining faces looked terribly young. After hurried introductions, the girls pulled Evie aside, leaving James standing with the G.I.s. One leaned towards him, almost shouting over the crowd. "Hey, want a cigarette?"

"Pretty dame!" the other observed, giving him a light punch on the arm. James fixed his smile in place and sidled towards the girls.

Mary had grabbed Evie's hand and spun her around. "Darling, you look wonderful! How did you manage it all?"

Sophia shook her head. "You're still in stockings and lipstick, while the rest of us are using gravy coloring and beetroot juice!"

Evie blushed and frowned. "It's Charles. He keeps finding it all somewhere, and he gets very put out if I don't use the things he gives me."

Mary laughed. "Sophie's just jealous. Honestly, I am too! But at least you get to show off the fruits of Charles's labors to your sergeant. I think it's working, too. Can't take his eyes off you!"

James quickly looked away at this, but he still saw Evie's blush deepen behind her brilliant smile.

"Oh, Mary! And who are your dates?"

"Oh, I don't know. They're just in and came up here on leave. One is Ron, and one is Steve, but I can't tell them apart. Can you, Sophie?"

Sophia just looked prim and disapproving, which James felt sure meant that she couldn't, either.

With a parting embrace, Mary and Sophia claimed their G.I.s and disappeared into the mass of people as the band began a few tentative strains that resembled music.

Evie and James made their way to the edge of the floor, avoiding the heavy crowds to protect his arm. He was gloriously free of the sling, but still under strict orders to treat the arm with care. They faced each other, both hesitating, and then James took her hand and put his on her waist, chiding himself for being nervous. Evie's hand slipped up to his shoulder and she smiled shyly at him. The noise and the bustle receded into the background.

They danced for hours with brief pauses to eat and drink. They got very warm and laughed a great deal—neither of them had been overly modest about their dancing abilities. Around midnight the band quit. Footsore and smiling, the dancers headed home.

As they rode, Evie's head drooped down on James's shoulder. James leaned back, content to breathe her in.

Sorry when the ride ended, he helped her down, and they walked, arm in arm, not talking, not needing to.

Too soon, the heavy oak door of Mrs. Heatherington's house appeared. Evie turned to him. "Thank you so much, James. I had a lovely time." A lamp had been left on inside, and a sliver of light peeped out around the edges of the blackout curtains. It bathed her face in a soft glow, and her eyes shone.

One week.

He took her hand, and leaned in, softly kissing her cheek. He began to pull back, but she moved towards him. It was all the encouragement he needed. He slipped his arms around her waist, and her arms went about his neck.

One week.

He leaned down, and kissed her warm, soft lips. He kissed her again, slow, and long, and deep. With a sigh, he rested his cheek on her hair and closed his eyes.

"Good night, Evie."

"Good night, James."

Seven

Out on Evie's windowsill, the little birds were raucously welcoming the morning when she woke. The sun shone in fitful bursts, but clouds on the horizon encouraged her to grab a red knitted jumper on her way downstairs.

As she followed the scent of breakfast, her great aunt's exasperated voice carried into the hallway and slowed Evie's steps. "Really, I don't know what you expected me to do. She's old enough to know what—" She broke off as Evie entered.

Charles looked up, and only his mouth was smiling. "I hear you had quite a time last night."

She forced her voice to remain cheerful, light. "Yes, there was a benefit dance over in—"

"Great Aunt Helena told me. If you were looking for a partner, I could have left town earlier."

"That's so thoughtful of you, Charles, but James asked me the same day Mary rang me up about it."

Great Aunt Helena examined the handle of her teacup, a sly smile tugging the wrinkled corners of her mouth. "I didn't hear you come in last night. How late did the dance go?"

Charles's shoulders became even stiffer.

Evie took a deep breath and her seat. *I've done nothing wrong.* "The band stopped playing at midnight. We caught a ride on Farrier's cart and were in at one—here by one-thirty at the latest—or earliest, I suppose." She yawned. "It was later than I've stayed up in ages, but it was awfully fun to dance again. Next time, Charles, I'll be sure to let you know what's up. Sophia's been asking after you."

He didn't answer, lips tight, spreading jam on his bread with more than necessary vigor. "I suppose you're still playing organ tomorrow?"

"Yes. I spoke to Father Carter, and he encouraged me to continue. And I do enjoy it." *And there's nothing wrong with doing* that, *either.*

His knife hit the edge of his plate with a clatter. "Well, then. If you *do* enjoy it, it certainly must be, whatever scruples others may have—"

"Charles..." She held out her hand towards him, but he ignored her.

"What about some cards, Great Aunt Helena?"

They left, and Evie finished her breakfast alone. For once she didn't mind the snub. When she had finished, she slipped outside, certain James would find her.

She wandered past the flowers in the garden. Tossed about by the rising wind, their red and gold and snowy white petals shone through the gloom. On reaching the little orchard, she looked back toward the gate and smiled to see James just coming through it. She stood on her tiptoes and waved—he raised his hand in response, grin spreading across his face.

He took her hand as he came up. "Good morning. Very tired?"

She stepped closer. "Not very. You?"

Smile broadening, he leaned towards her. Her breath caught in her throat.

"Hullo! Good Morning!" Charles's voice boomed, hearty and over-cheerful. Reflexively, she stepped back. He strolled over, smiling as if finding them together was the most natural thing in the world.

"Great Aunt Helena was just saying how she was longing for a game of bridge, and I thought the two of you might like to join us." Without waiting for a reply, Charles offered Evie his arm. She hesitated, and then, with a poignant look at James, she took it.

"Well, Charles, I suppose we might. James, do you play?"

"A little. I wouldn't mind trying it again." He gave her a quick grin and a shrug over Charles's shoulder.

At least we'll have some time together, she consoled herself. *And perhaps I can just lose quickly...*

Her patience wore thin as the game dragged on, followed by a tedious dinner during which Charles blocked any communication between her and James by maintaining a stream of wooden, pleasant, continuous talk. James sat impassive, but Evie was certain from the set of his jaw that he was silently seething, and just polite enough not to show it. On her other side, Great Aunt Helena also said little, but she watched, smirking.

The meal ended at last. Evie stood, bursting in to Charles's wall of words, "Yes, that's very interesting, Charles. Well, it looks like it might rain. I'd like to check the post before it does."

James stood. "Shall I walk you?"

"Oh yes, if you'd like company," Charles chimed in, beginning to rise.

James stopped him with a look. "Don't trouble yourself."

Charles froze half out of his chair and turned a chilly gaze on James before he rose the rest of the way. "I assure you, it's no trouble."

If they'd been dogs, both men would've had their hackles up.

Evie interjected with a nervous laugh. "Come now. It's only to the post office. We hardly need a parade. Charles, you were just complaining about your leg. Wouldn't you rather—"

"I know jolly well what I'd rather or rather not do, Evie," he snapped.

She recoiled. James stepped forward, putting himself between the two of them.

There was a pause, and then Charles deliberately smoothed his face and gave a careless laugh. "Sorry, *Sergeant*. I just never saw anyone so bent over a fellow wanting to check his mail. By all means, the two of you scurry along. I can walk over later. Great Aunt Helena, would you like me to push you anywhere, or shall I call Molly?"

Once they were safely out the door, Evie let out her breath with a whoosh, and then took James's arm.

He squeezed hers against his side, and asked, "So. D'you think he's happy for us, then?"

GREAT AUNT HELENA was feeling unwell the next morning, and the weather was wet, so she and Charles stayed home from church. Evie came to sit by James when she wasn't playing, savoring the time they had left.

She had been informed that she was expected home directly after service to help as needed.

Still, she lingered with James at her gate, twisting her hands. "It's all so silly. It's not as if Molly can't handle things. Still, I'd just as soon not press it today. After Charles is gone again, it's only Great Aunt Helena to contend with, and I think she likes you. At least she's never said she dislikes you, and if she did—"

"She probably wouldn't hide it." He reached up and tugged one of her curls, fingers lingering against her cheek. She clasped his hand as he lowered it, and he pulled her close for a kiss. "No, you go help your family. I'll see you tomorrow."

AS EVENING APPROACHED the wind rose, pounding against the windows and the French doors of the music room. It provided a fitting backdrop to Evie and Charles's arguing.

Boiling anger flooded Charles, threatening to drown him. He struggled to keep his voice calm. "What about the dress you needed?"

"Charles," she said, shaking her head, "I didn't need a new dress. I have some of Mother's things still, and all I needed was a skirt. Which

I made and am wearing."

"I went to some trouble to find that fabric as a gift for you. And you just give it away..."

She folded her arms, closed her eyes, and took a deep breath. "You said to see what I could do with it, and never indicated that it was a gift. I'm sorry if I misunderstood. I made a skirt, and Mrs. Smart can use the rest—"

"Oh, well, if Mrs. Smart can use it—"

"Yes, she can. With the children she's much more in need of—"

He pounded his cane on the floor. "Honestly, Evie. For all that you pretend to be so generous, I think you're one of the most selfish people I know."

Evie blinked and stepped back. "I...I don't try to make pretensions..."

Stepping after her, he leaned forward for emphasis. "Oh really? You can't help sticking your nose into everything around here, and even after all your running about..." He drew a couple of slim pamphlets out of his breast pocket and threw them down in front of her. "I found these."

"Those were in my room, Charles, what—"

"I was looking for you, and there they were. The Women's Land Army, indeed—what, are you going to go off to muck about in the fields?" He sneered. "Or maybe you're just getting ready to be a filthy little farmer's wife—scrounging around in the dirt with *his* brats pulling at your skirts. That's what you've been dreaming of, isn't it? After all we've done for you, you'll just turn your back on your family." Blood thundered in his ears as he waited for her reaction.

Evie flushed, and then went pale. She pursed her lips and spun away from him, headed for the door.

The anger cooled. *Blast. I've gone too far.*

Wincing as he took two quick steps to get in front of her, Charles put his hand on her shoulder. "Evie? Evie. I shouldn't have said that."

She wouldn't look at him. "No, Charles. You shouldn't."

Swallowing, trying to calm himself, he bowed his head. "I'm sorry, Evie. I am." He looked up at her. She was listening, at least. "You just make me so angry sometimes. You really must let me take care of you—we're just about the only family left for each other, aren't we?"

"Yes, Charles. We are." Her voice shook, knuckles white where they clutched the sides of her skirt.

Leaning in close, he lowered his voice. "Look here, I won't tell Great Aunt Helena about the pamphlets at present—they would only upset her. But you must promise to stay here. Others can and will venture out into the world over all of this current… unpleasantness."

She was silent for a moment, staring at his tie. "If everyone said that, I'm afraid we'd all end up speaking German."

He laughed, ignoring the fact that she had made no promise. "What if we head in for a nice cup of tea?"

"No, thank you. I have a headache starting and I would like some time alone, if you don't mind too much." She said the last as if it were habitual, not as if she were really asking. He chose to ignore this too.

"I don't mind, Evie. You take some time and think about what I'm saying." He squeezed her shoulders and released her.

She brushed past him, back stiff and straight, and he reminded himself that he must tread more carefully. *Especially after what happened this morning. She's just so frustrating. If she'd stopped playing, like I suggested, she would have been home, and it never would have happened. It's just as well I'll be gone when she finds out…*

THE SUN ROSE on Monday, and so did James.

Up with the lark. Or the starlings…

He grinned, then swallowed and dragged his hand through his hair. Two long strides took him the length of his room. Turning, he paced back to his bed.

It's good Charles'll be gone. I'll get a chance to talk to her... He shook his head and ran the words he needed to say through his mind again. They still didn't sound right, but they were the best he had come up with.

Twitching back the curtains, he inspected the angle of the sun, debating whether it was too early to walk over to Stoneglenn.

Better sooner than later, I suppose. Maybe she's up early too.

Striding with more confidence than he felt, he neared her front door before he was entirely ready to be there. He paused, then stopped and listened. His ears strained to catch a curious sound, carried on the wind.

Realization dawned, and he broke into a run.

He rounded the corner of the house to find Evie. She knelt, shoulders hunched, holding something cradled in her hands and weeping softly. Coming closer, he saw the damp, limp form of a baby bird, feathers half come in, neck twisted all wrong. She looked up, face streaked with tears.

"Charles moved the nest yesterday, while we were at church." Her voice was thick. "I didn't know until it was so quiet this morning. I...I suppose this little one fell out." Gently, she transferred the body into her left hand, wiping her eyes with the back of her right. "I'm sorry. I know it's just a bird..."

"'Are not two sparrows sold for a copper coin? And not one of them falls to the ground aprt from your Father's will.' Mum's favorite verse." James sat next to Evie and put his arm around her.

They waited until her tears had subsided, and then they buried the fledgling in the flower beds and looked for the nest. It took a good deal of searching, but they finally found it, pushed back in the far corner of the border hedge. The surviving birds were crying for food, mouths orange and wide.

"See? I wonder if they've been abandoned!" lamented Evie. "Oh, why did he do it?"

James said nothing aloud, but he recalled the stories of kittens and combs and a little boy who liked to punish others. *Was it because of me? Young Mr. Heatherington doesn't like when things don't go his way.*

They foraged in the garden for insects and found an assortment which the little birds thoroughly enjoyed. Evie had looked through Stoneglenn's small library when she had first discovered the nest and unearthed no books about birds (unless one counted cookbooks.) James promised to look at Thrush House. They decided in the meantime to move the nest into the kitchen garden to make it easier for Evie to keep them fed. With any luck, she could support them until they were able to do for themselves. This late in the year, it ought not be long.

It was nearly time for dinner, so James left Evie at the kitchen door, promising to call again in the afternoon.

When he was on his own he walked back to where Evie had found the dead bird. He had a nasty suspicion. The position didn't quite fit with the location of her window ledge. True, it had been windy, but her room was in the lee of the house.

One of the men in his company had been an avid hunter and had prided himself on his tracking ability. He and James had patrolled together frequently, and he had shown James several tricks to reading signs on a trail.

The turf was still soft from yesterday's rain, and there, he could see the marks of Evie's pointed-toed shoes where she had stopped by the bird. There to the side were his own prints. But there and there… He was quite certain that a third set of prints—men's shoes, shorter than his, but slightly broader—had come to the spot, squatted down where the toe prints were deeper than the heels, just in front of where the bird had been found, and then walked away. Next to these prints was a small round depression, about the width of a cane.

The grounds were empty, but anyone who had happened to see

James's face would have agreed that it was fortunate that Charles was several hours out of his reach.

JAMES PASSED his final check-up and was cleared to catch the train Thursday morning.

WEDNESDAY EVENING CAME, and Great Aunt Helena had the colonel, James, and Father Carter for supper. The table was quieter than usual. Evie sat pale and silent and picked at her food. She glanced at James from time to time, noticing that his face was calm, but he couldn't seem to keep his hands still.

The meal over, he murmured in Evie's ear, and they excused themselves from the party. Great Aunt Helena grumbled in a perfunctory way but conceded. As Evie exited, she heard her lean over to tell Father Carter, "They aren't much good for anything anyway."

The late summer sun was setting, a red eye beneath a blanket of low clouds, as James and Evie silently paced the grounds. A chill had crept into the air, and she hadn't grabbed a wrap, so he draped his jacket around her shoulders. She slid her arms into the sleeves and pulled the rough fabric close, inhaling the scent of his shaving soap from the collar and trying to memorize it. He pulled her arm through his and she leaned into him, taking comfort in his warm, solid nearness.

They passed the damp earth smells of the gardens and meandered through the little orchard, where the trees stood like silent sentinels against the growing dark. As they neared the house again, James cleared his throat several times. Evie was just hoping that he wasn't catching cold when he did it once more and stopped. He half turned towards her, sliding his arm free and catching her hand. Not quite meeting her eyes, he said, "Evie."

She waited for him to go on, but he didn't. "Yes, James?"

"Ahem. I—I wanted to—" He shuffled his feet and looked down.

"Yes, James?" Her heart-beat quickened.

Holding her hand a little tighter, he took a deep breath. "Well. We need to talk."

She shivered. Even with his jacket, the evening chill seeped through her thin dress. Still, she wasn't about to suggest they hurry inside. "What should we talk about?"

He took another deep breath, opened his mouth, paused, and then stared into the tree branches as if he might find help from above. Emptying his lungs in a great gust, he barked out a short laugh. "Dash it all, I'm not much good at this. Evie. You know what tomorrow is." He looked down at their clasped hands. "I—well, I know my own mind about you and me, and if I come back, I hope that, if you're still free, you and I—if you'll have me that is—" He paused, raked his free fingers through his hair, and laughed again ruefully.

Barely breathing, Evie waited.

He regrouped, taking another deep breath, releasing her hand and squaring his shoulders. "Evie. I don't believe it's right to bind a girl with any promises in my situation."

Evie blinked. *What?* She opened her mouth, but he held up his hand.

"Wait. I know that there are different opinions on this, but Evie, I just can't." He seized both of her hands and leaned close, eyes pleading. "What if you wait and I don't make it back? Or what if I'm wounded and you're stuck with an invalid? Or if I'm gone for years and you meet someone you prefer?" He shook his head. "I've thought and thought, and I just can't ask you to marry me."

Evie was silent for a long moment, trying to understand what had just happened. "You can't, but you're saying you would, if…?"

He pulled her close and held her, burying his face in her hair. His breath warmed her cheek as he said, "Of course I would. I…well, I love you, Evie. If I were here to stay, I'd marry you tomorrow, if you'd have me."

Closing her eyes, she savored the words. With a deep sigh, she wrapped her arms around his waist and leaned into him. She hoped that he could still hear her voice muffled against his chest. "And I love you, and I'm going to wait anyway, you know." She pulled back a little to wipe off the tears that had appeared on her cheeks. "I'll wait until you tell me you don't want me to anymore."

He squeezed her tighter and chuckled softly. "That's one thing you'll never hear from me. If God grants me my life, I'll come looking for you. First thing."

"Promise?"

"I promise."

WHEN EVIE RETURNED to the house, she went straight to her room and sat on her bed, staring at the walls. A hesitant knock on the door made her jump. "Come in?"

"Excuse me, miss," said Molly, peering around the door with a sympathetic grimace. "Mrs. Heatherington sent me for you."

Great Aunt Helena was sitting up in bed in a lace-trimmed dressing gown. The planes of her face were thrown into stark relief by the bedside lamp. "So, child. Am I to congratulate you? I rather think you might have done better sticking closer to home…" Here she paused, eyebrows raised, scanning Evie's face. When Evie didn't respond she gave a faint smile. "But I don't suppose there was much chance of that. If Roger had made it home...ah, well. At least your sergeant's an eldest son, and the colonel tells me the family land is good. You're still frightfully young, but I suppose he'll do, if he comes back."

Evie couldn't pretend to mistake her meaning. "We aren't engaged, Great Aunt Helena."

"What? What does he mean by it?"

Succinctly, she explained James's reasoning. When she had done, she sat on the edge of the old woman's bed and waited, exhausted.

Great Aunt Helena pursed her lips, considering. With a quick pat to Evie's hand, she nodded. "Well, he's a sensible young man, anyway." She sighed. "Not that I imagine it will make things any easier on you. Not really."

Turning her gray head, her eyes wandered to a picture of Uncle Raymond at her bedside. "When Raymond left me in 1914, I thought I should die." Her hard mask cracked for a moment, and Evie saw the woman of nearly 30 years ago gazing out of her dark eyes.

The impression lasted only a moment—with a shake of her head and a straightening of her shoulders, her indomitable Great Aunt returned. "But I didn't. I endured. And you will, too, child. Charles has the name, but you have my blood. And after all, Raymond came back." She smiled, a bitter twisting of her face. "Of course, he's left me here in the end."

Evie reached out and grasped her hand. Great Aunt Helena allowed the attention for a moment, and then turned her face to the wall. "Go away, now, child. I'm tired."

THEY'D SAID MOST of their farewells before reaching the station, but on the platform, James held Evie one last time.

The whistle blew. She slipped a small package into his hand, and then closed her eyes as he kissed her goodbye. He boarded, and she counted the seconds until his face appeared at a window, his hand pressed to the glass. Forcing a smile, she waved as the train pulled away, gathering speed, until it rounded a curve and he was gone.

Evie stood, staring at the empty track, lips moving in a silent prayer. Then she turned with heavy feet to return to the echoing, lonely halls of her great aunt's house.

CHARLES GLANCED UP from his desk at the wail of the train whistle. Checking his clock against the timetable on his desk, he allowed himself a satisfied smile.

The troublesome Sergeant Milburn was gone.

Part Two

8 September 1943

Dear James,

I hope this finds you well and safely on your way.

I've been keeping busy. The fledglings have all flown, but there is so much work in the garden that I can hardly keep up with it. (My tennis practice, sadly, is suffering. When you return you might want to keep your helmet on.)

Some distant relations of Great Aunt Helena's have contacted us, looking for a place to send their children for a while. One family's home was bombed out in the last raids, so they have been living together. Now both of their husbands have been called up, and the wives have "victory jobs" and, although the bombings are more sporadic, they would like the children out of London. Great Aunt Helena asked my opinion (I was surprised), and I think she may agree. Imagine—this empty old house with children in it again!

It may be that she feels I need something to do with my time. It came to her attention that I had some materials from the Red Cross and the WLA, and I think she was concerned that I might make a break for it and join the larger war effort. (It's not as if I haven't considered it!)

I had intended to write a really long, amusing letter, but I think that I shall stop where I am so that I still have something to write next time—you know how slow it is around here! I wish you were here. I pray for you constantly.

God bless and keep you, James.

Love,
Evie

"Who shall separate us from the love of Christ? Shall tribulation, or distress, or persecution, or famine, or nakedness, or peril, or sword? Yet in all these things we are more than conquerors through Him who loved us." Romans 8:35-37

"So. Who is she?" Lieutenant Harry Bradlock dropped to sit beside James, stretching his boots out ahead of him, digging his heels through the dusty Sicilian soil.

James froze, midway through folding up Evie's letter. "Sir?"

Bradlock nodded his dark, curly head toward the letter and pulled out a cigarette.

"Her name's Evie."

"Hm. For Evelyn? My Gran's name, too. Two chins and lots of whiskers, bless her. Hopefully yours is a better looker."

James pulled out the little pocket Bible that Evie had given him on the train platform and handed over the photo she had tucked inside.

Bradlock gave a low whistle. "Very nice."

"How'd you know?"

"Oh, you're a tough read, but that wasn't the look on a man's face when he gets a letter from his Mum."

James laughed and tucked the letter and picture away. "I should've known you'd sniff it out."

Bradlock grinned and didn't deny it. There was no point—anyone who'd been with him on the march to Messina knew he had instincts like a cat. The retreating Germans had set up an ambush around a blind corner of the road up in the hills. The forward scouts had seen nothing alarming. "Something doesn't smell right," Bradlock had said, and sent a patrol off into the trees to circle around, and sure enough, they captured half a dozen Germans with a machine gun and a sniper. The men had suffered only one wounded.

"So." Bradlock pulled a cigarette from behind his ear and lit up. "What's she like? Must be something if you loosened up enough to talk to her. Assuming you *did* talk to her."

"Evie is..." James scanned the brassy sky, searching for the words, and then gave up and shrugged. "She's lovely. When we make it back, you'll have to come over and meet her yourself."

"Oh HO! That's how it is? Fast work—how many weeks were you there?" He leaned forward to examine James's hand. "No ring?"

"No. I'll propose the day I get back, God willing."

Bradlock threw his head back, exhaling smoke like a chimney. "Pretty girl like that and you didn't speak up? Reminding them that you're off to die nobly for king and country is an awfully good way to get them to say 'yes', you know."

"That's why I couldn't do it."

Clapping James on the shoulder, Bradlock shook his head. "Milburn, you're a good man. Glad to have you at my back again. But sometimes..." He shrugged and heaved himself to his feet. "C'mon. We're up for more training with the new guns."

They climbed up into the Sicilian hills towards the training ground, James's long-legged gait matching the shorter lieutenant's quick step. The noises of the men and the intermittent blasts of weaponry led them on. A particularly loud explosion was followed by echoing shouts and cursing. They both winced.

"So, glad to be back?" Bradlock asked.

"Glad to see that so many of the battalion made it through."

"I reckon we're all glad of that. And what about our next outing?

You ready to see sunny Italy?" The lieutenant took a last drag from his cigarette and threw it down, grinding it underfoot. "It sounds like the advance has been pretty easy so far—at least on the Adriatic."

"Yes. I don't envy the fellows on the Mediterranean side."

"Umhm. Can't imagine why the Yanks didn't use their artillery to soften the beach up before the Salerno landing, poor devils. At least they made it in the end."

"Nothing like that on our side of the mountains?"

"No, not yet, anyway. Sounds like getting supply lines up is slow going, but I imagine Monty will have it sorted soon enough."

They reached the range in time to see one of the replacements preparing to fire.

"How's he gonna cock it?" Bradlock muttered. "That PIAT's almost as big as he is."

James silently agreed as the poor kid strained and struggled with the anti-tank gun until he was red in the face. He gave an audible gasp of relief as he finally succeeded, followed by a chorus of cheers from the other men waiting at a safe distance.

As the new soldier took position, lying on the ground, a couple of the enlisted men just in front of James bent their heads together, then burst into laughter. They looked like brothers in their matching khaki, though James knew better, having crossed North Africa with them. Both were medium height, both sandy-haired, and both stood as though they were out to a show rather than at a firing range.

The nearer, and slightly taller, Ed Turner got control of himself and leaned over to ask the other, Harold Peters, "How d'you think he'll handle the recoil?"

He was answered as the weapon discharged with a roar.

When the air cleared, it appeared that the soldier had left a furrow in front of him in the dusty soil. Coughing, he rolled over and stood to loud applause, a little stiff but with a grin that shone white through the dirt on his face. Turner and Peters cheered him on.

"What do you think?" Bradlock asked James.

"Tough kid—that must have smarted. Tiny though. Are they putting them straight into uniform after short pants now?"

"Could be. Glad to hear you think he's tough. He's going to be one of yours. Ho, Private!"

The new soldier came jogging over, mopping his face with a spotted handkerchief and snapping a salute. "Yes, sir?"

"Private Moore. What do you think about the PIAT now you've fired it?"

Even though the top of his head didn't reach the lieutenant's chin, Moore's grin was broad, crinkling his brown eyes. "Sir, I'd rather not!"

"Fair enough. Are you and the others settling in all right?"

"Yes. Only I think we're all just about ready to be done with training and move on to the real thing."

"That eager to get into the fight?"

Moore shrugged. "I figure now we're here, the job'll be finished soon. I'd like to get on with it and get back home."

The lieutenant raised his eyebrows and half turned to James. "Good-o, James. Sounds like we'll be in for a rest now that the new boys are here to take on the work. Private Moore, this is Sergeant Milburn. He'll be hanging around, just in case you need any backup."

Moore snapped another smart salute.

Was I ever that young? At twenty-three James was probably only a few years older. It seemed like an eternity.

Watching the next in line get ready to fire, he thought about the tanks that the gun was meant to stop, about the infantry waiting behind the tanks that would be working to overrun their positions, about the struggle to come, and he agreed with the private.

Best to get on with it and finish the job.

12 September 1943

Dear James,

I was especially wishing you were here last night. We were listening to the new Appointment with Fear program, and it was "The Pit and the Pendulum." Oh, it gave me goosebumps! It would've been better with you sitting next to me—I could've used a hand to squeeze!

Great Aunt Helena has made definite arrangements for the children I wrote of to come and stay here. We aren't certain what exactly we will do for those who are school-age. The children in the village and surrounding area have been travelling over to Farthington as our teacher shipped out a few terms ago, but I don't know if their families will want them sent so far. It sounds as if I may be gaining some teaching experience here, and at least get them through the current term. I am not entirely certain that I am up to the task!

We've just had word that a distant cousin who had been working in the UXB (disarming unexploded bombs) was killed. I had only met him once, but he had written about coming up sometime as he was working relatively nearby. I don't know if we will go to pay our respects. I think it unlikely.

We have seen little of Charles—work has been keeping him busy even on weekends. Great Aunt Helena has been cross about it, but I enlisted the help of the chemist's oldest boy to help Molly get her to and from church. He has also come to help get her out of doors on fine days, which is a blessing to all.

I try not to worry that I haven't heard anything from you yet. I suppose it's difficult for the postman to reach the front!

Be safe, James, God bless you.

Love,
Evie

James 5:11 "Indeed we count them blessed who endure. You have heard of the perseverance of Job and seen the end intended by the LORD—that the LORD is very compassionate and merciful."

EVIE FOLDED HER LETTER and gazed out the window, biting her lips. The clouds were hanging heavy on the horizon and the air smelled like rain.

Well, I'm not likely to melt. And it's now or never.

She dropped the letter into her bag, along with the package for Sophia. Creeping into the hall, she grabbed her coat and hat. She had just reached the front door and placed her hand on the knob when she heard a sound that made her cringe.

"Evie?"

Almost made it. "Coming, Great Aunt Helena."

Sitting in the library, newspaper still on her lap from her afternoon "reading" (as the old woman liked to call her nap), her great aunt's eyes were sharp as ever. "Trying to slip away?"

Evie smiled and nodded, keeping her chin high. "I left a note with Molly. Sophia's birthday was yesterday, and she'll be getting off from work shortly. I was going to bicycle over with her gift."

"By way of the Post Office?"

"Yes."

The old woman raised her eyebrows. "Any word from him?"

"No, but it's probably too soon."

Examining her folded hands, her great aunt nodded and pursed her lips. "You'll get soaked to the skin if it rains."

"Yes, but when else am I to see her? With the children coming next weekend—"

"Oh, go on." Great Aunt Helena leaned her head back in her chair. "You've been moping around here long enough. Go, but don't blame me if you catch your death. And what I'll do with six children if you do..."

"Thank you, Great Aunt Helena! I'll not be too late." Evie gave her a quick kiss and darted off.

Evie had barely raised her hand to knock on Sophia's door when her friend yanked it open. As Evie tried to regain her balance, Sophia wrapped her in a quick embrace, pulled her inside, and said, breathless, "You'll never guess what's happened!" Before Evie had an opportunity to try, she continued, "I've been called up!"

Evie froze, one arm still ensconced in a coat sleeve. "Never to the front?"

Sophia laughed. "No, silly. They aren't sending women to fight, you know."

"No, I know, but still, Madge went over running searchlights, and Betsy was doing secretarial work last year—"

"Nothing so far away. I'm to work in an airplane factory. I'm going to be billeted down in Manchester. I leave next week!"

Evie eased herself down on the sofa. She accepted the cup of weak tea that Sophia's mother pressed into her hands before vanishing into the kitchen, wiping her eyes with her apron. "Just like that?"

"It's war, Evie. They aren't going to ask if I mind."

"Do you?"

"Not at all." Sophia lowered her voice to a whisper as she glanced at the kitchen. "I'm ready for a change."

Evie nodded, and moistened her lips. "Then, I'm happy for you, Sophie. I just hope—"

"Well, I've done it!" Mary exclaimed, blowing in the front door, dramatically stripping off her jacket and hat and dropping them on a chair.

The other girls stared at her, puzzled.

She said nothing but smiled mysteriously and stuck her head into the kitchen. "Mum, I'm simply dying for a cup—oh, thank you!" She plopped down opposite Evie and Sophia and attended to her tea, avoiding their eyes.

Evie gave in first. "All right Mary. What have you done?"

Mary looked up, smiling in triumph. "I've signed on with the Red Cross. I'm going to train to be a nurse! I'll be sent off somewhere, oh, as soon as everything is sorted out."

Sophia stared at her sister, mouth agape. Evie managed, "Mary, did you really? You're only seventeen."

"Yes, and in a month I'm eighteen, and who's to say they won't start calling us up younger than twenty soon? I'm going to make my own decisions, and I'd much rather be wiping fevered brows of men in uniform than stuck in some dull old factory somewhere."

Sophia slammed her cup down on the end table. "Mary! Of all the—you always do this!" Face flushed red, Sophia stood, jostling Evie who barely managed to catch her teacup before it shattered on the floor. "I have something happen—*finally*—and you have to try to turn it all back on you…"

Mary smiled, red lips highlighting her teeth. "Surely, you don't think the war effort is all about you, Sophie. Even you can't be that self-centered. And if you thought I was just going to sit here after you'd gone off—"

Spluttering, Sophie raised her open hand.

"Please, stop." Evie stood up, moving between the two girls. "Please! Please, don't fight. Or, can you at least save it for when I don't have to see it?"

It took a moment, but finally Mary laughed. "Of course, Evie. I'm sorry, Sophia. I didn't mean to steal your thunder."

Sophia looked unconvinced but sat back down, pouting into her teacup.

"Oh, I've got your birthday present, Sophie!" Evie produced it, and Sophia, regaining her good grace with an effort, opened it, exclaiming over the colorful silk scarf. "It was one of Mother's, but I thought it would look so pretty with your hair."

"I love it. Thank you, Evie!" Sophia gave her a hug and swung the scarf around her neck with a smile. "I imagine I might be able to wear this in my dull old factory, or at least when I get off from work. I don't think I've ever seen the nurses I know out of uniform, wiping fevered brows or no."

Mary laughed good-naturedly. "Ah well. I think I'll look smart enough in my black stockings. So, Evie, Sophia's for the factories, I'm for the sick wards, what are you to do? Have you heard from your sergeant, yet?"

Evie looked down at her hands, temporary elation dampened. "No, not a word. But it's early days yet, and I hear it takes a long time for letters to reach the front. Weeks even."

Mary and Sophia exchanged a quick glance.

"Oh! I do have some news—Great Aunt Helena just agreed, we're to house six children. Evacuees. They're distant relatives and I'll be helping look after them."

"You know, Evie," Mary interrupted, frowning at her nails, "you don't have to stay there. There are plenty of jobs open now, good jobs, looking for single girls. You have a choice."

Evie paused for a swallow of her tepid tea. "I know, Mary. And I feel so guilty, staying behind."

"Nonsense," Sophia chimed in. "You work hard, Evie. You're doing what you can from there."

Unable to restrain a bitter laugh, Evie set her cup down harder than she intended. "Yes, from there. And how long haven't I been thinking that I ought to be somewhere else, somewhere I could...but Great Aunt Helena took me in when I had nothing, and nowhere to go. She's almost the only family I have left. How could I just turn my back on her?"

"HERE ARE THOSE FORMS you were looking for, Mr. Heatherington." Gladys plopped the papers in front of Charles and took a seat on the edge of his desk, crossing her long legs in his direction. "Is there anything else I can help you with?"

Charles leaned back and raised his eyebrows. "Just what did you have in mind?"

"Well, how about a date for this weekend?"

Charles considered the blonde. *She's not half bad, but it's probably time for me to get back.*

He'd deliberately kept his distance from Stoneglenn for a few weeks. Given some time to herself—now that Milburn wasn't around to distract her—Evie might appreciate *his* company a bit more.

And there was the matter of the birds—he was uneasy about that. He ought to have left it alone, but she made him so angry...

Anyway. She's had some time. I'd better get back to it.

"Sorry, Glad. I've got to get back up north this weekend."

She sniffed. "Visiting that chit of a cousin again?"

Charles gave her a winning smile and patted her hand. "Oh, you know. Family duties. I'll take you to dinner next week, though. Save a few of those sweet smiles for me?"

A smile spread across Gladys's face. Sweet mightn't have been the best term, and Charles suspected that her teeth were too even to be real, but her fondness for him had proved valuable. She reinforced this observation, reaching into her breast pocket and producing a message. "Oh, I forgot. Here, this was just left for you. Directly to your desk, as you asked." She pouted. "Not another girlfriend, is it?"

"Of course not, darling." He pinched her cheek, and she giggled. Then he took the paper and tucked it away.

Nine

30 September 1943

Dear Evie,

I hope that by now you've received some of my letters. Yours have come through regularly, but it doesn't seem from your last that any of mine have made it. Everything must go through censors to be certain that we aren't passing along information that would be dangerous—important to do, but it seems odd to think that someone else is reading my letters. (And apparently reading them very slowly. Am I really that fascinating a correspondent?)

I can't say where we are, but I imagine you'll figure it out. We haven't hit much resistance, but the sappers (Royal Engineers, if you don't know) have been kept busy. As the Germans have retreated, they've been busy laying mines, demolishing roads and bridges, and making travel as much of a nuisance as possible—I'll say this for the Jerries, they're thorough. The sappers do impressive work but keeping the supply lines up for all this mob is quite a task.

Having Italy out of the war hasn't helped as much as we'd hoped. There are partisans and small groups joining up with us here and there, but it looks as if Jerry had misgivings about his allies and took steps to keep them from becoming our allies as soon as the surrender took place. Nasty business.

One of the boys is brewing up on the little stove he built himself—you'd be amazed at the creativity displayed in making a cup of tea. I've got some biscuits from rations. A few of the fellows claim that they were left-overs from the last war. While I can't say for certain, they certainly taste like it.

All my love,
James

GOLDEN SUN BATHED the shores of southern Italy, lulling the senses, promising that no real danger could lurk in these lovely lands.

Crowds came out cheering as James's division passed through, smiling, waving, bearing flowers and pressing fruit, eggs, *vino*, and sometimes even chickens into the hands of the men. Real food and drink made a welcome change, and some of the boys were saying that maybe Italy wouldn't be so bad after all.

Lance Corporal Davy Llewellyn trotted up abreast of James's slowly moving transport, arms full, and called up for a lift. A couple of men leaned down, and he was hefted aboard, holding a pair of melons, a bunch of grapes, and, precariously, three eggs in one hand. "Look at these melons," he crowed.

Peters and Turner were gawping at a couple of *signorinas* smiling and waving from the corner. Peters muttered, "I'd like to get a look at *her*—"

"*Don't. Say. It,*" Llewellyn interjected, big fists closing around the produce, face as red as his flaming hair. He relaxed his grip in time to save the eggs, but his glare was still alarming.

Far from being cowed, Ed Turner roared with laughter.

Peters held up his hands and smirked. "Sorry there, Father. I promise, I'll be a good boy." He then leaned over to mutter something in Turner's ear that set him chuckling again. Danny Ryan sidled over to get in on the joke.

Still glowering, Llewellyn found a seat next to James, who relieved him of the fruit but declined to hold the eggs on the bumpy road.

"Father" Llewellyn had earned his nickname partially by his past. He'd been on the path to priesthood before meeting the girl who became his wife. His inflexible views on morality had clinched it. Still, while some were inclined to grumble about his beliefs, none were able to question his courage—or his luck (though Davy would likely snort and say it was no such thing). He had kept his battledress blouse with a bullet-hole through it; he was the living embodiment of the legend of the soldier, saved by the Bible in his breast pocket. Once a shell had landed directly in his trench. It had been a dud. The fellows who complained the most about "Father" stuck close to him when the bullets started flying, hoping to better their odds.

A moment later Lieutenant Bradlock vaulted up to join them, cramming in on Davy's other side. His dark brows shadowed his scowling face. James caught his eye and raised his eyebrows in a silent question.

Bradlock shrugged, irritated. "More supply troubles. It'll be slow going. Time for training, I suppose, but also more time for Jerry to get ready for us."

"Do you think there'll be much resistance?" James asked. "With all of the fighting in Russia—"

"They're saying it should be smooth sailing, and we'll be in Rome for Christmas." Bradlock shrugged again. Experience had shown that what *they* predicted may or may not be so.

He fumbled for a cigarette. His voice dropped low, so only the other two could hear. "With the Germans retreating, they're going to grab the high ground whenever they can. If we follow them into the mountains, we're going to be climbing up with them looking down at us, just like they did on Centuripe, and just like they did on that Salerno beachhead. And you know what that means." He gave a sardonic grin. "We won't be able to piss without Jerry knowing."

Grim silence stretched between them. Then, James shrugged. "Well, that realization is one thing that might keep the boys away from too much of the *vino*."

CHARLES MOVED BRISKLY through the dimly lit streets, cutting through a narrow alley littered with bits of rubble and refuse to reach a nondescript wooden door. He knocked, paused, and knocked again, a carefully repeated pattern.

The door opened a crack. After a moment, he was allowed in with a murmured greeting.

He wove past the roulette wheel, the baccarat game, and the gleaming bar. The room was dim with hooded lights and thick with the smell of good cigarettes and better liquor.

The big man smoking a cigar nodded as Charles slid into a seat beside him. "Welcome. It's been a while—everything going well?"

Charles accepted his cards from the dealer. "Oh, well enough. About to be better, I think." He pulled the missive Gladys had given him from his pocket and passed it over. "I've got word on some new merchandise."

"Ahhhh." The cigar glowed red with the man's satisfied exhale. "Good. Chester's was a long time ago. I'd started to think you were getting cold feet."

Charles snorted, looked at his cards and made his bid. "When have I ever done that? But I can't be too obvious, you know. If I get caught, it does neither of us any good."

"True enough. Well, this should square things between us—for the time being."

Charles frowned, not quite liking the tone of the last, but his companion gave a bark of a laugh and a slap on the back. "Cheer up. After all, if you wait long enough, you ought to be set for life, right? Why worry?"

Charles tried to smile, tried to recover the confidence he'd felt a moment ago. *Yes, I ought to be. I've done what needed to be done to be sure of it. The question is how long I can* afford *to wait.*

I've got *to keep working on Evie.*

Ten

20 September 1943

Dearest James,

In the last week the house has become louder than it has been in years. We have SIX children staying with us—little Leslie, who is 3, her sister Lilly-5, and then Tommy-5, John-6, Bonny-8, and Edward, who is 10. They are sweet children, and I have tried to make them at home.

I have a difficult time imagining that my cousins and I were ever this rambunctious. I suppose we had our parents to keep us in check. I have had to be very strict with Tommy and Johnny to keep them from jumping off the dining room table with pillowcases on their backs "parachuting." Lilly likes to tell tales on the others—you can imagine how that goes over. Poor little Leslie doesn't understand what's going on, and she clings to my or Molly's skirts most of the day. I wonder at her being sent away. In the early evacuations, children under five had their mothers, after all, and the others had teachers along. Still, if we can keep her safe, I suppose it's better than her being looked after by strangers or living in poor conditions.

I have never run so much, nor slept so well as I have this week! You have nephews—do you have any wisdom to share for busy little boys?

Mercifully, Great Aunt Helena seems to find the whole thing amusing and only complains periodically about the noise. Charles avoided the children when he was out last weekend.

Oh dear. Something just crashed to the floor, and I hear tears. I must fly—

Sending all my love, and prayers!
Evie

P.S. It was a plate. Apparently, the boys wanted to play discus, and then Lilly, who was for some reason shoeless, cut her foot on the shards. At least it wasn't a good dish, or it might take an act of divine intervention to save them from Great Aunt Helena! Even the old ones are impossible to replace. I think that this incident doesn't need to be mentioned unless I am directly asked.

Romans 8:38-39. "For I am persuaded, that neither death, nor life, nor angels, nor principalities, nor powers, nor things present, nor things to come, nor height, nor depth, nor any other created thing, shall be able to separate us from the love of God, which is in Christ Jesus our LORD."

JAMES'S SHOULDERS SILENTLY SHOOK as he read. Poor Evie. He hoped they didn't run too roughshod over her.

Charles was keeping his distance—good. He pictured the twisted body of the baby bird and shifted uneasily.

A drop of rain splashed on the paper. Glancing skyward through the thin, bare branches of the tree he'd found to rest under at the edge of the road, he sighed, carefully wiped the letter, and folded it away. Between Evie and his family, the packet of letters was bulging.

He pulled out the letter he had just finished composing for one last look.

1 October 1943

Dear Evie,

It is difficult to know just how much I can write about our day to day activities. We are in Italy, having crossed into Taranto on the 20th. The pace is slow. Perhaps that's just as well—our orders are unclear. At first it seemed that we'd be staying in southern Italy, gaining airfields. Now we are advancing indefinitely, and it seems that Jerry will defend Italy, or at least bedevil us as much as he can during his retreat.

Our lieutenant has noticed that I'm writing you again. He sends his best, and requests that you will write him some confirmation that you truly exist. He claims he does not believe that he has seen me speak more than two words to a woman. How you put up with a dull fellow like me, I'll never know, dear Evie, though I can't remember ever finding you difficult to talk to. I miss your voice, your laugh, your smile, everything.

Yours always,
James

He prepared it to post, and it joined the others before the wet spoiled it.

If autumn in Italy foreshadowed the coming winter, they were in for it. Everything was gray: the brooding October sky, the swollen rivers, the road, the Adriatic glimpsed to the right, the ever-present mud. The relentless rain soaked everything, transforming the roads into oozing mires and making the terrain increasingly slippery and treacherous. He pulled his collar tighter around his neck.

Peters, huddled under his coat nearby, echoed his thoughts. "So much for sunny Italy." His sandy hair was plastered to his head under his helmet. Turner, Ryan, Moore, and the others in the platoon grunted agreement or ignored him as they gathered themselves to continue their advance, reluctantly coming out from whatever shelter they'd found, shaking off rain and stamping mud from their boots.

"You were counting on a bathe in the blue seas, Peters?" he asked drily.

"Absolutely. Pretty poor holiday, overall."

Turner piped in. "I seem to remember you complaining that there wasn't *enough* water around in Tunisia. Never enough to drink and shave and wash."

"Never satisfied, that's me! 'Course," he added, throwing his arm about Private Reggie Cartwright's slim shoulders as he walked by, "if I had a face like Reg's here, I wouldn't have to worry about the shaving part." He patted the other's smooth cheek.

Cartwright brushed him off. "I shave."

"Sure you do, Reggie. Each hair individual," Turner laughed. "Aw, don't look so glum. Some of the girls like a baby face. Somewhere. I reckon."

"You were saying you wanted a swim, Peters?" Lieutenant Bradlock walked up. "You're in luck. We're coming up on the river—" he consulted the hand drawn map, using his body to shield it from the wet, "—Fortore. The bridge's been demolished, of course. Jerry's guarding the detour. Sounds like the forward troops are crossing under some heavy shellfire. So, it may be a bathe with fireworks as well. Quite the holiday."

"Wonderful news, sir," Peters said with a grimace.

"Air support?" James asked.

"Limited still, due to the weather. It sounds like they've got the crossing in hand, but we'd best be ready."

The sounds of the battle were barely audible over the sounds of the vehicles, the men, and the increasing rain. James kept peering ahead, but he couldn't see much through the downpour. Presently, Bradlock came jogging back from wherever he'd been. "All's well," he called. "The fighting's done. We've got the river."

"Where to next?"

"Little town on the way to Termoli—Serracapriola. Doesn't sound as if it'll be too much trouble."

Serracapriola was as gray as the rest of the world under the leaden sky. The structures and streets of what must have once been a pretty village bore the marks of their shelling and of the destructive German retreat: rubble and debris and carelessly thrown garbage.

James passed the gun emplacement that had troubled their advance, where the bodies of the Germans who had manned it still sprawled. The Italians who had neutralized them stood nearby, cheering the advance of the troops, waving liberated weapons. One gangly boy was wearing a captured helmet at a jaunty angle over his grinning face.

Over the sounds of celebration another sound intruded—the muffled roar of an explosion, somewhere in the town. The lieutenant pinpointed the location of the blast first, pointing ahead and to the right. "There."

Cries of anguish echoed from the spot.

Lieutenant Bradlock led the way. James, Davy Llewellyn and most of his section plunged into the winding streets.

Before the front of the building had been blown away, it had been a post office. Dust covered survivors huddled together, still reeling from the blast. A gray-haired woman sat on the curb, dazed, unaware of the blood streaking the wrinkled side of her face.

"Sharp's the word! See if anyone's inside!" Bradlock barked.

Bits of concrete and stone shifted underfoot as James led the others, heaving aside wreckage and clambering over rubble. They coughed and choked on the dust-filled air. Llewellyn covered his mouth and nose with a handkerchief.

Just inside, they found a man struggling to move bits of a broken doorway, right arm hanging limp and broken at his side. "La mia amore! Il bambino! Mio Dio, si prego…" he sobbed.

James and Davy hurried past him, and together heaved the debris away. James's stomach clenched as they uncovered a woman's shoe.

She had been nearly buried, face turned away, dark curls crusted in dust.

Her hair's the same color as Evie's.

James's hand started to shake. He closed his eyes and swallowed. As he forced himself to bend and reached down to help lift her to the stretcher bearers who'd come up and taken charge of the husband, he heard a strange sound.

Il bambino.

Carefully, he moved her aside. There, shielded by the mother's body, was the baby, half smothered by the weight above him, dusty but alive. He blinked up at James, and free of the crushing mass, opened his little mouth and howled his displeasure.

Steadied by the sight of life, James picked him up, checking his tiny limbs for injury. He blinked away memories of his little nephews whom he had held when even smaller than this and silently prayed that they were well and safe.

"There, little one," he said, holding the baby to his shoulder and patting the rounded little back as he continued to wail. "She saved you. You're safe now." He hoped he spoke the truth.

Emerging, James blinked the dust out of his eyes. He was nearly knocked down by the father, who tearfully embraced his son one armed and tried to embrace James as well, uttering thanks in rapid Italian.

Lieutenant Bradlock was speaking. "—time bomb. Word's coming back. Jerry left them all over the city on retreat. Civilians wounded—men and women and children."

"So much for their 'allies.'" Llewellyn grunted in disgust, wiping the grime off his face. "Jerry isn't playing very nicely, is he?"

Bradlock ground his cigarette into the soil with his heel. "Well, let's get on and take the game back to him, shall we?"

2 October 1943

Dear James,

Yesterday I received a bundle of letters from you, all at once! I'm sorry

I didn't write—I sat down and read every one of them! I've searched our library and the one in Thrush House for books on Italy, so that I might understand where you are better, but there isn't much. Colonel Bryce passed through Italy a few times, but he has little to say about its geography and more to say about the beautiful signorinas and the quality of the vino.

I've already been putting your advice into practice, and today things have been going much better, now that the children are kept more occupied, though I didn't institute as many press-ups as you recommended!

The colonel was expecting a new group of convalescents, and you know what trouble he's had keeping things up over there, so I took the children over to help. I'm proud to say that the hedges are reasonably neatly trimmed. The quality of the work improved once I moved the boys far enough away from each other that they couldn't attempt to fence with the tools. The weeds are pulled, along with a few flowers—Leslie couldn't tell the difference, but she did so want to help! Really, Ed and Bonny did the most, but the others were proud to think that they had helped. Then we had a picnic on the lawn with the colonel, and I managed to keep him from sharing too many inappropriate stories, though afterwards Tommy kept asking what a "harem" was.

I hope to visit Sophia and Mary today. They will both be moving out this week. I want to get Mary's birthday present to her before she goes, even though I am a little early. That reminds me—I don't even know when your birthday is! Let's see; if you joined in '39 you must be 22 or 23? It feels as if I know you so well, but we will have so many things to learn when we are together again. I can't wait, darling!

Love,
Evie

Joshua 1:9 Be strong and of good courage; be not afraid, nor be dismayed, for the LORD your God is with you wherever you go.

CHARLES GLANCED INTO the library. There was Evie, bent over the desk.

Writing again. She's more infatuated than I'd thought. And from the bundle in the post it looks like he intends to keep up his end of it. I'd hoped it was just a fling...still, it's only been a couple of months...

His frown didn't relax as he limped up the stairs, wincing each time he had to move his leg. The old wound was painful, and he hated how it slowed him down. Unbidden, he saw the firelit French alley again and Roger's white face.

Still. He stroked the fine wood of the banister. *It was worth it.*

He heaved a sigh of relief as he sat at his desk. The children ran about on the lawn below his window doing who knew what—noisy, spoiled things. And there, Evie was going outside to them. Pulling a sheet of paper out of the desk drawer, he paused to watch her, playing little games with the smallest, cautioning the bigger ones when they climbed too high, clapping for the exploits of all. In spite of himself, he smiled.

She really did grow up alright. This ought to have all been so much easier. It was supposed to be easy after France.

Pity Milburn had to show up and complicate things.

If only there were some way to show that he's wrong *for her. Something about him that would offend. If only I could be over there, and catch him at...well, at whatever he's doing. There are certainly enough sins for a man to commit, especially far from home. I wonder which he picks?*

Considering, Charles absently twirled a pen between his fingers.

Eleven

3 October 1943

Dear Evie,

We've just finished a bracing stroll. Jerry's been disinclined to leave roadways in any shape for vehicles, so we've had to hoof it while the sappers scramble to get everything else through. I imagine we looked a bit comical, carrying all the equipment on our backs like pack mules, the heavier bits like radios on stretchers between us. With any luck—

James paused and shifted further under the branches of his sheltering olive tree, dodging the rain drops. He squinted up at the low, gray clouds. They had said that the rain was due to stop. Once again, *they* were mistaken. Hopefully it wouldn't be too heavy—his feet were still soaked from the last bout. He wiggled his numb toes inside of the clinging, wet socks, hoping to coax some warmth into them.

A yawn surprised him. The last few days had been wearing as they traversed the broken ground from Serracapriola, clearing snipers and German rearguards out of the way while the Luftwaffe bombed their troop concentrations.

At the moment, he was on the far side of the river Biferno, near Termoli, until lately occupied by the Germans. His own battalion had caught a whole line of German troops and soft sided vehicles unawares and taken a good bite out of them, but now they were stuck, waiting. All their heavy armor and weaponry were stranded across the swollen river, waiting for a suitable bridge to be built. They had no tank support, nothing that they hadn't been able to bring across with them. A frigid drop of rain splashed on James's neck and slid down under his collar, and he shivered.

He looked up as Lieutenant Bradlock came by, talking earnestly with one of the majors. A moment later, he came over to James. He squatted and attempted to light a cigarette, cursing the match as one of the sporadic drops of rain slid through the dejected remnants of the olive's leaves and quenched its flame.

James shifted over so that he could get further under shelter, but the lieutenant shook his head and tucked the cigarette back into his pocket, muttering, "Woodbine. Still, might as well save it." He gave James a look. "It seems that there might be some trouble."

Trying to ignore the sinking feeling in his stomach, James matched his conversational tone. "Oh? I'd thought the force at Termoli was easily dealt with."

"Oh yes, *Kamfgruppe* Rau were taken prisoner before they could even fire a shot. No, the problem isn't in the city. Recce patrol just came back. Seems they've captured a motorcyclist with the Sixteenth Panzer division." He spat. "If he's telling it true, they've been traveling this way the last two nights."

"I thought recce said those tanks were back getting refitted after Salerno..."

"Apparently not. Rumor has it that some of the other patrols have been encountering tanks, too—" An explosion echoed, not too near, but not far enough. "If the Luftwaffe would just let up, a man could get time to think it all through."

"I'll ask them for you." James attempted to pull his collar up higher against the steadily striking raindrops. "Meanwhile, what are we to do?"

Bradlock pulled out his map and perused it. "We were due to

hand things over, of course, but the river's up and no one's going to be coming to relieve us. No one else is close enough to get in here, at least until the Irish make their landing—boats should get into the city tonight. Look, we'll need to stay here to plug the gap between these two battalions."

Shots echoed over to the left.

"Infantry against tanks. Well then," James folded his letter. "I suppose I'll save this for later, won't I?"

7 October 1943

Dear Evie,

I've just found my letter from 3 October, and while it's incomplete I'm sending it along. I'm sorry that it has been a few days since I have written. Things ended up a bit sticky here, but not to worry, all is well.

As I mentioned, Jerry has been hard at work demolishing bridges and roads, generally making things difficult, and we ended up on one side of a swollen river, with our armor on the other side when a number of German tanks who were supposed to be quite far away came to call. Facing tanks rolling at you while on foot is an excellent encouragement to pray fervently, but I don't want to worry you. We were able to hold our line; long enough to enable some others to pull back through it, anyway.

I don't know where we'd be without the sappers. Back in Messina, most likely! They worked tirelessly, despite the Luftwaffe, to bulldoze a ford into the river to get some of our own tanks across to us, and then before too long, off their boats and up the ridge came the Irish. I'm thankful for my allies tonight.

As a farmer, I thought that I understood mud. Never have I seen mud like this—thick, viscous and deep, bogging everything down. Right now, the thought of dry socks thrills me almost as much as the thought of seeing you again. Almost.

Love,
James

4 October 1943

Dear James,

I dreamt about you last night. You were standing in the rain, leaning up against a tank in your battledress with mud on your boots, trying to drink tea with water running off your helmet into the cup. There was a loud crash and you looked up, but then you laughed because you saw me. I was riding a camel. You asked, "Evie, what are you doing here?" and I told you, "I rode up from Alexandria and I'm bringing a boatload more for you all to ride on!" I was so pleased with myself, but you gave that very serious look you have, and asked, "What will we feed them?" I was completely flummoxed, and then I woke up. It was all very silly, but in a way, it mirrors how I feel. I wish I could do something real to help you.

Unfortunately, the crash I heard in the dream was real. The boys woke up early and attempted to build a trampoline out of chairs and a bedsheet. I am becoming so adept with bandages that I may need to consider a career in the Red Cross.

Speaking of, the new convalescents are arriving as I write this—five of them, and a couple pretty badly off. They're talking of reorganizing things over at Thrush House. Cook says Mrs. Jenkins has been in high dudgeon at the idea of someone else having a say in her house. The colonel doesn't seem overly concerned, as long as they will let him write.

It was Great Aunt Helena's birthday, so she, Charles and I had our portrait taken together—enclosed is a copy.

God bless you, and all of those with you, James

Love,
Evie

Isaiah 40:31 But those who wait on the Lord shall renew their strength; they shall mount up with wings like eagles, they shall run and not be weary, they shall walk and not faint.

(On an additional sheet)

Dear James,

I hadn't sealed my letter yet, and I'm so glad. Last night was, in a word, extraordinary.

Around bedtime a largish storm blew up, lots of wind and rain. I was in for the night when my door opened and in came Lilly with Leslie in tow. Lilly said Leslie had been frightened, although Leslie laughed, and Lilly quailed at every clap of thunder! I let them climb in with me. Then the two smaller boys piled in a few minutes later—what a mass of squirming limbs!

Finally, everyone was settled and getting warm and drowsy, then suddenly it was too warm. James, one of them wet the bed.

I think I may have flown, I leaped out of it so quickly! No one was unscathed, and the bed and bedding were soaked. Everyone needed to be washed and in clean pajamas. The whole time I was desperately trying to keep them quiet so that we wouldn't wake Great Aunt Helena. She or Charles might very well have murdered us!

At last, they were back in their beds and I returned to mine and realized that I couldn't use it. I ended up in a dressing gown on the sofa—the short, particularly hard one in the library, where we listened to the programs—because I thought it less likely that I'd be disturbed in the morning, and then when I heard people up I could slip upstairs.

No such luck. Cook came in for something early. I was disoriented and sat up and she screamed, and everybody over the age of 7 was wide awake.

I hope this made you smile, and I wish we were together so that I could see it!

Kisses, Evie

JAMES'S SOFT CHUCKLE at the midpoint of the story sounded loud in the silent room. The other men around the rough table—made of plywood supported on empty metal drums—looked up from their cheerless meal.

"Got some good news there, Sarge?" asked Danny Ryan, mustering up interest with an effort. His face was pale with weariness under his dark brown hair and freckles, and he cradled his cup of coffee lovingly.

"Letter from back home."

"From your girl?" asked Lieutenant Bradlock. He'd come down to pass along some new orders and had hung around.

Turner and Peters's heads shot up from their tins of bully beef. Davy just grinned and handed his canteen to Phillips, the driver. Ryan spat out a mouthful of coffee, catching little Moore in the splatter.

Ignoring Moore's sputtered imprecations, Ryan blurted, "The Silent Sergeant's got a *girl?* I thought you were writing your Mum! Lord help us, sir, I've never even seen you talk to a woman more'n five words—remember that blonde in Algiers?" he added as an aside to the lieutenant.

Bradlock threw back his head and laughed. "Do I!"

James ran his hand through his hair and grunted, "Wasn't my type."

"With legs like that, who cares?" Bradlock asked.

"Hear hear!" said Peters, raising his canteen in toast.

"What'd she do?" asked Moore looking up and forgetting the coffee.

Shaking his head, Ryan chuckled. "For some reason she took a liking to him. Hung on him all evening. Tried and tried to get him to talk to her. All she got was a 'yes' and a 'no'. Never seen a girl more disappointed." He looked back at Bradlock. "Wasn't it… yeah, Old Jonesy. He tried to help ease her pains—"

Peters slapped his forehead. "Right! Jonesy. I'd almost forgotten—bought it the next week, didn't he, Danny?"

Ryan's grin dropped. "Yeah."

The quiet was somber again. Bradlock lit up. Blowing a cloud of smoke to join the blue haze hovering around the ceiling, he asked, "So. What's so funny? I reckon we could use a laugh."

James hesitated, but the lieutenant was right. The Germans had continued to retreat after losing Termoli, but it was a fighting retreat. Their platoon alone had lost three men in the last two days: one to machine gun fire, one rushed away—leg blown off by a mine, and one to a sniper. The last, Bobby Sikes, had been proudly showing them the picture of his new son the night before.

The weather didn't help. The ever-present rain soaked everything, and the single intact room of the abandoned farmhouse they'd found to hole up in for the night was drafty and filled with the musty smell of mold and the rustlings and scurryings of smaller inhabitants.

Clearing his throat, James said, "She's been helping look after six kids, sent away from the city..."

The men enjoyed the story, especially Llewellyn and Henry Phillips, who had children at home. Llewellyn laughed till he teared up. "That's so," he finally managed. "Nothing wakes you up faster than that feeling at two in the morning."

"I dunno. When my boy had the 'flu in the wee hours, it was quite an eye opener," chuckled Phillips.

Ryan grinned. "My kid brother used to crawl in with me all the time when he got scared, got me at least three times."

Ed Turner rolled his eyes. "Why'd you keep letting him in?"

"I'd tell him off, but he'd have nightmares, and he's a sweet kid. He'll be seven now. Hey, is that a picture of her?"

Resigned, James handed it over.

"Little old, isn't she?" Ryan pointed to Mrs. Heatherington and got a couple of laughs. "Naw, she's pretty, sir! But who's the bloke?"

"Cousin."

"Civilian?"

"Wounded at Dunkirk and discharged."

The picture was passed around. Peters gave a wolf-whistle, and then, when Turner elbowed him, looked up to see that his superior officer didn't mind. James just raised his eyebrows, and Peters quickly passed the photo on.

Phillips held it a little longer than the rest, frowning.

"What's the trouble?" Bradlock asked.

Phillips forced a quick smile. "No trouble, sir. Just wondering how the sergeant caught such a pretty dame."

Shortly thereafter the men turned in, finding the softest bit of floor to kip on that they could. Soon the sound of regular breathing, and the less soothing sound of Ryan's perpetual snore, filled the space.

James sat up, working to get his kit in better order. He had just dislodged something sticky from the bottom of his canteen when he glanced up and saw Phillips standing before him.

"Excuse me," Phillips said, his usual confident grin muted under his wildly curly, yellow hair. He was a fearless and excellent driver, careening over muddy flats and rocky cliffs alike as those entrusted to his vehicles clung doggedly to the seats, playing it tough and trying not to flinch. He had been a regular in the army, transferred only recently over to James's division when an infusion of "fresh blood" was needed.

"Yes, Phillips?"

Phillips shuffled his feet and glanced over his shoulder at the sleepers. Turning back to James, he squared his shoulders. "I wondered, the man in your picture. Was it Lieutenant—or just Mister now—Charles Heatherington?"

James blinked. "Yes. Friend of yours?"

Phillips' brows lowered. "No."

"But you know him?"

"Knew. We were in France together. I was a driver with his company. Served with him until he was discharged. Didn't care to keep in touch. Look..." He squatted next to James and lowered his voice further. "May I be frank?"

"Please. And sit down."

"Thanks just the same, I'd rather not." He grimaced, as though from a bad taste in his mouth. "Look, Milburn, I wouldn't feel right not saying, if you're serious about her, watch out for him."

Ryan's snore hitched, and both men looked towards the sleepers. After a moment, the wheezes regained their steady rhythm, and Phillips nodded and continued. "He's what my Gran would've called 'a bad 'un'. Won't be a record of it—he always knew who to butter up. Helped that he was the sort of fellow who knew how to get what you wanted. Spread money around pretty liberally, at least at first. Later there was maybe some trouble, funny people around looking for him from time to time, civilians. Right before we started the retreat."

James exhaled through his nose and nodded. *Sounds like Charles. Slimy.* "What was he into?"

"Black market, maybe? I figured he got himself in debt somehow or other—maybe gambling. Whatever it was, his big brother wasn't impressed. Captain Roger Heatherington—now, he was a good officer. Well respected. Looked after his men."

Someone stirred on the other side of the room. Phillips glanced about and lowered his voice until James had to strain to hear him. "It was funny how he died. Had me drop him off while we were falling back from Arras and headed back towards town, looking for his brother. Next thing we heard he was dead, killed in an explosion." He shook his head. "A shame. What they were doing back there...well, I don't know. Pity the wrong brother made it out. Didn't like to say anything against your girl's family, especially not in front of—" he jerked his head toward the sleepers. "But I thought you ought to know."

"Thanks, Phillips. I appreciate it." The other man nodded and left him.

James leaned back against the rough stone wall and frowned at the dark beams overhead. He'd had his concerns about Charles, but this—this was much more than the childish spitefulness Evie had described.

The shady connections were bad enough, but the other hints Phillips had dropped...

An older brother who didn't approve of his sibling's dealings, an older brother suddenly dead, leaving the other wounded, but now the heir.

But why's he so set on Evie?

Perhaps Charles loved her. In James's opinion Evie was certainly loveable.

He thought of the baby bird and shook his head. Whatever that was, it was not love.

Charles liked to control—was it her lack of interest that kept him coming on?

Something didn't fit.

Evie. He closed his eyes, and pictured the gentle curves of her face, her wide eyes and how they lit up when she laughed, her soft lips... He shook himself and refocused on the matter at hand. *Should I tell her any of this?*

He scrubbed his weary eyes with his hands and shook his head, trying to clear it. *Even if there's something in all this, surely Evie's not at risk. After all, if he did—something—it wouldn't have anything to do with her. Evie's no threat to him, as far as I can see.*

Unless I tell her what Phillips said and Charles finds out. They're in the same house every week...

Still, it would be best if she's on her guard. If any of Charles's old connections show up…

If only I weren't so far away.

20 October 1943

Dear Evie,

The rain has finally stopped—dry socks ho! We've had some time to rest and reorganize, barring a few patrols here and there. It's been good to resupply. Food, fuel, equipment, (especially food!) are all streaming in, as well as additional transports, which I suppose we'll need when things are mopped up here.

Thank you for the picture. It was good to see your face again. Do you know, I think you've gotten even prettier, if that were possible? Please wish Mrs. Heatherington a happy birthday from me, if you think the sentiment would be welcome.

I hope that the kids are being good to you and that you haven't had any more midnight excitement. I hope you don't mind—I shared your story. I was holed up in a farmhouse with one of the sections, and they saw me laughing—some good cheer was much needed.

An odd coincidence—one of the men saw the picture, and he had served with your cousin, Charles. I must admit that some of the things he said concerned me. It sounds as if Charles was associated with some rather unsavory characters during his time in France—characters who enabled him to get ahold of things he might not have been able to otherwise. This sounded familiar, and I thought I ought to let you know, just in case it isn't all in the past. Please, keep this to yourself, Evie, and just be careful.

As far as doing something real to help me—you are, you know. Your letters give me something warm to think about on these cold nights. Whatever you do, just keep yourself safe. I wouldn't leave the men here short, but I wish I could also be nearer you—preferably somewhere we could watch the stars together tonight.

God bless you, too, sweetheart.
Love, James

EVIE SAT AT THE OAK WRITING DESK in the library, looking at James's last letter for a long time. Her pleasure in receiving it was dampened by the news it contained of Charles.

But was it really *news*? Hadn't she wondered just how a low-ranking government job could possibly enable him to get the things he was always able to find? Candy was rationed now, but somehow he'd provide Great Aunt Helena's favorite bon bons at least once a month. Just last weekend he had produced a new pair of stockings for her, even though silk and nylon were impossible to get. And there were his new suits and—

"Hullo, Evie!"

She jumped, hand convulsively clutching the paper before her.

Speak of the devil. She chided herself for the thought as Charles limped over to join her. *He's still Charles. Your family.*

"New letter?" His voice was neutral—at least he'd finally stopped sulking about her correspondence.

She managed what she hoped was a guileless smile. "Yes."

Cocking his head, he gave her a sympathetic grimace. "Poor Evie. It must be dreadful, waiting from letter to letter. C'mon, the sun's out. Let's take a walk. Fresh air, and all that."

"Thanks Charles, that sounds wonderful. I suppose I'd better check on the children, too—they've been quiet a long time!" She hesitated, glancing to the letter in her fingers. "Even with the sun, I've been chilly. I'll just pop upstairs and grab my jumper, all right?"

"Of course."

In her room, Evie grabbed her red pull over, and, after a moment's hesitation, tucked James's letter into the drawer of her writing desk. *Maybe there's something to it, maybe not.*

Returning to Charles, she took his proffered arm.

He led her out the French doors down past the gardens. They admired the flowers and headed into the orchard, where shrill voices betrayed the presence of the children.

Near the far side of the hedge was a large oak tree with low, spreading branches. Edward and the smaller boys had found some planks and tools in Mr. Fisk's shed and were attempting to construct a tree house.

"Look, Miss Worther, I can sit in it!" cried Tommy, as he did, nearly falling backward through a large gap in the boards.

"Hmm," said Charles, "let's take a look at this." He inspected the house from the ground, and he even took off his jacket and pulled himself up the old garden ladder the boys were using for their ascents (no mean feat with his bad leg). He and Edward discussed some ideas for improving the structure, he removed the hammer from Tommy's hand before it could hit his brother's shin, and overall, he was as engaged with and tolerant of the children as Evie had ever seen him. She smiled. It was good to have everyone at peace.

"Here, Miss Worther!" exclaimed Lilly, panting. She and Bonny had run up with a bouquet of wildflowers.

"Oh, thank you, girls! Where did you find these?"

"Bonny found a little hole in the hedge just back there," Lilly pointed, "so we reached them from the field." She frowned. "That's all right, isn't it?"

"Ye-es, just don't wander off, all right? We need to stay close to the house, in case—"

"In case of the Germans?" Bonny asked soberly, tugging on her long, dark plait.

"Oh, just in case. I'd hate to be looking for you and not able to find you! Is Leslie still napping?"

"Yes, Molly's listening for her."

Charles came walking up. "Well, that's that. We'll see if this house will stand, but at least I think they've got the right direction. Shall we continue on?"

Evie acceded. As they walked away, she squeezed his arm and thanked him in a low voice. "It was kind of you to show an interest in their work. It's hard on the boys, having so few men around. On the girls, too, really. Little Leslie came up to me yesterday, 'Mama, where's Papa?' Lilly just burst into tears, 'She's not Mama! Leslie's forgotten Mama and Papa!' Poor babes."

Charles squeezed her arm back. "You've kept them safe, helped them learn, and done your best to give them a happy home as long as it's needed."

They came back to the house by a circuitous route. Charles was favoring his leg a little more than usual. When Evie expressed concern, he admitted, "Frightfully stiff it's been with the weather about to change. And—oh, dash it all! I've left my jacket by the tree house." He grimaced. "Nothing for it. You go in, Evie. I'll head back."

"Nonsense, Charles! Rest your leg. I should really call the children in anyway."

EVIE WAS BACK in fifteen minutes, bringing the children in tow for tea. By that time her letter was tucked back in her desk, just as she had left it.

Thirteen

20 October 1943

Attn: Mr.H

We are in receipt of your inquiries and believe we have just the man for the job. We will arrange a meeting at your earliest convenience. In addition, we wish to cordially extend congratulations on your recent winnings.

X. J. S.

25 October 1943

Dear Evie,

If I were to write travel adverts to Italy I might say less about the sunny shores and ancient architecture and more about the many rivers traversing it. There doesn't seem to be any lack of them, flowing down from the mountains to our left, to the sea on our right. In the summer for the tourist with intact bridges to motor across, I'm sure that this is very pretty. We find ourselves appreciating the view of each one less.

"MORE SWIMMING?" Peters groaned as they approached the Trigno River. "The Irish at least have a bridge—"

"*Had.* Didn't you hear, it got blown?" Llewellyn fiddled with his boot laces. "Quit grousing—it's just a pleasant wade."

"You say so, Father, but I've already been baptized."

Knee deep in the frigid water, James agreed that "pleasant" was a poor descriptor, but what good did complaining do? *At least no one's shooting at us just now.*

Once they'd crossed and established their bridgehead, the lieutenant came over to divvy them up for patrol.

"Take a whole section, just in case, but don't get locked in a heavy engagement," Bradlock told James. "This is meant to be a quick stroll."

James nodded. "You think Jerry's waiting for us?"

"Word is he's holding San Salvo, the next objective. You just take a look and see what he's left for us on the way there. Out and back, and try not to go and get shot again, Milburn."

Gathering up Llewellyn's section didn't take long, and they set out under the approaching blanket of dark.

Once they were past their sentries, it didn't take long to feel the isolation of their little party, like a weight pressing against James's lungs.

As the trees closed around them, his ears strained for any unusual noise. The soft scuffs of boots on the leaf litter and stones, the small noises of their kit and weapons shifting—even the breathing of the men—seemed unnaturally loud.

There!

James jerked his head and rifle around to the left.

A moment later, he relaxed. The dim light had transformed the stunted, gnarled branches of an olive tree into a spindly human form. Embarrassed at how easily he had been spooked, he refocused and continued.

The trees ended abruptly in a small clearing.

James held up his hand, stopping their forward movement. Past the clearing, the trees recommenced, with a ridge rising dark behind them.

I don't like the look of that.

Danny Ryan appeared at his elbow, breath coming in heavy gasps, eyes wide and staring. "Sir, this is bad news. We'll be exposed out there—if they've got that ridge they can just pick us off..." He wiped sweat from his brow despite the chill.

James nodded. "Settle down, Danny. We'll circle around to the left, see if it's a narrower gap. Keep your eyes open."

Treading softly, they moved through the wood. The stillness felt ominous; not a breath of wind stirred in the thick, rain-scented air.

They reached a narrower point for their crossing without incident and peered across in the last tattered remains of light. Nothing moved.

James had just signaled forward and stepped beyond the tree line when he heard what might have been mistaken for a bee buzzing just past his face.

He'd been through too much to make that mistake.

As he dropped, splinters showered him, bursting out of the tree trunk overhead. He heard the others hitting the ground as the forest across from them opened up.

"Back, back!" he hissed, scooting into the shelter of the trees on his belly until he was able to get behind a large enough trunk to sit up. The fire lasted a few more moments, then cut off. The eerie silence resumed.

"I think we've found the enemy," gasped Llewellyn from a neighboring tree.

"Take roll—are we all here?" *Please, God.*

Ryan, Peters, Turner, Llewellyn, Rogers, Cartwright and Moore all sounded off, all unharmed. James breathed again.

"What do we do, sir?" Moore asked. The little replacement's hands were steady as he checked over his rifle.

James wished his own nerves were as steady. "Sounds like there's a machine gun emplacement up there. We aren't ready to take them, and they aren't coming to us. We'll report in and see what the orders are."

Ryan let out his breath with a whoosh, trying not to look too relieved.

"Next time out we ought to do something to mute Father's hair—it's like a signal flare. That must've been how they saw us," Peters grumbled.

"More likely they heard *you*, mate. I don't think an elephant going through could find every dry stick to step on like you do," Turner said.

"Quiet," James interjected. "Come along now, before they throw something heavier."

Taking care to stay under cover, they began their withdrawal to the bridgehead.

Traversing ground they'd covered once was less anxious work, and James could almost feel the tension leaving the men. The deepened dark was also a relief, a shelter from unfriendly eyes.

Davy Llewellyn had just turned towards him, opening his mouth to speak, when James froze, signaling the others to do likewise.

There was a gully off to their right. From within it had come a small splash, followed by a muttered curse. The word was unfamiliar, but the language had a guttural sound that James recognized.

He crept towards the gully, covered by the sparse underbrush, willing them all to follow and move silently.

The clouds parted, faint light revealing the tops of three helmets, smooth and rounded, like turtle shells.

"HALT!" James commanded.

Three pale, dirt-stained faces looked up.

One man, if man he could be called—his face looked as though it hadn't yet seen the growth of a beard—tried to raise his gun.

Crack! Moore fired. It went wide, but the young German soldier and one of his companions dropped their weapons and raised their hands in surrender.

"Rogers?" James asked, keeping his rifle carefully trained on the nearest of the three. He had lowered his rifle, and his eyes were hidden in deep shadow under his helmet, but his stance was ready, James fancied, for any opening or show of weakness.

Broad-faced Rogers stepped up with a grin. His uniform fit his bulky frame uneasily—he always looked as if he ought to be in a jumper and gum boots, striding across a moor somewhere. His German, however, was flawless. "Yes, sir."

"Tell them to climb up, but to keep their hands where we can see them, or they will be shot. Moore and Cartwright, you climb down once they're clear and get their weapons. We'll take them back to the bridgehead."

"Right-o," Rogers replied and relayed the instructions.

The Germans complied. The youngest made it out last. As he passed James, he paused for a moment, gave him a look, and spat on his boots.

Peters gave an exclamation of rage and raised the butt of his rifle, but James held out a hand to stop him.

"Don't let him rile you, Peters. Can't blame a man for being angry when he's beaten."

The soldier James had been watching—the one who hadn't surrendered at once—turned at that and looked James full in the face. He spoke in very good, if slightly accented, English. "Beaten, you say? No, no we are not beaten. Three of us you will take away, but when you reach our *Winderstellung*," he shrugged and smiled, a cold, cheerless grimace, "a thousand of you will break upon it, and still our armies will fight on."

James stared back at him, face impassive. In a moment the other broke eye contact and muttered something to the young one, who laughed. Ignoring this, James gave the order and they moved out.

Falling behind, he gestured for Rogers to come back with him. "What were they muttering, there at the end, Rogers?"

The young man grimaced. "Just talkin' about you. Nothing complimentary, I'm afraid."

"Ah. And 'Winderstellung'? What's that?"

"Winter Line."

James nodded slowly. He'd heard some talk, mainly through Bradlock, about the Winter Line further on through which the Germans were pulling back. What he had heard had an ominous sound.

Returning to the bridgehead, they learned that the other patrols who had returned had also had clashes with the Germans. The resistance looked to be strong, "…but now that we've seen where they are," Bradlock concluded, flicking his cigarette butt into the icy waters, "we'll knock 'em out, sooner or later."

James hoped it was sooner as the weather worsened.

Dug in deep, with the rain pouring down in sheets, taking what shelter he could on the muddy river bank, the night and the next day passed in soggy misery.

The Germans didn't seem to mind—any movement brought down artillery fire from the heights ahead.

Through it all, James tried to sleep, or at least to think of pleasant things—getting home, taking Evie around to meet his family, a hot drink at his mother's table. Nothing he tried could distract him from what was coming. Word had come down: tonight they would begin their advance.

NIGHT FELL. The water slowly rose in James's trench, seeping into his boots and soaking his trousers, leaving his feet and legs heavy and numb. Gritting his teeth against the chill, he methodically checked his kit for the hundredth time. Rifle, bayonet, pistol, entrenching tool—all the essentials were in place and in good working order.

"All set?" Davy Llewellyn asked, flopping down next to him.

"Yes. You?"

"Just finished the prayers."

"Good to hear it. Your earthly gear is in top shape, too?"

Davy snorted. "What do you think? My old dad used to say, 'spiritual doesn't mean stupid.'" He took a drink from his canteen. "James, d'you think the diversion will work? I imagine the railway station is pretty well held. Do you think we'll be enough to draw out more forces from San Salvo?"

"We'll have to be. The fellows are counting on it for tomorrow night." He stood, shaking his legs and stamping his feet, trying to wake them up. "C'mon. It's time."

He and Llewellyn made their way over to where the lieutenant and the rest of their platoon were waiting, and he checked in with the other two section leaders. The men stood about, wrapped in what layers they'd been able to contrive to keep out the chill and damp, and loaded with all the necessary gear of war.

They waited. Bradlock held a cigarette between his lips, unlit, not that a match would easily light in this weather even if it were safe to carry a glowing flame about. Ryan, just behind him, fiddled obsessively with his boots. Ed Turner tested the keenness of his bayonet's blade with his thumb while Peters looked on. Cartwright and Rogers were silent dark shapes. Moore muttered to James as he walked by, "No chance of a brew up before we head out?"

The signal came.

Small details kept James focused and helped him ignore the knot of fear in his belly. *Don't care much for the lack of cover. Or the mud.* His boots squelched as he slogged through the morass, eyes scanning ahead, ears straining past the sounds of the men and tap of raindrops on his helmet. *At least the rain should have Jerry keeping his head down tonight and mask the sound of our approach.*

The sharp report of rifles burst out to the right. Returning fire was followed by the muffled blast of a grenade. His eyes tracked that way automatically, though he could see nothing except the occasional tracer bullet.

Or not.

He quickened his approach, Llewellyn and Peters in his periphery, doing the same. Time was running out. Jerry knew that he had company coming to call.

A burst of small arms fire exploded directly ahead.

James dropped, bullets buzzing above. Up again, he pulled the grenade's pin, counted, threw.

The blast was muted by the mud and rain, but the fire paused for a moment.

Bent low, wishing he were smaller, he dashed forward as fast as he could with mud-caked feet. More grenades were lobbed on his left and right. One exploded nearby in answer and Peters bellowed a curse.

We must be nearly on top of them—

Figures loomed ahead through the mist and the dark.

James knelt and took quick aim. For a moment he was back on the farm, firing at empty tins lined up at the far end of the back garden, calm and sure. One dropped, then another. He felt rather than heard the bullet that nearly took his left ear.

Back on his feet, pressing forward, the world was reduced to a few scattered perceptions.

Moore's voice roared a challenge.

Llewellyn's red hair looked almost black in the dark, plastered to his neck under his helmet.

Peters jostled his right arm.

I hope the others made it—but there was no more time.

He flung himself forward.

27 October 1943

Dear Miss Worther,
We have had bad news.

THE CASCADE OF TEARS wound its lazy way down the curve of Evie's cheek and dripped off the tip of her nose. Her hair hung down on either side of her face, dark curtains to shut out the fading evening light.

Leaning against one of the little apple trees in the orchard, she wrapped her arms around herself as if to keep from breaking to pieces as she sobbed, gasping for breath. The rocks and dirt dug into her knees, and the roots of the tree she leaned against made an uncomfortable refuge. The ache deep in her chest blunted all other sensations.

The letter had arrived today from Lilly and Leslie's mother. Her husband, the girls' father, was missing in action. She intended to come up the following Sunday to tell the girls herself.

Evie had kept her face and manner composed around the children with an effort of will, but they were asleep now.

Missing. Not dead, no finality offered, no certainty that their father's suffering was ended.

"Dear God," she whispered, "How will they bear it? How can their mother bear it? Oh, God, please, I couldn't bear it if…"

Those first weeks after James had gone, when no letters arrived, had been torturous. She had struggled to remain cheerful and not to worry, but specters of U-boats, of the Luftwaffe, of shipwreck and blood and death had haunted the edges of her consciousness. Almost worse than these was the nagging thought, *I had him such a short time—what if it wasn't real? What if he didn't love me like he said he did?*

When that first packet of letters arrived, she'd gasped in a deep breath of air, the first full breath she had taken since he left.

He was alive. He hadn't forgotten her. All was well.

The sobs slowed. Evie pulled out a handkerchief, struggling to hold it in her trembling fingers. She wiped the tears away, gulping in a shaky breath. "If he were to die, Father, it would break my heart. But please, please, don't let him be dragged away, lost, somewhere we won't ever know..." her voice broke. "Please keep him safe. Please keep them all safe. God, let this end, please!" She leaned her head against the rough bark, looking up through the few remaining leaves at the darkling sky. A headache starting behind her eyes, she sighed, closing them.

A gentle pat on the shoulder startled her, and her eyes snapped open.

Cook smiled down at her, wearing her going-home jacket and hat. "Come along, Duck. I was headed home, but you could use a cup of tea. Mr. Fisk won't mind."

Obediently, Evie stood, brushing her hair out of her face and smoothing her skirt. *Keep up that stiff upper lip—that's what Father always said.*

Cook clattered around the kitchen, producing a couple of biscuits to go with the tea. She asked without turning, "He's not sent you bad news, has he?"

"Oh, no. It's not James—Sergeant Milburn." She gave a brief explanation of the truth. Cook shook her head.

"It's a terrible business, not knowing. Had a cousin whose man was lost in the last war. She never knew what happened. Near broke her heart. It's hard on the young ones. Hard thinking about them that are over there still, in danger all the time." She patted Evie's hand.

"It is. It's terrible." In spite of her resolve, a lump filled Evie's throat, and she cast her eyes down. "We...we must do everything we can to help the poor little dears."

"Yes. Of course." Cook squeezed Evie's hand and then released it to put a cup of tea and the biscuits close by. "I'll make sure to plan a good dinner, and I'll lay aside some extra tea..."

As she continued (and showed no inclination to pause), Evie couldn't help smiling. How like her old friend to try to cure pain of the spirit with the catch-all remedy of a cup of tea and some good victuals.

After the musings had gone on for some time, Evie said, "Thank you, Cook. Don't feel that you need to stay on. I think I'll write a letter and then go to bed."

"Yes, Mr. Fisk will be wondering. Try not to fret yourself. They'll pull through, and your young man's a strong one. I daresay he'll be fine, God willing."

When the other woman had gone, Evie forced herself to eat, though the lovingly made biscuits were dust and ashes in her mouth. She couldn't stop thinking about little Leslie, with her red-gold curls, and Lilly with her brown bob, how they both had the same large, brown eyes—their father's eyes, their mother had said.

She almost gave in to melancholy again, but she shook her head and spoke aloud, "This will do no one any good, Evie. You mustn't dwell on it." Straightening her shoulders, she put the lights out and headed up to her room through the chill dark.

Passing the children's doors, she squelched the urge to peek in on them.

Waking them up past bedtime won't help matters.

She readied herself for bed, forcing herself to go through all the motions, brushing her hair carefully, telling herself that she was calm. Finally, she sat down to write.

30 October 1943

Dear James,

She stared at the paper. What could she write? She didn't want to worry or trouble him, and she was in no state to pretend to be cheerful.

She stood and paced the room. The four walls were suffocating. She opened the window, savoring the clean chill of the night. As she put her hand on her desk, her fingers found the worn cover of her Bible.

She flipped it open, and there it was: Psalm 27. "The LORD is my light and my salvation; whom shall I fear? The LORD is the strength of my life; of whom shall I be afraid?" Taking a deep breath, she bowed her head, and prayed again for patience and peace.

30 October 1943

Dear Evie,

I hope it doesn't shock you too much to hear that I am considering a change of profession. Some kind of excavation maybe. As I lay completely still in a hastily dug trench shortly after my last letter, admiring my construction skills at leisure for the entire day, I thought I ought not waste this talent. Any thoughts?

I'm spouting nonsense. If I meant to complain, the worst part was the fellow in the hole next over grousing about how dull it was, as if Jerry's greatest crime was depriving us of entertainment. Even that wouldn't have been so bad if his need for movement hadn't kept Jerry's attention focused so keenly in our direction.

During all of this, out came one of their aid wagons, flying the Red Cross, and their medics asked to remove their wounded and dead. We acquiesced on the understanding that they wouldn't betray our positions. Seemed like decent fellows. Our RAMC's are just as dedicated, running into the fray with nothing but their Red Cross for a shield. It makes me wonder if the dictators were removed this whole mess could be sorted out by the reasonable people without the necessity of firearms.

I must close this and get a letter written home. Mum commented in her last that I haven't been writing as often. Apparently, I have been distracted writing elsewhere. They will understand when they meet you, and seeing you, they will immediately forgive me, I'm certain.

Love, James

Evie put the letter aside with a weary smile. It was good to hear from James. It was also good to sit for a moment. Her feet and head were aching after helping the children sort through some of their more worn things. It had taken the whole morning to find what could be mended and patched, and what needed to be added to the rag bag.

She stretched her arms over her head, joints popping.

Just how can *those boys wear holes in their knees so quickly? And where could Bonny have lost her stockings? Maybe in summer I'll just have them all go barefoot…*

A sharp knock on the front door interrupted her thoughts.

Molly was busy tending to Great Aunt Helena, so she called over her shoulder, "It's all right—I'll get it!"

She stood and stretched again, shivering. It was difficult to keep the sprawling old house warm as November brought a chill edge to the air.

Buck up, Evie. It's not going to get warmer any time soon.

Grabbing her jumper and a basket of clothes to be mended, she trotted down the stairs. The knocker sounded again, impatient.

Sounds like Charles.

He had written that he would be coming this weekend and she had been surprised not to see him earlier. Setting her load down, she opened the door, and then stepped back.

A stranger stood in the doorway.

He was average height, but on the bulkier side of average in build, with pale gray eyes and ashy hair—even his skin seemed strangely colorless. He was so non-descript that he seemed to blend in with the stone pavement on which he stood, a chameleon in uniform. He stared at her with a broad, unassuming smile and flat, expressionless eyes, and said nothing.

"Hello…?" Evie managed.

Charles stepped out from behind the apparition. "Evie! Good morning. Ah, Private Andrews, this is my cousin, Miss Worther." He spoke heartily with large theatrical gestures. One man had too little presence, the other too much.

The stranger took Evie's proffered hand in a brief, clammy grasp. She resisted the urge to wipe her hand on her skirt after.

"Miss," he said in a soft, inexpressive voice.

She mustered a gracious smile. "Welcome, Private Andrews. What brings you up this far?"

Charles answered, "Oh, Andrews and I met up through my work. He's just been called up, going to be sent over to reinforce our front in Italy."

Evie's hands gripped each other convulsively, thoughts winging to James. She struggled to keep her face serene as Charles continued. "I invited him over for a last good meal beforehand."

"How lovely. I'll let Cook know, and shall I have Molly make up a room?"

Charles jumped in again. "Oh, no, he won't be able to be gone overnight. Dinner will do very well."

Private Andrews stood silent through all, smooth faced and blank eyed, smile fixed and bland.

He kept nearly the same expression all through the meal, making the conversation very dull. Instead, he focused on eating, each bite slow and deliberate as if mealtime were serious business. He answered a direct question or two, but Charles generally beat him to it.

Evie found it all odd. *James is quiet. This man is.... secretive.*

After the meal, Great Aunt Helena decided to rest.

Keeping her most polite smile fixed in place, Evie ventured, "Since the children are helping Mrs. Jenkins over at Thrush House, I had hoped to walk into the village and practice my music a bit, Charles. If you and the Private don't mind." *Please, don't mind! I don't want to be rude, but that man makes my skin crawl!*

Charles's smile was quick and bright. "Certainly, Evie. Take as long as you like. We'll entertain ourselves."

Really? She searched his face for sarcasm, for irritation, for any of Charles's normal reactions to her personal plans. She saw nothing.

Evie had made it nearly to the lane when she realized she had forgotten two pieces at the piano. Returning, she let herself in the front.

Voices were coming through the sitting room door, which stood slightly ajar.

Anxious to avoid interrupting Charles and his guest and anxious to avoid more uncomfortable lack of conversation with Private Andrews, she stepped lightly.

She didn't intend to listen but couldn't quite block out the words.

"So, you see, old man, it's really very simple. Give me *something* to work with and I'll be more than able to make it worth your while. As you can see, I'll have the means soon enough."

A dim, masculine murmur answered Charles. Presumably Andrews had asked a question because Charles said, "Oh, anything will do. It's all a question of character. One falls, another rises, everyone is satisfied—you see? I'll be happy to smooth any financial necessities arising from the project, as long as you can get results."

Evie slowed her steps as she passed until her conscience pricked her.

Really, eavesdropping? You're worse than the children.

She sped up, collected her music, and left via the kitchen door.

Even though she tried to banish the conversation from her mind, she couldn't help wondering as she played. What was "the project"?

Her fingers paused. Could this be related to James's letter of months ago, a sign that Charles was involved in something he shouldn't be?

But if Andrews were someone 'shady,' would Charles bring him to the house? Surely not! And in any case, he'll soon be gone. There can't be any cause to worry James, can there?

She frowned, chewing on her lower lip as she practiced, hardly hearing the notes she played.

That evening, Charles approached her. "Evie, could I have a word?"

She followed him into the library, and he closed the doors behind them. He turned to her, a frown creasing his brow, and folded his arms.

"Evie, I've been worried about you. It's been wearing on you, hasn't it, worrying about your sergeant over there in Italy?"

She looked down, unable to meet his eyes. She stalled, sitting on a chair covered in a hideous green print. She traced the curlicues of the pattern with a finger. "It's difficult, being left behind here, but really, I'm all right, Charles."

He sat down opposite her. "You can't fool me, Evie. I've known you too long. Not knowing—that's what's worst, isn't it? That's one reason I had Andrews over."

Evie looked up at him but said nothing.

He continued, "I debated whether I should tell you, but he will be one of the reinforcements in Milburn's division, perhaps even in his brigade."

Her breath caught. "How can you possibly know that?"

Charles shrugged. "I've made friends privy to a few of these details." He leaned forward and took her hand. "I could see him tomorrow if you wanted to send a letter or something small for him to carry along.

I thought you might like to send a letter privately for once, without the censors reading it."

"Charles, that is…that is so thoughtful of you," Evie managed through her astonishment.

Is he actually trying to help me?

"Also, well, he doesn't look like much, but word is Andrews's pretty good in a scrap. Did well in training, anyway. If he ends up near enough your sergeant, well," Charles shrugged, "we can't go over to help him ourselves, but if we can at least send someone…"

He laughed in a self-deprecating fashion and raked his fingers through his hair.

Like James used to.

Evie blinked away the sudden stinging in her eyes.

Charles didn't seem to notice. "It made more sense in my mind. Maybe having contact with Andrews won't make any difference, but," he released her hand and spread his out before him, "it's hard to know what to do to help. I do want to help you, Evie. I hope you know how much."

"Oh, Charles, it's a kind thought, and I appreciate the gesture. I've just sent out a parcel, but maybe, if Cook still has that brandy—in any case I will work on a letter at once." She reached across and squeezed his hand. "Thank you."

Head full of the letter she would write, Evie hurried out of the room, with only one glance over her shoulder. Charles sat still, leaned back in his chair and smiling.

Fifteen

9 November 1943

Dearest Evie,

Thank you for the socks and gloves. They were just what were wanted with the winter beginning here, and different food is always a pleasure, especially when it's made by you.

I'm sorry that I haven't written since the second, but I am well, and seeing some new terrain. We've liberated another city and are camped out beyond it. It's an impressive landscape, but it's hard to appreciate it just now as the view's been hard-won.

Word from the upper echelons is that Rome ought to be in our hands by Christmas. Christmas in Rome, wouldn't that be something? I have to admit, I'm skeptical. Forward progress hasn't been exactly swift. I know that it's all in God's hands, I just wouldn't complain if he'd turn that hand against Jerry a little harder and spare us another winter away from home.

Love,
James

Evie tucked her letter away and took a sip of her still scalding tea, burning her tongue in her impatience for its warmth. The days were rapidly getting colder. At least the warm things she had sent had reached James intact. Hopefully the little bottle of brandy she had sent along with Private Andrews made it through.

Outside the diamond-paned window above her desk, another swift flock of birds flew over, presumably looking for warmer climes.

I wish I were flying away, too, off to…where? Somewhere. Somewhere I could do MORE. It's so hard to be sitting still here, when everything's happening elsewhere.

I wonder where James is now…

Movement below caught her eye. The three little girls were huddled around something—it looked like something alive.

"What are they up to?" she asked herself, and then stood as Bonny, looking up and meeting her eyes, waved for her to come.

"Please, please, Miss Worther, can we keep him?" Bonny pleaded as Evie hurried up, still pulling on her mittens. "He needs a home, just look at the poor thing!"

The scrawny tabby kitten in her arms mewed piteously. It would have been perfect timing to match the girl's plea, except for the fact that it was mewing as it was struggling to escape. Three of its needle-sharp claws were snagged in her coat, one was in her dark braid, and her hands bore long red scratches.

"Oh dear, where did you girls find it?"

Lilly pointed. "Just back there, under the hedges. He's so lonely, Miss Worther, and it's winter. We'll take care of him, I promise!" She gave Leslie's foot a kick.

"Ouch!" cried her smaller sister without pulling her fingers out of her mouth. Lilly leaned over, put her mouth to her ear, and in a fully audible whisper urged, "Tell Miss Worther you want to keep kitty too!"

Turning those velvety brown eyes up to Evie with her sweetest expression, Leslie lisped, "Please, Miss Worther?"

Evie sighed and examined the girls' discovery. The kitten looked healthy enough, but its ribs showed beneath its gray-striped fur. "I'll ask Mrs. Heatherington. I imagine he'll have to stay outside—"

Bonny chimed in at once. "We can make him a little home in the old carriage house. There are sure to be mice and things in there for him to catch!"

"—and we'll have to figure out what to feed him until he's big enough to hunt. After all, there's no rationed pet food," Evie said.

"He can have *my* milk!" Lilly exclaimed, jumping up and down.

"We'll see."

The boys came around the corner of the house, three dark heads close together. They straightened abruptly when they saw the cluster of females and set about looking innocent.

Evie opened her mouth, and then closed it. *I don't even think I'll ask.*

"Edward, Edward, we found a kitty!" cried Leslie, running up and tugging on the big boy's sleeve. Obediently, Edward let her pull him forward, and he admired the little creature.

"What a jolly little fellow. Will we keep him, Miss Worther?"

"I'm going to speak to Mrs. Heatherington—"

"I wish he were a dog," said Tommy, frowning. "I used to have a dog. They're more fun."

"Brutus was the best dog ever," agreed John. "I wish we could've kept him."

"Oh, did you have to give him away?" Evie asked.

John shrugged. "No, the war started, so we put him to sleep."

"Oh..." Evie bit her lip.

He joined the other children, gathered around the tiny kitten. It didn't have enough mass to satisfy all the small fingers trying to pet it, and it was trying to burrow into Bonny's shoulder.

Evie wrapped her arms around herself. *Poor little dears. They've had to give up so much, through no fault of their own, and then to lose their animals, too, and it does seem to need a home...*

She sighed, and said, "I suppose, if he stays in the carriage house, and if we can keep him fed without shorting anyone else, I don't know why we can't keep him."

There was a general cheer, and then Bonny piped up, "But what shall we call him?"

There was a moment of silence, then Tommy gave a decisive nod. "His name is Brutus the Second, of course!"

Brutus mewed.

21 November 1943

Dear Evie,

Jerry has been quiet, though we've only been visiting him by patrol. It's been pretty cold, and the mud keeps getting deeper. Thank goodness for those new socks! Not to worry—with any luck and some fair weather, the sappers will have us keeping our feet dry soon.

Do you know, when I'm back home, you and I should go walking in the rain. We should splash in every puddle and get as untidy and wet as possible, just for the sheer pleasure of being able to walk into our house and to be clean and warm and dry at any instant. What do you think?

I believe I'd better close this before I spout more foolishness.

All my love,
James

P.S. Word's coming in, we'll be busy for a few days. I'll write again when I'm able. God bless you!

James folded up his letter, tucked it in his pocket, and hurried over to join the others, skirting some loose piles of debris. They'd assembled in an abandoned barn, if three walls and no roof could be called a barn.

Lieutenant Bradlock's cigarette dangled between his unsmiling lips. "All right, here it is. The bridgehead across the river is in trouble, and it needs to be expanded. Looks like it'll be up to us. We'll cross over in fighting patrols to set our forming up points for the battalion's attack. They'll be firing the Bofurs gun for us with tracers every few minutes. Just follow them, and you'll know you're going the right direction. I've got a few pictures of the terrain—the CO "borrowed" them from the HQ."

He spread the papers out in the flickering light of candles and lit smokes. "Jerry's likely got some surprises waiting for us, so we'll try to slip in as quietly as we can under the regular artillery fire. Yes, Turner?"

"How high's the river?"

Bradlock took a long, last drag on his cigarette and flicked it away. "Too high. We'll go in with the light stuff, wading—"

"Moore, I suppose it'll be swimming for you," Peters threw in, smirking down at him.

Bradlock silenced him with a look and continued, "—since we can't safely carry in the heavy equipment."

Ryan half raised his hand. "Pardon me, sir, this Sangro River, isn't this that Wintersteller they've been talking about?" Rogers rolled his eyes and laughed at the mispronunciation. No one else found it particularly funny, and Ryan continued. "How're we going to break that with rifles and bayonets? When'll they be bringing in the big stuff?"

Bradlock's lips were pressed in a thin line. "That depends on the weather, Danny. If we can just get two dry days, the bridging can be done, and we'll have all the backup we need. With any luck, by the twenty-third."

"And if the rain doesn't let up?"

"If the rain won't let up, we may be on our own for a while. This is a big push. Jerry thinks he can hold us here. It's up to you to show him different. That's all."

The men separated, muttering to each other, and checking their kit to see that all was in order. The lieutenant pulled James aside.

"Have you got your patrol sorted out?"

"Yes. We'll get the job done."

"Good." Bradlock pulled his spare cigarette from behind his ear and frowned down at it. "I don't like going into this blind. Watch out for mines. If I were Jerry, I'd have planted 'em all over where they'd been cleared before. The other side of the Sangro isn't likely to be a friendly place. Get over, get your assembly point, and don't get yourself killed if you can help it, Milburn."

"I'll do my best." He pulled out his letter for Evie. "Would you mind dropping this off for me, since you'll be heading that way?"

"Not at all." He took the letter with a grin.

"And Harry? Try not to get yourself killed, either."

24 November 1943

Dear Evie,

Things haven't gone as well as we'd hoped.

RYAN GAVE A GRUNT of protest as Rogers, Davy Llewellyn, and James landed on top of him.

"Sorry, mate," Rogers gasped, "that's what you get for being first down."

Anything Ryan may have replied was muffled by another spray of German "burp gun" fire over the rim of their sheltering shell hole.

When he had breath, James barked, "Llewellyn, any grenades?"

"Two."

"Gimme one. We need to clear them out ahead or we're pinned down. I'll break right, you try from the left. Rogers? You have ammo?"

"Some, it's running short."

"Don't waste it, but keep them looking this way, won't you?"

"Right-o."

Taking a deep breath, James rolled out of the hole into the sparse, rough undergrowth, staying as low as he was able. He scrambled up the escarpment, digging his boots into the earth and using his elbows and hands to propel himself forward. A blinding flash lit the pitch-black sky, dazzling his eyes. He hesitated, fingers trembling against the cold, hard dirt, blinking. With a shake of his head, he pushed himself forward.

Lucky thing those blasted burp guns are loud enough to follow.

Nearly close enough. He jerked his hand back as rocks and earth peppered it, thrown up by automatic fire impacting inches away.

Almost there! He pushed himself up, boots slipping on the loose earth. Head bowed low, he sprinted the last few yards. A thin ribbon of flame burned across his collar bone, but he was pulling the pin...

The grenade flew true and, with a satisfying burst echoed almost simultaneously by one from Llewellyn's side, the troublesome guns were stilled.

He hit the ground again, ready for the next attack. Silence.

Behind him, he heard the heavy breathing and the crunch of boots and the rattle of equipment as the others in his platoon scrambled up to join him.

He turned and counted the shadowy forms. *All here. Thank God. Hope the other sections are doing as well.*

His hands began to shake as the adrenaline wore off. Trying to stay in control, he clenched them into fists. The black sky was shifting to charcoal gray. Dawn would come soon. "We'll dig in along this rise. Keep an eye out. Jerry might try one more go before light."

Peters spoke up. "Can I check if any of these stiffs have spare rations on them? Only we're running short—"

"Be quick. We'll need to be in deep."

"I hope he finds some," grumbled Reggie Cartwright as he dug, sweat streaking the sparse bristles on his pale face. "Unless they get some stores out to us yet tonight, we'll be plenty hungry tomorrow." Digging alongside him, little Moore grunted agreement.

"The problem is the river," Llewellyn said for the hundredth time. "As long as they've got to use the Ducks to ferry everything down by the coast, we're going to be short. Once the bridges are built—"

"Built again you mean, Father?" Peters jumped down to work.

The bridge closest to them was just coming visible in the growing light. It had been built to span the river and allow the main attack to come across. Now it stood completely useless, surrounded by the swirling flood that had swept down from the mountains and expanded the banks. They and the other men of the bridgehead across the Sangro were isolated, waiting day to day on sporadic supplies delivered by amphibious trucks. Along with the shortage of ammunition and food, their artillery forward observation officer had been killed and their radio batteries were running low.

"Keep your voices down." James scanned the dark ahead. "No need to give them a target."

Turner called over to Peters in a stage whisper, "Hey, you find anything? I could use some *schnapps*."

Peters shook his head. "Nah, nothing."

"Figures."

The cold gleam of pre-dawn lit up their weary faces, pale under the dirt. Three days of constant fighting, grinding through the German defenses, showed in the stoop of their shoulders as they dug.

One by one, as they decided that they'd dug deep enough and sank down to rest, James gave the familiar reminders. "All right. You know the routine. Those on watch, keep sharp. The rest of you, try to sleep while you can." *So that we can wake up and do this all over again. And even if we get beyond this escarpment, what's next? More pillboxes, wires, fortifications—how can I possibly keep them alive?*

He rubbed his hands over his eyes, dirt-coated skin rough and dry. *Best not think about it. Just get 'em to the top and then... we'll see.*

His watch dragged by as he struggled to keep his heavy eyelids from closing. When Davy relieved him, however, James tossed and turned on the hard earth.

He finally gave up and pulled out his little pocket Bible. Thinking of Evie, he found his way to Psalm 27. "Wait on the Lord: be of good courage, and he shall strengthen your heart; Wait, I say, on the Lord!"

Well, we've got plenty of waiting ahead. Don't let me fail them, Lord. And please, if that river could just go down, we'd certainly appreciate it. Amen.

Charles frowned, picking over the tray of cigarettes.

Red lipped smile wilting, the girl holding the tray fidgeted. "Aren't you finding what you'd like, sir?"

"There isn't much selection."

"Word is there's a war on. Sir."

Gripping the edge of the table, Charles half stood. "Why you little—"

A hand, solid as cement, clapped him on the shoulder, and he sat. "Easy now," growled the big man beside him around the cigar clenched between his teeth. He tossed the girl a coin and an apology. She took both and ambled off to a friendlier table.

"What's the matter, Heatherington? You aren't losing as badly as last week."

Charles pulled out one of his own cigarettes and lit up, deliberate, calm and collected. "Nothing. And who's to say my luck won't turn?"

"Only experience. That last job paid well, though, so I shouldn't think it'd put such a bee in your bonnet."

Lowering his voice, Charles leaned towards him. "Andrews. He's made it over, but I haven't heard a thing since. Are you certain he's reliable?"

"'Course. There's more going on in his pate than those eyes let on. Mind you, you didn't want to pay for one of my more…experienced boys."

"One of your thugs, you mean."

"Careful, Heatherington. Don't start thinking you're above the company you keep. Thick as thieves, you and me!" He threw back his head and laughed.

8 December 1943

Dear Evie,

I'm sorry that I've been such a terrible correspondent lately. Good news. The Germans had put a great deal of stock in their Winter Line, which we've now pierced.

How far we will be able to carry the advance is beyond me. For the time being, I am out of it. My division is being rested at Campobasso, up in the Apennine Mountains. Compared to the front it's a regular paradise, with a theater, cinema, and clubs. I'll be terribly spoiled.

I sent a small parcel your direction today for Christmas. Hopefully it will make it on time.

I'm up for a shower and then dinner!

Love,
James

10 December 1943

Dear Evie,

There has been a change of plans. We will be needed to hold the line in the mountains this winter. We are busy making preparations. At least we've had time for a wash and a meal. I will write to you again soon and let you know more.

Love,
James

15 December 1943

Dear Evie,

We are settled in to our new quarters, such as they are. Jerry left some notes to welcome us to some of the ruins he left behind—very thoughtful. Not to worry. It's not being on leave, but it could be worse.

SHARP COUGHS RATTLED in James's chest and tore at his throat. When he got his breath back, he blew on his hands to warm them, shoulders hunched against the frigid wind.

He and his platoon had taken up the forward positions on the line the night before and expected to stay in them for five days, before moving back for a brief respite.

Llewellyn's section had claimed one of the best spots—the burned-out shell of an old farmhouse. James stretched his arms and then his legs. *Wish I could stand.* He knew better, though. Their shelter was situated near the crown of the hill, and Jerry was too close to allow a careless act like raising his head above the level of the ruined walls.

He shivered, and considered moving closer to Ryan, who had lit a small fire to keep the works of the machine gun from freezing up, or Davy Llewellyn who was trying to brew up tea in another corner. Wrapped in every layer of clothing they possessed, the others sat about, too cold to attempt a card game or reading.

"What would be your fancy if you could pick?" Ed Turner quizzed Peters. "A hot meal, a warm night's sleep, or a dance with a girl?"

Peters ruminated for a moment. "One dance?"

Turner nodded solemnly.

"What's the girl look like?"

Shaking his head and grinning, James turned his attention back to his letter, but the ink in his pen had frozen. He shuffled over to warm it by the fire, coughing again.

Ryan glanced up at him as he approached. "Patrol tonight, sir?" His voice was deliberately casual.

James considered. Patrolling had been difficult. The nights had been clear, affording little cover from enemy eyes, the snow was deep and difficult to traverse, and Jerry had been active. The platoon over the next ridge had lost an officer two nights ago, presumably captured on a brief jaunt from their OP back to the main position—vanished without a trace.

Still, tonight the weather looked promising—cloudy, which would cut down on the glare off the snow, but no new snow threatening. "Yes, unless there's a change." He broke off, coughing.

Llewellyn grunted. "Good. Don't want Jerry to get too comfortable."

"Forget about Jerry, I'm wanting a stroll to warm up a bit," Peters said. Turning back to Turner he added, "All right, but only if she's a blonde."

James's cough continued to trouble him into the evening as the time for the proposed patrol approached. After a particularly bad fit, he looked up to see Llewellyn standing over him. "Jimmy, you can't go out tonight."

"Oh? And why not?"

Moore answered, grinning. "All due respect, but you'd make us a target, wouldn't you, with that hacking?"

"But..." James grimaced. *I hate sending out patrols that I don't lead. Not that they can't handle themselves, but if anything happens, if I'm not there, if someone dies because I wasn't there...* He shook his head, coughing into his hands.

Can't afford to think like that. "All right. Davy, take a couple of men. You needn't go too far but see if you can't get a look at what's going on beyond that ridgeline. Keep sharp."

Dark came, and Llewellyn, Peters, and Moore set out. The cold was so bitter that even writing was difficult, necessitating many pauses for ink and fingers to thaw. James finished the address on a letter home and was about to snuff out his candle.

A shot rang out, then another.

James dropped his pen and paper and seized his rifle, standing in a half crouch. Ryan was already peering over the broken stones, cursing under his breath. James joined him, and they squinted into the hazy dark, looking for any movement.

When the shapes first appeared, James wasn't sure what to think. He could discern Peters's silhouette—he always wore his helmet at the same angle—and the shorter one must be Moore, but where was Llewellyn?

The already icy world froze solid around him.

Not Davy.

The men came closer. They were dragging something between them.

James's stomach twisted. Discarding caution, he vaulted a low section of the broken rocks.

"Is he wounded?"

"Fatally, I'm afraid," answered Peters, but his voice was all wrong, nonchalant and cheerful.

What?

Davy Llewelyn came into view, stumping along at the rear of his patrol. The prone form, dragged between Moore and Peters, was a fair-sized pig, shot cleanly through the head.

"Wha—" James began, but Moore interjected.

"We saw him wandering about in no man's land, and he looked awfully furtive."

James's face didn't twitch, "The pig looked…furtive?"

Moore nodded vigorously. Llewelyn just shook his head. Peters continued, "You know Jerry and his camouflage. Well, we figured it was best not to take any chances. And now…well, I suppose there's nothing to do but…"

James sighed, and waved them on. He had always liked pork.

A WEEK LATER James pulled his collar up as he left his billet, letters secure in his pocket. He had been lodged at the very edge of the camp and had a cold walk ahead of him. Still, his winter gear gave some relief from the bitter chill of snow and the perpetually swirling sleet, and with warmer lodgings, his cough had finally eased.

Bending his head against the wind, he felt a moment of sympathy for the men who'd relieved them. Casualties were coming in—harmed not by German bullets, but by exposure.

Out of the cold white just in front of him, a figure appeared. Startled, he stepped aside, narrowly avoiding a collision. "Pardon," he muttered.

"Sorry, sir," the other said at the same time.

His voice caught James's attention for its sheer expressionlessness. He glanced down, and he was no longer surprised that he had nearly missed seeing him. The other's pale, drained face blended in with the wintery white.

Private...Andrews. The one Evie sent the brandy along with.

Too cold for conversation, James just nodded in reply and continued on, not considering until later that it was odd to see Andrews out in the cold, apparently walking aimlessly since he was so far from everything else in the camp.

December 30, 1943

Dear James,

It sounds as if we are in for some changes. They'll be reopening the school in town soon! I'm not certain what that will mean for me, as I won't be needed to—

EVIE STARED AT THE DRY, forlorn Christmas tree and struggled to think of what to write. James's name blurred on the page, and she lowered her face into her arms.

"Child?"

She started, raised her head, and wiped her eyes, fixing a smile on her face. Her great aunt peered around the corner, Molly pushing her chair. She took in Evie's state in a glance. "Push me over, Molly, and then make yourself scarce."

Once Molly had gone, Evie asked, voice steady, "What can I do for you, Great Aunt Helena?"

"You've been unhappy."

Evie bit her lips, then nodded. "Yes, I suppose I have."

"Has something happened?"

"Nothing new." Evie rose and paced. "He's still up in the mountains, and nothing seems to be changing, nothing at all. I suppose that's the trouble." She laughed bitterly. "Nothing changes, I contribute nothing—it seems like it's never going to end."

Her great aunt frowned. "I'd hardly say you contribute nothing. Between all the work you've done in the village, and the children—"

"I know…I know." Evie scrubbed her hands across her face. "And I've tried not to complain. I've just been…restless, I guess."

"What, is watching the children becoming too tiresome?"

"No." She threw up her hands. "They're dears, and I've been happy to try and help them have a home. It's given me some purpose. But now, well, I don't feel like I'm really necessary here, especially if the school reopens like they've been talking about. With only one little girl here all day, am I really necessary?" Walking over, she knelt by her great aunt's chair. "I know that nothing I do will really make it all end faster, but—"

The old woman rolled her eyes heavenward. "But you've been longing to jump into the fray for years. Nothing I've done seems to content you."

Unwilling to be baited, Evie took a calming breath. "No, I suppose not. Though you must admit, everything you've done has been designed to keep me here."

"Is it so bad here?" Her great aunt's voice was weary, uncertain, and so unlike her usual stringent tones that Evie paused, surprised.

"No. No, it isn't, and I'm sorry. I owe you so much, and you've been very good to me. I'm going to be nineteen, though." She reached for the old woman's hand. "Don't you think it's time?"

Pulling her hand away, Great Aunt Helena leaned forward, gaze piercing. "For what? For you to put yourself in harm's way? How many have you and I lost? Is it so wrong for me to wish you safe, child?"

Evie leaned back on her heels. "I don't want to do anything foolish."

"All right, then." Folding her blue veined hands, the old woman sat back in her chair. "What is it you want to do? Be specific."

Evie gathered her thoughts and then nodded. "I would like to help our soldiers. I can't do much for James, but if I could help the wounded..." She squared her shoulders and took a deep breath. "I've been thinking about this, Great Aunt Helena, and I have a plan."

10 January 1944

Dear James,

I have sent another parcel that I hope will brighten the winter days.

It has been a bit cold, especially in the bedrooms, as we are, of course, conserving fuel, and this drafty old house doesn't hold heat. Great Aunt Helena spends a great deal of time in her room, wrapped well and drinking her tea allotment. Charles has come through again and provided her with some extra, for which we are all grateful.

The children and I have been spending these chilly days around the kitchen table working. Cook, bless her, doesn't mind, and always finds a bite for them or a job to keep them busy. The first they appreciate, and the second I certainly do! I've been teaching the older girls how to knit and received an extraordinary hat from Bonny as a thank-you. It was sweet of her, and it has been a great benefit in keeping me from becoming vain. No, you will not be receiving a picture of it, and if you dare suggest it, I shall ask her to make one for you!

The school in town will be opening for the remainder of winter term as they've finally found a teacher to take on the post. He's long retired, and rather deaf, but he is experienced, and with the objection of having to transport the children removed, the older ones will all be attending there. With only the littlest about, Molly and Cook have volunteered to keep an eye on her during the day, as I will likely be busy.

Thrush House is expecting more convalescents, bringing the total up higher than it's ever been. They're planning to expand their operation, and the Matron to head it all up has already arrived. (Mrs. Jenkins is not thrilled.) They've still got the same Red Cross nurse about who was here when you were. They are hoping to have another to help, and they'll be filling the other positions with VAD nurses, one of whom will be me! Great Aunt Helena finally agreed, albeit reluctantly, to let me sign up. I braced myself for all the possibilities of where I might be assigned when, lo and behold, it was next door! While it wasn't what I was expecting, I am excited to have the opportunity to help, and I suppose it will be good to come "home" at the end of the day. I'll admit to you, James, I am a little nervous to be working with strangers at an unfamiliar job. I hope that I do well.

Stay safe, and God bless you! Sending love and kisses. I hope that next winter we can sit by the fire and stay warm together!

Love,
Evie

Matthew 28:20 "Lo, I am with you always, even to the end of the age."

Seventeen

February 5, 1944

Dear Evie,

I am well, and in a much warmer position. The snow on the mountains is beautiful from a distance.

I think that you will do very well as a nurse. I healed up right quickly when I met you, after all. You're not going into full time nursing, are you? Only they're not allowed to be married—or has that rule been let go because of the war?

If I have my way we'll keep plenty warm together next winter, fire or no.

Love,
James

EVIE SCRUBBED HER HANDS. Nancy, one of the Red Cross nurses, tapped her on the shoulder, and she moved aside with a sigh. She knew that her hands were clean, but the greasy ointments left them feeling oily for hours.

"I checked that dressing, Evie. You did a good job there. Sure you don't want to train to be a regular nurse?"

"It would be very interesting, but I'm not sure how I'd handle it all."

"But look how far you've come already! Your first day when you saw some of those burns you turned positively green!"

"It has gotten easier," Evie admitted. "Of course, some of the worse ones are looking better—I imagine that helps."

"Always. Check on the beds in the big ward, won't you? Make sure they're all comfortable, and I'll see that the kitchen's starting to make lunch." She paused as she headed out the door and turned back, smirking. "And don't let them spend too much time trying to chat you up, dear."

Obediently, Evie headed for what had been Colonel Bryce's trophy room. The stuffed heads and bodies of various exotic animals and the impressive display of armaments had been moved out and put in storage upstairs to make room for two rows of hospital beds and all of the accompanying paraphernalia. There were six other men in individual rooms who were more able to care for themselves and would soon be released, either back to the war or back home.

She stopped first at the bedside of a young RAF pilot who had crashed during a training exercise. Miraculously, he had escaped with only two broken legs and some rather nasty burns.

"Good morning," Evie said, smiling cheerfully.

LAC Winters put aside the paper he was reading and gave Evie his most winning smile. "Good morning, Nurse. It's a pleasure to see you again."

"How are you feeling today?"

"Well enough. Got an itch in my cast that I can't get to, which is driving me mad. I don't suppose you could give us a scratch?"

"Hmmm, I don't think so, but maybe we can find a stick or something..."

He laughed. "Anyway, a pretty girl to talk to gives some pleasant distraction."

Giving him a mild smile, she busied herself checking his pillows, water, and the state of his dressings.

He picked up his paper again and, without looking up, asked, "So, is your boyfriend abroad just now?"

"Yes, he's in Italy." She caught his grimace out of the corner of her eye.

Rallying, he leaned over to ask, "I don't suppose you've got a cigarette?"

"I can see if there are any in the Salvation Army package."

"Nurse, you're an angel!"

The next bed over was a Corporal Evans, who thought himself a great flirt and on her first day had tried for a pinch with his good arm when her back was turned. She had spoken sternly to him, and today he was all politeness. Still, when she walked past she kept an eye on his hands.

She didn't need to worry about his neighbor. PFC Thompkins hadn't spoken a word since he'd come in. Half of his face and head were bandaged, and one of his arms was gone below the elbow. He spent most of his time asleep.

Evie tried to make him comfortable, and then moved on to another burn victim, then one with some extensive shrapnel wounds and so on.

By lunch her feet were aching, but several of the men needed help eating, and then there was cleanup. Afterwards she rolled bandages, and then pushed several in wheelchairs out to the garden, and when she was sent home after her twelve hours, the children mobbed her to tell her about their day and to pull her in six different directions for play.

At last, she climbed the stairs with leaden limbs and collapsed on her bed with a sigh. She rolled her head towards the paper laid out on her desk for today's letter to James, but she couldn't pull herself off of the blessedly soft mattress.

I'll get up extra early tomorrow, she promised, before drifting off, smiling in spite of her weariness. Exhaustion was welcome. It made the waiting easier, feeling like she was moving forward, doing something worthwhile.

And even Great Aunt Helena can't complain. Where else could I be so useful, and so safe?

10 February 1944

Dear Evie,

I notice that you didn't say much about your work at Thrush House in your last. Don't worry if it's a bit unsettling. I am sure that just seeing your smile and having someone as sweet as you about cheers them all greatly. Just be sure that you mention me frequently so that none of them get their hopes up too high. And don't think less of me for being envious that they will get to see you every day.

It looks like we'll be doing some travelling soon. Good thing that I've just been issued some new boots. I was beginning to show off your knitting expertise right through the leather. Here's to a change of scenery!

LLEWELLYN WHISTLED THROUGH HIS TEETH as they came over the ridgeline. "There it is. That's what all the fuss has been about."

Staring down at the forbidding landscape in the fitful February sunlight, Peters shrugged. "Doesn't look so bad. After all, they said months ago that we're to take Rome by Christmas, so how bad can it be?"

"Ah, but Christmas of what year?" Turner chimed in.

"That's the question. I was hoping for '43, but we're past that aren't we? The brass didn't say—hope we're not shooting for '44."

"Well, maybe if we ask very nicely they'll move it to this Easter. One holiday's good as another, I say."

Spread out below them was the flat, three-mile-wide valley of the Rapido River. Water reflected the fitful sunlight in marshy pools—the Germans had flooded a great deal of the valley in order to hinder the Allied advance. The road traveled straight and sure through the olive groves, that stood still naked from the winter's chill, until it reached an abrupt mountain wall. At the top, a vast, honey-colored stone structure stood, with windows like gaping eyes peering out through the ruined walls—The Monastery of Monte Cassino.

The monastery of St. Benedict, a bastion of the Christian faith, lately devastated by heavy Allied bombing, was now a stronghold for forces that would replace the crosses of that faith with their own crooked abomination.

"Which are the points we're holding?" Henry Phillips asked from behind the wheel of the Jeep, squinting into the early morning haze.

James peered ahead as he climbed in. "I'm not certain without a map. There, see the ruins below the monastery? I think that's Castle Hill. We've got that, though I hear they spend plenty of time under siege. And I think that's Snakeshead Ridge along there...If Jerry's holding any of those high points, though—"

"He's got an awfully good view, hasn't he? Whew. I feel like that monastery's watching us, even from here."

"Yes." James marveled at the shape of the mountains. Thrown up across the way like a half-built wall, they hardly looked real.

No wonder Jerry picked this spot for his Gustav Line. I've never seen a better situated place for observation and defense. God, help us.

Phillips shifted the car into gear. "Excuse me, sergeant, but get that leg in. I won't be the one to answer for it if we hit a mine and you..." James obediently folded his leg into the Jeep, setting his feet on the sandbags packed into the bottom of it.

Davy Llewellyn leaned forward from the back, speaking loudly as the Jeep began its descent. "When's the attack going in?"

James shook his head. "I'm not sure. I imagine we'll be briefed soon. Got to be ready in case this one makes the gains."

Llewellyn snorted, "Third time's the charm?"

"We'll see."

Two battles had already failed to break the line at Monte Cassino.

First, in January, the British and French had gained some ground to the right and the left, and the Americans of the Fifth Army had pushed their weary advance forward to try to break the line in the center, only to suffer a horrific loss of life at the Rapido.

Shortly after, the attempt to flank the line with an amphibious assault to the north at Anzio had stalled, leaving 70,000 men trapped on the beachhead, unable to advance. Months later they still held on, isolated through the bleak winter, struggling to maintain their hold and not be flung back into the sea.

In February the New Zealanders had moved through the valley and Indian divisions had moved through the hills to attack the German lines. Fighting courageously, they suffered crippling losses without the reward of breaking through and gaining their objectives. In dreadful conditions, suffering hundreds of casualties, they had remained. Unable to dig in to the hard, rocky soil, they'd constructed rough stone shelters—sangars—to protect themselves from shelling and the flying rock shards scattered violently with every blast.

And here we are.

Their division had been moved over from the stalled action on the Adriatic side of Italy to assist, waiting and watching for the third battle to commence. Waiting to see if the New Zealanders and Indians could make the necessary gains and, if so, to pass through them and engage Jerry in his stronghold.

Evie's feet felt as though they might fall off. One more check of the beds and she'd be free to go home.

She'd been asked to stay late as Nancy had fallen ill. The men in the individual rooms were settled, though it had been a bit of a scramble. Two of them had gone into the pub at Farthington, which was allowed, but had come back worse for it. Evie and Lynelle, another VAD, had hustled them to bed before Matron could see their state. With any luck, they'd sleep it off.

The lights were dimmed in the main ward, and she could hear from the regular breathing that some of the men were already asleep.

Not all, though. "Nurse?" The call came from the far side. She passed the other beds, thoughts wandering to James, hoping he was safe.

She arrived at Corporal Evans's bedside, "Yes, what do you need?"

"A kiss goodnight?" he asked, with a hopeful grin.

Evie sighed and shook her head.

"Can't blame a bloke for trying. A drink of water, then?"

"Yes, of course." She backed away, not trusting his innocent face and gave a cry as an arm encircled her from behind and she found herself caught by Winters. Nearly.

She twisted out of reach as Evans laughed uproariously, waking a few others who told him in plain language what they thought of the noise.

Evie nearly laughed as well, but forced a stern face and said, "Now, really—"

"WHAT is going on here?" Charles's voice thundered.

Evie jumped and swung around to see him, standing in the doorway. "Charles, what are you doing here? You really can't—"

He lowered his voice, but the anger quivered in it. "I came to see you home, Evie. I came up because I wondered what was keeping you. I didn't expect…"

He choked on the last word, staring, not at Evans and Winters who were offering a chorus of explanations such as "a bit of fun," and "not meaning any harm," but at Thompkins.

Thompkins, silent as always, had half sat up in his bed at the commotion. His eyes shone dark and inscrutable in the dim light. His half-bandaged face gave him a ghostly appearance.

Evie took advantage of the pause. "I'm ready now." Hurrying over to Charles, she called a goodnight over her shoulder, took his arm, and exited the ward.

Charles walked in heavy silence all the way to Stoneglenn. Evie would have been grateful, if it hadn't been so unnerving.

Finally, she spoke. "Charles, I know that it may have looked—well, a little—but really, they're just terribly bored, and they don't mean any harm. I was just tired and didn't have my wits about me."

"Hmm? Oh, yes, Evie. You really ought to be more careful. Some fellows can be a little rough. If you need me to speak to any of them—"

"No, thank you, Charles. Matron keeps a close eye on things most of the time. It was just—"

"Yes, yes." He opened Stoneglenn's door and paused at the bottom of the stairs. "I suppose you'll want to sleep now. It must have been a long day."

"Yes. Thank you, Charles."

Evie made her way up the dark stairs, wondering. To let the whole thing go so easily wasn't like Charles at all. She glanced back as she got to the landing. He wasn't following her. Almost lost in shadows, he had sat down on a small bench in the foyer, head bowed, his bad leg stretched out in front of him.

AFTER BREAKFAST the next morning, he waited until Great Aunt Helena left the room. "Well, Evie. I haven't asked. How has your work at Thrush House been going? Last night's foolishness aside—there's no need to go into all of that."

"Very well, thank you. I'm learning so much, and it's nice to feel as if I'm doing something useful."

"One of the fellows looked familiar, but it was hard to tell in the dark, and he had all of those bandages on his face. He looked like a Paul Rivers, capital fellow, in my company in France."

"No, his name is Richard Thompkins. He was injured in a bomb explosion, poor man. I've never heard him speak."

"Not at all?"

"No, not a word."

"Was his voice damaged in the explosion?" Charles's voice was politely curious.

"I'm not sure. I thought so at first, but Nancy said the other day that he doesn't talk, not that he can't."

"Hmm. Poor fellow. I wish it was the man I'd remembered. It would be nice to visit with someone from back then." He gestured to his leg. "Sitting out is frustrating."

"Yes." Evie tried to be cheerful for her cousin. "You're doing good work, though. Keeping food on everyone in the country's table is no mean feat!"

Charles smiled and gave her a friendly pat on the knee. "Ah, Evie. You always think the best of everybody, don't you?"

She smiled back at him, but her brow furrowed. "I try to, Charles."

25 March 1944

Dear Evie,

This one will have to be quick—it looks as if I will be busy for a while. Please, don't worry if you don't hear from me. It will likely be difficult to write, but I'll be fine. Other fellows have been holding the positions we're taking up for a long while, and we're just giving them a breather. It should be better than scraping out new ground. In a way, it's a relief to know that we won't be left in uncertainty about Jerry's position. Apparently, we will be close enough that if one of us sneezes, we might very well hear a "Gesundheit!" in reply.

DEATH HUNG HEAVY ON THE AIR. Even the cool twilight breeze couldn't carry it away from James's aching nostrils.

The worst of the stench came from the mules. Essential for the transport of supplies in the difficult mountainous passages, their pack mules were easy prey. The "Mad Mile" of road, ranged by German artillery, offered up its daily victims, and what was to be done with the bodies? The rocky soil offered no good burial sites. Even liberal application of lime didn't help with the odor.

The mules were bad enough. Best not to consider the bodies of the men sprawled across the narrow no man's land between the armies.

The stench of the dead mingled with the smells of the living. Unwashed bodies coated with sweat and dirt gave off a by-now familiar aroma. However, Cassino's exposed positions also didn't even allow for digging proper latrines.

Hungry as he knew he ought to be, James had a hard time mustering up enthusiasm for the tin of bully beef in his hand. He examined the meat, half suspended in the congealed fat, then looked away.

Shifting, he eased his cramped legs, careful to keep his head below the level of his sheltering stone sangar. He glanced at the sky, wishing for the dark.

Not that dark is so much better. When we can move, so can Jerry.

He sighed and poked at the beef.

Don't want to waste it, but maybe they'll get hot food up tonight. Meat pies again, maybe. Whoever thought up packing 'em in hay so they'd keep warm ought to get a medal.

Maybe there'll be another letter tonight, too…

He set the tin down and pulled the newest letters out. Three had come since he'd been on the line—two from Evie and one from home. His eyes scanned her handwriting, not even reading the words. Just having something to look at besides the desolation before him was restful, even the hurried curlicues of her penmanship.

The new photo she'd sent him peeked out from the envelope. Pulling it out, he tried not to worry about how thin she was looking behind her brilliant smile.

I hope she's keeping well. Between the children and nursing, she looks tired. At least she hasn't mentioned any troubles with Charles—it was likely nothing to worry about…

His head snapped up as a clatter sounded from the hillside ahead—small rocks tumbling down the slope. Folding up the letters and tucking them away, he reached for his rifle.

"What was that?" Ryan hissed. He sent a quick spray of fire from his machine gun across the hill's crest. Silence answered him.

Little Moore, crouched nearby to help him reload as needed, grumbled. "I almost like it better when they shoot back." He scanned the horizon. "At least I know where they are."

"I'm sure if you ask 'em, they'll oblige," Ryan replied, rubbing his bloodshot eyes.

James noted that his hands shook. *I'd better make sure Ryan gets some rest.*

They tried to rotate sleep, but the constant shelling made real rest impossible. The *nebelwerfers* were the worst. The six barreled German guns, dubbed "screaming meemies" by the Yanks, produced an unearthly shriek, unnerving even the most stoic. Ryan went pale as milk at the sound of them.

It's all wearing on him. He'd best stay back from the patrol tonight.

As if reading his thoughts, Davy Llewellyn asked, "Patrol tonight?"

James shook himself out of his reverie and rubbed his weary eyes. Perhaps Ryan wasn't the only one tired. "Yes, of course. Look, with ammo so scarce, we are only supposed to fire on Germans within twenty-five yards. So, tonight we are to set up an ambush halfway to their line—in no man's land. There's a burned-out tank at the spot, a few trees for some cover, but we'll have to keep sharp. Jerry's been active. Ryan? You'll stay behind. Get some sleep. Llewellyn, you, too, in case he needs to be up to fire."

Ryan nodded, trying not to look relieved.

Llewellyn protested. "I'm fit enough. I'd rather go than sit."

James shook his head. "Not this time."

Llewellyn said no more, but as dusk fell and the others were making their preparations, James worked his way over to him. "Davy, I'd rather you came, too, but Ryan isn't looking well, and I need someone fresher to make sure he gets some rest—he'll listen to you. An exhausted gunner doesn't do anyone any good."

Mollified, Llewellyn promised to look after the younger man.

As dark fell, James set out, taking Moore and collecting Cartwright,

Rogers, Turner, and Peters from their sangars just down the hill.

It was a good night for patrolling. The weather was fair, the moon hadn't risen, and the stars were dimmed by tendrils of smoke drifting lazily skyward.

Eyes straining through the dark, they inched over the rocky, uneven ground, moving forward and down.

Reggie Cartwright, close on James's right, disturbed a loose rock. It clattered down the slope, landing with a ping against an empty tin.

James grimaced and hoped that no one had been listening.

There didn't seem to be anyone alive out tonight, only the lingering dead. At his feet, a limp hand gleamed pale against the dark rock. James stepped around and did not look deeper into the shadows.

The hulking form of the ruined tank loomed just ahead.

With a few terse gestures, quieted breath and muffled footfalls, they found their positions.

They waited, shadows in the dark.

The German patrol was nearly as quiet as they had been, but one man must have stumbled. As the rocks clacked, he let loose a quiet but no less vehement guttural expletive. Another shushed him.

Placing one foot and then another, James edged around the side of the tank.

The stealthy footsteps on the other side paused. Jerry knew something was up.

James hardly drew breath. He listened to his heart beat and willed himself calm.

Stick to the plan. Finish the job. Get the boys back safely. Just wait. Stick to the plan…

The footsteps resumed.

Their silhouettes, darker shapes against the dark night, came into his line of sight. He counted seven men, walking half crouched, weapons readied.

They never thought to look up.

Moore's throw, lobbed from atop the Sherman, was perfect. The grenade landed in the middle of them.

The blast threw them back, doing for at least two. Sharp cries in German echoed against the rocks but were drowned as James and Cartwright fired from the front and Turner, Rogers, and Peters from the back.

Two ducked the crossfire and vanished into the night. The others tried to stick it out. Only one got a shot off, and it was over.

Releasing his pent-up breath with a whoosh, James moved forward, scanning the shadows for the two that got away.

He'd nearly made it to the fallen forms when the first shell fell.

Rocks shattered just uphill.

He broke into a quick trot, anxious to gather the others. "Quick—c'mon, this way—"

Peters's hiss stopped him, frozen in the growing cacophony. "Sergeant!" He was standing over Reggie Cartwright.

Oh, please God, no.

The boy slumped against the shell of the tank, a dark stain spreading across his belly. Another explosion echoed from the other side of the Sherman, making the whole structure shudder and creak.

In two paces, James reached them and slung Cartwright's arm across his shoulders. "Hurry now. Use what cover you can. Move."

"But—" began Moore.

"Move it!" he snarled. Without another word, they did.

He followed, half dragging a groaning Cartwright along.

Another shell whistled overhead, bursting near enough that his skin cringed, expecting to feel shrapnel strike. None did, and they lurched toward the slope they'd just come down.

"Up we go. Hang on, Reg."

"I'm slowing you down," Cartwright gasped.

James ignored him, saving his strength for the climb. Dirt and loose stones slid out from under his boots. He stumbled, and Cartwright let out a gasping sob.

Another mortar burst, this one further downhill.

A few more yards—

The shriek set his teeth on edge. The *nebelwerfer* shells were going to fall too close.

He flung Cartwright to the ground, himself beside. Pressing his body into the earth, he scrabbled at the rocks with his fingertips as if he could dig in quickly enough to make a difference.

WHOOF. One of the shells impacted close enough to feel, and bits of shrapnel pinged off of his helmet. His shoulder throbbed in memory.

One, two, three, four, five, six…that's all. Get up, James, get UP.

He heaved himself to his feet, grasping Cartwright's arm.

The other man didn't respond.

Falling back to his knees, James rolled him over. Reg's eyes were blank and staring, empty.

Llewellyn and Moore were watching for them when he came, staggering over the ridgeline, Cartwright slung across his shoulders. They ran to relieve him of his burden.

"Shall I get the stretcher bearers?" Moore asked.

James just shook his head.

He heard his voice, cold and tired, saying, "It's too late."

I couldn't save him. I can't save any of them. God, help us.

30 March 1944

Dear James,

The flowers are blooming, and the early seeds are in. I hope that warmer weather is bringing some relief to you, and that the mud isn't back and becoming a difficulty.

We went over to Thrush House this Sunday afternoon and gave a bit of a concert to the men—piano and some singing. Those that could joined in on the hymns and songs they knew. I will have to try to schedule more visits in the future.

Missing you terribly, and sending all of my love,
Evie

"CHARLES?" Evie peered around the door of the library. Dinner was about to go on the table, but he had disappeared outside shortly after breakfast. She had thought she heard the door a few moments ago, but he hadn't made an appearance.

He stood near the fireplace, holding a couple of sheets of paper. Shoulders hunched, a frown creased his face. His hand moved toward the grate which had a small fire burning merrily in it.

A fire in the grate? Why would he have it lit with no one in here?

"Charles?"

He started, and his head jerked around as his hand stayed frozen above the fire. "Evie! What are you doing here?"

Her surprise at his tone must have shown on her face because he tried again. "I'm sorry, Evie, you startled me. What can I do for you?"

"It's time to eat. What—is everything all right?"

His chuckle sounded forced. "Oh, yes. I've heard from Andrews. He says that your sergeant is—or was, by now—headed on to the line for a bit, but all are doing well and keeping healthy."

"Oh. That's good news, at least. Shall we go? Great Aunt Helena will be waiting—"

"Yes, I suppose…yes, I'm coming."

As she turned she saw Charles hastily put the letter into the grate before he followed.

Why in the world would he do that with something so unimportant?

Evie ate quietly, thinking about that letter.

Am I just being a snoop? But really, if the letter were what he said, why burn it? And if it weren't, why lie? And there are those things James wrote me about…but it's none of my business. Is it?

Charles and Great Aunt Helena retired to their rooms after eating, and the children dispersed outside.

Evie hesitated in the hallway, listening to the receding footsteps. Almost before she knew it, her mind was made up. She hurried towards the library on soft feet.

The fire in the grate was nearly dead, and the letter was, for the most part, ash. However, one large piece had not fallen directly on the flames, and before she could think better of it, she pulled it out.

It was broken and smudged, the words difficult to decipher.

…will not be too displeased that I have been so unsuccessful. He appears………………..respe……and no one will say anyth……………………… front soon, so maybe your troubles……………….. in another way.

None of it made any sense.

She dropped the scrap on the dying flames.

It was none too soon.

Steps sounded at the door, and Charles walked in. Once again, he looked discomfited to see her. "Evie, what are you doing here?"

She tried to laugh it off. "That seems to be the question of the day! I thought that I had left my book on the mantle here, but it seems I was wrong." How easily the lie came!

Spying and lying. What's got into me today?

"Oh, and what book are you reading?" He spoke with his eyes fixed on the grate.

Why is he so concerned about me seeing that letter?

"*Emma*. It's terribly funny, and I'd just gotten to the best part."

"Ah." He met her eyes at last. Were his relieved, or was she imagining it? "Well, I'll keep a look out for it. What will you be doing this afternoon?"

"I was going to take the children for a walk. It's such a nice day. Would you like to come?"

"Thank you, maybe another time. The old leg, you know?"

"Oh, of course. Well, I'll see you later."

She left the room but glanced back once she was well out into the hallway. Charles had turned to check the grate again, then pulled out a handkerchief to mop his face.

JAMES DIPPED HIS HANDS into his helmet full of water and splashed his face. The dislodged dirt ran in rivulets down his fingers. He scratched his growth of beard, and he resolved that he would shave tomorrow. Tonight, his hand wasn't steady enough for a razor.

Waiting for their relief to come had made the day seem endless, but in time they arrived, and he and the rest of his battalion had begun the march down the mountain. He had spared only a glance about to make certain the others he was responsible for were there, deciding as he did that they looked a sorry lot. Bone weary, the men plodded, feet hardly lifting from the ground, barely speaking, eyes fixed ahead, toward rest. Reaching his transport, James had fallen instantly asleep.

The sleep hadn't been enough, but through the weariness, he was grateful.

He was grateful to be off the line for a while, to have any place to sleep other than a ditch behind the indifferent protection of a low, stone wall, and even for the next can of bully beef waiting for him to quell some of the hunger gnawing at his guts.

He was grateful to still be alive. Unlike Cartwright.

James sighed and closed his eyes.

It didn't register for a moment that there were voices drifting over from behind a row of Jeeps. It sounded like Rogers, voice weary and flat, speaking to someone else whose voice was not familiar. James couldn't avoid hearing Rogers's voice rise in affront.

"You bloody fool. I'm dead tired, and I'm not sure what it is you've heard, but it sounds like a pack of lies to me. He's a good officer, and no one I know will say different."

The low murmur of the other voice responded, and Rogers rejoined, "No. Never shied away from a patrol, or hid and just came back later, and I know plenty who have. Leads himself, wouldn't send anyone to do what he wouldn't." He spat. "Carried one poor bloke back up to the line himself the other day."

Again, an inaudible question.

"What?" Rogers exclaimed. "No, never. No, no more drink than anyone else in any case, and if he has a nip from time to time... No, not women neither. He never even visited… Where are you getting this tripe from? And what business is it of yours, anyhow? I think you'd better be off."

A moment later Rogers came storming around the corner. He started when he saw James and flushed. "Sir. I didn't know you were here. Did…did you just get in?"

"Only just."

"And…how are you feeling?" The words tumbled out awkwardly.

James managed a smile that was more grimace. "About dead on my feet."

"Me, too." The other man hesitated, as if he were about to ask something, but decided against it. "Have a good rest."

Weary as he was, two thoughts niggled at the back of James's mind before sleep came.

Why had Rogers looked so guilty when he saw him standing there? And did it have anything to do with that odd, half-heard conversation?

Nineteen

1 May 1944

Dear Evie,

I'm sorry I've been lax in writing, but for once it was because I have been busy with pleasant things, so I hope that you'll forgive me. We made it to the rest camp safely and have been sightseeing.

Despite her wartime scars, Naples is a beautiful city. Standing at the edge of the Via Roma and watching all of the people go by is almost overwhelming after weeks surrounded by khaki and mud.

Sunday, I and a couple of mates wandered in to the grandest church I've attended, all pillars and space. The music didn't seem to come from any source, it just filled the whole place. I wish you could have been there. The choir sang, and it was like hearing angels, truly. (My, aren't I becoming poetic?)

Afterwards, a family in attendance, the Campinellis, invited the lot of us over for dinner. They were very kind—they have little and shared it all with us from an open heart. Their son is off fighting with the Partisans, which is a source of great grief and pride to them. They also have one daughter, who has the misfortune of being very pretty. (I say misfortune because her father talked about how, when Jerry was in town, he wouldn't let her leave the house for fear of attracting unwanted attention.) Things have improved, but I could tell that he has still been keeping a sharp eye on her with all of these young fellows in uniform about, and with good reason. No fewer than three of the boys I know have gone gaga over Luciana, trying to impress her with stories or gifts they find, while she just smiles seraphically. A couple of us have a small wager going as to whether any of them will ever manage to get a date.

Several of us motored over to Pompeii. Seeing the ruins was interesting, but eerie, thinking of those people, going about their daily lives, unaware that disaster was about to strike.

I've been invited to the Campinelli home again tomorrow evening. I think that Signor Campinelli likes to have me along in the party because he sees that I pay his daughter no notice. At any rate, I find myself seated next to her frequently. I may try switching places with Moore. Of the three, he's the fellow I think likes her the best.

I suppose that it is bad form to be talking about how pretty a different girl is when writing to you. I'd feel badly about doing so if you didn't know that I think you're the loveliest girl in the world, and the only one I want to see—you do know that, don't you? I laugh at these others, gawking and falling over themselves, but I assure you, I am fully prepared to make as much of a fool of myself over you when I'm back, and anyone may laugh who wishes to.

All my love,
James

JAMES SET HIS PEN DOWN and considered his letter. It was all true, but he had been careful to stick to the pleasant aspects of leave.

Naples and her people had suffered. When the Germans retreated, they had poisoned the water supply, sabotaged the sewers, and burned precious documents.

On the way to the pub tonight, he'd pressed a few coins into the grubby hands of the children begging on the street corners, while skirting around the men standing alongside them, calling to offer him a "nice girl." The poor girls were likely just one of their ragged relations and looked more forlorn than provocative. Clusters of displaced persons clogged the sidewalks, lost and hopeless.

He rubbed his eyes to dislodge the images and then took out a clean sheet to write his family. Leaning back, he stretched his shoulders.

I wonder what they're all doing tonight. By the time I get back, the boys will seem nearly grown…

Squelching a wave of home-sickness, he scanned the room, searching for a familiar face.

Across the way, a table of local men dealt out cards, heads wreathed in blue smoke. A few local girls were hanging around, with their entourage of uniforms trying to chat them up. In the corner, a balding man struggled to coax something like music from a dreadfully out of tune piano.

His eyes rested for a second on a singularly unobtrusive man seated in profile to him with another group at a nearby table—Private Andrews.

The man puzzled him. He was like a shadow, the more so because of his ethereal appearance. Yes, a shadow was a good comparison, and it seemed as if this one had attached himself to James—at any rate, he seemed to be there whenever James looked for him, just one of the crowd, but always *there.*

Odd fellow.

A hand landed on James's shoulder with a thump. He started and then looked up to see Lieutenant Bradlock. Bradlock chuckled. "Jumpy, aren't you? C'mon, Milburn. No need to sit alone—I'm for the card table. Join us."

"Thanks, but I'm writing home. I'd like to finish before it gets too late. Maybe then."

The other man pulled a face and continued on his way. The group gave him a loud greeting, and Geoffrey Small, one of their MPs, dealt him in.

James tried to focus on his writing again, but the words blurred before his weary eyes. Getting off the lines for a few days was a relief, but they all knew they'd be back soon enough.

Wonder if I'll make it through this time. I wonder who won't…

He looked up as the wooden legs of the chair across from him grated across the floor. Expecting to see Bradlock or one of the other men, he was startled to see one of the local girls.

Granted, she was a little old to be called a 'girl'. Her hair was so dark that it was almost black, glossy and long, her eyes were deep liquid brown, and her red lips curved upward invitingly. Her scarlet dress was cut invitingly, too. As she leaned forward, James quickly flicked his eyes upward.

She must've found the wrong table.

"Hello. Might I trouble you for a light?" She held out her cigarette to him with a languid hand. He obligingly fished out a match. She leaned even further forward to get the first puff of smoke. James examined the part in her hair.

"Thank you. I'm Sabine. What is your name?" Her accent was hard to place—not Italian, nor English nor French—she just *was.* She lounged in her chair, exhaling a thin stream of smoke and waited, smile playing around those red lips.

James cleared his throat and cautiously introduced himself.

She nodded to the papers before him. "Writing to family? Maybe to a sweetheart, yes? How long has it been since you've been home?"

He cleared his throat again. "Oh, it's been a while now."

Face grave, she shook her head. "It is very lonely, being far from home. I haven't seen my family in five years. And the world, it can be so cold." Again, she waited, watching him.

"Well. Yes, I suppose that's true."

If she was disappointed by his reticence, she didn't show it. She settled back in her chair, smoke wreathing her head in lazy circles. "I had three brothers, all but one in uniform. I haven't heard if they are well, or if they even live." She smiled up at him. "You remind me a little of my oldest brother. Christoph was always very serious, very determined. It was terrible, trying to get him to take a break, have a little fun. But really, if we can't enjoy life, what's the use of living it?"

Her foot rubbed up against James's leg, and he jumped, jerking away.

Tossing back her dark hair and exposing her long, graceful neck, Sabine laughed. "Are you always this nervous around girls, Sergeant?"

He shifted, trying to regain his composure. "I have a girl back home already."

To his astonishment, Sabine merely nodded, dark chocolate eyes fixed on his. "I thought you must. You look like a man missing someone. I thought 'he must have left a sweetheart behind.' How long has it been since you saw her, since you held her in your arms? Many months?"

"It's been a while." *Nine months. Nine months since I've seen her.* He looked away, pursing his lips.

Clunking with each note, the pianist's fingers plunked out the first notes of "I Wonder When My Baby's Coming Home."

Sabine's chair creaked as she shifted forward and put her warm hand over his. "You miss her very much. Is she a pretty thing? Tell me."

"I don't see...I'm not sure what brought you over here..." He pulled his hand away and ran it through his hair. Shaking his head, he started to gather up his papers. "I'd best be..."

"Wait." Sabine took a long drag and glanced about, her face altered. Casting her smooth manner aside, she tilted her head forward, eyes locked onto his, voice low and hurried. "To be honest, Sergeant, a few of the men about tonight, they have been more attentive than is comfortable. It would help me to be out of their line of sight for a while. Won't you talk with me?"

Then she leaned back, laughed, and the mask slid back into place. "Also, it's nice to sit by a man who doesn't look like a wolf after a nice cut of meat! Come, tell me, what kind of a girl did it take to draw you out? I will make it easier—do you have a picture of her?"

That change in her demeanor, the plea for help, worked where nothing else would. After considering for one more moment, James pulled out his latest portrait of Evie, in her VAD uniform, smiling in the sunshine. His fingers left it reluctantly as he passed it over.

"Ah! Look at her." Sabine took another long drag. "Fresh and pure as can be—and a nurse! A good girl, yes?" She leaned forward, a wicked smile playing about her lips. "Did she even let you steal a kiss?"

He avoided her eyes. "Well—"

"Ha! She did! I like her better for it." She leaned back. "You didn't answer before, and I can't tell with that awful uniform—is she pretty? What caught your eye? Oh, come. We must talk about something, you know, if you're to be my protector."

He stared at the picture, searching for the words. "When she smiles...it's...it's like her whole heart is there on her face. She beams out of those blue eyes, and it's like I'm the most important person in the world to her. I don't know. I'm no good at descriptions."

"No! That's very good! You'll be a poet for love yet, I can tell. Was she your nurse? That would be romantic."

"No."

"Well? How did you meet her?"

Tired as he was, he laughed. He told the story of the tennis ball, and Sabine laughed with him.

The laughter warmed him. "It's good to talk about her," he said, after a pause, "but—"

Sabine nodded, "But now you miss her more."

Wearily, James ran his hand through his hair and rubbed his eyes. She caught his hand before it returned to the table, and held it, squeezing his roughened fingers gently.

"You don't like to say much, yes, but I know the old saying, 'still waters run deep,' and I can tell it is so for you. You care deeply. And she, I am sure she feels the same." The curtain of raven hair fell down on either side of her face, and impatiently she shook it back. "It is hard to be so lonely for someone."

He was silent, staring down at the photo, willing the ache in his chest to ease, half wishing he could just forget, just for a while.

She squeezed his fingers again and lowered her voice. "I can tell that you are a good man, and I am sorry for your loneliness. Perhaps... perhaps tonight I can help ease this."

James blinked once, twice. Carefully, he disengaged his hand, and looked up at this woman he didn't know.

"I think you misunderstood me, Miss. I am—"

"Yes, I know, you are thinking of this girl." She smiled, gentle, understanding, sure of herself. "You are true to her in your heart—this is very good. Very honorable. Also, though, you are a soldier, you are far from home and you have suffered much. Do you think she would wish you so unhappy? And perhaps she is lonely, as well. Who is to say that comfort in loneliness is so bad?"

She was very lovely, beautiful and exotic, as she pretended to understand him. He was repulsed.

"Where are they?"

Sabine blinked. "Who?"

"The men who were bothering you. Where do you suppose they've gotten to?"

For the first time, she looked uncertain. "I...I imagine they've—"

"What, frightened off by me sitting here? If that's all it took, I suppose you'll be all right now." Gathering his letters, he stood. "Goodnight miss."

As he turned toward the door, he caught Andrews's pale eyes, with a thin frown line between them, watching him. Ignoring him and Sabine's protesting, "But—" he left.

The chilly night air was welcome as he set a brisk pace back to the hotel room he was sharing. *What was that all about? Someone's idea of a joke?*

No one else was in yet, and he prepared to sleep. After an unsuccessful hour, he pounded his pillow in frustration.

When his eyes closed he saw Evie. He could smell her scent, feel her in his arms, taste her kisses…exasperated, he stood.

After pacing round the small space, he sat down and penned a brief letter, having no other way to relieve his feelings.

Dearest Evie,

Did you know there's a strange condition that some of the men who've lost limbs go through, where, even though the limb is gone, they still can feel it there? Evie, that's how I feel tonight. I keep looking up, half expecting to see you, you seem so near. What I wouldn't give to see you and touch you—I'd have to grab hold of your hand at once and find a willing member of the clergy to do the rites for us immediately. Then I'd not have to let go of you again. Be ready, my girl, I may dog your steps like an old hound when I come home, and I hope you'll have pity on me and treat me well, even if I'm a bit tiresome. Keep writing—some days it feels like your letters are the only sanity in all of this madness.

All my love,
James

9 April 1944

Dear James,

Happy Easter! I don't imagine it was a day of chocolate eggs for you, but I hope that you still found peace and joy in it. Oh James, I could hardly play the hymns today, the church was so beautiful with flowers, and there's something about Easter, it's as if even the most indifferent singers could raise their voices and they sounded like they'll sound someday in heaven!

Charles has brought some treats to hide about for the children. He has really been very kind to them these last months. Maybe seeing that there are others who need our care is helping him to work on his own character? He's been much more interested in my work at Thrush House, as well; he even came over with the children and I to the little service Father Carter did for the men this afternoon.

God bless and keep you,
Love,
Your Evie

John 11: 25–26 Jesus said to her, "I am the resurrection, and the life. He who believes in Me, though he may die, he shall live. And whoever lives and believes in Me shall never die."

April 9, 1944

Dear Evie,

Happy Easter! I hope that today was jolly for all of you. Did you manage to find Easter eggs for the children? Mum always spoiled us on Easter. After egg rolling (with three boys it often resulted in one or more of us rolling after), we'd have a huge hunt, and once we were good and sick from the sweets, it would be time for the feast. Her Simnel cake was second to none.

This year was a bit different. There were worship services, and many a man whom I'd never heard a religious song out of produced some lovely hymns, but the most extraordinary thing that happened was that Jerry stopped shooting. You have to understand, out here it never really ends. Artillery, small arms fire—it's the backdrop we live to, and we just hope it doesn't come too close. Today, silence. We kept it silent on our end, as well. It has been lovely, if strange. Have I become so used to gunfire that I will miss it when it's gone?

The thing that comes to mind, Evie, is that if we can agree with Jerry to this extent, if we can agree to the importance of Christ's resurrection day, then what are we all doing here? If there are Christian men over there, how can they be fighting for this monstrousness?

God bless and keep you. I wish I could've sung with you today and seen the church all decked out in flowers.

Love,
James

SHADOWS DRAPED THE WALLS of the main ward at Thrush House. The Easter festivities were long over, but Richard Thompkins lay awake in bed, silent as always.

Fingers hesitant, he reached up to touch his face. Under the bandages, his skin felt foreign and strange. They'd offered to take the bandages off. He had refused.

Who could stomach looking at me?

Mum and Sarah still wrote, but they didn't come. They said it was because of their wartime jobs. He knew it was because they couldn't bear to see the monster he had become.

The staff had been talking again, whispering about moving him to a psychiatric hospital because of his lack of speech.

What do they want from me? When the doctor came, I answered all of the questions.

With a low growl, he pulled the bandages back into place. It was over, whether the doctors knew it or not. He was finished. Finished with people trying to fix him, finished with the guilt. Here, he could stay, and be quiet. Here, he could die, for all he cared.

The quiet tread of her shoes announced her presence before she came into his line of sight.

It was that nurse again. She'd been making night rounds lately.

He lay motionless and willed his breath even as she passed by. Once he was sure she wouldn't see, he opened his eyes, just a slit, and watched her checking the other beds. He liked that nurse. She didn't feel the need to fill his silence with chatter like some of the others. Her smile reminded him of Sarah. His beautiful Sarah—

What was he *doing with her? Twice now, he's been here with her. He still has his limp, but that's no surprise.*

Richard had forgotten many things, but he hadn't forgotten that night.

Closing his eyes, he slipped away, back to France.

What a shambles it had been. Blood and sweat and smoke, explosions ringing in his ears, fear shaking his hands and bitter on his tongue. Realizing that the lines had shattered, the blitzkrieg was punching through, driving them back further and further towards the coast, threatening to engulf all of them.

And then, there was the night, the night at Arras, the night he couldn't forget.

With panic knotting his stomach, he realized he'd gotten behind his company. Where were they? There was too much noise, too many broken buildings.

Breathing hard, trying to get his bearings, he found himself standing at the mouth of the alley.

For a second—a breath—there was silence.

In that brief lull, as he frantically looked about, he heard a pop. A little sound. In the general cacophony he shouldn't have even noticed it.

Looking to his right, down the alley, he saw the silhouettes of two men, illuminated from behind by flickering flames.

As he watched, one slowly slumped to the ground.

Then, the world exploded.

He was flung backwards, breath leaving his lungs in a painful blast.

Rocks dug into his spine as he gasped and then rolled to his side, amazed to still have all of his limbs.

He looked up, as one man came lurching out of the alley, clutching a bloody mess of a leg. He called out for help, and Thompkins heaved himself to his feet and gave his shoulder so that Lieutenant Charles Heatherington and he could escape.

In the scramble he hadn't thought much more about it, assuming the second figure in the alley was German, until they reached the aid station, and he heard Heatherington telling the major how he and his brother had been trying to get out, how his brother, the captain, had been killed, and his leg had been injured in the explosion.

He had listened, frozen in disbelief.

It was all confused, but I know what I saw, you bloody liar. Your own brother...

Back in the present, he shifted his shoulders, trying to get comfortable. The missing arm confounded him still, and his conscience bothered him. He had always felt rather sorry for not telling anyone about what he'd seen. Time had passed while he debated whether it was worth the risk—his word against Heatherington's. He'd told himself that he had other things to worry about, more important than starting a kerfuffle with one of his superiors over something he had no proof of anyway. In the meantime, the lieutenant had been discharged, he'd moved on to working at the landing field, and the whole thing was relegated to the past.

Still...

Tompkins shifted again, and looked towards the far end of the room, where that nice little nurse was finishing up.

He considered how Heatherington had stood so near her today when they sang, and how he had taken her arm when it was time to go. He'd glanced back as the two of them left, grazing Tompkins with a sharp, wary look.

What's she to him? Does she know? He closed his eyes, welcoming the darkness, praying for dreamless sleep. Instead, he saw Sarah's face.

Ought I tell her?

Twenty

15 May 1944

Dear Evie,

Once again, I have to ask you not to worry if you don't hear from me for a while. I am well, just looking to be busy. With any luck, next time I write I won't have any interruptions for quite some time.

RUNNING HIS HAND through his hair, James stared at the paper. The expectation in the air around him was palpable, distracting.

Four days ago, the last—*dear God, please let it be the last*—great strike at the enemy line through Cassino had begun. Over a thousand guns joined voices for the 11 p.m. barrage. Far back from the front, James had felt the air vibrate.

Now, his division had been ordered forward. They were to advance through the lines and drive Jerry out of his stronghold, into the Liri Valley beyond.

He analyzed the situation for the hundredth time. The men were seasoned, the plan was sound, and the numbers ought to be sufficient to break through.

Still, one had to face facts. It would be a battle of attrition. Many men had died in the last four days, and many more would die. The trick was to make Jerry lose more men and quickly enough so that he would have to give up.

These might be the last words I pen to her… and the words would not come.

The men handled the tension in different ways. Lieutenant Bradlock mingled, chatting and laughing, making sure that orders were all clearly understood. The only sign he gave of nerves was the long trail of cigarette butts he left in his wake. Llewellyn had completed his letter home already and was teaching Moore the intricacies of Piquet. Peters and Turner were raucous, joking and making nuisances of themselves. Ryan had been pretending to sleep for at least an hour, his lips moving silently from time to time, perhaps in prayer.

James stretched, looking up to heaven. *Lord, I'm not particularly afraid of dying. I'd rather that than…*

His thoughts flicked to Rogers and their last patrol together.

The night had been perfect. The moon gave just enough light to see by. The artillery's smoke screen, nicknamed "Cigarette," protected them from Jerry's sight. The smoke didn't choke them, and they were far enough over that the casings from the smoke shells were not likely to land on them. It was always disheartening to be in danger from one's own artillery.

Scrambling up the steep, rocky cliffs, they meant to find a vantage point to observe one of the big hotels of Cassino town that Jerry had holed up in. If luck was with them, perhaps they'd see something of use or intercept a German patrol. The area had already been swept for mines and cleared of a few nasty surprises.

It should have been an easy patrol.

As always, James took point, with Rogers, Moore, and Turner spread out behind.

Approaching a bend in the primitive excuse for a path, he had paused for a moment, just a moment, to look over the edge of the precipice to his right. He thought he'd seen some movement. He had just decided that he was mistaken when the path ahead exploded.

"God, oh, God," cried a strained, shrill voice—Rogers.

James ran, Moore close at his heels. Turner had dropped to a crouch and kept back, scanning the area for threats.

Rogers lay, clutching his face. For a moment, James thought the shadows were confusing his eyes, but no, shards of white bone gleamed in the moonlight where Roger's right lower leg ought to have been.

"Schu mine," Moore hissed, fumbling for a tourniquet.

James reached for the wounded man's hands. "Rogers, let me see—did it get your eye?"

His voice a strained gasp, Rogers answered. "Y-yes. I can see out of the left, but the right—It doesn't seem to be bleeding too much. My leg—"

"Never mind. We'll get you back down. Moore—no, Turner, you're taller—we'll balance better. Moore, you cover us, keep sharp. Ed, help me carry him."

Ed Turner turned pale as he nodded. He'd never developed a stomach for blood.

James positioned himself by the shattered stump of the leg to try to spare him.

The struggle down the jagged, rocky landscape was nightmarish—more so when Rogers passed out, his broad form becoming dead weight.

They had made it eventually and found proper stretcher bearers who got Rogers to the dressing station. He had been sent farther back to a field hospital, foot and lower leg gone, one eye gone, and the other damaged.

James silently cursed the schu mines and whoever had thought them up. The casings were primarily wooden so that they could evade minesweepers, but there were a few small metal parts that were blasted into the air with the explosion, often finding the faces of the men they robbed of limbs. Ugly creations, meant to maim, not to kill. After all, what good was a soldier with only one leg? And what was more difficult—caring for wounded or burying the dead? Jerry's logic, cold as it was, was sound.

He lowered his face to his hand. *It should've been me. Why did I let him get ahead of me?*

Bradlock brought him back to the present, coming over to sit, puffing away like a smokestack. "Any word on Rogers?"

Swallowing the guilt, pushing back the regret, James nodded. "He'll live, but he'll have some nasty souvenirs to take home." He glanced up at the haze above the lieutenant's head. "Trying to help the smokescreen along?"

"Just doing my bit." Lowering his voice, he added, "I'm ready to go, Milburn. I'm sick of this place, sick of those hills staring down at us, sick of those smug Bosche, dug into their lines, so sure we're going to break against them. It's time to be done with this. Push 'em back, get the boys at Anzio back in the game to cut them off, on to Rome and then…" He flicked away the spent butt and reached for the spare he had behind his ear. "Then, I suppose, we'll see. They'll have to give up some day because we won't."

"No, sir. We won't."

Bradlock nodded to the letter in James's hand. "What are you going to tell her?"

"I can't decide, exactly."

The lieutenant nodded again and stared in the direction of Cassino, though from their position to the rear they could see nothing of interest.

James's eyes followed his. "Any word?"

"Nothing new, but things seem as good as we can hope for. Alexander planned it well. With all the camouflage, smuggling in the Poles and the Canadians, the false trails for more amphibious landings…if Kesserling was expecting this one he's got to be almost omniscient." He grinned. "At any rate, we'll see soon enough! Drinks in Rome?"

"Absolutely."

Bradlock moved on.

Card game done, Davy Llewellyn came over to sit next to James. "Want to play a hand?"

Wordlessly, he held up the letter. Llewellyn nodded and made to stand.

James held out a hand to stop him. "Davy, I've been thinking. If anything happens to me, I know they'll let my family know, but I haven't really let on about Evie to anyone."

"How long have you been writing to this girl? Keeping your own counsel is one thing—"

"I know, I know. But that's not the point. Would you write to her for me, if it were necessary?"

That gave the other man pause. "Yes, of course I would. If it's me, would you mind writing to Muriel? They'll let her know, but I'd rather she hears from someone who was there."

"Of course."

"Aren't you two a couple of sentimental geezers," snorted Peters, coming up from behind. Davy rolled his eyes. "Tell you what, if both of you go, *I'll* write the letters. I'm going home no matter what—wouldn't rest easy in this rocky ground."

Llewellyn snorted. "I shudder to think what you'd write."

"Oh, don't worry. I'll be sure to let her know that you weren't any fun at all, Father, and that you did your utmost to keep us from having any, as well."

Impatient with their attempts at banter, James rose and walked off, away from the concentrations of men and mud and mules, longing to find some green grass and a semblance of peace.

He stopped beyond a row of olive trees which gave the illusion of solitude, inhaling deeply. The air always tasted sweeter when you might not be breathing it tomorrow.

The death and devastation of Cassino hadn't prevented the forward march of spring on the land. Delicate leaves reached towards the warming sun from the tips of the olive trees, wild corn grew all around, and poppies bloomed, red as blood.

Poppies. The flower brought to mind the poem James had learned as a boy, the poem from his father's war. He remembered being called to recite, hands behind his back, mouth dry and eyes lowered, heart pounding. He still knew every word.

In Flanders Fields the poppies blow
Between the crosses row on row,
That mark our place; and in the sky
The larks, still bravely singing, fly
Scarce heard amid the guns below.

Flanders was far away, but still the poppies bloomed. The crosses stood here, too—row on row like a perverse parody of a garden, planted in the areas where burial was possible and where the names of the dead were known. How many others lay, scattered across France, North Africa, Sicily, Italy, and all of the other battlefields he hadn't seen: Burma, China, Pearl Harbor, Bataan, Singapore, Stalingrad?

It's a miracle that any of us have made it through this far. But we can't stop now. Whether we live or die, God, don't let the fight be in vain. Preserve our loved ones, and if you will, bring us home to them. And, as it seems the only way home is through that line to the north—

Wheeling around, he strode back. It was time to finish his letters and check his kit one more time. One wait, at least, would soon be over.

One way or another, they would no longer be waiting behind this line tomorrow.

May 20, 1944

Dear James,

Brutus has found his Portia, (named by Edward, who is really very good at history) so now we have a large number of kittens inhabiting the carriage house. Just how many is uncertain. Portia is very protective of the litter, and we never see more than two at a time. Thankfully, the new parents are good hunters, so I can dissuade the girls from sneaking their milk ration down to the little family. At least most of it. Bonny always looks very innocent after tea, and I think she may be stashing some in an old scent bottle that she keeps in her pocket. I have decided not to notice this.

EVIE PAUSED and chewed on the end of her pen. Her mind kept returning to James's last letter. It had sounded so…final. He was in the midst of something big, and there was nothing she could do for him.

Waiting. All of my life seems to be waiting.

"Miss Worther, that is not food and not to go in your mouth!" piped Leslie.

Evie jumped, then laughed. "You're absolutely right, Leslie. Here, are you done with your drawing? Let me see."

Gray clouds blanketed the sky this Sunday afternoon, occasionally hurtling raindrops groundward. The children were all piled atop each other in the library, reading or drawing pictures on bits of paper they had scrounged from informational government pamphlets. Bonny was writing a story using the margins of old newspapers which she announced had "very gruesome pirates in it!"

Admiring Leslie's artwork though she wasn't sure what it represented—it resembled an octopus hiding in a field—Evie said, "What a big girl you're becoming!"

Tommy called out, "Well, I'm bigger!"

"I'm as big as Goliath!" declared Johnny, standing on the back of the sofa.

"Johnny! Get down! Be David instead."

He obliged. "Oh! Tell us a Bible story."

"Yes, the one with the great storm, since it's raining." Leslie crawled into Evie's lap.

So much for writing.

Putting down her pen, Evie held the little girl, and Lilly, Tommy, and Johnny came to sit at her feet. With great animation, and a great many interruptions, she shared the story, concluding, "And he said to the wind and the waves, 'Be still!' and they *were* still. With only his word, the Lord made the storm stop."

Leslie leaned her head back against her shoulder. "I wish He would make the war stop that way."

Evie blinked the threatening tears back. "I do, too, love. But He knows best." She gathered the little girl into a hug, and stared, unseeing, out the rain-streaked window.

HER MELANCHOLY HADN'T FADED as she began her shift at Thrush House on Monday. She did her best to hide it, but Winters, nearly ready to be released, noticed immediately.

"No smiles today, Nurse?"

Evie tried to oblige him. "I'm sorry. I'm just a little tired."

"You've not had bad news?"

"No, not really. I'm certain everything is fine."

"Your fellow's over in Italy, isn't he? Is he by that Gustav Line they've been talking about?"

"Yes. His last letter—"

"Was it the 'don't worry if you don't hear from me for a while' one?"

"…Yes."

Winters leaned back. "I always wondered if saying that helped or made the waiting worse."

"I'm not sure, either. But worrying does no good, and let's take a look at your dressing. I think that last one's almost ready to come off."

"Of course. That'd be grand," he said, holding out his arm, obediently allowing her to change the subject.

"Wait." Evans looked up from the magazine he had been perusing. "You've got a fellow in Italy, Nurse? What about the dark-haired chap you were singing with on Easter?"

Out of the corner of her eye, she saw Thompkins' bandaged face turn towards her. "Oh, that was my cousin."

Evans and Winters exchanged a look and raised eyebrows.

"First cousin?" asked Evans.

"No, it's kind of convoluted. Here now, hold still. There, that should hold for now. Hang on, I need another bandage."

She walked over to the press to get one. From behind the door she heard Evans mutter. "You saw? Hope her boy doesn't make it back from Italy to find his bird flown."

"It's time for you to get discharged. You're so bored you're gossiping like an old woman. Besides, you're just wishing she were flying away with you, instead."

She closed the press just in time to see Evans pull a face and go back to his magazine. Ignoring him, she finished the dressing, washed, and went over to Thompkins's bed. "Good afternoon! Would you like to sit up for a while?"

He stared at her, then nodded.

She supported him as he sat up and repositioned his pillows. "You know, the weather is very fine, and the doctor said you should get some fresh air. Would you like to go out for a bit today?"

To her complete astonishment, Thompkins answered her, his voice harsh and scratchy from disuse. "If you'll walk with me, Nurse."

She blinked, then beamed a smile at him. "Of course! Just let me finish my rounds in here."

Evans and Winters exchanged a startled look. Evans called over, "Rich, haven't heard you talk in a good old time, not since we got in here."

Thompkins glanced at him and shrugged but did not respond.

"Known him ten years, but I guess it takes a girl…" Evans muttered.

Venturing outside for their walk, Evie stopped frequently for Thompkins to rest. She walked beside him, ready to offer support, soaking in the golden afternoon sunlight. They came to a stone bench set under an oak tree. The gnarled branches were covered in pale green spring growth. Thompkins looked tired, so she suggested that they sit.

Wordlessly, he did. Just as she was becoming drowsy in the warm silence, he startled her with a question.

"Your cousin—how did he hurt his leg?"

Why would he ask that? Charles said he didn't even know him. "In France. He was in the BEF. He was caught in an explosion during the retreat, along with his brother."

"What happened to the brother?"

Evie stared at him. Something in his voice… "Roger was killed."

The silence between them stretched long. Then Thompkins' voice grated out once more, "Were you fond of him?"

"Of who? Of Roger? Yes, of course. He was…we all looked up to him. He was so good, always watched out for everyone else. I've just… hoped that it was quick." She bit her lips, startled by the old emotions.

I will not lose control. I am here to work, not to cry.

Thompkins nodded slowly. Slowly he asked, "Have you ever wondered—"

"Evie?" Nancy leaned out Thrush House's door, looking about for them. Evie waved. Nancy called, "Tea time! Hurry in."

"All right," Evie called back. She turned to Thompkins. "I'm sorry, they'll need me to help set up. Can we talk while we walk?"

He stood silently, wincing, and they made their way back towards the house.

"Please, what were you going to ask me?"

Whatever it was, it seemed the time had passed. He would say no more.

LYING IN THE DARK that night, Thompkins considered.

She doesn't know. Is it worth ruining her peace of mind? And what happens if he finds out that I know?

Frozen with indecision, it was a long time before sleep found him.

18 May 1944

Dearest Evie,

We've broken through. A cobbled together Polish flag is flying from the ruins of the Monastery on the hill.

All my love,
James

4 June 1944

Darling James,

The word has just come in that Rome has been liberated! How wonderful! I didn't hear all of the details—it sounded as if it were the Americans in first. Oh, I hope that this means that the Italian campaign is drawing to a close!

The children are calling. Everyone is so excited about the news. I think there is more coming on the wireless, I will write more later.

God bless you, James! Write soon!

Love,
Evie

Philippians 4:4 Rejoice in the LORD always. Again I will say, rejoice!

4 June 1944

Dearest Evie,

We are making good progress. It was heartening to pass through the mountain positions that have plagued us for so many months, and even better to see Jerry driven along ahead of us.

Word has just come in about the liberation of Rome. We aren't there yet, and I wish that it had happened under more fortunate circumstances. The American general, Clark, was to have used his men from the Anzio beachhead to cut off the German retreat. Since he marched north instead, our old foe Kesserling has been able to save a large number of his forces. I'm afraid that we will be paying for this victory in the future.

I'm sorry for the gloomy thoughts. Now that we have our first Axis capital, maybe things will move more quickly. It is certainly good to see Jerry in a real retreat, rather than just removing to the next hill ahead or to the next river. As we travel, we see the wreckage left behind—trucks and tanks, blackened and blasted by our good old RAF boys.

We're moving out. I'll write again soon.

Love,
James

CHARLES STOPPED IN THE DOORWAY of the library, staring. "Evie, what in the world are you doing?"

She balanced, barefooted, on a narrow chair, fumbling with something at the top of the library window. As she turned to answer, the chair wobbled, and she flung her arms out for balance. "Oh!"

He lunged forward, but she slapped both palms against the wall and steadied herself. "I'm alright!"

Wincing, he adjusted his leg, tempted to berate her for worrying him like that. The beaming smile she sent over her shoulder stopped him.

"What do you think, Charles? Our first Axis capital!" she crowed, clapping her hands and then freezing as the chair shifted underfoot.

He walked over and steadied it for her. "That's good news," he allowed. "Pity the Yanks got in first, and pity it's taken so long. Still..."

"Oh, Charles." She sighed. "Help me get these curtains down, won't you? I don't know how the children managed to get them so dirty."

Charles reached up and easily detached the curtains, which sported fingerprints in various shades of brown. "Ugh. Are you a washer woman now?"

"We'll send them over to Mrs. Smart. Helps her earn something, and it's one less task around here." Once she had climbed down safely, he handed them to her.

"Of course. You have been busy, haven't you? You're looking tired, Evie. I hope you're finding time to rest."

She motioned him over to the next window, and he followed. "Oh, I do, Charles. It's hard to rest, though. It all just keeps on going on and on and on..."

He took down the curtains she indicated and then patted her shoulder. "How's life as a VAD? Do you still like nursing? Convenient that you're so near home."

"Yes, it is, and yes, I do. I'm learning so much, and it's good to be able to help...at least to help some of them." Her voice fell on the last.

He paused, studying her face. "What—but you haven't lost patients, have you, Evie? By the time they send them up here they're stable, aren't they?"

Piling the curtains on one end of the sofa, she picked up one and started folding it. "Well, we lost one man. There was an infection, and we didn't find it in time. He just faded away. It...well, it was hard. It made me grateful that I'm serving here. I don't know what I'd do in London."

"Good heavens, no. We couldn't have you going there."

"And then there was Richard Thompkins—the man you thought was named Rivers? It was strange, it almost seemed like he knew you, and when he spoke to me—"

The words burst out of Charles before he could stop them. "He spoke to you?" Evie's hands froze mid-fold, and she stared.

Taking a deep breath, he continued in calmer tones. "I thought that was the poor fellow who couldn't speak."

She blinked. "Well, I thought so, too, until one of his last days here. He talked so seldom and seemed depressed. They moved him out this week to a facility with a psychiatric ward to try and help him."

Nodding, Charles walked over to the bookshelves and ran his finger across a few of the titles without seeing them. "This war is making plenty of poor devils like him. But...you say he knew me?"

"Oh, he didn't say much. Just asked after you as if he knew who you were, so I thought.... But then Nancy came out for tea, and that was it, he didn't say a word about it again. Maybe I misunderstood." Her hands began moving again, smoothing the creases on the cloth. "I'm going down to visit Sophia soon, if I can manage it. His new hospital is close by. I had thought of dropping in, just as a familiar face. As far as I can tell I'm the only one he ever spoke to, so I feel like I should try—Charles, are you all right? You look positively ill!"

"I feel ill. I think that fish we had for dinner may have turned. I need some fresh air." *Air. I need air. I need to think!*

6 June 1944

Dear James,

What a week it has been! Now all of the news is about the landings in Normandy. With troops back in France, you in Italy, and the Russians coming from the east, surely the Germans must give up their defense of Europe soon, mustn't they?

BONNY TIPTOED to the library door and peered around the frame, holding her breath. Miss Worther sat in the far corner, shoulders hunched as she bent over the desk, pen scratching across a sheet of paper.

She must be writing to that sweetheart she won't talk about.

Tugging on her dark plait, Bonny considered and then nodded, satisfied. She slipped through to the music room and out the French doors, the bottle of milk carefully concealed under her bulky jumper.

The June days were too long for the growing shadows to offer much concealment. She skulked towards the carriage house through the little orchard, traveling from tree to tree. She imagined she was a soldier like Daddy, evading searching German eyes.

At the last gnarled trunk, Bonny turned back to study Stoneglenn's frowning face. The windows that dotted the stained stone were empty, blackout curtains in place. Even the other evacuees were absent—the little ones in bed, her brother Edward and the other big boys listening to the night's programs.

Good. Miss Worther's not likely to put up much fuss, even if she saw me. But I shouldn't like to be caught by Mr. H…

Thrush House was about as good a place as they could've landed when Mum sent them away from the bombings, but old Mrs. Heatherington didn't care much for children. Miss Worther was nice, but she was always busy at the convalescent home. Weekends like this, when Mr. H came by, were the worst.

Bonny hated how Mr. H's eyes never changed expression, even when he pretended to smile at her. He was always suddenly interested in what they were doing when Miss Worther was around. Once she had gone, he went back to scolding them whenever he decided they were "underfoot."

The rotter can make a big house like this feel smaller than our old flat. At least out here, I can get some quiet.

The main doors of the carriage house were shut. Opening them would mean wrestling with rusted hinges while standing in full view of the house. There was, however, a little door on the far side, partially hidden by an old rubbish heap and some weeds.

Bonny tugged it open, then waited for her eyes to adjust to the dusty dark.

She had been the first to think of the old carriage house as a retreat. It was all but abandoned, and the empty stalls were dim and mysterious. The corners were cluttered with interesting old pieces of wood, rusty tools, and bits of harness, and it had an excellent old beam in the ceiling on which she and Edward had managed to hang a rope to swing back and forth.

Miss Worther hadn't forbidden them to play in the carriage house. However, she had suggested that they only go in during the daylight—and with an adult. She also wasn't likely to approve of Bonny's giving part of her milk ration away.

But, if she doesn't know...

Bonny glanced back one last time and darted inside, pulling the door almost closed behind her.

The new kittens slept in a back corner on some tattered old horse blankets. They knew Bonny's step and came, mewing and scrambling over each other.

Bonny played with them for a bit, cuddling their warm bodies and teasing their tiny paws. Their mother, Portia, kept to the shadows, and Bonny couldn't spot Brutus, the tom. She spent a few moments trying to call him and peering through crannies before giving it up.

I suppose I ought to hurry back before I'm missed.

Still, Bonny took her time wiping out the discarded dish she used for the cats' milk, careful of the large chip in the rim. She refilled it, and the kittens jockeyed for position, lapping the treat greedily.

The crack of light by the door slowly faded, the light turning rosy with sunset. The others would notice she was gone.

Bonny sighed. She stood, stretching, trying to think of one more reason to stay. Nothing. She took a reluctant step towards the door and then froze.

A low murmur drifted from the direction of the orchard—were those voices?

Men's voices.

One sounded like Mr. H.

If he *sees me, I'll catch it for sure.*

Bonny ducked far back into the corner, crouching, hoping the shadows concealed her.

"We can talk in here," came Mr. H's slow drawl as he opened the door. "No one uses it anymore."

He left the door open, the last beams of light reaching towards, but not quite illuminating, Bonny's corner.

A bulky shadow nearly filled the doorframe. The glowing end of a cigar failed to illuminate the stranger's face. "You sure? Door wasn't locked." The rumbling growl of his voice sounded like the butcher's back home.

Mr. H. sniffed. "The evacuee brats probably broke it." His head swung around, eyes skimming over the shadows. Bonny's skin crawled as they passed her corner, but after a moment he turned back to his companion. "So. You have a solution to my problem?"

"Half of one. I can't get anyone down there soon enough, and there are people about who make it not worth the risk. If it didn't have to be a rush job—"

"There's no time to spare."

"So you said. What's the bloke got on you, anyway?"

"That information wasn't part of the deal. And if you aren't going to help me, I don't see that we have anything more to—"

"Oh ho! Settle down now." The shadowy stranger flicked the ash off of his cigar, his voice amused at the panic in Mr. H's voice.

Bonny smiled. Mr. H always acted so big. *Sounds like he's gotten himself in some trouble. Serves him right.*

She strained her ears, more curious than frightened.

The big man took a long drag on his cigar. "I have some stuff that'll do the job. I've got a friend on the staff, found out his medications..." He listed off some names that sounded like gibberish. "Just get one of the bottles and dump it out in the loo—it'll look like he took 'em all, and then give him this in his drink. He'll be none the wiser—well, until it's too late anyway." He gave a harsh laugh.

Wait—what? What, he can't mean—

Mr. H held the little glass vial up to the light. "They won't be able to tell the difference? What if they do an autopsy?"

"Who'll be asking for one? He's a mental patient. He'll be just another victim of the war."

"Why can't you handle this? After all, it's your field—"

The cigar glowed bright. "Not just mine, from what I've heard. Just how did your big brother end up in that alley?"

There was a long silence. Stabs of pain shot through Bonny's foot, cramped from her sustained crouch. She held her breath and tried not to move, waiting for Mr. H's answer. There must be some answer—none of this could be what it sounded like.

"What...that was...that was an accident."

The other man snorted. "Lucky accident. In any case, you can't afford me. You've had some losses."

"Nothing that I won't win back. And besides, I've got backup. When I inherit—"

"When Auntie kicks off you mean? An' a tough old bird she is." The cigar wiggled as he shook his head. "No. You already owe me, and I've done the hard work for you, getting this, getting it planned out. You're not worth any further risk to me—not without more coin, anyway."

"I've paid you more than enough. I could've gotten this much help from any two-bit swindler—"

"Careful, Heatherington." The man's growl made goosebumps rise on Bonny's arms. "Let's not forget how things stand. If I were to call your debts in today, for instance..." He pulled a knife out of his pocket and flicked it open. Even in the dim light, the silver blade flashed as he trimmed his fingernail. He left the blade open and held it between his body and Mr. H's.

Bonny's mouth went dry, but Mr. H didn't sound concerned. "More fool you, if you did. What would you stand to gain?"

The shadow chuckled; the knife clicked shut and vanished. "True enough." He turned to go. "Still, I wouldn't expect any more favors. Clean up your own mess."

Bonny hardly dared breathe as the men's silhouettes filled the doorway. She clenched her sweaty palms together.

Just at that moment, one of the kittens rubbed against her leg.

She jumped.

Her shoulder bumped the wooden wall. A board, leaning against the wall, slid sideways.

She grabbed for it—too slow.

It teetered, scraped against the wall, and then fell to the floor with a clatter.

Both men spun about, staring towards her hiding place. "Who's there?" Mr. Heatherington's voice cut the air. The other man's hand flew to his pocket.

Silence.

Oh God, Oh God, please...

Bonny bit her lip until she tasted blood. Closing her eyes, she imagined herself as a statue.

The image of the knife danced behind her eyelids.

Mr. Heatherington took a step towards her dark corner—

Please!

—then another.

A terrifying yowl rent the air.

Cursing, Mr. H and the stranger jumped back. Bonny nearly toppled over.

The tomcat, Brutus, streaked across the floor to her corner, yowling and hissing. Shaking with shock and momentary relief, Bonny stifled a hysterical laugh.

"Blasted cats," muttered Mr. H. "If I had a free hand, I'd drown the little beasts."

"Hardly good sport. We'll find better…" and the two men were gone, shutting the door behind them with a click.

Bonny's heart pounded a frantic rhythm as she waited to be certain they were gone. The silence stretched long, but she did not move. *What if they come back? What if they find me? What would they do if they knew I heard them?*

At last, legs cold and cramped, she could hold her pose no longer. She drew air into her lungs with a little sob and plopped down on the ground.

She scooped Brutus onto her lap as he came near.

"Good kitty."

A few deep breaths later, she scrambled to her feet. Brutus mewed in discontent.

I've got to get back to the house before anyone notices I've been gone!

She didn't want to give Mr. H any reason to wonder where she had been tonight.

Twenty Two

4 July 1944

Dear Evie,

It's official. We've been relieved. I'll begin the journey down to Egypt later today, and we should have a good long stay with rest and refitting. We will have a stop off at Rome along the way. It'll make a nice change to see a city whose ruins aren't from shelling. Strange, though, passing through all that ground so quickly—it took long enough on the way up. Time to go—

Love,
James

20 July 1944

Dear James,

Rome and Egypt! I am so glad that you will be off the line for a while, and having a rest, and what fascinating places to see! Egypt especially has always seemed so romantic and mysterious, but perhaps this is just because I haven't been anywhere near it. I hope it is lovely.

Colonel Bryce asked after you, and when I told him where you would be on leave he immediately launched into some very colorful stories and told me to warn you about the shoe shine wallahs and not to buy anything the merchants claim came out of a tomb. He said the families manufacture these items each evening for sale the next day. Whether this is true or not,

I will leave to you to discover!

What a pity you couldn't have gone down in the winter for a chance to warm up—it must be very hot there just now. Oh James, I'm just so glad that you'll be somewhere safe.

Love,
Evie

Matthew 11:28 Come to Me, all you who labor and are heavy laden, and I will give you rest.

10 August 1944

Dear Evie,

It has been a relief to relax, and to have a shower and a change. The lines were getting pretty ripe. I hardly recognize some of the other men, and half of the sunburn I had was just dirt. I'm a pretty handsome fellow now, my girl! I'll have to have a photo taken and sent to you, so you don't forget it. Regular meals are nice, too, and there's talk of an ENSA show. I'll let you know if we see anyone famous for this one—some of the men have come to call them the "Every Night Something Awful," but I figure it takes some guts to be out here, and, in any case, some entertainment is better than none.

All my love,
James

To SAY THE HEAT was oppressive would be akin to calling a lion a large cat. While technically true, the description fell far short of the reality. Heat shimmered in the air around the canvas town at Qassassin. Rumor had it that one man had managed to fry an egg on a stone outside of his tent.

James felt pretty well fried, too, and kept reminding himself how he had longed for heat during the last two winters in the cold rain and mud. The reminders didn't help much.

Flopping onto his bed and folding his arms behind his head, he stared up at the canvas ceiling. Mercifully, there was another layer of canvas above it, keeping the direct heat from the interior of the tent and saving him from a complete cooking.

He considered the last few days.

Rome had been beautiful. He hadn't attended the audience with the Pope, but he had visited St. Peter's and had sat in at Mass in the great basilica, savoring the peaceful loveliness of the music and the surroundings. The front seemed like an entirely different world, a nightmare, half-forgotten.

Rather than a passenger train, they'd been loaded onto sweltering cattle trucks for the journey back down Italy. Stops meant a frantic exit to relieve oneself or to fill oneself up with tea to be discharged at the next stop down the line.

Passing back through Cassino had been eerie. White tape still bordered the train tracks to mark minefields. Beyond, the summer foliage effectively camouflaged the blood-soaked ground that they'd spent the winter fighting for. The memories couldn't be covered up so easily—they lingered like pale ghosts of the lost.

James shifted, using his cuff to wipe away the bead of sweat that crept down his temple. Heat aside, it was good to settle down in Egypt. Though only a temporary town with very few permanent buildings, the camp was well organized and pleasant. Having regular showers available was enough of a luxury. To also have a NAAFI to shop at, a cinema, and clubs left James almost overwhelmed.

They'd been offered leave to either Cairo, Alexandria, or Ismailia. Most of his mates had selected Cairo, as he had, and there were already plans in place to view the pyramids and, of course, to ride camels. *I'll probably look a fool, but Evie'd enjoy a picture of it.* Imagining her laughter at his expense made him grin. The grin turned to a yawn.

Might as well kip for a bit. Davy promised to stop by, and we're not to leave for a few hours. He shifted to his side, giving the sweat on his back a chance to dry. *It's one way to get through the hot part of the day, anyway.*

He had nearly dozed off when the sound of voices, singing with gusto, passed his tent. The loudest sounded like Peters, singing nearly on key. *There they go again.*

More voices joined in, laughing as they belted out "The D-Day Dodgers".

As the men's voices pierced his thin canvas walls, James rolled over, licking his dry lips. He tried to ignore the knots the song always brought to his stomach. Another verse, another joke about the easy life they'd lived so far in Italy—

Hmph. Easy. Maybe Lady Astor would like to come up in the mountains with us for the next round and see just how easy it is…

When Lady Astor, back home, had started flapping her politician mouth and calling them the "D-Day Dodgers," off in Italy shirking the real war in France, naturally they'd all been outraged. One clever fellow had put their feelings into song, though the joking words couldn't hide the undercurrent of frustration they all felt.

How many D-days have we seen now, between North Africa, Sicily, and Italy?

Not that these seemed to matter to the brass.

The day after Rome was taken—finally, after months of work—the campaign was a backwater in all the papers because of the invasions in France. Montgomery had left months ago for the same campaign, taking many of his favorites with him. The ill-fated landing at Anzio had been a rush job because of the transports being needed in France. And now that they were finally making headway, chasing the enemy before them, several of their best divisions had been diverted for *another* landing in the south of France, diminishing their numerical superiority and slowing down the campaign yet again.

From a neighboring tent, another man shouted out a stringent encouragement for the singers to quiet down, including a few creative suggestions about the nature of their parentage. In response the volume increased.

When they'd finally passed out of earshot, James rolled over, trying to get comfortable again. The song kept spinning through his head.

Breathing deep, he tried to reason through it. *All right. It's frustrating. But we're here to do a job. If it's not the job that makes the headlines, well, they can take their papers and—*

He rolled over again. *Think about all that, and you'll never sleep. Blasted heat. Hope we'll find some shade in Cairo.*

10 August, 1944

Dear James,

I hope that you are having a lovely time on leave and keeping cool!

I am getting some leave of my own. I have this weekend off, and I'm going down to Manchester to visit Sophia! Her landlady has given permission for me to stay over, so we can have a good visit. She's threatened to take me dancing with her and her new boyfriend, Elmer.I don't want to dance without you.

Unfortunately, Mary is working nonstop at her hospital in London and won't be able to come up at all. I almost feel guilty going, with all those signs looming over the train platform—"Is your Trip Really Necessary?" Not guilty enough to stay behind, though!

I can't believe Great Aunt Helena didn't put up more of a fuss, but once she had checked that Sophia has a shelter, she seemed content to lecture me about all of the dangers I'm likely to face. Apparently, I am to be wary of pickpockets, lecherous Americans, loose women who will want me to join their ranks, and feral dogs and rats, as well as bombs.

I am hoping to stop by one of the local psychiatric hospitals. It's just down the road, and one of our patients from Thrush House was sent there. As far as I can tell, I am the only one he spoke to while he was here. I feel sorry for the poor man, and being right there, I thought I ought to at least say hello.

It is so nice to write to you and know that you are safely away from the fighting!

Love always,
Evie

Jer 29: 14 I will bring you back from your captivity; I will gather you from all the nations and from all the places where I have driven you, says the LORD.

THOUGH IT HAD BEEN four years since Evie had ridden the train, she felt that she managed not to betray how awkward she felt, alone among strangers.

The carriages were a bit shabbier than she remembered, the eyes of the people a bit more tired, and their cheeks more sunken. She found a seat in a quiet compartment and pulled her jacket closer around her shoulders; the unheated cars were chilly.

She reached the proper platform in Manchester without incident and took a deep breath as she stepped down into the throng.

I'd forgotten how busy it can be! Silly, Evie, it's probably not even that many people. I've just gotten used to Thrush.

After years tucked away in the countryside, the smells of smoke and petrol and dust and people assaulted her nostrils.

She steeled herself and commenced the short walk to Sophia's lodgings.

It looked like a pleasant part of town—or it had been. She tried not to stare at the houses standing with windows shattered or doors missing from the frame, giving the appearance of a skeleton's grin. Others bore dark streaks from long-quenched fire. War had been here.

Her stomach clenched. Some things she'd forgotten, but not the terror of the raids. She quickened her pace.

Sophia's house was still whole, brick with white trim, in a row of similar ones. Though the paint on the trim was dingy and the windows were taped to avoid shattering, the walk was neat and there were curtains at the windows.

"Evie!" Sophia met her at the door with a glowing smile and an embrace, her wet hair in a towel. "Come in! We've just time for a bite, and then, what do you think? We're going dancing!"

"Oh, Sophie, I don't know. I didn't bring—"

"Oh, pooh, don't worry about clothes. After a week spent in our work gear, the boys all go gaga just seeing a skirt! Come along and meet Mrs. Kenwich!"

A tall, spare woman with a mouth disinclined to smile but with kind eyes, Mrs. Kenwich made Evie welcome. Evie, resigned to Sophia's scheme, helped to set the table while Sophia fussed over her hair at a mirror in the corner. "I had to wash it—it was dreadful! But there wasn't time earlier, and now it's unmanageable! Never enough soap to be had." She frowned at her reflection. "Thanks for being a dear and helping with that. I won't be much longer, and then tonight you can meet Elmer!"

When Evie didn't express her delight, Sophia glanced over her shoulder with a reassuring smile. "I know you don't care to dance with strangers much, but Elmer will ask you if I tell him to, and there are a couple of other boys from work who are very nice. Plenty of uniforms about, too. We'll have a jolly time. Then you said you wanted to do some shopping Monday. The queues will be dreadful, you know, but if you want to—is there anything else you were planning on?"

"Just to visit you, though I had thought about going over to Thornridge—the psychiatric hospital, you know. One of our patients from Thrush House was transferred there, and being right here, I thought I'd stop over. Maybe tomorrow afternoon?"

Sophia turned around completely, eyes wide. "Ooh, go over *there?* My friend Madge used to be a VAD over there. She said lots of them were simply loony. Once her stint was up, she started at the factory, instead. She says she likes it much better. Ooh, the stories she tells, Evie! If you go in there, you're much braver than I am."

Evie frowned at the plate she was setting on the table. "I'm not afraid, I just find it all sad." *And I feel like I ought to talk to Thompkins again. When he spoke to me—and Charles's face when he realized he'd spoken—something isn't right.*

If Charles was in some kind of business he oughtn't be, maybe Thompkins knew something about it. Maybe he'd even been involved. That could explain why he hadn't said much to her—a guilty conscience keeping him quiet.

The strangest part was his bringing up Roger. Could Roger *have been involved in something illegal?*

Surely not. Roger was so honest. I don't remember him lying once, not even hedging to stay out of trouble, but I was so much younger. Maybe I missed something...

Nothing made sense, and she couldn't rest easy until she'd at least tried to understand.

The meat pie that Mrs. Kenwich served, though filled with more vegetables than meat, tasted delicious after a day's travels. Still, Evie ate sparingly, keenly aware of the fact that she was eating off their ration books and not wanting the two ladies, generously urging seconds on her, to want for food later this week on her account.

Since Sophia wouldn't be deterred from her plans, Evie was grateful that she had packed an extra dress, though no stockings. Sophia had the solution for that—they applied gravy coloring to their legs to darken their skin, and then they took turns drawing a line up the back of each other's legs. From a distance at least, they would pass inspection. Evie had a little powder and lipstick still from Charles, which she shared.

Powdered and preened, arm in arm, they walked down the road in the dusk. Sophia chattered away about her week's work, where the best goods were to be found, and what Evie should expect at the dance. Evie was content to listen and to wonder at the changes that a train ride could bring.

The dance hall was already filling up. There were a number of men in uniform—local men and troops sent over from America. To the side, a few younger boys still in school clothes milled about near older men just cleaned up from the factory. Slightly separated, girls of all ages, shapes, and sizes chatted and practiced steps and covertly glanced over at the boys to see who might ask them to dance.

The band struck up a catchy tune. Evie found a chair near the edge and watched Sophia, quickly snatched up by one of the American enlisted men, jitterbugging enthusiastically.

She grinned and looked down at her hands. *Maybe it's been good for Sophie and Mary to be apart. Sophia finally gets the attention. She certainly seems to be having a good time.*

The floor slowly filled from dance to dance as more couples joined. Many of the men lingered, building their courage up with some liquid fortification before approaching first the girls and then the floor. The color and the noise and the scents of cheap cologne and perfume swirled and eddied around her, and she felt like a stone in a stream, quietly watching the world go by.

She was startled out of her reverie by a slightly spotty young man, American by his uniform, standing in front of her and trying to look confident, but shuffling his feet as he asked her to dance.

Oh dear. But he looks so hopeful—

She stood up, and he beamed at her. He leaned over to half shout in her ear, "Do you know how to jitterbug?"

Evie laughed and shook her head.

He spent the next two songs trying to teach her a few steps and was a good sport about the process. He told her she was doing swell and was very gallant when he went off to find a new partner, though she was privately sure he was hoping for someone with more natural talent.

She headed back towards her seat, but Sophia waved her over, clutching the hand of a young man with heavy, dark hair and eyebrows, and rounded shoulders. "Elmer, this is Evie!" she called out over the noise. Elmer gave her a wary smile and Sophia pushed him towards her. "Elmer, dance with Evie, won't you? She doesn't know anyone, and she's terribly shy."

Elmer didn't look particularly extroverted himself, but he shuffled over and attempted a dance, mustering a polite smile any time they couldn't avoid eye contact.

Heading back to her chair a second time, Evie was surprised by the call of "Nurse!"

She looked round, and there was Corporal Evans, beaming at her. He strode over, neatly done up in regular uniform again, well and whole and looking little like the wan man who had lain in the bed at Thrush House.

"Out of uniform? You've escaped the backwater, I see," he said.

"Yes, for the weekend, at least. I'm visiting a friend. What about you?"

"Flying bomber raids these days. I've got the weekend off, as well—been visiting some friends and family." He seized her hand. "C'mon, let's dance."He was an excellent dancer and led Evie well enough that she managed the fast steps rather better than usual. The next dance was a slower number, and he kept hold of her, gliding across the floor. "So, who's the friend you're visiting?"

"A girl from Farthington. Sophia Turner. We've known each other since childhood, and she's working in the airplane factory. Since the hospital, Thornridge, is so near I had thought to stop in and visit the other man who was at Thrush House—Richard Thompkins—you knew him, didn't you?" Evans' face darkened. "Why, what's wrong?"

He avoided her eyes as he said, "I hate to dampen the evening, but, well, I had the same thought. Went to visit Rich this week. I'm sorry to tell you, he's passed away."

"Oh no." Her feet froze, and Evans nearly stumbled over them. "I'm sorry. I just—I don't understand. He'd looked like he was healing so well."

The corporal hesitated, but after a minute he admitted, "It wasn't his injuries. Just last week... well, they found a whole bottle of pills gone afterward. It looks like...he just couldn't take it. I'm sorry to be the one to tell you."The song was over, and he walked her back to her seat. She sank into it. Evans offered to get her something to drink. Numb, she managed a nod.

Suicide? They'd said he had psychological problems, but I never thought—oh dear God, how could it be? Is there something I should have done? I didn't think—

Evans returned, pressing the drink into her hands.

Taking a sip, she struggled to gather her wits. "Thank you."

He sat down next to her and draped his arm around her shoulders. "It really is terrible, isn't it? Poor devil. Just goes to show how short life is. How fragile. I think about it every time I go up." He squeezed her shoulders and shifted closer. She stiffened. "You know, Evie, if you're not doing anything after this—"She leaned away and stared at him, mouth open, unable to believe that he was *really* trying this, but just then Sophia came up, Elmer in tow, complaining about how hungry she was.

"I'm sorry, Corporal. My friends are here." Detaching herself, she escaped.

Evie found a new chair, the evening's fun drained away. She sat alone, arms crossed tight, watching Sophia and Elmer—who had gone off to dance again—appear sporadically in the crowd.

Oh, James, I wish you were here.

She was grateful when it was time to go back to Sophia's to escape for a while into sleep.

12 August 1944

Your patience may be rewarded tonight.

A. Andrews

ANDREWS STARED at the scrawled note and debated. Ought he send it, when he wasn't even sure if his idea would work?

Yes, he'd better. Heatherington was an impatient man. Best to let him know that something was in the works. Perhaps it would satisfy him for a while.

Once the letter was safely posted, Andrews ambled down the dusty Cairo street, ignoring the noise and the smell and the heat, focused on his purpose.

The men were still in the pub. Good.

They'd been drinking more than they ought to, and their angry voices carried to the small table he found adjacent to them.

"—and then he charged me five times the price. Five times!"

"What, you think these drinks cost the same for the natives? No, it's all a game—but we'll get our own back tonight."

One of the men, his bulk seemingly better able to hold his liquor, said, "Quiet down, now. No need to broadcast it." He leaned his head in and the others mimicked him. Andrews had to strain his ears. "Tonight's a go—we've got enough fellows. We'll make quite a stir. But we've got to be quiet about it. Don't want them to find out. I've a score to settle with Kamal, over in the junk shop. Don't want him waiting for me, do I?"

"What do we say when the MPs catch wind of what's going on?"

The big man laughed. "Don't get caught. And if you do—tell 'em you've been to the pictures."

The unsteady party left. Andrews waited a few moments and then followed, a pale shadow. He knew Kamal's shop. The man was notorious for the deep enjoyment he took in helping the newly-relieved troops spend their pay.

His mind moved quickly behind his expressionless eyes. Riots in Cairo would bring chaos. In chaos there was opportunity. If the rumored plans for tonight went through, if these men went after Kamal, if he followed after and made sure there was enough damage done—enough for some serious charges—and if he could get the MPs and Milburn there—

It was a bit complicated, but he'd handled worse. If it worked, he might just earn his pay.

12 August 1944

Dear Evie,

I've learned some new things in Cairo. Everyone is required to have a picture taken on a camel, preferably in front of the Pyramids. Enclosed is a copy of mine for you. What do you think? I'd say, given a turban, I might make a pretty convincing native. The Pyramids really were very impressive, as was the Great Sphinx, all moldering away in the desert, standing up as a testimonial to the fact that in the end "we are but dust." I'm enjoying the variety of food, especially dates and bananas.

The city is busy, and we stick close to our mates. The natives are very eager to help us dispose of our pay as quickly as possible, by honest means or dishonest. I can see what the colonel meant—the tendency to haggle and bicker and bargain is wearing on some of the men, still tired from all of our work these last months.

I'm planning to go to the cinema tonight. An American comedy is playing, Arsenic and Old Lace, with Cary Grant. We should have some laughs, and maybe find a pub after.

"Are you ready?" Davy Llewellyn asked, sticking his head around the doorframe. He looked rather alarming; his sweating face was flushed almost to the shade of his hair. He tugged at his collar and mopped his face with a handkerchief.

James put his pen down. "Yes. Where're the others?"

"I don't know where most of the blokes have gone to. C'mon. It's got to be cooler in the show."

Walking through the streets of Cairo, they were accosted by smells of dust, animals, unfamiliar spices, and sour sweat. The usual crush of people crammed the narrow streets: vendors hawking their imitation "artifacts," bar keeps trying to attract people for libations, fruit stand workers, pickpockets, shoe shine wallahs—and everywhere, knots of men in uniform.

Something about the military groups seemed odd today. Rather than moving through the crowd, they were standing about in twos and threes, some talking earnestly, others watching the crowd with closed faces.

James sped up his steps to walk beside Llewellyn. "Have you heard about anything happening today?"

"What? No, nothing."

Llewellyn mopped his face with his handkerchief again and then used it to wave away a boy insistently tapping his arm.

The boy held up his wares. "Good dates—you buy? Good dates!"

"No, thanks, son. No dates today. Run along, now."

The boy turned his attention to James, who shook his head and kept on walking. He glanced over his shoulder and saw the boy accost the next group of soldiers.

The cinema was nearly empty. Only a few locals and a scattered assemblage of troops were there, ready to be entertained. James frowned in the dimmed lights, mind rattling around the strange feel of the city outside. Tensions had been high, and many of the men were disgruntled. To risk life and limb, to finally go on leave to recuperate, and then to be taken advantage of at every opportunity didn't sit well.

Is something going to happen—some sort of retaliation?

The picture began, and he lost himself for a while in the absurd story. Just when Boris Karloff appeared, leering on the screen, he was startled back to reality by a tug on his sleeve.

He turned to see the young date seller, staring at him with large, dark eyes. He leaned over and whispered, "Look, I really don't want to buy any dates."

"No, please, sir. I follow you here—you are an officer, yes? My uncle Kamal, he is in trouble with some of the men. Please come, please help!" The boy's face was distressed, his voice an anguished hiss carrying over the sounds of the picture.

Again, James frowned, and his worries returned. If there was trouble, and he turned his back on it—

Llewellyn was still immersed in the film, and not wanting to bother him, James slipped out of his seat to follow the boy.

They left through a side door, and James followed the boy's retreating back down a series of alleys and side streets. There were people about, but not as many as on the main thoroughfare, and they were all local, watching him hurry past with weary or wary eyes.

They stopped in front of the sagging striped awning of a shop with grimy windows piled high with "artifacts."

The boy pointed. "In there. Please, sir, hurry!"

James peered through the open doorway. The shop appeared empty, though it was difficult to be certain with all the shadows cast by cases of dull brass bracelets and small statuary.

He turned, but the boy had vanished into thin air.

Where did the scamp get to? Scanning the street and seeing nothing, he turned back to the door.

"Hullo?"

There was no answer.

A sharp prickle traveled down his spine. Something was off.

He took a step into the silent dark, then two.

The scent of foreign spices and cheap cigarettes surrounded him.

Straining his eyes, he scanned for any sign of trouble as he moved toward a small display table.

The silence was broken as shouting echoed down the street, followed by the sharp crash of breaking glass.

What the—

He turned toward the door, and as he did, his foot swung and struck something on the floor—something that gave a little. Something like a pile of rags or a sack of rice, but it wasn't.

The shopkeeper lay face-down, blood slowly seeping from a wound on the back of his head.

Shaking off his shock, James crouched, feeling for a pulse. More shouts echoed down the street, and was that gunfire?

Trying to focus, he pushed his fingers under the man's stiff collar.

He's just bent the wrong way. If I could roll him over—

The shopkeeper was not a small man, and James grunted as he heaved him over, trying to support his head and neck, still-warm blood smearing his hand.

"Hold it right there!"

James jerked his hand up to shield his eyes as blinding light flashed—electric torches. He blinked rapidly, trying to clear the spots from his eyes. "Wha—"

"None of your lip, now. Just stand up, nice and easy." The voice growled, deep and very English.

He eased himself to his feet, keeping his hands visible. As his dazzled eyes cleared, he saw the red banded hat of the Military Police. "Just what do you think you're doing in here?" the deep-voiced MP demanded, dark mustache bristling. "Another trouble maker! You're crawling out of the woodwork tonight! Check him."

Another MP, who resembled a stick insect, knelt by the shopkeeper. "He's alive, but he'd better get to hospital if he's to stay that way."

"Think you can just do whatever you want, don't you?" spat mustache man in James's face. Turning to the other MP he said, "Better go and get some help then. I can handle this one."

As he left, James willed himself to remain calm. "Sir, I don't know what happened. I was at the cinema—"

He snorted. "Just like all the trouble makers we've taken in tonight—innocent as can be, spent the night at the pictures."

James continued. "—and then I was brought here by a boy who'd been selling dates on the street. He said there was some trouble with his uncle and asked me to help. I found the shopkeeper like this."

"Yeah? And just where is this date-seller?"

"He ran off when we got here."

"And just left you here, blood on your hands, but innocent as can be, eh? What was his name?"

"He didn't say."

"Why'd he ask you?"

"He seemed to think I outranked whomever was causing the trouble—I don't know. He looked like he needed help. It was all off, but I couldn't leave a kid—"

"Regular Good Samaritan, ain't ya? C'mon. Let's go." He escorted James to the door. "Say what you like, the fellow who tipped us off had a different story. We'll see what's what. Rioting in Cairo, of all the cheek—"

The fellow who—what? What is *this?* Shocked silent for the moment,

James went without further protest.

The noises of disorder intensified as they exited the shop—shouts and cries, and the sporadic pop of small arms fire.

James's guard marched him to the corner where the main road intersected their side street. As they came out onto the thoroughfare, they heard a call, "Hold on there!"

Two more MPs came walking up. The shorter of the two squinted up at James.

Recognition and relief washed over him. *Geoff Small. He ought to listen to reason—*

Geoff looked over to the mustached MP who had him in custody. "What's the problem here?"

James's guard planted his feet. "Caught him roughing up a shopkeeper. Man's still unconscious. I'm taking him in."

James was about to reply heatedly that he had *not* been caught doing anything, but the other man—he thought his name was Adams—caught his eye and gave a miniscule shake of the head.

"You don't say?" Geoff stepped up and examined the patch on James's sleeve. "He's one of ours. We'll take it from here."

James's guard spluttered, mustache vibrating. "But—look here—"

Adams already had James by the arm. "Thanks. We'll see to him." Before the guard could protest further, they marched him off.

James began to explain. "I know this looks bad, Geoff, but I didn't—"

Geoff motioned him to silence until they'd reached the corner and turned onto the next narrow, dusty street. There, they stopped.

He gave James a measuring look. "Milburn. What've you been up to? Never seemed the sort to go looking for trouble."

"It found me. A kid on the street said his uncle needed help and brought me to the shop. The shopkeeper was already down."

"What? Why would he do that?"

"No idea. Maybe he was just causing trouble—"

Geoff laughed. "Pretty weak, but we've got enough to contend with."

More shouting and the sound of breaking glass echoed from a nearby street. His smile faded to a grim line. "Beat it. Quickly."

James hesitated.

"Look, there's plenty of trouble tonight from fellows more inclined toward it than you. Anyway, I know Kamal's shop—who's to say some of these fellows don't deserve it?"

Adams made a sharp sound in his throat, and Geoff shrugged, then started off after him toward the nearest disturbance. "Get out of here—unless you'd rather we take you in? I know you, Milburn, but think anyone else'd buy that story?"

Probably not. Turning in the other direction, James headed back to the cinema on heavy feet, wondering. Llewellyn was just exiting.

"Milburn! Where'd you disappear to? Missed the best part—"

"C'mon, Davy. We don't want to hang around tonight."

"What? What's—" Another crash of glass sounded from a street over.

"Riots." James started walking, and Llewellyn hurried after, too distracted by the noises of disturbance to ask more. That suited James's mood.

Someone gave them a tip. The date seller? Why would he do that? Someone else? Who'd try to set me up?

They returned to their lodgings, avoiding the noisier streets where the riot was in full swing. Coming up the stairs in front, they passed Private Andrews.

James turned his head as he passed, watching the other man. Andrews stared past him, face blank, unreadable.

Who is *Andrews?*

With a chill, he recalled their first introduction, when Andrews brought the letter and the brandy from Evie. If he'd met Evie, had he met Charles? Had Charles sent him to be a shadow, to—what?

This is ridiculous. Andrews hasn't ever done anything against me, Besides, Charles'd have to be mad to go to that kind of trouble over a girl who doesn't want him.

He told himself these things—and more—but the sense of unease lingered.

Twenty Three

1 Sept 1944

Attn: Messers S, J, X

I'm certain it has come to your attention that the difficulties regarding my finances, as well as other private matters, have been satisfactorily resolved.

That being said, it is my sincere hope that we can recommence our business relationship, which has until now been so mutually beneficial.

In anticipation of your acceptance of this proposal, I am enclosing information regarding the next shipment of the items you had requested last month, assuming that they are still in demand. Please respond at your leisure with details regarding where we can meet to discuss specifics.

C.H.

Charles fidgeted with his pen, rereading his letter to "Mr. Smith" for the third time and wondering why he still felt uneasy.

He was safe. Thompkins had been the only witness, and now he was dead.

Did I forget anything? Any evidence?

He had visited the hospital in an official capacity, ostensibly to check on the food supplies, making sure that all was in order and following regulations. Convenient, how Thompkins's bed number had been listed in the records.

How simple it had been! The wards were hectic, understaffed. He'd just had to stall until Thompkins was in treatment, plant the empty pill bottle, add the contents of the vial to the water on his waiting dinner tray, and it was done. The other man hadn't even seen him.

Neat and simple. No one suspected a thing.

To be certain, he'd left some important paperwork behind in the office. The next day he returned to retrieve it and to hear the news of the patient suicide. He had expressed his grief and concern, breathing a silent sigh of relief.

Safe.

He reread the letter, trying to focus on the words. The memory of Thompkins's face intruded. Charles put the paper down and rubbed his temples.

He was a nobody, damaged and depressed. I practically did him a favor.

He wiped his hands on the legs of his pants.

It wasn't supposed to be this way. It was just supposed to be Roger, and then I'd be set for life.

It's strange. I didn't worry like this over Roger.

Perfect Roger, everybody's favorite. Noble Roger, whom everybody admired. Responsible Roger, predicted to rise quickly in rank and do them all proud.

Roger was always in his way.

The thought had first come to Charles the day he'd heard about Peter's ship sinking. *With Peter dead, it's just Roger between me and inheriting. But if he were to die—*

At first, he had shied away from the thought, horrified at himself. *He's a prig, but he's my brother. Besides, if I were caught—*

Then the Blitzkrieg came. There was confusion, movement, danger—it would be so easy for a man to just vanish.

The catalyst came the night Roger confronted him.

Roger had been displeased to find out that his little brother had been gambling and dabbling in other disreputable businesses. Roger had ordered him to stop, threatened that he would make him.

Idiot brother. You could never make me *do anything.*

During the retreat from Arras, he'd waited, far behind the company. Roger came looking for him, as soon as the others were safe.

Always look out for the others first, don't you, big brother?

When he'd found Charles, he was angry. Accused him of being irresponsible, ordered him to rejoin the retreat, quick as he could.

When Charles had drawn the Luger, Roger hadn't comprehended.

When the bullet felled him, he still had disbelief and confusion writ across his face.

There should have been no witnesses. He hadn't seen Thompkins until he left the alley. At the time, muddled by pain and concerned about the enemy's fast approach, he hadn't worried. After all, it was unlikely that the man had seen anything.

But then, that night in Thrush House, seeing Thompkins's face again, Charles had been certain. Thompkins remembered. Thompkins knew.

But he's gone now. He's gone, I'm safe, and it's over.

Unless—unless Evie—

He buried his face in his hands.

Evie paced the upstairs hall, worn carpet muffling her footfalls. She passed Great Aunt Helena's door, and then her own door. Reaching Charles's at the end, she paused, and walked back again.

Great Aunt Helena was napping, the children were in school, and she had an hour before her shift was to begin.

The lack of occupation was the trouble. In the brief moments of silence, worried whispers crept into her mind, piercing her uneasy peace.

Thompkins tried to tell me something about Charles. James's friend said something about France, too, and then there was that Private

Andrews—Charles is *up to something. I know it—but what?*

Walking the length of the hall again, she came back to his door. Were there answers beyond it? The dark wood hid them, silent and uninformative.

He uses his desk when he's here, and there's a locked drawer, just like on mine. I wonder—

"Excuse me, Miss."

Evie gave a low cry and nearly jumped out of her shoes. "Oh, Molly! Sorry, what—what are you up to?"

Molly grinned over the pile of bedding in her arms. "Just airing out Mr. Charles's room. He doesn't like me in there when he's here. Today seemed like a good day to do it, before he's back tomorrow. I've got to move quick, though. Your Great Aunt is restless—I don't expect she'll sleep long."

"Let me help."

The room was neat, almost sterile, but Molly ran a dust cloth over all anyway as Evie stripped the bed. She tried to be discrete as her fingers probed under the mattress, tucking in the fresh sheet. Her tentative search revealed nothing out of the ordinary except one dirty sock fallen in the shadows beneath the bed."Molly?" Great Aunt Helena's voice echoed down the hall.

"Oh, bother." Molly hurried off. "I'll be back."

Evie stood, frozen in the middle of the room. She stared at the handsome, wooden, and completely clear desk as she reached back and fumbled for a hairpin.

The locked drawer was her best bet.

Inserting the hairpin into the keyhole, she almost giggled aloud from nerves as she realized she had no idea what to do next. She wiggled it around experimentally.

The novels make it sound so easy—

Nothing gave.

Molly's footsteps echoed down the hall.

She froze.

They passed Charles's room, the door at the end of the hall for linen storage opened and closed, and they passed back towards Great Aunt Helena's a moment later.

Evie sighed, and pulled at the hairpin. *Stupid. I ought to have known better—*

The drawer shifted and opened a crack. It was unlocked.

Gasping a breathless laugh, Evie gently slid it open.

Papers were stacked nearly to the top of it.

She sifted through them, trying not to disturb them too much. Organized Charles would likely notice anything out of place. They were filled with lists of figures, nonsensical to an untrained eye. There were a few sheets regarding his discharge from the Army—and there, at the bottom of the drawer—

Pictures.

Photos of their family smiled up at her. Great Uncle Raymond and Great Aunt Helena, standing in the orchard, laughing. Evie's and Charles's parents, picnicking on the grass. The cousins, flopped about, done up in fancy dress for a play they'd put on. Charles standing proud in his uniform. And the last was a picture of Charles, about fourteen, and Evie, about nine or ten, proudly holding up the fish they'd caught. Charles had been teaching her how to manage the line herself—

Evie blinked away the sudden damp in her eyes.

She stacked the pictures and papers up again as they had been and closed the drawer. Giving the room a quick glance to make sure all was in place, she left, shutting the door. It was time to get ready for her shift.

He's my cousin. Yes, he can be irritating, but he's my blood, and I've wasted all of this time being suspicious and peevish. I don't have any evidence of anything—I don't even know that Thompkins had something more he wanted to tell me.

She tidied her hair and freshened up her lipstick. Pausing to look at the tube, she rolled it around in her fingers. Charles had brought it for her last week, having found it…somewhere. Shaking her head, she set it firmly on her dresser.

Who knows if he's really been in bad business? There are authorities looking out for that sort of thing—they're much better at it than I am. If Charles is doing wrong, they will deal with it. Even if he is doing…something not entirely legal, what would I do if I found evidence? Turn him in?

He's my family.

Evie closed her eyes tightly for a moment, and she decided. She would stay out of it.

"BONNY?" Edward leaned around the corner of the library door.

Bonny jumped inside her skin. "Ed—what? What do you want?"

Ed walked to stand in front of her, arms crossed.

He always tries to look like Dad—man of the house. Sometimes this annoyed her. Today, she just wished Dad were really here. *He'd know what to do.*

"Bonny, what're you doing in here?"

"I just want some quiet."

Ed snorted. "Come off it. Something's worrying you."

"No, Tommy's driving me wild—"

"Don't give me that. You keep sneaking off alone, staring at nothing, jumping when someone comes into the room—"

Yes, because it might be him.

She sighed and looked out the window. After a moment of hesitation, she said, "Did you hear Miss Worther and Cook talking about her trip the other day? She was trying to keep it quiet with us around, but Cook kept going on, and she mentioned a suicide—"

"Yes, one of the fellows from next door. Sad thing, but he'd been sent off to the loony bin, so I suppose it wasn't such a surprise." Ed shrugged. "What—is that worrying you?"

"Yes…well no, it's just…what she said about it. It reminded me of something."

"What?"

Oh, just Mr. H and some mysterious stranger planning to kill someone and making it look like a suicide.

"Bonny?" Ed had walked forward, He put his hand on her arm, brow furrowed. "Bonny, you can tell me if something's wrong, you know. Maybe I can—"

Bonny shook her head. "It's nothing. C'mon. The rain's stopped. Want to get outside?"

Twenty Four

10 October 1944

Dear Evie,

The Italian mountains look just like I remember them. I'm glad to see them again, in a way. The three-day drive to get here was so terribly wet that we couldn't see much of anything. My stomach is pleased to be back on solid ground—well, fairly solid mud—again.

It looks like there will be some big moves soon. Maybe we will get a few more hits at Jerry before the year is out.

THE COUGHING INTERRUPTED JAMES, shaking him in its violent grip for a few moments.

Once he got his breath back, he tried to regain his train of thought. *The censors'll probably cross that last bit off anyway...*

He scrubbed his hand through his hair and across his eyes. *I shouldn't be this tired. C'mon, James, it's just a little cold. Buck up—*

"Milburn! Ready to roll out?" Llewellyn's cheery smile faded as he came to face James. "You look terrible."

"Thanks." James tried for an offhand grin, but as he stood, the coughing returned.

Llewellyn stood by until he finished. "You'd better get that looked at."

"It's just a cold. Once I get used to the weather—c'mon. We'd best be off."

Llewellyn shook his head. "Stubborn. If I outranked you—"

"Davy, we've only just got back." James looked his friend in the eye and willed himself to look strong. "I'll not leave you all to move up while I sit back here having the doc shake his head and tell me I've got a cold."

"Hmph. Well, if it isn't better soon—"

"Then I'll get it looked at. Let's go."

21 October 1944

Dear Evie,

It looks as though I'll be getting some extra leave, of a sort. The switch back to cold and wet hasn't agreed with me, and I've been feeling poorly. Not to worry, but I've been sent back for a while to get over a bit of a cough—pneumonia they say, but it sounds much worse than it is. Don't worry, I'll behave myself and get some rest, and be back on my feet in no time.

Love,
James

21 October 1944

Sir,

It may interest you to know that the gentleman you have been so concerned about has been recently sent back off the line for medical attention. It appears that he has a good case of pneumonia. Is there any type of care or attention that you would like me to give him?

A. Andrews

SITTING IN HIS ROOM at Stoneglenn, Charles folded the letter, pinching the creases and considering.

Pneumonia. Wouldn't it be perfect if—?

Resting his elbows on his desk, he absently stared out the window. The children were playing below, enjoying the brief appearance of autumn sun. Evie sat under a tree nearby, just visible from this angle. She held a fluttering piece of paper.

Ah, he's written her. I wonder if she knows? He locked Andrews' missive inside his desk drawer until he could destroy it and went down to join her.

Evie looked up and smiled as he approached, but the rims of her eyes were pink, and her lips trembled. "Hullo, Charles—Oh, Bonny!"

The biggest girl came, racing around the tree, and then planted her feet and froze as she noticed the adults, eyes big. The smallest, running behind, crashed into her. Amid the howls and tears, Evie started to rise, saying, "Oh girls, do be more careful—"

"Don't worry, Miss Worther, I've got her." The big girl spun around, dark plait whipping behind her, and picked the little one up, apologizing and soothing and hurrying away.

Charles shook his head. "Wild little—"

"Maybe, but they're just so glad to be outdoors. It's a lovely afternoon, isn't it?"

He leaned against the tree and watched the children run. The littlest was back in the game, though the big girl had vanished. "Yes, especially for November. It's good to see the sun."

"Yes."

Her voice sounded dull and distant. She was thinking of *him*. Charles decided to push.

"The change of seasons is hard on the health. It's good to see the children all looking so well, and you, too. Of course, you were hardly ever sick, even as a child." He looked down as she made a gulping sound. "Why, Evie, what is the matter?"

The tears welled up in her eyes, and she looked away to hide them.

He crouched down to her level, careful of his leg, using the tree for support, and put his hand on her shoulder. "Evie, tell me. What's the matter? Is someone sick over at Thrush House, or—" He paused and looked at the letter, held loosely in her hand. "Oh, no, you haven't had bad news from—"

"James is ill. Pneumonia. He tries to make light of it, but it's bad enough that he was ordered back to get rest and treatment. Oh, Charles." Here she turned her face, twisted in misery, towards him. "I...I just hate...not knowing, being so far away..."

To Charles's utter astonishment, Evie leaned into him. He put his arms around her, and she didn't resist or pull away but let him embrace her. It wasn't a lover's embrace, and he was careful not to make it anything that would be inappropriate from one cousin to another, but he found it surprisingly pleasant to have her put her head on his shoulder as she allowed herself a moment to weep.

See, this could all work out well. If only he *weren't in the way.*

He released her as soon as she had done and offered her his handkerchief, which she accepted with a rueful smile.

"I'm sorry, Charles. I don't mean to make such a fool of myself. It's...it's difficult enough already, but to have him sick, and I can't do anything..." She spread her hands out in front of her helplessly. "And then...Father...it wasn't pneumonia, in the end...but..." She pursed her lips and stopped.

He risked the intimacy of tucking a loose strand of hair behind her ear. "It's not like the last war. And he knows you're back here, praying for him all the time. That's something, surely."

"Thank you, Charles." She took a deep breath and stood, as did he. "You've really been wonderful, you know, with the children and Great Aunt Helena and everything, on top of your work. I'm sorry to be all weepy—"

"It's understandable. Come. Let's find a cup of tea, hmmm?"

"That sounds lovely." Calling the children to come in, Evie walked beside him, holding James's letter, but listening to him as he shared some amusing stories from his week to take her mind off her worries.

Well. That was promising.

ANDREWS'S TIME WAS RUNNING OUT.

He'd taken as long with the delivery as he dared, but odds were he'd be missed soon. Between that and the fact that Milburn had shown improvement under the doctor's treatment…Listening for any unusual sound, he entered the ward, treading quickly and carefully in the dim light. It reeked of disinfectant trying in vain to cover the stench of illness.

He'd hung around enough to know the sound of Milburn's cough—deep, rattling in his lungs. It was silent now. He must be asleep.

Heatherington's terse words cycled through his mind. "If you can aid in a satisfactory resolution to his illness, it will be greatly appreciated."

Sure enough I know what you mean, Heatherington. And I could surely use some of that appreciation…

Euphoria washed over him as he thought of just what it would mean to finally be free of the debt to the cigar-smoking "Mr. Smith," but he buried it. Dug a hole in his mind and buried it deep—it didn't bear thinking about until it'd happened.

He stopped at the foot of Milburn's bed. The man's breath rasped in his lungs, but it was regular and deep—asleep indeed. He lay on his side, a small dark object next to his limp fingers, as if he'd dropped it in his sleep.

The gold letters of the little book revealed that it was a Bible, and the photos spilling out from its pages smiled up at Andrews. *That girl. The one Heatherington's so worried about, or so he says.*

Her monochromatic, blank stare followed him as he reached over to the next empty bed for a pillow.

Taking a firm grip, he held it in both hands.

Milburn stirred.

Andrews's fingers clutched the pillow until his fingers ached and held his breath—a statue.

The sick man settled.

Exhaling softly, Andrews took a step forward. He stared at the other man's face, watching for any movement.

He took a deep breath. He raised the pillow. He hesitated.

This isn't really my line. Not what I signed on for, debt or no debt. He took half a step back and then shook his head, gathering himself.

Just do it. All your problems will be over. He'll get you back home—he promised—and then—and then—

Taking a firmer grip on the pillow, he clenched his teeth and moved forward.

Footfalls at the other end of the ward sent a jolt of fear through him—*they're making rounds!*—and he set the pillow down, plastered on his imperturbable smile, and strolled out of the ward in the other direction, nodding to the man coming in.

Safely back in his quarters, he waited for his heart to stop pounding and then penned a brief note.

If I'm to attempt medicine, I will need additional compensation to pay for the training I will need.

He considered it for a moment and then nodded. That ought to be clear enough. If Charles Heatherington wanted to raise the stakes, he was also going to have to raise the payoff.

10 December 1944

Dear Evie,

Things to be thankful for: you, the end of that dreadful cough, and a return to the lines to find things in good order. I remind myself of these so I don't complain about the cold. I find myself thinking longingly of Egypt's heat, where I thought longingly of the cool mountains, naturally. At least we have some shelters and aren't ordered to go out into the snow too much. Visibility is too good and snow too deep for much patrolling. Don't worry. I have no intention of heading back to hospital, and I am keeping well wrapped up and behaving myself.

Christmas is on its way, another Christmas away from home and away from you. It makes it hard to be jolly, but we will do our best. If we aren't too numb, maybe we can sing loudly enough to be a bother to Jerry that night. Or maybe he will sing back to us. One never knows.

God bless you, Evie.

All my love,
James

BLOOD SEEPED THROUGH the bandage on Charles's hand, staining the letter he had written. With a growled curse, he pushed the paper away and fumbled in the desk drawer, looking for another bandage. He didn't find any, so he improvised with a handkerchief.

For all their bleeding, the cuts weren't deep, though he'd have to explain the hole in the plaster where he'd punched the wall. At least he'd been able to repair the chair leg. It was also good that his landlady hadn't been home to hear him when he'd first opened Andrews's latest—he was half surprised the neighbors hadn't come by to see what was wrong.

He pulled a clean sheet of paper over, took a deep breath and a quick drink, and put pen to the paper a second time.

Pvt. Andrews,

If you think for one moment that I am going to pay additionally for anything you do at this juncture, you are a greater idiot than I could have imagined. All your attempts to be of use have failed, you have given me nothing to work with, and now, by vying for more, you have even missed this opportunity. I could have done better hiring one of the pack mules! If you expect to gain anything from this, you will simply have to take some action, gain some kind of result, or we will be finished, and I will find a way to handle matters myself.

C.H.

1 January 1945

Dear James,

Happy New Year! Perhaps this will be the last New Year that we are apart. I hope that I won't be too tiresome at closer quarters. I hope that we get a chance to find out soon!

We have been glued to the wireless, waiting to hear updates on the fighting in the Ardennes. Hitler just can't keep going, can he? The children are all sick. I never imagined how many handkerchiefs and how many sheets one would have to wash to keep up with six sneezing children. I am tempted to keep a tally, as I'm sure the sum would be impressive. I am well, just tired and missing you terribly.

Mary has come home for a visit, and she is stopping by soon. I will write more later.

God bless you, James, Be safe.

Love Always,
Evie

Isaiah 40:31 But those who wait on the LORD shall renew their strength; they shall mount up with wings like eagles, they shall run and not be weary, they shall walk and not faint.

Evie put down her pen and massaged her temples. She was healthy, only this headache wouldn't leave her in peace. Her cold hands felt good against the throbbing.

Everything was cold. Between coal shortages, threadbare clothing, and the coldest winter in fifty years, she'd nearly forgotten what it felt like to be thoroughly warm. The poor men in Thrush House who were unable to move about shivered under their blankets, and she laid out the children's' clothes the night before so that when they woke they could dress under the covers rather than in the icy air.

"Evie?"

Looking to the door, Evie called in response, "In here, Mary."

Mary entered and came at once for an embrace. Her face was thinner, and her eyes looked tired, her golden hair up in a tight victory roll.

Evie stood and gave her another hug. "Welcome home! How was Christmas?"

Shrugging, Mary said, "Drab, compared to the old days, but Mum appreciated having me home. Dad's written just today that he is doing well. He's been busy with all of the incidents lately." Her father had been in construction, and he had gone down to London to work with the rescue crews once the V1 rockets, Hitler's vengeance weapons, started falling. He had just made plans to return home when the first V2 rocket fell from the sky.

"Have any been near you? They say so little in the news—"

"Yes, they keep it all pretty hush-hush, but I suppose better that than help Hitler to improve his aim. There have been some close enough. They're frightfully loud when they hit, but you're grateful to hear them. It means they've missed you. It's not like the buzz bombs—at least those you could hear coming." A pained look flashed across her face. "There was a bad hit right before I left. We were running like mad to find beds. Families were there, Evie, out to do their holiday shopping. It was...well, I'd rather not talk about it."

"No, of course not." *Oh, Mary. I can't imagine. How awful...*

She forced a cheerful smile. "Not to put you right to work, but do you want to help me sort clothes? We've done a drive to send some things down for people whose homes have been damaged or destroyed."

"Goodness, Evie, you're still doing WVS along with nursing and minding the children? I suppose you're still doing music, too. No wonder you look done in."

Evie shrugged as she led Mary into the library, weaving around piles of donated items. "Well, the war's not over yet, is it? And the word we hear from people leaving the city—the conditions sound dreadful. All of the families, homeless in this cold—"

"Yes," Mary mused, holding up a yellow dress to get a better look at it, "it's rough. At least there are places for them to go, and the WVS is busy down there, handing out food and everything. I had to take the tube last week and stepped over dozens of people sleeping all about down there all in their little spaces…what do you think of this dress? I think it'd just fit."

"Now Mary—"

Mary laughed and threw the dress over to Evie, who caught it and began folding it. "Yes, yes, I know. It's not for me, though you ought to know, Evie, it's not as if my closet's overflowing. Now, if there were a decent corset in here somewhere I can't vow I wouldn't try to pinch it. Mine's in a dreadful state. I don't suppose you have a cigarette?"

"Sorry."

"Hmm. I bet one of the boys next door would give me one for a smile…any Yanks over there?"

"A few."

"I'll take the Yanks any day. Better uniforms, better cigarettes, better pay."

"Mary—" This time Evie's look of reproof was more serious.

"What, hadn't you noticed?"

"It just seems a little…disloyal."

Mary's eyes and mouth took on a hard line that Evie hadn't seen in them before. "It's not disloyal to our boys, it's just speaking the truth. A girl's got to look out for herself. The way the world is just now, no one is going to do it for her. I'm going to have some fun while I can. I don't see it all getting any easier, do you?"

Evie looked down at the pile of nappies she was folding and bit her lip. "No, I don't suppose so."

Mary laughed the serious moment away, patting her friend's arm. "Don't fret. We're going to be alright, you and I. I won't do anything really stupid, and you'll likely be settled in as a happy little housewife having dozens of babies and keeping chickens before next Christmas." Mary looked at her sidewise. "You're still planning on it being with that sergeant of yours?"

"Yes, of course, although dozens of babies before Christmas might be a tall order. Why?"

Mary moved to a pile of shirts. "Oh, no reason. I ran into Charles on the way up to the house. We stopped to talk a bit. A few things he said—"

"Oh, Mary, you're not singing that old tune, are you? He knows how it is with James and me."

"Hmmm." Mary avoided her eyes and started on a stack of shirt collars.

"No, really. He's been very kind to me and the children. It's as if he has finally grown up. I've been able to actually enjoy spending time with him again."

"Hmm. Enjoy how much?"

Evie threw the last nappie at her with an exasperated grin. "Mary! Can't I visit with my own cousin without you turning it into some kind of—Hullo Bonny, have you finished your lessons?"

The girl had come in the room quietly and was watching her with wide eyes. Her nose was bright red from constant blowing, but she obediently showed Evie her work. Evie looked it over and praised her for it. Bonny took it back, but stayed, standing and watching her with an odd expression, tugging on her plait, lips pursed.

Evie put a hand on her shoulder. "Is there anything else you need, dear? If you weren't so drippy I'd have you come and work with us, but I suppose we don't want to risk sending illness down with the clothes."

"Certainly not," Mary agreed, looking for the moment like a prim and proper nurse.

Bonny shook her head. "No, Miss Worther. I thought I might see if Cook had anything in the kitchen."

"Of course! If nothing else, it's warmer in there." Evie gave the girl a smile, which she returned.

As Bonny retreated, the two young women resumed their chat, and she heard the visitor say, "Well, I'm glad that you can be fond of your cousin again. And I'll take your word for it that nothing else is in the air. Whether he will or not remains to be seen."

"Oh, Mary."

Bonny sighed. *I was right not to tell Miss Worther about what I overheard. After all, she* likes *Mr. Heatherington, though I can't imagine why. He's such a phony. She probably wouldn't believe me if I told her. And if she told him, what would happen, then? Best to keep quiet.*

If only keeping quiet didn't knot her stomach so, if only every time she saw Mr. H she didn't remember and wonder—

She looked up and froze.

There, walking towards her, was Mr. Heatherington. He was reading something, but he looked up, took her in, and then looked back down again dismissively. As he passed, she shivered.

I wonder if he really did *kill that man.*

1 February 1945

Dear Evie,

Lost a fellow who'd been with us since Africa yesterday—Ed Turner. Poor devil was just looking for a warm place to kip. There was a haystack at the side of the road. He knew Jerry likes to booby trap them, but he must've gotten careless.

It's hard, especially when the end is so close we can almost taste it. Geographically, we've nearly run out of Italy, and with Jerry's offensive in France quelled, he just can't keep the fight up much longer. If only he could get that thought through his thick head.

My platoon's wise-cracker told me the other day that I ought to just leave him back from patrols, as he's not going to stick his neck out too far—doesn't intend to go down so close to the end. I think he was only half joking. Of course, Ed's death reminded us that even if he keeps his neck in tight, Jerry is still playing to win, and we must, too.

Sorry for the gloom my dear. Send me some more funny stories with the kids, or another picture, won't you? And I'll write you soon, and more cheerfully.

Love,
James

James debated taking Danny Ryan along on patrol. He had always been a bit nervy, but in the days since Turner's death, he had been jumpy as a cat.

Not the sort of mentality you want at your back with a rifle.

Still, at least I know Ryan. Half of the replacements have just been rushed into infantry to fill the gaps.

He's never been a shirker. He'll be all right.

I hope.

Not long after they set out, they found the house.

Its shattered remains cast eerie shadows on the snow in the near dark. The looks of it didn't bode well for finding any survivors, but James stayed alert. It wouldn't be the first ruin to be booby trapped or to hide an ambush.

All was silent as they stepped over the rubble. Bits of smashed crockery crunched underfoot. Torn papers rustled in the breeze of their passage.

They found the remains of the family in the next room.

"Merciful God," Llewellyn breathed, and crossed himself.

Ryan cursed and then turned and stumbled back the way they'd come. "I can't. I can't—"

"Moore, go keep an eye on him," James barked.

He couldn't take his eyes away from the remains of a mother, father, and two children. They had taken shelter under the wooden table, but it had offered them little protection from the blasts. James's stomach turned surveying the pitiful forms, broken, long past bleeding. One of the children was just an infant, thin arm stretched out pathetically towards them, begging for help even in death.

"Good God, have mercy on us," Llewellyn repeated, shaking his head.

The sound of Peters's sharp guffaw broke the silence. He'd lowered his rifle and stared at Llewellyn, shaking his head. "Why bring him into this?" He gestured to the crucifix, still incongruously hanging from a bit of intact wall and then down to the remains. "When has He shown mercy? Didn't show much to them, did He?" An edge crept into his voice as he observed, "Hasn't shown much to us, either." Llewellyn looked him over. "You're still alive."

"For now, Father. But how many aren't? Who's next? You keep

preaching about God—where is He? Look at them, they were children, and poor old Ed—" He broke off in disgust and spat into the dirt.

Llewellyn put his rifle down and stepped towards him, fists clenched.

James, who had been frozen in place, moved, ready to stand between them, but there was no need.

Davy bent down and picked up a twisted piece of metal, part of a shell. He waved it in Peters's face. "Give credit where it's due, man. Did God manufacture these? Did he send them raining down on this family?" He threw it aside to clatter against the wall. "When we see good done—what do the papers call it?—a "triumph of the human spirit." We help the survivors and we praise it as "humanitarian aid." Good things happen, and people are mighty proud of themselves and ready to take the credit. But when evil happens, where does the blame go? You ask how *God* could do this?" His voice had risen; he didn't shout, but it reverberated with a sound like thunder. "*God* didn't do this. It was men. Men like you and me."

Llewellyn turned and stalked out the door. After a moment, Peters shrugged and followed him.

James came last, steps quick as he remembered Ryan.

Ryan hadn't run far. He sat outside the door, head between his knees, eyes closed, rocking back and forth as Moore stood awkwardly by.

Peters paused and snorted in disgust. "Looks like you've lost another one, Sergeant. They'd better end this soon, or there'll be none of us left."

"Milburn, we've got to talk."

James put down his paper. Davy's voice was light, cheerful, but his eyes were serious.

Trying to match his tone, James forced a grin. "You heard we're going on another patrol? Come to hear my confession before we go in?"

"Not really." He eased himself down to sit, grunting as he positioned stiff muscles. "More to give one. I'm worried about you, mate."

James shrugged. "About me? I'd be more worried about Ryan."

Llewellyn opened his mouth and then paused to examine James. He nodded. "Yes, what'd they say about Danny?"

"Battle fatigue. He's out of it, for now at least."

"Hm." His hand rested on James's shoulder. "Maybe it's for the best. Better it happens when we're not under fire."

"Yes." James looked down at the paper again. "I shouldn't have taken him. I knew he wasn't coping well—"

"And that," Davy raised his hand and lightly smacked James's shoulder for emphasis, "that's exactly what I'm talking about, James. You've got to stop blaming yourself."

"For—"

Lewellyn counted on his fingers. "For Tommy. Sikes. Cartwright. Rogers. Turner. Ryan, now." He spread out his hands. "All of 'em. You carry 'em on your shoulders—I can almost see it."

"I—" James took a breath, kept his voice even. "I was supposed to look after them. I told them to go, and they went. And yes, of course, it bothers me, Davy, but I don't *blame* myself—these things happen, I know they do—"

"Shut it. I've shared quarters with you enough. I've *heard* your dreams. It's no good telling me it hasn't been eating at you. And you can't let it."

James barked out a laugh, bitter and tired. "I'll try." *But I let them down.*

Llewellyn read his mind, somehow. "You didn't fail them. You've tried your best—it's near a miracle you've lived this long, with the risks you take. It's war, James, and...well, God knows when it's our time."

"Davy, why does He? Why does He let it happen?" In the dusk, James's voice was thin, tired, plaintive, but the failing light lent a privacy to the conversation and allowed him to succumb, for a moment, to weakness.

Llewellyn blew out a heavy gust of air. "Sometimes I reckon I left my studies too soon, before I got all those answers. But I figure what

I said to Peters is true—this mess is the doing of people. There are evil people, and someone's got to stand up to them, and God didn't promise to fight our battles for us. He didn't knock Goliath down with fire from heaven. He used David, who had the guts to stand up and do it. God helped him, sure, but—"

"But we don't just get to sit back and let him sort it out?"

"That's how I see it."

"But all those boys, Davy, and the families, and—"

Llewellyn's hand warmed his shoulder. "I know. I know. That's why I try to remember, our hope isn't *here.* And, well, I suppose with most of this, we might not see the reasons, or the good behind them, this side of heaven. But, after all Jesus has done for me, I'm taking it on faith."

James sighed and nodded. He stood, ready to be done with the serious talk. "Be that as it may, you don't go and get hurt, Davy."

There was a long silence. Finally, Davy gusted a soft laugh into the dark. "It's not in my hands. But," he conceded, "I'll do my level best. Murial'd never forgive me, otherwise."

3 February 1945

Pvt. Andrews

To say I am disappointed by the lack of news I have received from you is a gross understatement. When you agreed to enter my employment, you led me to believe that you had at least a modicum of intelligence and resourcefulness to call upon. I have seen neither. It appears that time is running out, and if you don't have the wits to produce any information worth paying for, you needn't expect to receive any more notice from me.

C.H.

JAMES'S STOMACH TURNED over and over, his shoulders tense, breathing tight. Tonight, on this patrol, he was afraid.

It's stupidity, sending us out after all of our losses lately. The new boys are so green, who knows how they'll cope—God, I can't lose more friends. I can't.

He moved to the front as they ventured into the claustrophobic dark. The starlight was faint, and the moon had not risen. The silence pressed down, unbroken by a bird call or a rustle in the rocks.

At a crunch of rubble to his right, he swung about, coiled to spring.

Breathe, James.

It was only Private Andrews, pale face gleaming in the dark as he nodded, that bland, stupid half smile of his still in place.

I thought his platoon was meant to be farther over... perhaps he's lost his way.

He'd meant to check up on Andrews after Egypt, to find out more about the man who was always there, but first the pneumonia and then the war had driven it out of his mind.

It was all foolishness, anyway. I've barely seen him in months.

He nodded to the other man and continued forward, placing his feet with care. Sound traveled easily across the river. Andrews's boots crunched against a stone, close behind him. An echoing sound came from ahead.

James froze.

What was that?

Andrews stood, still as a statue, almost at his elbow, breath coming low and quick.

Starting forward again, James's ears and eyes strained in the dark. He sniffed the air for tobacco—there was nothing.In his peripheral vision, Andrews shifted even closer.

James quickened his step, uncertain if the uneasy prickle at the back of his neck was generated by the sounds from ahead or behind.

It was *all foolishness*—

The silence shattered.

A mortar exploded just to the front.

Shots broke out from ahead and to the right, followed by small arms fire from the left.

Rifles answered from behind and feet scrambled, and men grunted and cursed as they flung themselves into cover.

Andrews pushed past, scrambling for a half-erect wall, silhouetted against the sky by the flashes from ahead.

James followed.

Gasping, he dug his feet into the soil as he nearly collided with the other man.

Andrews stood, frozen, rifle drooping from his fingers, staring at the bayonet that pierced his torso.

A tall form—crowned by a rounded shape, like the shell of a turtle—stood silhouetted before him.

The German pulled his bayonet free. He lunged for James.

James was faster.

He shouldered Andrews out of the way. A burning pain slid across his left hand. Something solid glanced against his arm as he swung his own bayonet home.

Heart racing, he regained his balance, head swinging left and right, searching for threats.

Sounds of the engagement were already dying away as Jerry disappeared back into the dark.

Andrews. He was still standing but only just, shoulder pressed to the ruin. His white hand clutched at the wound, dark rivulets running through his fingers.

Fumbling for something to stem the flow, James called for aid.

Andrews was still alive, though not conscious, when the stretcher bearers arrived.

ARTHUR ANDREWS DRIFTED. He half thought he was back in his uncle's shabby rooms, recovering from a blow.

When Uncle had come home drunk, railing at the world in general and reached for the leather shaving strop to vent his angst on the thin, silent boy, Arthur had nowhere to go except into his own mind. He'd made a safe haven there.

Silent, expressionless, two thoughts had warmed and sustained him. One: the old man would pay. Two: once he left these rooms, he would leave for good, and he would never, *never* be in want of money again.

Naw, I can't be back there. I got out years ago. Something tasted metallic on his tongue, but he ignored it, remembering.

The old man had paid, though not at his hand, throat cut in a drunken brawl in the alley behind the pub next door.

Arthur had sat, waiting for him until two days had passed. When a lady of his uncle's acquaintance had finally thought to check on the boy, he was already creeping down the dark hallway to the stairs. On hearing her footsteps, he lowered his head so that she would not recognize him and continued on.

He had no need of her. He knew the space under the loose floorboard where his uncle kept what monies he hadn't drunk away, as well as a fine silver christening cup and his dead aunt's wedding band.

Leaving had not been as liberating as he had hoped. His first goal had been met, but not as he wished. His second constantly eluded his grasp, and in desperation he had found himself scavenging in the underbelly of society, accruing debts, running errands for men like Smith. And then, Charles Heatherington…

Heatherington. The memories flooded back. It had been a simple job. Watch the sergeant. Find out his vices. Get evidence and send it back. In exchange, he'd been promised more money than he'd ever seen. Easy, and then he'd be independent, his own man at last.

How did it get so complicated? Bother that Milburn for being such a dull old dog. Couldn't find anything worth my time. Couldn't even trump something up in Egypt or with that woman in Naples…

Heatherington's letters spoke of his anger and impatience, and he'd seen it all slipping away, everything he'd hoped for, vanishing…

And then—the patrol. The patrol tonight—I could've done it tonight. Finished the job, if it hadn't been for—

The pain of the wound prodded him fully awake and his eyes flew open. He heard his voice cry out as if it were coming from far away.

Another voice answered, "…more morphine!"

"No," gasped Andrews, "I've got to—got to speak to him—the Sergeant. James Milburn!"

THE CASUALTIES WHO WERE to be sent farther behind the lines were being loaded up into whatever transports were available when James reached the aid station.

"You've not much time. He'll need surgery, but he was so insistent, and since I knew where you'd be—" the stretcher bearer, O'Malley, spoke quickly, trying to keep his red cross emblazoned helmet from slipping over his eyes. It looked like a Yankee helmet, but this was no time to ask where he'd gotten hold of it.

"Thanks. Though I don't know why he's so keen to see me—"

"Well, you did just save his life, so I hear. Some fellows get sentimental."

James wouldn't have thought that Andrews could have gone any paler, but his face was ghostly, eyes wide and staring as he fought the effects of the morphine. He tried to sit up, his frantic hands reaching for James to pull him in close.

"Steady on, lad." O'Malley tried to ease him back down, but he fought.

"Milburn!" He gasped James's surname like a prayer, clinging to his collar.

Putting his hands on the other man's shoulders, James bent down next to him. "I'm here, Andrews. Settle down now or you'll make it worse."

"I've got to tell you," the pale man panted. "I've got to *warn* you. I owe you now—I'll not die with another debt—" He gave a sharp, agonized cry, and his hands clenched.

One of the medical men nearby muttered something about surgery. Andrews frantically waved him away. "Not yet, not yet! Milburn. You've got to watch out for Charles Heatherington. He's not to be trusted."

What? Leaning in closer James searched the man's wild eyes. "What do you mean?" O'Malley checked the dressing from the other side, his face grim. "We've got to get him moving back—"

"No! Listen, Milburn." He pulled James even closer, breathing in his ear. "You've got to know. He hired me…to watch you. Sabotage you if I could."

"Why?"

"It's money, and this girl—this girl you'd been hanging around. He needed something to make her throw you over."

James stared. "What? That's…" The words stuck in his throat. *Well. I guess I wasn't being as stupid as I thought.* His fists clenched. *Of all the manipulative little—*

"There's more. When you had the pneumonia, he said he wouldn't mind having you out of the way permanently. But I didn't. I didn't…" the morphine was kicking in and the stretcher bearers were impatient. His hands grew weaker and he lay back down, muttering.

Contact broken, the stretcher bearers wasted no more time, whisking him away.

James stood watching them go, rooted to the spot.

What madness is this? Is Charles really this determined? But why? Money, he said—that doesn't make any sense. The money's going to Charles anyway. But Evie—I need to warn Evie! What if he tries something on her end?

But he's there.

If he's had someone spying on me, is he watching her? Is he reading her letters? Does he know about me meeting Phillips and what he told me?

If I try to warn her, will I be putting her in danger?

```
We regret to inform you—
```

CHARLES PERUSED THE LETTER and then closed it and locked it in his desk drawer with a sigh.

Andrews is dead. Well, that's the end of that.

Looking at the other missive he had received and at the list of figures on it, he considered with a grim smile. *At least he won't have to be paid.*

Outside, the sun was setting, throwing long, purple shadows across Stoneglenn's lawn. One shadow moved—Evie, walking home. Even at this distance, he could see the weary slump of her shoulders. If he hurried, he could meet her on the way and accompany her into the house.

If that avenue is closed, well, I'll just have to manage things myself.

Twenty Six

3 February 1945

Attn: Mr. H

We would like to congratulate you on your recent stroke of good luck. Your winnings will be more than sufficient to expunge your previous debts. You are again welcome at any of our sponsored events.

X. J. S.

Great Aunt Helena raised her glass, and Evie and Charles followed suit. The wine was a deep, rich red that she had kept squirreled away since well before the war. They drank in silence.

Today was Great Uncle Raymond's birthday. Great Aunt Helena always drank a toast to him on this night before retiring, more silent and morose than on any other evening during the year.

Shifting in her chair, Evie tried not to show how the heavy silence smothered her

Her first year present for the ceremony, just a young thing with little idea of what her life here would be like, she had tried to offer comfort. "Dear Great Aunt Helena, I miss him terribly, too. You know though, he is in heaven, with Jesus and the angels, and Father and Mother, too. I'm certain they wouldn't want us to be sad for them."

Her great aunt had given her one stony look and sent her up to bed. It only took that night to teach her to keep her peace.

When Molly came to take the old woman to bed, Charles followed, and Evie drew a deep breath and allowed herself to relax.

The children were in bed, and she wasn't ready to sleep, so she slipped off to the library. A number of books needed to be re-shelved.

Fishing several books out from sofa cushions, she shelved them and then turned back for the stack on the corner table. Her gaze traveled to the doorway.

Charles stood there, watching her.

She jumped—he'd been so silent, she hadn't noticed him arrive. "Oh! Charles."

Smiling, he walked over. "Always a grim night, eh, Evie? What are you up to now?"

"Just putting some books away. They've been piling up. I must speak to the children..." She turned to put the next few in place.

Charles chuckled and leaned up against the shelf just at her left hand, standing so near that she could smell his aftershave and the scent of his favorite cigarettes. She avoided his eyes, but she could feel them studying her face. Uncomfortable, she smiled at him and started to turn, but he stopped her with one hand on her upper left arm. Leaning his cane against the shelves, he took her right hand, stroking it lightly with his thumb.

"You know, Evie, you've changed. You've really improved these last years. No, I mean it. You were a pretty girl, always, but all this work you've been doing hasn't harmed you a bit. You're a beautiful woman now." He moved his hand off her arm and reached up to touch her cheek.

Warmth flooded her face, and she turned it away. "Thank you, Charles, but I don't—"

He kept his voice low but spoke with forceful urgency. "Evie, darling, lovely Evelyn, I know this is something we haven't spoken of in some time, but how can I hold myself back? Have I no chance of ever winning your heart? Things have been—well, I wondered if, just perhaps, you may have softened to me. Tell me, Evie, isn't it true? You must know how I feel about you." He tried to draw her closer, but she pulled back.

"Charles, please! You know that James and I—"

"You've made no promises—you admitted that yourself. You're under no obligation. You—"

Meeting his eyes, she said, "I love him, and I told him that I would wait. That ought to be enough."

He snapped his mouth closed and gave her a measuring look. More gently he said, "Of course. But what if he doesn't return?" She looked away, but he tugged on her hand, and she met his eyes again. "The war isn't over, and who knows what will happen? Or what if things are different between you when you meet again? War changes a man, and can you say it hasn't changed you, too?" He leaned closer, brown eyes warm and pleading. "Can you at least give me some hope?"

You have to tell him, Evie. You have *to just say it and make him understand. Oh, I hate to hurt him, but*—She took a deep breath, steadying her voice.

"No, Charles. I'm sorry. I will always care for you. You're the last link to my childhood, and I appreciate all the kindness you've shown me. But you and I wouldn't work. Not ever. I—I always hope to be your friend—" she stammered as he drew back, his eyes icy cold.

"I see. And our history together, or how hard I've tried these last years to be what you wanted—all of this means nothing?"

Closing her eyes, she shook her head. "Charles, of course that's not what I mean, but really, if we were at all suited to each other, don't you think it wouldn't have to be such hard work?"

His grip on her hand tightened, as did the line of his mouth.

"So, I'm simply deficient, then—"

"No, Charles—"

"While he is simply—"

"Stop it, Charles!"

He seized her upper arm again in a vice-like grip and leaned in close. Evie gasped and tried to pull back, hitting her elbow against the bookshelf. The alcohol smelled heavy on his hot breath as he said, low, "What if I won't take no for an answer?"

At the look in his eyes, her stomach clenched, and her palms began to sweat. Again, she tried to step away from him but had little room to move, blocked by shelves and the table.

Willing her voice calm, she said, "Charles, you're hurting my arm. Please stop and step back. I've made my decision, and I'd ask you to respect it."

Her heart pounded in her ears for one breath, then two, three.

Footsteps sounded on the floor above, and she glanced up at the ceiling, reminding herself that she wasn't alone, wondering if she should cry out—

Charles released her and stepped back. His face was stone, his eyes betrayed nothing. "Well, dear cousin. I hope you never have cause to regret that decision." The quiver of anger in his voice belied his words. Turning, he left, slamming the library door.

Evie dropped to the sofa, shaking. Abruptly, she stood back up and almost ran through the adjoining door into the music room and out the French doors.

Her breath crystalized ahead of her in the dark, but she welcomed the cold. It felt clean on her limbs and the shock of it distracted her from her mental turmoil. Hurried steps led her into the orchard. The trees stood, naked in the winter night. Leaning her forehead against one, her breath coming in sobbing gasps, she listened to her heart pounding against her ribs.

Oh James. I wish you were here. Charles frightened me tonight.

She tried to shake the thought away. Charles could be sly, impetuous, and hot-tempered, but he'd never been violent.

At least, he never had until tonight. She rubbed her arm—it would sport a bruise tomorrow. *But…he was just disappointed. And angry.* She shivered. *But he's still Charles. He'd never do me any real harm.* Her breathing slowed, and she repeated this assurance. Of course, Charles wouldn't do her any harm. How could he? He was family—her family.

Rubbing her arm again, she stared back at the hateful house, trembling with more than the cold. Stoneglenn had never felt like home, but it had never felt unsafe before.

CHARLES STORMED UP TO HIS ROOM.

Who's that girl think she is? Ungrateful tart, what will it take for her to see reason? After all I've done for her—if she weren't family, and if the old Auntie didn't keep holding that money over my head, I'd—

He slammed his door and pulled out his cufflinks, throwing them across the room. He hadn't been this angry since the night Roger came to his billet to confront him.

That anger had been cold as he folded his hands and pulled on a repentant face to hide the murder in his heart. This was hot—rage that burned.

Family or no, I'm through playing games.

15 February 1945

Dear Evie,

We're just getting situated back on the line after a bit of rest. Here's hoping that at last we've got Jerry's back against the wall.As my old dad always liked to say, keep that stiff upper lip. I am sorry to hear that things have been difficult with the family. The general feeling over here is that things will be over soon. We still have a big push left, and plenty of work to do convincing Jerry that he's beaten, but his time is running out. If God spares me, I'll be back with you soon, and if I have my way, you'll never feel unwanted or uncomfortable again—how about that? Maybe it's too big a promise, but if there is any way I can keep it for you, Evie, I'll do it.

Love,
James

"What do you think?" Moore's half-whisper carried over to where James was trying to sleep.

Peters snorted, and whispered back, "I think that it's the stupidest leaflet Jerry has sent over yet. Not even an interesting story—just more blathering about how the Yanks hog all the girls.' He paused, and paper rustled. "Hmm, nice looking dame, though. Maybe I can just tear off the other bits and keep her around."

"Don't you think about anything except girls?"

"What've you got that's so much better?"

There was a long pause. "So, how're you gonna tear it?"

James rolled over, trying to block out the sun and the conversation. Llewellyn spoke for him, calling over, "Gents, I'm glad you've come to a resolution. Now can you please shut up?"

There was another long moment of silence. Then Peters whispered loudly, "Be a good boy, Moorsey, Father's terribly cross."

Moore sniggered. Llewellyn growled.

James sighed and then spoke up. "One of you *is* keeping watch?"

He could almost hear Peters's nonchalant shrug. "New kid's on it. Aren't you, Ack Ack?"

Opening his eyes to slits, James watched to see how Peters fared. The "new kid," a former anti-aircraft gunner shuffled into the infantry because of the growing shortage of manpower, had arms that would've done a blacksmith proud.

Peters was safe. "Ack Ack" ignored all of them, keeping his post by the machine gun, eyes scanning for any activity. His given name was Grant, but Peters had dubbed him Ack Ack after the guns he had been trained to fire. "After all," Peters had reasoned to James, "what's the point of learning names for all of the replacements? They'll be gone after the next run-in with Jerry anyway."

The Germans were close—uncomfortably close—and had been continuously raiding over the River Senio in rafts or on bridges or in tunnels through the flood banks. While the Allies had returned the favor, the fact remained that survival here depended on two things: getting well dug in and staying awake. James hadn't slept in nearly forty-eight hours and was fading fast.

Hoping to keep the peace and get some rest, James called out to Ack Ack, "Good work, Grant. Peters and Moore will help, too. Keep a sharp eye out, don't let Jerry get the jump on us. And Peters, if you don't help out and don't let me get some sleep, you may just wish he had."

Peters feigned nonchalance as he took a more watchful position, tucking the German propaganda leaflet into his breast pocket.

James closed his eyes. Word had come down that the big push to and over the Po River was coming any day now. With luck, they'd push Hitler out of Italy entirely, and smash enough of his forces that they couldn't regroup in the Alps. Until then, it was just another wait, and it was time to pass some of the wait in blissful oblivion.

He shifted on the hard ground. Sleep was difficult to come by, even in his weariness. He worried over Evie and still hadn't reached a resolution on how to warn her about Charles's activities without potentially increasing her risk.

Is she safer just not knowing?

He woke to the *thunk* of— *What was that?* Peters was laughing, and cheering Moore on.

Opening his eyes, James stared. "Where did you get *that?*" The two men had a PIAT. They'd propped the anti-tank gun on the ground at a high angle and were just firing a second round.

Moore grinned. "Look! In place of a mortar! Let's send Jerry another one!"

The sun was nearly set, and deep shadows blanketed the land. James reckoned he'd had several hours sleep and felt more himself. He looked over to where Davy Llewellyn was just starting a brew up.

"Enough to go around?" James yawned.

"First cup's for you."

He nodded his thanks and, when the tea was ready, warmed his hands around the cup. "Any activity?"

Peters answered. "A few mortars. Ack Ack thinks he heard something a bit ago in the water. Moore and I decided to send over some deterrents. Encourage Jerry to keep his head down."

"What did you hear, Grant?"

The big man looked down from the wall. "Splashing. They haven't raided in this section for a few days now, have they?"

James nodded. "Get ready, just in case. Better safe—"

"—than skewered on a bayonet," Peters finished.

The shadows deepened, and full dark came. There was still no sign of German raiders. The hot food was delivered, and Lieutenant Bradlock brought the mail.

"New duties, sir?" James asked.

The lieutenant laughed. "Have to keep busy somehow." He sobered. "I'm stopping by all the positions. We're to be ready to move very soon. Things are going fast, and you know McCreery—when he says we're not to let Jerry have any rest, he means it!"

"Things are going well, then?"

"Looks like." Bradlock squatted down next to James and took a swig from his canteen. He leaned forward, speaking low. "I've been wondering, though. Have you thought anymore about what that bloke, Andrews, was saying?"

James glanced around, but no one seemed to be listening. Besides Bradlock, Davy was the only other person he'd related the incident to. He shrugged, scrubbing his hand through his hair. "I don't know. The thought of Charles hiring someone to make trouble for me all the way over here—he'd have to be off his rocker."

The lieutenant shrugged. "It's pretty far-fetched, I grant you. You've run into some funny business here, though. That set-up in Egypt, for instance."

"Alright, I'll give you that." James rolled his eyes heavenward, thinking. "But where'd he get the money to make something like that happen? It sounds like he'll be in for quite a bit when the old aunt passes, but now—"

"Waiting on an inheritance, hmmm? Seems like it'd make more sense for him to aim for the aunt if he's that sort, doesn't it?" Bradlock shrugged and sent a column of smoke towards the dim stars.

James laughed without humor. "Phillips told me a while back that he half-wondered if that was why the eldest brother met his end—"

"What?"

James filled him in, and he whistled. "Well. You didn't mention that before." He shook his head and took another drag. "I dunno, Milburn. You'd better watch your back. I can't help thinking the whole thing smells off. Have you written her about—" Bradlock froze. If he'd been a dog he would've sniffed the air. "Did you hear—?"

An explosion threw up mud and silt at the top of the embankment. Grant gave a groan as he collapsed.

Llewellyn cursed and scrambled up to man the machine gun, calling Moore to assist him.

A stick grenade came sailing over the side.

While James was still trying to get his legs to move, Bradlock caught the grenade and threw it to the rear. He flung himself forward in the same motion, taking James down with him.

James grunted as his jaw met earth, just as the blast reverberated in his ears. Something pierced his calf. Ignoring it, he heaved himself to his feet.

Peters was down—wounded or dead.

Llewellyn sprayed the land on the other side of the embankment with fire.

Shots echoed from the dugouts on either side.

James scrambled up beside Davy, rifle in hand. Bradlock followed, and they peered over the edge.

The enemy swarmed below. A shadow held another grenade aloft. Taking quick aim, James felled him. As the shadow dropped, his grenade exploded. Two other dark forms fell. Bradlock gave a whoop.

Llewellyn hollered for someone to help him reload, but there didn't seem to be a need. Within moments, the noise had faded. The still forms of the victim of his own grenade and one other unmoving shape remained. The others melted back into the night.

James heaved a deep breath and slithered back down the embankment.

He made his way over to Peters, who was struggling to sit up, face dark with blood. "I'm all right," he insisted, if a little unsteadily. "Just some shrapnel and a couple of cuts."

"Still, I want it looked at." James moved over to Grant, intending to take his pulse. There was no point.

Peters came up behind him. "See? Told you there was no need for names."

Coming gingerly down the embankment, Bradlock grunted, holding his arm.

"Are you hit?" James called.

"Just a scratch—your leg's bleeding."

He looked down absently and then took a closer look. "Shrapnel. Could've been worse. Thanks for the save."

"What about you, Father, Moore? Any blood?" Peters called out.

"Nothing here," Moore said, still keeping a careful watch from the top.

"No, not me." Llewellyn slid down and rummaged through the remaining ammunition stores.

"No, not me," Peters mimicked and shook his head as he dampened his handkerchief from his canteen and dabbed away the blood with a shaking hand. "Never you, is it? I should stick closer by you. If you don't make it out of this alive, then I'll know there's no God in heaven."

With a sharp cry that made them all jump, the redoubtable "Father" Davy Llewellyn spun about cursing, and cuffed Peters hard across the cheek. "Idiot!" he raged, face as red as his hair. "Don't you put that on me. Don't you dare put that on me."

James stared, open-mouthed. "Lance-Corporal," Bradlock began, finding his voice. Llewellyn threw his hands into the air, breathing hard.

"I'm sorry. I'm sorry sir but—If I die, Peters, I'll be singin' God's praises, right in front of him. If I live, God help me, he knows I want to see my wife and the little ones, but I—I'm not afraid to see him, and you believing or not—what difference does that make to whether he *is*? A lot of us are going to die out there yet—how can we face it if we don't have hope for after…" Shaking, he turned back to the ammunition.

Moore whistled low and busied himself with the machine gun. The others stood about until James broke the silence. "C'mon, Peters. Let's get to the aid station."

Staring at Llewellyn's back, Peters blinked, then nodded.

"WHAT DO YOU MEAN I still owe?" Charles heard himself shouting. He knew he ought not, but he couldn't stop. He gripped the crisp paper of his newest bill until his fist ached.

The big man opposite him shrugged, unruffled. "What, did you think all Andrews's pay went to him? There are handling fees, expenses—"

"Rubbish. The man was useless."

"He was a valuable asset, and he died working for you." Lighting his cigar, Smith inhaled the foul-smelling black smoke with relish. "This is your first warning. I'm sure you'll see reason when you take some time and think about it." He played with something in his pocket. "Just not too much time."

Lips pressed into a thin line, Charles nodded.

Smith took another drag. "Well. Now he's dead, have you thought any more about managing things closer to home?"

"I've tried. Thanks to Andrews's ineffectiveness, Milburn's still in the way."

Smith snorted. "Are you sure removing him would make a difference?"

"Absolutely."

The big man laughed. "I don't know, Heatherington. If the girl was willing, I don't think we'd be having this conversation. Since she's obviously not," he took another deep drag, "doesn't it make better sense to let soldier boy be and take care of the nearer threat?"

Charles moistened his lips. "No."

"It'd be simple to manage. Quick and painless even, if you like—"

"I said, no."

"Coward."

"I don't need to prove anything to the likes of you. I think I've shown I have nerve enough, but I'm no thug. And blood still means something."

"Want to know what I think?"

"Not partic—"

"I think it's your brother all over again. You just want to prove you're really the best—"

"STOP TALKING ABOUT ROGER!" Charles shouted, incensed, spittle flying from his mouth. He clenched his fists, forcing himself under control, struggling to return his breathing to normal. He spoke through his teeth. "He has nothing to do with this. I'll not be analyzed."

His companion stared at him, puffing on his cigar. "All right, then. What's next?"

Charles's anger melted away. He moistened his lips, avoiding the other man's eyes.

"What? No plan? You know you can't wait on this forever, unless of course you want to try your hand at the tables again, see if your luck's improved—"

"I have a plan. I'm just waiting for the right moment."

Pulling his shiny knife out of his pocket, Smith smoothed the edge of this thick, grimy thumbnail. "Fair enough. Just remember what I said. Don't wait too long."

The two of them left the carriage house in the dusk, Smith heading for the gate.

WATCHING THE FORM of the big man pass down the path, trailed by cigar smoke, Bonny's hand shook on the curtain.

Dear Jesus, it's him again. What does it mean? Is somebody else going to die? Please, I'm afraid...

14 April 1945

Dear James,

I had the most terrible dream last night. Please write back quickly and tell me you're all right.

Darling, I know you can't always write, and that you warned me things would be busy. I am terribly selfish. Every family has someone at risk, and I know that I don't have the worst wait of all. I see it in the children's eyes. Lilly and Leslie are still so small that they aren't as aware, but the older ones—especially Bonny—look so worn and tired with waiting. She's hardly talking at all these days, and her school work is slipping, and I don't know what I can do for her. Children shouldn't have concerns like these.

Yes, I know how selfish I am, but please, James, write back quickly. No matter what, know that I love you. No matter how long it takes, I'm waiting for you.

Yours always,
Evie

15 April 1945

Dear Evie,

Tomorrow is the day. Keep us in prayer, darling.
All my love, always, no matter what,

James

JAMES LEANED AGAINST the heap of stones, gasping for air and coughing on the dust kicked up as the machine gun pounded into the earth above him.

Llewellyn hit the dirt next to him with a grunt. That was two—where were the rest? Keeping his head down, James shifted his body, trying to get a better line of sight. The knots of men were scattered, crouched in what cover they could find.

The world was drowned in cacophony: blasts of grenades, pops of small arms fire and the ever-present rattle of the machine gun.

The machine gun. That's the real problem.

They had made it this far on bayonets and grenades and survived three counter attacks, but men were being cut down trying to get up to that monster. It had to be dealt with.

He checked his rifle and made sure he had a grenade easily to hand.

"Davy, I'm going up that little gully to try to get up to the machine gun nest. Stay here and give me some covering fire."

Llewellyn shook his head. "All due respect, sir, the rest of the lads are making enough ruckus without me. Two have more chance than one. I'll come along for the run."

"Insubordination?"

"Are you going to write me up for it?"

James ran his hand through his hair and scrubbed it across his face. With a sharp exhale, he nodded. "Maybe later. C'mon—when we get up there, you take it from our side, and I'll circle round and try to draw fire."

The "gully" was barely that, and the machine gunner had a fair view all along it, but it was the closest thing to cover available.

Speed or stealth? James compromised and ran, bent almost double.

Five yards to the dip, then down.

A moment later, Llewellyn joined him.

Off they ran again, attempting to make themselves into the smallest, fastest targets they could. The machine gunner hadn't zeroed in on them yet, but it was only a matter of time.

Twenty yards to go.

The blood pounded in James's ears.

The first of the bullets zipped past. He tried to run lower. Flame kissed his left bicep—a graze.

Llewellyn came up abreast of him. He sent a few blazing rounds from his Thompson the machine gunner's way. The fire paused.

Five yards to go.

Each breath burned James's lungs. His muscles screamed as he began the last steep climb. The Germans had built up the position to give it the high ground.

Grabbing the grenade, he reached for the pin.

"Look out!" Llewellyn slammed into his shoulder, knocking him to the ground.

The whole world exploded in a blaze of white light.

"James?"

He couldn't quite believe it. "Evie? What—"

"It's alright, darling." His head was resting on her lap, and she was gently smoothing the hair off his brow. It was lovely. He struggled to open his eyes to see her, but he couldn't quite manage it. She shook his shoulder.

"James, you need to wake up."

"Evie, can't I just stay—"

"Not yet, darling. Quickly! Get up!"

The shaking no longer felt like her gentle fingers and more like the earth was shaking and groaning as explosions ripped the air.

James's eyes snapped open.

His eyelashes tore as the lids peeled apart. The metallic stench of blood choked his nostrils, and his face felt sticky and stiff.

He lay on his back, head downhill, looking up at the blazing machine gun.

Moving inch by inch, he eased himself into a better position.

The gunner and his support didn't glance his way. Apparently, they thought him dead.

Not yet, anyway.

He put his right hand down, and there was the grenade he'd been holding, miraculously intact. Pulling the pin, he counted, rising to a low crouch.

Wait, wait, ready, and NOW!

He lobbed the grenade up in a high arch, and it landed neatly just to the rear of the gun. There must have been some extra ammunition back there. The explosions were impressive, jarring his head back against the rocks. Something struck his left arm.

He heaved himself to his feet. Up came Peters and Moore, running for all they were worth.

"Well done, sir, on we go! Look, they're retreating up ahead already—c'mon, Peters!" Moore cheered, enthusiastic, ready to go on the hunt.

Peters stood stock still a few feet away, staring at something on the ground—a huddled, bloody form.

"Oh, please God, please no..." James whispered. He scrambled over.

Davy Llewellyn lay still, lifeless eyes staring, body ravaged by the explosion that had nearly done for them both.

"Davy—" The world rocked beneath him, foundations shaken, and he fell to his knees.

Davy can't be dead. Not him. He could've died so many times, but he was never going to, not really—God, why couldn't you let him make it home?

No, It's my fault. I let him come. He saved me—

A hand gripped James's shoulder, hard, keeping the world from crumbling to bits. He turned.

Lieutenant Bradlock stood there looking at Davy—what had been

Davy—face grim and set. Then, he looked away, back at the other men.

His orders seemed to echo in James's ears from a great distance away. "The enemy is in retreat. Let's take it back to 'em, boys."

Moore nodded soberly, checked his rifle and started forward, followed by the others.

Leaning down, Bradlock simply asked, "Milburn?"

James squeezed his eyes shut, pushing the pain down. It compressed into a hard knot, deep inside—not gone, but strong and hot enough to push him forward. "I'm coming. Peters?"

Peters didn't move. "I didn't think—how could it be him—"

James barked, voice harsh, fueled by the pain. "You have your orders, Private! Let's finish this."

He tried to push himself to standing and flinched and nearly fell. Only then did he notice the bleeding mess that had been his left hand.

"BONNY? Won't you take me to see the kittens?"

"What, Leslie?" Bonny was deep in her book as the pirates were just about to catch Jim Hawkins. Not to be deterred, Leslie inserted her face between Bonny and the pages.

"The new kittens, Bonny. I want to see the new kittens. Lilly does, too, don't you, Lilly?"

Bonny pushed her aside. "The kittens are in the carriage house, you aren't allowed alone, and it's nearly tea time."

Leslie's voice took on a wheedling whine. "But you could take us down there. You used to go down there all the time, until you saw the ghost."

Bonny's eyes snapped up. Over one curved arm of her chair she could see Mr. Heatherington's back as he sat at the writing desk near the window. *Is he listening?* "Don't talk nonsense, Leslie. There's no ghost."

"Tommy said you saw one with the last batch of kittens. You came back from bringing them milk and you were all white and frightened looking and then you wouldn't go in the carriage house alone anymore, even though you used to sneak in all the time."

She couldn't look away from Mr. Heatherington's back. *I wish I could see his face. Oh, Leslie, shut up, SHUT UP!* "Tommy was just trying to scare you. Miss Worther told us not to go in there alone, didn't she?"

"Well, yes—"

"Because it's old and there are dangerous tools and broken bits and things, right?"

"Yes—but you still used to. I remember, and I kept your old milk bottle."

"Well, Miss Worther caught me. And so, I stopped. And I wouldn't have gone down this late, anyway. The days are still so short, and I wouldn't like to go down there in the dark." *Please, let it go, Leslie, please!*

The little girl looked unconvinced and started to open her mouth again.

Mr. Heatherington broke in. He stood, folding his papers and then looked over into Bonny's eyes as he spoke. "That's wise of you. You should, of course, always listen to the adults charged with keeping you safe. It's the best way to avoid any number of unpleasant things."

Leslie stared at him, sucked on her teeth a moment, and then darted away. Bonny did her best to meet his gaze.

Don't look away. Don't look guilty. Don't let him know you're afraid.

Mr. Heatherington smiled at her. He put both hands on the head of his cane and leaned forward, confidentially, affecting friendly curiosity. "Of course, we used to pretend that old carriage house was haunted, too. Tell me, did you ever see anything to frighten you down there?"

She moistened her lips and shook her head. "Just a couple of rats."

Speaking low, he leaned in a little further. "We used to play that there was a ghost of a fat man, a giant of a fat man, smoking a glowing cigar down in that old carriage house. He didn't visit you, did he?"

Can't catch me that easily. She screwed her face into a look of wide-eyed confusion.

"No, Mr. Heatherington. Never anything like that. Ed tried to scare me about a woman in white once, but it was just the laundry that had been hung out to dry." She shivered theatrically.

He watched her for a moment more and then nodded. "Very well. Run along to tea now. I hear Cook calling."

Bonny put down her book and did as he said. She may have imagined it, but she thought she could feel his eyes boring into her back until she was out of sight.

30 April 1945

Dear James,

I'm in a hurry tonight; Charles and I are going in to Farthington to the cinema.

EVIE PAUSED TO CHECK the time. She had a few minutes left.

The invitation to the cinema had come as a surprise. Out of the blue, Charles had approached her yesterday. He had apologized for how he'd behaved the night of the proposal and how he had avoided her since, adding, "And, well, it's been difficult not to be jealous, feeling about you as I do—but that's best left unsaid. I think it's wonderful how true you've been to him, and I'm sorry for being so childish." Then he'd asked her to go and see a show with him, like in the old days.

She had hesitated. The bruise on her arm was long faded, but the memory of his expression—of his anger—had lingered. Still, it would be good to be at peace with him.

Testing the waters, she'd asked, "Charles, are you sure you can get away? You've been working so hard, even on the weekends."

"As hard as I've been working, I think I deserve a holiday, and I doubt anyone will object."

"Well..." Then she had remembered something and relaxed. "All right. Mary and Sophie will be so pleased to see you, too. They're both in town for the weekend—I'll let them know to meet us."

She had thought a flash of annoyance crossed his face, but it passed so quickly that she couldn't be sure.

Glancing at her little clock, she put her pen down. As she hurried through her door, pulling on her wrap, she nearly collided with Bonny, who stood just outside.

"Oh! Be careful, Bonny!" She paused. The girl was tugging her plait and biting her lip. "What is it?"

"Miss Worther—" the girl began. "Could I talk—"

Charles voice called from the foot of the stairs. "Evie? Are you ready? I've brought the car around—"

The girl stiffened, her lips snapping shut.

"Just a moment, Charles!" Evie called. "Of course, Bonny, but can it wait? Or can Molly help you? Mr. Heatherington and I are supposed to be going out—"

With a quick nod, Bonny turned and vanished in the direction of her room.

Evie watched her go, frowning. *Oh dear. Maybe I should have waited.* "Evie?" Charles's voice had an impatient edge. With a sigh, Evie hurried down the stairs, resolved to find the girl later.

Charles drowned any concerns she had with his eagerness to talk as they drove. She tried to listen and told herself to stop wondering just where he'd gotten the petrol to run his car.

Things are just settling down between us. Don't borrow trouble, Evie!

If he noticed her distraction, he didn't show it. "I tell you, Evie, things are looking up." He slapped the steering wheel for emphasis. "Naturally, there will be struggles as we establish peace, but you just watch. I'm going to do very well. I've got the instincts for it. It's all about knowing when you've found the right time to move, when to buy, where to sell, and who's willing to make a good deal."

That caught her attention. "I didn't realize the Ministry of Food was involved with much buying or selling."

"Ah. Well." He tapped his fingers energetically on the wheel. "My duties take on many forms, but you wouldn't be interested in all that."

Wouldn't I? Ugh—stop! You promised yourself you'd leave it alone!

Mary and Sophia met them at the cinema, each with an American G.I. on her arm. Sophia looked particularly pleased about this as she greeted Charles.

Charles was cordial, but Evie could almost see the old complaint about the Americans running through his mind, "Over-paid, over-sexed, and over *here.*" He had warm smiles for the girls, however, and behaved himself, even engaging in a few minutes of small talk.

They found seats, but Charles couldn't seem to relax. He kept drumming his fingers on his knees and fidgeting. Even after the film started, he couldn't keep his eyes on the screen, turning his head to study the different faces in the cinema.

About halfway through the first show, he squeezed her hand, leaned over, and said in her ear, "Need to stretch my legs. I'll be back."

Evie rather wished he hadn't gone. The film, *The Uninvited*, was eerie enough that she would have liked James's arm to hang on to. Sophia was taking full advantage of it, looking like she was going to climb into her G.I.'s lap at every creak of the haunted house.

When the lights came back up, the seat next to Evie was still empty. She bade goodbye to the others and set off through the dissipating crowd to find Charles. The dark made her nervous as she moved further and further away from the comfort of other people. She had nearly walked past the narrow alley between the bookshop and the grocer before she heard his voice, cutting through the night.

"I told you. I can't get any more just now, but with this new job and what she was willing to loan me—how can you still expect more?"

He sounded angry. Some wooden pallets were blocking her view, stacked next to a bin that stank of decomposing vegetables, and she hesitated at the alley's entrance.

A deep, rough voice answered Charles's deliberate, cultured tones. "You hired my boy, and he did his best, God rest him. Now it's time for you to pay the piper."

Shifting her stance to peer around the pallets, she could just see Charles's face in the dim light, and the broad back of the man to whom he spoke.

"Yes. I hired the man to do a job. I will not pay as it's not finished."

There was a pause, then the deep voice answered, cold as ice. "Careful, Heatherington, you don't want to jeopardize our partnership. After all—"

Just then, Charles glanced at the alley's mouth and caught sight of Evie. He coughed, and the other man turned around. He was a bulky sort of man, whose dark suit's buttons strained to hold all of him in. Standing almost a head taller than Charles, his small, dark eyes and jowls resembled a bulldog. A black cigar dangled from his thick fingers.

Evie tried not to squirm as his eyes slowly raked her up and down.

Charles stepped around him. "Ah, Evie. Show over? This is a business associate of mine, Mr. Smith."

She swallowed and tried—and failed—to smile. "How do you do?"

Mr. Smith nodded with a smirk. He turned back to Charles.

In a low voice she could only just catch, he growled, "Remember what I said." He turned back to spare Evie a nod. "Miss." He strode past her into the growing night.

Silently, Charles took Evie's arm, and they walked back to the car. His lips were pressed thin in his pale face.

"Charles, is everything all right?"

"Oh, yes." He forced a laugh. "It's a frightful bother and a frustration when a business deal you thought wrapped up leaves…loose ends."

Again, he was silent. It was a silence she would have welcomed at other times. Tonight, it felt ominous and squelched the urge to ask him further questions.

Charles seemed to be in a hurry to put distance between himself and that alleyway. Evie's fingers tightened on the edges of the car's seat as he sped over the dark roads. The ruts made her teeth rattle.

When a particularly large bump jarred them both, he glanced over to apologize and eased off the speed. He draped his arm over her shoulders, giving her a quick squeeze. With a wooden laugh, he said, "Couldn't have you falling out, could we?"

She looked over at him, but he was watching the road. A shiver crept down her spine, but she forced herself to laugh, too.

Relieved to reach Stoneglenn, she hurried up the stairs and nearly collided with Molly, who was waiting at the door.

"Sorry, miss." Molly bit her lip and pulled a bit of paper from her apron pocket. "They brought this over just after you left." She held out the telegram.

"Oh." The world slowed, nearly stopped, and Charles and all of his concerns evaporated as Evie reached out to take it with icy, trembling fingers. "Thank you, Molly."

Twenty Eight

30 April 1945

Dear James,

Oh, darling, I'm so sorry to hear that you've been wounded—but will you forgive me if I say I'm thanking God, as well? When I saw that telegram tonight I was so afraid that it was the worst.

I wish I could come to you, or that, somehow, we could get you here—do you need anything? What can I do? Please, if you can, write soon.

Sending all my love and prayers,
Evie

James ignored the muted sounds of celebration coming from outside the hospital. Fidgeting with the pen in his hand, he scoured his brain for the next words he ought to write.

2 May 1945

Dear Mrs. Llewellyn,

I am very sorry to have to inform you

James threw down the pen. He raised his left hand to rake across his hair in his habitual gesture—the pain reminded him of the truth.

The surgeons had been able to save his fingers, except for the tip of the index one, which was missing down to the first knuckle. They were waiting until the bandages came off to find out if they'd all still work properly. *And if they don't, how am I going to manage the work around the farm?* He grimaced and pushed the thought to the back of his mind. *At least I've got my right hand and can write letters properly this time. Not that it's doing much good.*

This was his fourth attempt at fulfilling the promise he'd made to Davy back at Cassino. Each letter was wrong—too familiar for a woman he'd never met or too stiff for the wife of his dead friend—or this one, just too cold.

He didn't have the words. He didn't know how to convey in writing what this had meant to him. To lose Davy, their rock—here, at the very bitter end.

Today, May 2, the fighting in Italy was officially over.

It was just a few days too late for Davy.

James lowered his head to the crook of his arm. *Dear Father in heaven, why now? Why* him*? He did nothing but serve you and tried to get us all to do better. Now his wife—their children—three children who will hardly know the man their father was…*

The sobs ambushed him, shaking his shoulders, breaking all his resolve. He'd not cried at the service, hadn't taken the chaplain up on his offer of a visit, had kept the pain quiet until he'd nearly thought he could live around it.

Now, writing Davy's widow, something inside James broke. He wept like a child.

Do I tell her it was my fault? If I hadn't let him come, if I had just ordered him to stay back—if he hadn't saved me. So many, Lord, so many lives lost, and shattered—please, how can it be right again?

"Sir?"

James's head snapped up, blinking. Peters stood at his elbow, shuffling his feet.

Clenching his fist and dashing the back of it across his eyes, James regained control. After a few deep breaths, he answered.

"Yes, Peters. Hullo."

"I was just stopping by to see—well. You've heard the news, sir? Fighting's over. Here at least—"

James forced a smile. "Yes. Good news." He held up his bandaged hand. "Wouldn't want you all getting into trouble with me useless in here." *Not that me being there helped Davy any.*

Peters gave him a weak grin. "Couldn't have that, could we?" He nodded toward the wound. "How is it?"

Shrugging, James said, "Could be worse." *Though I can't do a thing with it yet. Useless. Just like me—*

Peters nodded. He looked down and cleared his throat. "Well. Look, I wondered—are you going to send a letter to Father—I mean Lance-Corporal Llewellyn's—wife? Only, I remember you said you would, if—"

James laughed, sharp and bitter.

"Yes. I'm trying to write it now. I don't quite know what to say, nor how to say it."

After an awkward pause, Peters nodded again. "You and he were good mates. I reckon she'll be glad to hear from you, whatever you say."

Too wrung out and weary to care if Peters were the right man to ask, James said, "What if I tell her the truth—that it was my fault he was up there?"

"Your fault?" Peters snorted. "All due respect, but don't you think you're giving yourself a bit too much credit?"

Of all the responses Peters could have given, this one took James by surprise. "What—?"

"Well, this war wasn't exactly your idea, was it?"

"Of course not, but running up that hill was. I told him to stay back, but—"

Peters was shaking his head, and said, "But nothing. I knew him, too, you know. If you were set on running up that hill to save the day, you'd have had to tie Father up to get him to stay behind. More fool him, I say, but there it is." He shrugged.

James turned the idea over in his mind, then shook his head. "I—I could've ordered him."

"Then you'd be dead. The rest of us, too, most likely." Peters shuffled his feet, cleared his throat again, and continued in a low voice. "Look, I know I'm not the one to say this, but don't you think you might be asking the wrong question? How would *he* have wanted you to take this?"

James sat for a moment in silence, staring at his wounded hand. "He—Davy would've said I ought to trust God's will. That there was a reason, even if I can't see it."

Peters nodded. "Sounds just like Father. If he was here, you'd be getting an earful for all this fuss."

Recalling Davy's lectures, and the way his hands swept the air when he was confronting anything he considered foolishness, half a smile crept across James's face. "Probably. And—thanks."

Peters hitched up one shoulder in a shrug. "But about the letter?"

"Yes?"

"I wondered—I wrote a bit of a note, and I wondered if I could send it along with yours." He held out the neatly folded missive. "You can read it first if you want. Make sure it's all right."

As he walked away, James unfolded the letter.

Ma'am, I wanted to write to you about your husband. I'm sorry for your loss, and that your children won't get to know him. He was a good man, brave, and never shirked. He reminded me of my Da, always trying to keep us good boys doing what we ought to and pointing us back to the right way when we'd let him. Before he'd sleep each night, if he were in a dry place, he'd take out the picture of you and the kids and put it next to him, right up where he could see it first thing. I thought you'd like to know. I gave him a hard time, but I always considered him a friend and would be honored if he thought the same of me.

Wishing you all the best,
Harold Peters

Refolding the letter, James set it aside carefully. He set his unfinished letter to Muriel Llewellyn on top of it.

Soon. I'll finish it soon. First, though—

He pulled out a clean sheet.

Dear Evie,

Thanks for your letter. I'm fine, really, though I'll likely have a few new scars—sorry you're getting such a banged-up fellow for all of this waiting. At least it's my left hand this time, so I can write.

I'm sorry to tell you I've lost a good friend—Davy Llewellyn. It's been a blow. I'd promised to write his wife, but I haven't yet found the words, especially as his last act saved my life. I wish you could've met Davy. He was a man of great faith, and you would've liked him. I don't know why God took him, so close to the end as we've come, but he would've wanted me to trust—it's a hard thing, Evie.

I've never said much about it, but thank you for the passages of Scripture you've sent in your letters. They've been a great comfort and an anchor in all of this I couldn't have done without. Sometimes I've felt like I have seen too much for there to be any answer to it, though I always prayed pretty fervently when dug in and the shells started coming down. I still don't have the answers, but I am living for the day I can be with you again, and we can try to make sense of this life together.

Now that the fighting's over in Italy and I'm useless with this hand, perhaps it will be sooner rather than later? The doctors are still saying the same as I wrote you in my last—that I'm to be sent home for good. I can hardly believe that it's so.

Until then, I'm always
Your James

2 May 1945

Attn: Mr. H

We regret to inform you that, due to outstanding debts and recent losses, we will no longer be able to honor any ongoing business arrangements. If these matters are resolved, we will be willing to enter discussions.

X. J. S.

"EVIE?" Charles peered around the library door. Evie sat at the writing desk, her head bowed, shoulders shaking. "Oh, Evie." He hurried over to her, putting a hand on her shoulder. "I—I'm sorry, are you alright?" *Don't suppose Milburn's finally kicked off? That would be something…*

Dashing her hands across her face, she sat up, beaming through the tears. "Oh, it's all right, Charles. I…I think everything is going to be alright now. Have you heard? They've declared the fighting in

Italy over...and..." She held up a letter, then put it down to take the handkerchief Charles offered.

He leaned against the writing desk next to her and glanced down at the letter.

"You've heard from him? What's the word?"

"He's healing. The doctors have said—they've decided that he's to be sent home, Charles. Permanently."

"Wonderful." The smile stretched painfully across his face. "I suppose you and he—?"

She blushed. "Yes. We're planning to meet when he gets in and then take the train to meet his family."

"Well, then. I'm happy for your happiness." He leaned down to kiss her cheek. "Is there any word on when?"

"Not yet—maybe a few months? It seems like everything moves so slowly!"

A few months. Not much time, then, but enough. I'll just have to speed things up—unless I can get some assurance from Auntie dearest. "Yes, it must. But at least you've got some idea of an end in sight. I'm happy for you for that, Evie."

She stood and hugged him. "Thank you, Charles. I just—I can't believe it's finally happening. I've got to see Great Aunt Helena—"

"I'll come with you. I've got some things to discuss with her, myself."

The two of them found their great aunt sitting in the music room, as the oldest girl—Bonny—attempted to play one of the songs Evie had taught her.

Squelching his impatience, Charles gritted his teeth and fixed a smile on his face until the last hesitant note was played. He clapped with the others. As Evie hurried to the old woman's side, letter in hand, he strolled toward the window to wait his turn. *She's got to agree to a loan this time. She's got to—and she's got to stop playing games. After all, I'm Uncle Raymond's heir. It only makes sense for her to follow through and—*

His thoughts were interrupted as he passed the piano and glanced over at Bonny. The girl immediately dropped her eyes and hurried around him.

Worry settled into the pit of his stomach. *That girl. Sneaky thing. Didn't seem to know anything, but if she really did used to sneak into the carriage house...* He thought about the night he met with Smith—the night he agreed to kill for the second time—and about the moment when he'd suspected that someone was listening. *But, it was just the cats—*

His eyes followed Bonny as she left the room. He glanced back to his Great Aunt, who was nodding to Evie's hurried, joyful speech, but was watching him with an unreadable expression.

Twenty Nine

HELENA HEATHERINGTON LEANED her head back in her chair, eyes half closed, watching Evie read stories with the children before bed.

Her Evie. It was difficult to remember that Evie was no longer a child herself. Sometimes she still saw her the way she'd looked on her first night here to stay.

The child's eyes had looked too big for her wan, thin face as she sat, silently moving the food about on her plate. She had always been small for her age. Lost in the massive dining room chair, she had looked less than her fourteen years, hardly any different than she had two years previous, at the last family gathering before Raymond's death. This did not help put her great aunt at ease.

She and Raymond had never been able to have children, a loss which she had only mourned for his sake. Children made her uncomfortable.

Still, she had felt it her duty to issue the invitation to her great-niece. After all, who else was left? And even if she didn't quite know what to do with the girl, she certainly had the means to provide for her.

She had tried, that first night. She had cleared her throat and tried to sound friendly. Even she had been able to tell her voice came out stiff and formal. "Well, child. This is your home now, and I wish for you to be comfortable and to feel safe."

Safe. At the word, the child had looked up. "Thank you, Great Aunt Helena. Where is your shelter?"

"I haven't got one. Our location is not likely to be of much interest to invaders. The house is old and strong, and if I'm to die, it will be in the comfort of my own bed—not half-buried in the garden."

The child's eyes had grown even wider at this pronouncement. Helena had wondered just how many air raids the child had lived through and shivered. For the first time, a protective spark lit in her aging heart.

One of the girls—Lilly—laughed, bringing Helena back into the present.

She sighed as she considered.

I ought to have done this sooner, but I'd hoped things could just stay in the family. If only Charles had been what he ought to have been. If only Roger had lived. Now—now, I've got to know. *I feel I haven't much time left, and I've got to make things right. She's got to be taken care of.*

She opened her eyes completely.

"Child?" Bonny, Edward, Leslie and Lilly all looked over. Tommy and Johnny were too busy trying to look as if they weren't shoving each other to notice the call.

The old woman gestured to Bonny, who walked over and sat in the seat she indicated. The others trooped out with Evie to ready themselves for bed.

Bonny tugged at her plait. Helena suppressed a smile. She could almost see the child's mind whirring, wondering just what infraction she was being called over for.

"Child, I have noticed that you don't much like my nephew, Mr. Heatherington. I would like to know why." The question was asked in clipped tones—a command, not a request.

Bonny avoided her eyes, examining the room's corners. "Ma'am, I don't—"

"Don't pretend to be stupid. Unless I miss my guess, you are by far the cleverest of this brood we have running about. If you dislike Mr. Heatherington, I imagine it is for a good reason. You will only offend me if you withhold the truth." Helena folded her hands and stared at her.

The child took a deep breath, obviously choosing a safe answer. "Mr. Heatherington doesn't like children much."

The old woman snorted. "Neither do I, but you don't avoid me in the same way you avoid him. Why?"

"I don't avoid—"

Helena stopped her with a wave of her hand. "No lies, please. I am beginning to doubt my belief in your cleverness. I am an old woman, I am unwell, and I want to leave my house in order. I have my own reasons for wondering about my nephew. If you have a reason, please, speak it."

Bonny hesitated. The words trembled on the edges of her lips, but her eyes—her eyes were dark, frightened. "You won't tell him I told you?"

"Naturally not."

The girl sighed, thin shoulders drooping. "I used to take milk to the kittens in the carriage house. One night, Mr. Heatherington came in with another man..."

"Evie?" Great Aunt Helena called her from the hall.

"Coming!" Evie hurried out of the library to where the old woman sat, waiting in her chair. Her great aunt's face was thin and tired. She felt a pang of worry.

The old woman's voice had lost none of its authority, however. "I wondered if you could do something for me."

"Of course. What do you need?" At her great aunt's signal, she took hold of the handles of the wheelchair and guided it towards the dining room.

"Evie, what would you say to a short trip?" The words left the old woman's lips grudgingly.

"A trip? What do you mean? Of course, if there's something you need me to do—"

"I have some papers I would like delivered to my solicitor's office in Leeds and no one else to take them. I thought you might enjoy the task and a change of scenery."

"But—doesn't Charles usually—"

Her great aunt glanced over her shoulder through narrowed eyes. "Don't you think you can manage?"

Evie blinked. "Of course I can. I just wondered—"

"Also, I've been in contact with Mrs. Connors. As she and her sister have stable lodgings and as it appears that things are winding down, you will be taking her children along so that they can return home."

"Oh." Evie sank into one of the dining room chairs. "So soon?"

Great Aunt Helena raised an eyebrow. "Won't it be a relief to have four fewer running about the house?"

Moistening her lips, Evie nodded. "I suppose—if she feels it's safe, it will be good for the children to return home. Wouldn't it be better if I took them all the way down to London? You can't want them to go alone—Ed and Bonny are responsible but—"

"No, no. In spite of all of the damage they've done to my crockery, not to mention my gardens, I would still like the children to return home safely." Her lips pursed after the last word, and she paused. "Their mother will meet you in Leeds, and I will send money for all of their tickets back home.

"And Lilly and Leslie?"

"Their mother is still sorting things out—it sounds as if there may be some word on their father. They'll stay on for the time being."

Evie swallowed and nodded, the pain of another separation numbing her limbs. She'd known it was coming but—

The old woman cocked her head. "You are going to be able to manage it, aren't you?"

Shaking herself, Evie nodded. "Yes. I will have to speak to Matron.

Things aren't too hectic. Five of the patients have just been discharged."

"Good. You'll be careful, of course."

Evie reached across the table and, squeezing her great aunt's hand with its tissue-paper thin skin, she smiled. "I'll be fine."

Her great aunt hesitated for just a moment and then gave a brisk nod. "And Evie? I'd like you to keep this trip—the visit to the solicitor, I mean—just between us."

Evie blinked in surprise. "Oh. Of course, I can do that." She bit her lip. "Great Aunt Helena, please, tell me. Is this to do with Charles?"

The old woman stared at her, measuring. She looked away, and Evie felt certain that she'd been found wanting. "Don't worry yourself, child. This matter is better kept private until I decide what must be done."

Evie couldn't suppress a small, impatient noise. "But—"

The old woman sighed and massaged her temple. "I know I haven't always been what you've needed, but I've done what I thought best for you. In this, I'd just ask you to trust me."

Evie's nails bit into her palm. "But, Great Aunt Helena, if you need me—or if there's anything I need to know—you will trust me, too?"

"Yes, of course." The old brisk tone returned to her great aunt's voice. "Don't fret, child. Everything is going to be fine."

Evie smiled through tight lips. The smile faded as Molly came and pushed the wheelchair out of the room, and she stalked back to the writing desk. *She knows something. Oh, why won't she trust me for anything more than nannying…*

Her throat closed suddenly as she thought of saying goodbye to Ed, Bonny, Tommy and Johnny. Hastily digging through her pockets for a handkerchief, she tried to tell herself that it was for the best. *Bonny especially has looked so unhappy. They'll be home, and they'll be safe.*

A sob slipped out, and she bit her lip. *And oh, how I'll miss them…*

8 May 1945

Dearest Darling James,

Father Carter is ringing the bells, and even in our little hamlet everyone is out of doors talking about it and celebrating, and the farmers have driven in to celebrate, as well. Happy Victory in Europe day!

I can't believe that after everything, one phase is finally over.

Surely Japan will surrender soon, and then we can finally get everyone home! Oh, James, I can hardly believe it's true—after almost six years of war, it's become such a part of life that the thought of it finally being over is almost unreal. Will the children even remember what peace is like? Lilly and Leslie just keep asking questions—most of which I can't answer!

The other four are safely home. The house seems so empty, James, and though they nearly drove me mad some days, I miss them terribly—with you coming home soon, it's the only blot on today.

I'm being called away. Mr. Churchill's speech is on the wireless.

All of my love
Evie

CHARLES LEANED HIS HEAD into the kitchen. "Mrs. Fisk?"

Cook looked up, startled by her proper name. "Yes, Mr. Heatherington? Isn't the news wonderful—"

"Have you seen Miss Worther anywhere?"

"No, I think she may have taken the children into town for a walk. She said they needed to get out, with all of the excitement over VE day, especially now the weather's improved. I thought it was a good idea, as well. They've the fidgets something awful. That Leslie almost knocked over my flour this morning, and you know how it is trying to replace food." She shook her head. "No good at all. And how are—"

"Yes, yes, thank you. My great aunt was looking for her and it doesn't seem that she can wait."

"Ah, she's in that mood again. Always in a hurry these days. Not sure what she's in a hurry to get to, mind you, she just wants it all done and done now. When she sent down for tea the other day and I took a moment to make sure there was enough of everything, she nearly had a fit, Molly says. I suppose it was because she had company, but still, at her age she oughtn't—"

"Company?" Charles's voice was sharp. "What company?"

Cook's eyes widened. "Just a gentleman—well, not a *gentleman,* you understand—but a man in a rather shabby coat and a hat. He came, and they talked in her room, not even Molly was there, and took tea and that was that."

Charles contorted his face into a jovial expression and Cook relaxed somewhat as he strolled over and patted her floury hand. "Go on, you must have some idea what it was all about? I don't think anything gets past you and Molly, does it now?" *Stupid, fat, old bird. Is she blushing?*

"Ah, Mr. Charles, we know a few things that go on, but not all. I can tell you, he's likely to come again from what he said as he left, and he carried a bag, the kind men keep papers in. I figure he's from London by his accent, and just carries his things with him in case of an air raid while he's away."

Charles kept his smile in place with an effort. "Yes, I imagine you're right. But why would she be meeting with someone from London?"

"I think she said once that Mr. Heatherington—the late Mr. Heatherington I mean—had some property or somesuch down there. Perhaps it's been damaged in the bombings, and she's being kept informed."

Daft old woman, why would she keep that private? It's not her will, or she would have solicitors in. That Bonny—I wondered—but she's gone now, so that's unlikely. It's not about Evie, or she would've told me. She's hardly telling me anything, anymore. "Well, that's all very interesting, I'm sure. I'd better go and find Evie."

Outside, he continued his train of thought. *If it's not her property, and it's not Evie—has she got someone nosing about after me?*

His blood ran cold. *And if she has, and if he finds anything, what will she do?*

20 May 1945

Attn: Messrs. X. J. S.

I have received your many notices. I must remind you of our many fruitful years of working together and beg you for more time. At the very least, give me a month. If interest is needed I will be perfectly willing to provide it. As to the hasty course of action recommended by Mr. S, I can only stress that it would be foolish in the extreme, and unlikely to end up benefitting any of us. You know that I am good for the money, given the time. Please consider the advantages of patience.

Respectfully,
C.H.

3 June 1945

Dear Evie,

I'm sorry to hear that your great aunt's health has been declining. She's fortunate to have a seasoned nurse like you about, but seriously, Evie, she and you will be in my prayers.

I've had good news. The doctor's been so pleased with my progress that, by the time you get this, I might be sailing your way. The timing couldn't be better—my lieutenant has just been granted a leave home. It'd be nice to have a friend to sail with.

It's been strange, adjusting to peace. I'm not sure I've managed it yet. I made quite a fool of myself yesterday—I and a few others were on a lorry and had stopped by a crossing. We heard a shot, just a farmer shooting at a dog or some such foolishness, and out into the dirt half of us went. If another motor had been coming we'd have been run over. I think one of the others pulled his stitches.

I hope you'll be patient with me as I learn to live a normal life again. I'm sure you've seen some of this in your VAD work, but I thought I ought to—

James dropped the pen and ran his hand through his hair.

Ought to what? Warn her that the nightmares haven't stopped, that I can still see all their faces most nights? How do I tell her that I want to come home but I can't imagine what it'll be like to be happy? He glanced down at his heavily bandaged hand. *And what if the doctor's wrong?*

What if the therapy doesn't help, and I don't get my strength back? If I can't do all of the farm work…

He sighed and put the letter in his pocket for another day.

Half standing, he changed his mind and sat back down. Taking the pen out again, he began another, more pleasant, letter.

Dear Mum,

Good news. The doctors say I should be able to head home soon—in fact, I might be sailing by the time you receive this. I can't wait to get home and see all of you.

I would like to bring a visitor along with me when I come, who I hope you will welcome into the family. Her name is Evelyn Worther (Evie), and I met her when I was convalescing. We have been corresponding, and I hope to introduce her to you as your soon to be daughter-in-law.

You always complain that I omit too many details in my writing, so I have thought long and hard to answer the most pressing question that each of you will have.

Mum: Yes, she is a very nice girl. She even plays organ at the church. And yes, she can cook.

Dad: No, she hasn't any farming experience, though she tends a nice garden.

Hal: Dark brown hair, blue eyes, and yes, she's pretty.

George: I have never heard her opinions on cricket.

Janet: She likes children. She's helped take care of six refugees from the cities. I think you and she will be great friends.

For more detail, you will have to wait and meet her. With your approval, I will see if she can meet me, and we will come down on the train together. God willing, it will be soon.

Much love,
James

Folding it up with a satisfied grin, he decided on a shorter letter for Evie. The other would keep. The pen raced across the page, as if the speed of posting would increase the speed of the events outlined.

Dear Evie,

The doctors and everyone else who matters has confirmed it. Evie my dear, I'll be home soon.

Love,
James

"CHILD?"

Evie paused her trek down the hall to her bedroom and peered around her great aunt's doorframe. The single, dim lamp flung deep shadows into the corners of the room, and she hesitated, wondering if she'd imagined the call. Her doubts vanished when the old woman coughed, raised a thin, white-clad arm from the bed and waved her in.

Feet almost silent in her slippers, Evie padded over. "What can I do for you, Great Aunt Helena? Are you thirsty?"

The old woman nodded her gray head against the pillows that propped her up. Evie searched the clutter of bottles on the bedside table until she found a water glass. Her great aunt struggled to push herself to sitting; Evie sat beside her to offer the support of her arm.

She's gotten so much weaker, just in the last few weeks. The aroma of lavender sachets tucked around the room provided only a thin veil over the smell Evie had come to know too well at Thrush House—the sour scent of illness.

Another fit of coughing shook the old woman's frail shoulders.

When it passed, she gulped the water, then pushed the cup away. "Alright, child. Don't fuss." She turned a beady eye on Evie. "You're up late. Writing more letters?"

Evie smiled and nodded. "Yes. I hadn't written one yet today."

Snorting, the old woman settled back down into her pillow. "Yes, well, I'm rather starting to think you're spoiling that young man of yours—still a sergeant?"

"He is."

"Hmmmm. Has he proposed yet?"

Rearranging the blankets more comfortably, Evie shook her head. "No, not yet. Remember, he wanted to wait..."

Her great aunt snorted again. "It seems more like he wants *you* to wait. Well, if I were you, I'd start hinting in those letters that maybe waiting too long isn't in his best interest."

"Aunt Helena—"

"Child, patience is all well and good, but really, if he means to take you on, *I* at least would like to know for certain."

Evie rolled her eyes, glad the dark masked it. "If he doesn't mean to, I can't imagine what he's doing writing all of those letters." Trying to lighten her tone, she patted the old woman's frail hand. "What, are you afraid you're going to be stuck with me in the end?"

"No, I suppose not." Her great aunt turned her face away and was silent for a long moment. Finally, with a sigh, she turned back to Evie. "Well. When he finally does propose, I think you'll find I planned a rather extraordinary wedding present for the two of you."

"Oh? Have you?" Evie laughed. "I hope you aren't planning to finally foist those awful Baroque candlesticks off on me—the ones with the cherubs that Great Uncle Raymond used to joke about. Remember?"

Her great aunt tilted her head back and laughed until she coughed again. Evie supported her for another drink. When she was able, Great Aunt Helena shook her head. "Good night, child. Get some rest."

Evie rose, then hesitated, curious about her great aunt's real meaning.

The old woman had already turned her face away, and closed her eyes, her breathing a deep, regular rasp.

Cigar smoke clouded the air, dimming the light in the already gloomy office. "Why are you here, Heatherington? Unless you're ready to pay up."Charles glowered down at the toes of his polished shoes, sullied by the grime on the floor. "I can't. You know I can't. The man you sent to see me made that very clear."

"Well then."

"He indicated that you are becoming…impatient." His teeth clenched. "I had hoped you might consider my request and give me a reasonable length of time to prepare—"

The big man's fingers drummed on the desk. "Two months is a bit much."

"I—" Charles fidgeted, beating his hat against his leg. He flinched as it brushed one of the fresh bruises. "Surely not if you end up with full payment. It won't be any longer. I want it finished before Milburn gets back. I don't know if he's had any suspicions, but if it's all done—" He swallowed. "He'll have his own life to get on with."

"Not so high and mighty now? Are you going to do what I said you ought to all along?"

"I know what I need to do."

Smith flicked cigar ash toward him. "Tell me."

Lifting his chin, Charles tried to inject his old confidence into his voice as he explained.

Nodding, Smith said, "Not bad. But why not speed it up? Save the interest? It doesn't all have to be this convoluted—"

"Don't be an idiot."

The fingers of Smith's free hand wandered over to stroke the knife on his desk top.

Charles modulated his voice. "I'm the heir. Where do you think they'd look first? And if they look too deep, who will cover for me? You?"

Smith's laugh sent a great puff of smoke towards the ceiling. "Fair enough. But the extra time—if I push for it, and buy you the time, you'll be able to pay it off? You're right, I won't stick my neck out for you."

"You won't have to. I've been working on it for a while now. Soon enough, it will be done."

The big man nodded. "And the girl?"

"I've kept an eye on things—no solicitors have been about. That means the girl doesn't matter."

"And if that changes?"

"If that changes—" Charles stared at the streaked window behind the big man. Cobwebs draped the corners. In the center of one, a fat blue fly buzzed, struggling against its inevitable fate. "If that changes, I'll do what must be done."

Mr. Smith slid a small parcel across the desk. "Well, take this anyway. Just in case."

Thirty One

15 June 1945

Attn: Messers X. J. S.

Circumstances have changed. Our business dealings should be satisfactorily resolved within the next week—two at the most.

C.H.

Evie finished stitching the dress hem, the black fabric a shadow draped across her lap. Shaking out the wrinkles, she held it up.

It will have to do.

She slid the needle back into its little flannel book. Then she checked that all the pins in the pincushion were equally spaced. Next, she turned her attention to the thread, winding it just so, reluctant to have the job done.

Busy hands kept her mind occupied, providing some relief. Idle moments let it all come rushing in.

The children had returned home last week.

Great Aunt Helena had passed away last night.

She would be reunited with James tomorrow.

The partings from the children had been a painful joy. Leslie and

Lilly's father had made it home at last. He had come up with their mother to collect them. His face had looked gray and tired and he was still wearing his uniform, but his expression when he embraced his girls forced Evie to turn away and fumble for a handkerchief.

Without the children, Stoneglenn's rooms felt hollow, desolate. Even Great Aunt Helena had commented that the quiet felt odd, somehow.

Now her voice was silenced forever. Molly had discovered her death when the old woman didn't ring at the usual time this morning.

Spying a loose thread, Evie opened her sewing kit again, looking for her scissors. *She wasn't young, and she'd been so ill these last weeks. If only she'd let me call in the doctor sooner—but she was always so stubborn. Immovable as these old stones. I always thought she'd dig in her heels and Death himself wouldn't be able to move her.*

To have her gone—and more, to have her gone so quickly and quietly, faded away to a memory in the dark of night—was surreal.

Evie slipped the dress over her head, cold fingers fumbling with the buttons.

It's true though. She's gone. She's gone, too. Thank goodness Charles was here. The thought made her laugh through the threatening tears. After months of studying and analyzing Charles's actions, wondering if she could trust him, it was strange to be grateful for her cousin. Still, he had earned it.

He had been wonderful, solicitous and kind, and had helped make all the necessary arrangements. Where she faltered, he stepped in and carried the burden of decision-making for them all. The funeral would be this afternoon. She'd been surprised at the rush, but Charles had said, "Father Carter thought—and I agreed—why wait?"

He was right—no one else will be coming up. We might as well say our goodbyes.

She moved to the looking glass and brushed her hair. Dark-circled, weary eyes stared back at her.

Yes, it's good that Charles was here.

I can't believe that a few months ago I'd have suspected him of anything, but after all—for all of my watching, for all of my suspicions—what did I find? Nothing at all. Maybe James was mistaken. At least I'll be able to talk to him about it soon. Oh, dear…tomorrow…

Tomorrow afternoon she was to meet James at the Leeds station. She'd kept reading and rereading his last letter until the creases in the paper were almost worn through.

Dear Evie,

When you get this, I shall already be traveling toward you, a Mister rather than a Sergeant.

Would you still be able to meet me? I can't wait a moment longer than necessary to see you again, dear, darling Evie. If you are willing, we can meet at the station in Leeds—you've said you know it a little, and it's central enough for us. From there, we can travel to Lancashire and my home to meet some people who are very anxious to know you. Since hearing of your existence, it has been difficult for Mum to wait to meet you. She may be more excited for your arrival than for mine.

I don't know when I'll get mail in again, but we can discuss the details when I arrive, face to face.

Charles had been calm and civil about the whole thing, and had even offered to travel with her, as he had business in Leeds. She supposed he would be visiting Great Aunt Helena's solicitor. As the heir, his money troubles would be over. As just another relative, she would likely be out on her own. It was time to find her way in the world.

And now came the question. Would it be with James?

The comb fell out of her trembling fingers and clattered on the dressing table. She pressed her hands against its comforting, solid wood and bowed her head.

I haven't seen him in two years. We've had our letters, made our plans, but Lord, I haven't even seen him in two years. What if, when he sees me again, it's not the same? What if we've changed too much? What if—

CONSIDERING ITS HASTE, Great Aunt Helena's service was well-attended, but Evie could hardly attend to Father Carter's words.

Tomorrow. Tomorrow, he comes. Tomorrow.

She could eat nothing. Cook and Molly exchanged worried glances over the kitchen table where they all had tea together, the need for formality gone.

She went to bed early and then paced the floor, unable to sleep.

Tomorrow…

Tomorrow. Charles handed Evie into the train carriage.

Tomorrow all of my problems will be solved. Just get to the solicitor, make certain that everything is as it should be, and see if we can't speed a few things up with the estate. Surely by tomorrow Smith'll see that I've got things sorted out. Just in time, too.

His bad leg catching on the edge of a compartment door, he stumbled and winced. It was stiff still, since that last visit by Smith's men.

"Oh, Charles, are you all right?" Blue eyes wide, Evie reached to steady him. Her color was high—cheeks red in her pale face. *Pretty. Not that there's any point in telling her. He's back, and that's the end. It doesn't signify—soon I'll be free.*

"I'm fine. What about this compartment?"

"What? Oh, yes." She entered it and sat, hands clenched on top of her unopened novel. Sitting next to her, he considered asking to borrow it, just for a distraction. Neither of them would be seeking much conversation on this journey. Leaning over, he caught sight of the cover. It was by that woman mystery writer, titled *A Family Murder*.

He sat back. *Maybe I'll just watch the scenery.*

The landscape flashed past the windows, colors dimmed by the engine's smoke. Tapping his feet, he tried not to dwell on the past, tried not to worry about the future, tried to think of what he'd do when the money was his. He closed his eyes.

Mine at last. I've waited long enough. The old bat held on longer than I'd have ever thought possible—

"Charles?"

His eyes snapped open. "What?"

Staring down at her clasped hands, Evie said, "Before we get there, I just wanted to thank you again. For all of your help. With everything."

"I was happy to—"

"How did it happen, Charles?" Eyes filled with tears, she clasped his hand.

"What—"

"How could she just...go? So quickly, too, at the end. She'd been looking a bit better, and then the weekend came and..." She bit her lip.

His stomach turned. *And what, little Evie? Just what are you getting at?*

Taking a breath to steady his voice, he freed his hand and passed her his handkerchief. "I was shocked, too—but she wasn't young, you know, and she'd been ill for nearly a month. Isn't it a mercy that she didn't have to suffer?"

"Yes. Yes, I suppose you're right." She turned to stare out the window again. "Everything's just been so...hard."

He patted her knee. "Maybe it doesn't have to be anymore."

Just, don't ask more questions. Let it be, Evie. This is almost over.

He bade her farewell on the platform. "You'll be alright? It's an hour or more until his train's due, isn't it?"

She mustered a pinched smile. "Yes, if he catches the one he expected to. Will you be coming back here after your meeting? Maybe we'll see you—"

"Maybe." He leaned over and gave her a cousinly kiss on the cheek and then hurried off, eager to finish this meeting, to claim his due at last.

JAMES SAT AT THE EDGE of his seat, staring out the window, feet pressed against the floor as if he could will the train to move faster. His fingers drummed on the cardboard box containing the civilian clothes issued at his demobbing. He had considered changing out of uniform before traveling, but after six years the dark suit looked foreign and uncomfortable.

For that matter, I half feel like if I put it on an MP would catch me and haul me off for failing to report in. Feels like this must all still be a mistake, and I'd best hurry back before I catch it. He raked his right hand through his hair and then smoothed it down. Evie would be seeing him soon.

Harry Bradlock didn't deign to look up from his paper. "Settle down, Milburn. You didn't have the fidgets this badly when we were pinned down on the Sangro."

"I know it's just…it's been a long time."

Nearly two years. I'm finally going to see her again. What if— He tugged at a loose bit of the remaining bandage over his left hand. Trying to flex his fingers, he flinched.

"She's waited this long. Written you a couple novels worth of letters. After all that effort she's not going to take a look and run the other way, now is she?"

James managed a weak smile. "I hope not."

The train slowed. James sprang to his feet, reaching for the luggage rack to find his balance.

Grinding his teeth, he resisted the urge to push his way through the crush exiting ahead of him.

Reaching the doorway at last, he scanned the faces on the platform.

There! His breath caught in his throat.

There she was, a little thin and tired, dressed in black, a small frown creasing her forehead.

Her eyes met his. The frown disappeared. There she was, his Evie.

The crowd leaving the train and the passengers waiting to get on separated them, but he was tall enough to keep his eyes on her, and she stood tiptoed, waving and beaming.

He raised his hand to wave back, but Charles had appeared at her elbow.

Taking her arm, he leaned down, saying something in her ear. She frowned over her shoulder at him and shook her head, but he pulled her back, into the press of people behind.

Just before the crowd blocked him from view, Charles looked up, and locked eyes with James.

James had a sudden sick feeling in the pit of his stomach.

The two of them disappeared.

When Evie saw James, the world froze, her breath caught for a moment, and then it restarted, her heart pounding as if it would burst.

There he was, just as she remembered him, tall and lean and strong and alive. She waved over the crowd, wishing she could pass through them all and run to him at once.

"Evie," Charles's voice was in her ear and his hand was on her elbow.

"Charles? What—?"

"Come along, Evie. I need to talk with you." His grip tightened.

"No, Charles—James is—"

"Sorry, old girl, this can't wait."

"Charles, you're hurting my arm—"

Ignoring her, he pulled her back through the crowd, away from the station and all of the people.

Away from James.

JAMES'S BATTLEFIELD INSTINCTS screamed *danger!*

What's he doing? Something's wrong—I've got to get to her—

Dropping his box, he plunged through the crowd, elbowing Bradlock aside.

"Ouch! What the—" Bradlock saw his face and seized his arm. "Milburn, what's the matter?"

Not stopping to answer, James ran.

"CHARLES, STOP! Where are we going?"

Evie planted her feet, trying to stop. Her cousin was heavier and stronger. He propelled her forward, holding her upright with his left hand. He wasn't carrying his cane. Though he limped, he gritted his teeth and walked on. His right hand was in his coat pocket.

"Come along, Evie. My meeting with Great Aunt Helena's solicitor was faster than I anticipated." His voice was pleasant, but his smile was stiff. "It's funny, he hasn't been willing to talk to me much these last months. Has he contacted you at all?"

"No, why would he? Charles, where—"

He kept talking over her, "No, I didn't suppose so." He forced a laugh. "He still was pretty close-mouthed, but he saw fit to drop some hints that, well, really made everything much clearer. I should've known, but I always hoped she'd be reasonable—and that things could've been simple. Come along, Evie. I've left my cane just back here."

He steered her into an alleyway between two warehouses—a grim, gray place. The buildings had no windows into the alley, and only a scatter of boxes showed that the space was ever used. It smelled of old cabbage and refuse.

Her fingers scrabbled for purchase on the crumbling bricks of the corner building but found none. "Wait, Charles, back there? Why?"

Without looking at her, he continued forward. "You know, Evie, you really should have just agreed to marry me in the first place. It would have made everything so much simpler and more pleasant. After all, I always liked you." His immaculate coat sleeve caught on a crate—he tore it free without a second glance. "I tried and tried to work this out any other way. Fool that I was."

His voice froze her heart. "Charles, what's in your pocket?"

Halfway down the alley now, he peered about in the shadows and then nodded. "Now, well, now I haven't any choice. And it's all your fault." He shoved her forward and she stumbled, then turned to face him.

His hand came out. He was holding a pistol.

JAMES BARRELED THROUGH the crowd, Bradlock calling from behind. He cast his eyes to the left and the right, looking for any sign of Evie or Charles. There was nothing, no indication of which way they might have gone.

Away from people, he guessed. *Dear God, please. Please let me find her in time. Please, don't let me lose her, too.*

Choosing a direction, he ran through a row of warehouses, praying it was the right row. A scream echoed ahead.

"SHUT UP," said Charles. Evie took another breath, and he slapped her, leveling the gun.

"Dear God," she whispered, hand to her cheek, "Please." *If I could get the gun*—but her feet were rooted to the ground.

Charles laughed, a high, wild sound. "What, think he'll spare you? He didn't spare perfect Roger, nor that old bat Great Aunt Helena."

"Great Aunt—what do you mean, Charles? What did you—" His jaw hardened, and he gripped the pistol tighter. Evie shook her head. "It doesn't matter. If I die I'll be with Mother and Father, but what about you, Charles? If you're this lost, what hope will you have when your time comes?" She held out her hands, beseeching. "Don't *do* this!"

He cocked the hammer. "Sorry to disappoint, Evie. No choices left."

JAMES FOLLOWED THE SOUND—next alley down. He stopped at the corner and peered around.

Evie, face pale, hand to her blooming cheek, stood staring at Charles with wide, frightened eyes. Charles's back was to him, gun leveled at her.

What I wouldn't give for my rifle.

Evie held out her hands to Charles, as quietly—*quietly*—he eased himself around the corner and moved toward the other man.

"Don't *do* this!" said Evie.

Charles cocked the hammer. "Sorry to disappoint, Evie. No choice left."

James sprang.

AT THE SAME MOMENT, Evie and Charles became aware of him. Charles swung around. The shot went wide. James slammed into him, grappling for the gun.

Evie screamed, "NO! James!" She grabbed at Charles's arm but was knocked to the ground, striking her head on the brick wall.

Dazed, she struggled to find her feet.

The two men were locked together, wrestling for control of the gun. James was taller and wiry, but leg notwithstanding, Charles was broader and still powerfully built. They slammed into the wall on the other side of the alley.

BANG. The gun fired.

Both men fell to the ground.

All was confusion.

Footsteps thundered down the alley—all the noise had attracted some attention.

Bright red blood hemorrhaged out onto the pavement.

Evie heaved herself up and ran a couple of staggering steps and then collapsed by the prone forms sobbing, "Dear God, no! No, no, no, please no, not *now!*"

Then, with a groan, James pushed himself up, blood-stained and covered in dust. "James..." she gulped. "James...you're..."

He gathered her up into his arms, stroking her hair and shushing her sobs as she clung to him. "It's all right now. It's all right. You're safe. I'm here."

Charles did not move again.

Thirty Two

JAMES FELT LIKE A SCHOOL BOY, summoned to the headmaster's office as he waited before Chief Inspector Wilton's desk.

Bit more serious than that, though, isn't it?

He tried to ignore his sweating palms and the stink of the blood on his uniform. He tried not to worry about how pale Evie had looked when they led her off. Instead, he studied the Chief Inspector. The man had thin, graying hair and a fatherly aspect, but his sharp dark eyes were shrewd as he studied James over his half-glasses. James blinked when he realized he'd been asked his name.

"Sergeant—no, sorry, I've just been demobbed. Just James Milburn, sir."

"And what happened in that alleyway, young man?" Wilton folded his hands on top of his desk, and leaned forward, using his best paternal smile.

James gazed back, willing his voice calm. "Well, sir, I think it goes a few years back."

The Chief Inspector's bushy gray eyebrows rose higher and higher on his forehead until it seemed they must disappear into his hairline as James outlined his knowledge of the last three years' events regarding Miss Evelyn Worther and Mr. Charles Heatherington. He concluded, "I was trying to get the gun away from him when it went off. I can't tell for certain which of us pulled the trigger. I'm just thankful the muzzle wasn't pointing at me at the time."

"Certainly. Not terribly sorry it happened, though, are you?"

James's lips compressed. "I am sorry it all came to this, and for the pain it will cause Miss Worther, but no, I won't be shedding any tears for him. Sir."

Wilton nodded slowly. He took his glasses off and rubbed his eyes. "You say this will give Miss Worther pain, though?"

"She'll be sorry for his death. He was her cousin. No matter what he became, she will be sorry for it." A flush of warmth made him smile despite the grim circumstances. "She's got a soft heart."

Replacing his glasses, Wilton gave James a pointed look. "You haven't said just what your relationship is to Miss Worther."

"We met when I was invalided back in '43. We've kept in touch by correspondence. I intended to propose today. Hasn't really been a good chance."

Wilton's lips stretched into a grim smile. "No, I imagine not." He examined a paper on his desk. "One last thing. You said you saw Mr. Heatherington grab her, didn't know where they were going, and yet you found her in an alley several streets over in enough time to prevent her murder." His eyes pierced James. "Can you explain how you managed this without any foreknowledge of his plans?"

James stood silent for a long moment. "I knew she was in trouble. I ran, took my best shot at finding her, she screamed." He hesitated and then looked the Chief Inspector squarely in the face. "When she screamed, though, I was almost there. I was praying, you see, the whole time, that I'd find her before she came to harm. Personally, I believe I was answered." He gave a crooked grin. "I'd never have admitted that a few years back."

The Chief Inspector raised his eyebrows but said only, "Very good. Thank you."

WITH SHAKING HANDS, Evie held her compact mirror close to her face, applying a little powder to cover her pale cheeks. She fished in her purse for her lipstick, pulled it out, and then froze. The makeup had been a gift from Charles.

She dropped it in the waste bin and followed the officer who'd come for her.

Chief Inspector Wilton got up to help her into the chair across from his desk, making sympathetic noises about the shock she had suffered. She managed a weak smile in response, but she couldn't help noticing his sharp eyes. She took a deep breath, clasping her hands together. *I've got to hold myself together. For James. Dear God, please, they can't blame him for...for...*

The Chief Inspector interrupted her thoughts. "Well, Miss Worther. Feel up to talking a bit?"

Evie swallowed. "I'll do my best to be of any use. It's just all been so horrible." Her voice broke.

Wilton fished out a handkerchief and handed it to her. "Tell me about today."

She regained control of herself and described what had passed.

Wilton steepled his fingers, eyes never leaving her face. "Charles Heatherington had asked you to marry him, then?"

"Yes. He...he was angry when I refused."

"Why did you refuse?"

She hesitated.

"After all," he encouraged her, "he *is* dead. And we need to know why."

Nodding, she said, "He and I...our personalities just didn't suit. Also—" She bit her lips and squeezed her hands tighter.

Wilton leaned forward. "Yes?"

"I had reason to believe that his business dealings... may not be quite right."

"Oh?"

She told about the man in the alley at the cinema. At her description, the Chief Inspector held his hand back to his assistant who produced a photograph as if by magic. "Is this the man?"

Her eyes widened. "Yes. Charles said that he was called Mr. Smith."

Wilton chuckled. "Among other things. What else can you tell me?"

Taking a deep breath and gathering her thoughts, she described how Charles had always been able to find unattainable items, about his recent money worries, and his dependency on Great Aunt Helena. "And—"

"And?"

"And—" Heat flushed her cheeks and she looked down. "I was in love with someone else. So, I couldn't marry Charles, you see? He even asked if James were, well, if he didn't make it back. But I said no." Her eyes filled, and she blinked, trying to will the tears away. "I just can't understand why he would try to…to kill me."

"Men in love have done things like that before. 'If I can't have her, no one can,' and all that rot."

She shook her head. "But that's just the thing—he wasn't in love with me. I'm sure of it. He tried to be pleasant, to act as if he were, but he never…even at the end, he said he didn't want to kill me because he'd always liked me—" She held out her empty hands. "Oh, I don't know how to explain it." Choosing her words with care, she added, "I'm just so thankful that Sergeant Milburn was there today. He saved my life." *And he should be released. Please, please, say that he'll be released…*

Wilton studied her and said nothing for some time. When he finally spoke, his comment took her aback. "I notice you're wearing black."

"Yes. My Great Aunt Helena just passed away the night before yesterday." *Was it only two days ago?*

The Chief Inspector nodded. "I'm sorry to hear that. This is the great aunt from whom your cousin was expecting to inherit?"

"Yes. Well, not exactly. He was heir to her husband, our Great Uncle Raymond. But Great Aunt Helena was in possession of everything up until her death—Oh." The pieces all fell into place, and Evie stiffened, her eyes wide as the world dropped away beneath her. "Oh, no."

She was dimly aware of the Chief Inspector at her elbow, barking for someone to bring water. He touched her arm. "Miss Worther, are you all right?"

Raising a shaking hand to her mouth, she nodded. "Yes. I think—" She took a deep breath. "I think I understand everything."

JAMES TRIED TO TAKE IT as a good sign when he was led into a small conference room rather than a cell. It was dominated by a table that was rather too large for the space and a number of stiff metal chairs.

He was debating whether to brave sitting in one of them, when the door opened again and Evie entered.

"James?" Evie breathed his name and then wove around the chairs to him.

Wrapping his arms around her, he started to ask, "Evie, are you—" but she shook her head, her face buried in his chest. He closed his mouth and just held her.

The door opened again, and, to James's surprise, Harry Bradlock entered. "You forgot your box." He plopped it on the table. "I didn't find where you'd run off to until I heard shots. Then you were both being taken away. You all right?"

James nodded. "Thanks."

Harry returned the nod, then fished out a cigarette. "Had a chance to vouch for you to the Chief Inspector, anyhow. Seemed a decent fellow. Said I could wait with you." He took a long drag and blew a blue cloud towards the ceiling. "Any word on what's next?"

James shook his head and guided Evie over to a chair. He sat beside her, and she clung to his arm like a capsized sailor to a life ring. Bradlock sat across from them, giving a satisfied grunt as he noticed the newspaper on the table. "Only a day behind. Well, that's better than in sunny old Italy, isn't it?"

The door opened again, and they all looked up. Chief Inspector Wilton and another officer entered.

"Mr. Milburn, I see that your friend found you. Feel free to change after this. No need to walk through town looking like a casualty rather than a victor."

James nodded. "Thank you."

The Chief Inspector sat a few seats down from them. "Good news. Based on your evidence and everything we've been able to gather, you'll all be free to go. There'll be the coroner's inquest, of course, but that should be that."

Relief washed over James, and he struggled to keep his face calm as he nodded again.

Evie shifted, rousing herself. "Chief Inspector, was I—did you find out why—?"

Wilton nodded. "Very likely the motive you put forward is correct. The solicitor should contact you soon to clarify matters."

James looked down at her. "Motive? Evie, what—?"

Bradlock directed his gaze at Wilton. "Solicitor?"

Looking to Evie first, who nodded, the Chief Inspector steepled his fingers and leaned back in his chair. "More evidence may come out, but it seems that Mr. Heatherington had made a great deal of money with illegal goods during wartime, and then lost more than he made through extravagances, gambling, and the like. The 'Mr. Smith' you described to us," here he nodded to Evie, "fits the description of a rather nasty underworld figure we've been watching for some time—fingers in gambling, black market, even some murders, I'm afraid. Not that we've been able to make anything stick."

Bradlock caught James's eye and raised his eyebrows. He mouthed the word *Egypt*.

Wilton continued. "Bad business. It seems that young Mr. Heatherington had gotten himself deeply in debt, and his debts were being called on him. He was banking on his inheritance to bail him out. It was his last hope."

James nodded and said slowly, "But he couldn't get his hands on it, not while his Great Aunt was alive—" He stopped, startled by the implication.

With a shudder, Evie looked up at him, her face a mask of misery. "That's what I—but do you think he really did—?"

The Chief Inspector looked down at his folded hands. "With his death it may be redundant, but I will see if there is any call to have her body exhumed."

Evie gave a choked little sob, and James covered her hands with his own as he gritted his teeth. *The slimy, selfish—So he couldn't wait, could he?* If he'd felt any regret about what happened in the alley, it evaporated.

Wilton cleared his throat, and James looked back at him. The Chief Inspector's face was apologetic as he continued talking. "I'm afraid there's more." He held up a file. "We were paid a visit by a Mr. Parker. Miss Worther, do you know him?"

Evie shook her head, then paused. "Parker, yes. He was coming around to visit with Great Aunt Helena. She had him looking into... something." Her mouth took on a bitter twist. "She wouldn't discuss details with me, though."

"He's an investigator. From London but works for your family's solicitor from time to time. Your great aunt hired him several months back. It seems that she was suspicious of her nephew's financial activities." The next words left Wilton's lips reluctantly. "She had also been looking extensively for any reports she could find regarding his elder brother Roger's death."

James inhaled sharply through his nose. *Phillips guessed it, after all.*

Evie sat straighter and leaned forward. "But Roger was killed in France, before Dunkirk—"

Wilton nodded. "That's true, but the details are sketchy, and at least one witness—a young man in a pub after the evacuation—was overheard mentioning suspicions. He was quite intoxicated at the time, though, and unfortunately, Richard Thompkins has since died, himself, so couldn't be questioned—" He leapt to his feet and started forward. "Miss Worther?"

Evie had gone white as a sheet.

Bradlock jumped up, as well. James kept his arms around her as he pushed her head down. "Breathe, Evie, just breathe."

When she had some color back, he turned on the Chief Inspector. "See here, can't this all wait? Hasn't she been through enough today?"

Evie interjected, breathless. "No, James. I'll be alright." Turning to the others, she explained her history with Thompkins. Bradlock summed up their reactions by kicking his chair back and giving a long, low whistle.

Evie nodded and then asked the Chief Inspector, "Please, what else? I'd rather know it all."

Wilton shrugged, sitting back down. "There's not much more you don't know, aside from a few nasty details you don't need to. The idea was that with the middle brother's death in '39, only Roger was in his way, and it's awfully easy to stage a death in a war zone."

She closed her eyes. "Oh, Charles! How could he?"

"But why attack Miss Worther?" Bradlock asked. "She didn't know anything about all of that, and—pardon me, Miss—but why would such a cold character go to such lengths over a girl throwing him over? It seems a bit...excessive."

Before Wilton could speak, Evie, eyes still closed, answered, "It wasn't me. It was the money."

James shifted so that he could see her face and shook his head, baffled. "Money? But you don't have any."

"No," she agreed miserably. "I didn't. But," she looked at the Chief Inspector, who nodded, "it's all about Great Aunt Helena's will, you see?"

Blinking, James shook his head. "I'm sorry, Evie, but what bearing does that have on anything? You'd always said that Charles was your uncle's heir."

"Yes. He was Great Uncle Raymond's heir." Evie sniffled, and blew her nose. "But Great Aunt Helena—she asked me, oh, a few weeks ago, if you'd proposed yet. When I said no, she said some, well, rather rude things. You know...I mean knew her. Then she told me she had an extraordinary wedding present for us. I had no idea what she was talking about and made some joke about candlesticks—stupid of me, really."

"You see," Chief Inspector Wilton supplied, "Mr. Heatherington was heir to the house, land and a bit of income uncontested. He was from Mr. Raymond Heatherington's side of the family. The *money*, however, was all on Mrs. Heatherington's side, and while it was assumed that it would go along with the house, it was hers—free to will away."

James stared. "So, she left the money to—"

"All of the details will come out when the will is read, but Miss Worther is likely to come out quite well from it," said Wilton with a smile.

Bradlock asked, "But how would Charles have known today then?"

Evie shrugged. "That's why he came down on the train. He had an appointment with Mr. Browning, the solicitor. He must've given him the hint..."

"And with you being unmarried and having no will, the money would go to your next of kin in the event of your death," finished the Chief Inspector.

"Charles." Evie buried her face in her hands.

James's heart ached for her, and his hands twitched, helpless to ease her pain. He put one on her shoulder and watched her, grim-faced.

Bradlock spluttered, slapping his hands on the table. "But surely not if he murdered her. I don't know how he thought he'd get away with it. Milburn saw him walk away with her. He must've been pretty desperate."

Wilton tapped the file before him. "He was. We've found that the gun belonged to one of Mr. Smith's associates. Way I figure it, once he got her out of sight he planned to make it look like the attack was by a third party because of his shady associations, a tragic result of his poor choices. Shoot her, then just wound himself would be my guess. If he managed not to get arrested, he could get the money, pay his debts, and possibly escape with his life. If he didn't pay his debts he was likely as good as dead anyway."

Bradlock nodded, crushing his cigarette out in the ash tray. "All right. There's motive for today. But it still doesn't explain why he was so fixed on marrying her—or I suppose it does if he was worried that the old woman might split the money and he planned on needing it all—"

Evie raised her head, wiping her eyes, and nodded, "He knew that if the inheritance were divided, or if in the worst case he were disinherited, I was the only other relative that she was close to."

"So, if he married *you*, he believed that he'd be sure of all of the money, no matter what else happened." James's arm went around her shoulders, and she leaned in to him. Wearily, she nodded once more.

He looked up with a frown. "Chief Inspector, is there any reason we need to stay here any longer?"

"Just let us know where we can reach you for the inquest and for the will settlement for Miss Worther."

He nodded. "Thank you. C'mon, Evie."

She looked up at him. "Where—what should I do, James? I don't know *what* to do, now."

"Just leave it to me. I'll be back in a moment."

He changed his clothes, and they collected their belongings. A handshake with Bradlock on the station steps, a quick wire sent out, and James led Evie back to the train station. She followed willingly, too drained to be curious. He didn't even release her hand to pay for the tickets—he tucked it under his arm as he took out the money.

When she heard him name the station she started.

"James, where are we going?"

"Home."

That woke her out of her lethargy. "Wait—to *your* home? I know we had written about going there to meet your family, but tonight? James, I can't just show up at their door like this—"

"Watch your step." He guided her around a stack of waiting baggage. "Don't worry about it. Mother likes company, and they're expecting you. I sent off that wire to let them know we'll be late, so they won't worry. My sister, Janet, will loan you some things until we can figure something better out. I know them. By the time we're there, they'll have it all arranged."

She frowned, considering.

He smiled, satisfied. *Good. Now she has something to think about besides today.*

She looked up at him, eyes dark with worry, but then her smile broke through, the smile he'd ached to see all of these months, and she said, "Well, if you're sure. I haven't anything left to fight you with even if I wanted to, and I could certainly use a change of scenery." Her smile faded, and she shivered.

They found an empty compartment. Evie sighed and leaned her head on his shoulder. He passed his arm around her and buried his face in her hair.

"I was worried that I'd be too nervous to even talk to you."

She laughed. "So was I. I didn't know how it would be...I suppose all of this broke the ice quickly, anyway."

They fell silent as the train pulled away from the station, gathering speed, putting distance between them and that blood-soaked alley.

He thought she had fallen asleep when she said, "James?"

"Hm?"

"Thank you. For finding me."

"Well. Of course."

"I can't believe—"

"Try not to think about it."

She turned her face to look up at him. "I can't help it. Months ago, you warned me about Charles, and I wondered, and then I decided—I *chose*—not to think about it. If I had done something, if I'd spoken up, maybe he wouldn't be—maybe he wouldn't have—" She bit her lip.

He reached over to touch her cheek, brushing away the tear that trembled there. His finger lingered on her soft skin.

"Charles made his choices, too. You did the best you could, Evie, and if he'd gotten the wind up sooner, I wouldn't have been there."

She shivered and pressed in closer to him. "It's all so terrible. Do you ever—I mean, with all you've been through—how do you bear it?"

He dropped his hand to her knee and looked into his empty palm, searching for the answer. Her fingers stroked the bandage and the livid scar that traveled across the exposed flesh. "Your poor hand," she murmured. "Look, never mind. I'm sorry. If you don't want to talk about it—"

"No, it's all right. It's—it's not something that just goes away. The dreams are pretty bad sometimes." He smiled and squeezed her hand, making light of it. "But then, I always had you to think about when they woke me."

Laughing a little, she sat up and freed her hand, looping her arms around his neck. "You know, this wasn't really how I imagined welcoming you back home."

"No?" He reached up and stroked her cheek, tracing the contours of her face.

With a rattle, the compartment door opened. "Might be some empty space in here—" a man grumbled over his shoulder and then turned and saw them.

Arms frozen around Evie, heat flushed James's face. After a startled pause, the stranger smiled under his gray mustaches, tipped his cap and said, "Welcome home, son," and beat a hasty exit.

"Well, then," said James, and Evie laughed, and he pulled her up on his knee and leaned in to kiss her, and it was as if all of the years apart had never been.

When Evie was back beside him, James pulled her head to his shoulder and put his arms around her, reassuring them both that they were together and safe. "Try to rest?"

She yawned. "All right. Thank God, James—"

"Yes."

"EVIE? WE'RE HERE."

Evie blinked the sleep from her eyes sat up. The train was just pulling into the station, and the moon shone through the window. James took her arm, and they disembarked, stretching stiff, cold limbs. The air smelled fresh and green, and stars were liberally sprinkled across the velvety black sky.

A man waited for them under the wan light of the small, dark platform. Evie tried not to stare. He was so like James, only twenty years older, that he could only be his father. Tall as his son, still lean, gray just starting to streak his temples, he gripped James's hand with his own strong, browned one, and thumped his shoulder. With that same serious face that James so often wore, he said, "It's good to see you, son."

"It's good to be home, Dad. This is Miss Evie Worther."

"Pleasure to meet you, Miss." He shook her hand and she returned his sentiments, a little bemused at this calm greeting between father and son after long absence. "Your mum's keeping some food warm—we'd best be off."

He had a small cart waiting for them and they were quickly situated, Mr. Milburn holding the reins, James next to his father, and

Evie beside him. Mr. Milburn produced a rough woolen blanket for Evie, to keep out the night's damp chill.

James's arm around her probably saved her from a spill; she was still dreadfully tired, and only the frequent jolts of the country road kept her from falling into deep sleep. As it was, her head was continuously drooping and then jerking up as a bump woke her. The men spoke very little. *Like Father, like son,* Evie thought in one of her lucid moments, but the quiet was not uncomfortable.

An especially large jolt woke her, jarring her teeth together, as they drove up to the front of the farmhouse. It was ablaze with light, and there seemed, to her dazzled eyes, to be a crowd awaiting their arrival.

"Here, Miss!" A curly-headed young man in uniform, presumably James's brother, helped her down. She leaned against the cart's side, clumsy and awkward in her weariness.

Then came the cry of "James!", and as he jumped easily down, he was enveloped in embraces. Evie was fairly certain she identified his mother, sister, and nephews in the tangle of arms, with the young man she had seen and a smaller copy there on the outskirts, thumping their big brother on the back, and a couple of friendly, shaggy sheepdogs running about everybody's feet making nuisances of themselves.

James broke out and took her hand, and everyone was introduced to "Miss Worther," and then they were brought inside, her coat taken, a blessedly warm cup of tea pressed into her icy hands, and a comfortable chair found for her by the fire. Supper was produced like magic, and though it was far past bed-time, the plate of hot food placed on a little table at her elbow was welcome.

Evie was shown nothing but kindly solicitude, and noted (perhaps due to James's quickly sent message earlier in the day) that she was asked no questions that did not pertain to her present comfort. She was free to observe this happy family celebrating its son's return with nothing being asked of her—for this she was grateful.

She ate and drank, watching the nephews tumble over their eldest uncle like a pair of exuberant puppies as he wondered over how much they'd grown, and watching his mother fret over his weight and his color and the scar on his hand that he hadn't written home about. She watched his father find a quiet chair on the other side of the fire where he read his paper, pretending to ignore the fuss, but frequently glancing up at his son, the ghost of a satisfied smile crossing his face. Evie was convinced: this was a good place, a home.

"Pardon me, Miss Worther." Evie looked up to see a young woman who could only be James's sister. She was older than Evie, tall and fair like her brother, but her eyes were greener, and her face was softer. "You may not remember from the crush outside. I'm Janet, James's sister." Her smile was warm and welcoming, and Evie liked her immediately. "I know you didn't come prepared for a stay, so I brought some things over for tonight and tomorrow, and if you're staying past then, there are a few nice shops the village over that I don't often have excuse to visit!"

"Thank you so much. It's very kind of you." In a lower tone, Evie confided, "I do hate to be a bother."

"Oh, you aren't a bother at all, dear. I can't wait to talk more, but if you don't mind me saying so, you look done in. Shall I have Mum show you where you're to sleep?"

On cue, Mrs. Milburn came bustling over.

"Ready to sleep, my dear? Tut, you look exhausted. Come along, I'll show you to the room we've made up."

Evie looked for James. He had moved to the other side of the room and was talking with his brothers. Suddenly shy of approaching him, she turned and followed Mrs. Milburn up some stairs and along a dark corridor to a small, pleasant room with a bed made up in white, and a few necessary items of clothing and toiletries arranged on a dresser.

"Thank you so much—" Evie began, and then she heard a quick step in the hall. James came up and gave his mother a kiss on the cheek.

"Got her all set? Thanks, Mum. I'll just say goodnight." Mrs. Milburn beamed at them both and departed.

James's cheeks were flushed, and an irrepressible grin lingered in the corners of his mouth. It faded as he examined her face, and his eyes grew serious. "Are you going to be all right?" he asked, taking her hand.

Evie pulled on a brave face. "Of course, thanks to you. Your family's lovely."

His grin returned. "You like them?"

"Mmmhmm. Very much."

Stepping a little closer, he looked away, scrubbed his hand through his hair, then looked back at her. "You know, if you'd like—Dad was just saying, there's a little house just down the lane up for sale. It could use some work, but..." He shrugged, cocked his head, and waited.

She blinked. "A house?"

"Yes, with a bit of garden. Easy walking distance..." He dropped his eyes. "What do you think?"

Her breath caught in her throat, but she swallowed hard and smiled. "Oh, well...it does sound nice. Are you...are you thinking of setting up there?"

His head jerked up. "Well, yes. At least, I would if you'd like to come along." He moistened his lips and looked down at the floor, then raised his eyes to hers. "Maybe it's not the best time to ask, but... would you, Evie? Marry me?"

She flung her arms around his neck. "Oh, James, yes!"

They didn't speak again for quite some time. When she had her breath back, she interjected, "I do have one condition."

He leaned back and looked at her. "What's that?"

"Please—let's get married soon. I'm so very tired of waiting!"

He threw back his head and laughed. "Yes."

Acknowledgements

When I first put pen to the paper, I imagined that, with just a bit of research, I knew enough about the Second World War to tell this story.

It didn't take long to realize just how little I knew.

While my characters and the English villages of Thrush and Farthington are fictional, I wanted to make sure that the events in the story *could* have happened to real people.

That's where the real historians came in. The fascinating and heartbreaking tales preserved by authors like Fred Majdalany in his Cassino: Portrait of a Battle, Richard Doherty in his The Eighth Army in Italy 1943-45: The Long Hard Slog, and Ken Ford's Battleaxe Division: From Africa to Italy with the 78th Division 1942-1945 shaped and directed James's physical journey through the real difficulties and dangers of North Africa, Sicily, Italy, and Egypt. Others, like Maureen Waller in her London 1945: Life in the Debris of War and the BBC's "People's War" archives shaped my portrayal of the British home front.

While research books were essential, *this* book would never have come into being without the aid of some truly wonderful people.

I had many fantastic readers at all stages of the book who offered advice, encouragement, and support. I can't thank them enough. I made some tremendously helpful contacts online, like author Sarah Higbee who helped clear up some misconceptions I had about life in the U.K.

Special thanks must go to Bekah, Shanna, and—of course—Mom,

who read this at its earliest and ugliest, and to Mara and Jean Lee, who took it on in the later stages and provided invaluable constructive criticism.

The credit for final edits, formatting, and the beautiful cover go to my friend Amanda Ruehle, for whose expertise and help I am so thankful.

I am also grateful for my husband Todd, patient listener, expert comma catcher, and professional child wrangler, he kept me sane through the process and saved me from some silly grammatical gaffes.

Finally, thank you, Reader, for coming along on this journey. If you'd like, feel free to walk with me a bit farther via my blog:

thenaptimeauthor.wordpress.com.

I always love visitors!

Soli Deo Gloria!
Anne Clare

Made in the USA
Monee, IL
21 November 2023